LADY LIEGE

A Serving Magic Book – Volume Three

TONI CABELL

Endwood Press LLC © 2021

All rights reserved.

No part of this book may be reproduced in any form or by any electronic or mechanical means, including information storage and retrieval systems, without written permission from the author, except for the use of brief quotations in a book review.

CHAPTER 1

"Are you ready this time to pronounce me fit for duty?" asked Linden, knowing full well she was capable of leading the Valerran mission. Overcoming Reynier's objections, however, required a stamp of approval from her healer. Reynier looked for any excuse to keep the Liege far away from battles—whether magical or military—convinced that keeping Linden safe from harm was his top priority. Linden, of course, disagreed.

Her personal healer and best friend sighed, frown lines marring her smooth brown complexion. "If I say you're not fit for duty, you'll go anyway," said Jayna. "You've healed well enough from the wounds Mordahn inflicted, but I still don't think you should go."

"You know what's at stake. And why I have to go." Images of the final battle inside the Valerran Museum, where Linden, Jayna, and their friends barely escaped with their lives, still haunted Linden nine months later. The last of the Serving mages had hidden themselves in the museum, the only remaining holdouts against the wave of Fallow sorcery overtaking Valerra. Serving magic had been dealt a resounding defeat that day; it gnawed at her, a wrong that screamed out to be righted.

Linden had another reason as well. She'd received reports about the resistance deep within Valerra, and a certain leader who bore a striking resemblance to her brother, injured during the war. "I have to find him, if he's still alive."

Jayna handed her a tincture of healing herbs to drink. "I understand you want to find your brother and help him if you can. But I don't have a good feeling about going into Valerra. Or about you having to face Mordahn again. Some of the wounds you carry aren't physical."

Linden grimaced as she downed the bitter medicine. She couldn't argue with her friend. Mordahn's dark sorcery scared her to the core. Sometimes Linden would wake up in a cold sweat, convinced Mordahn had managed to crossbreed her into a grotesque creature, or ordered another troop of undead soldiers to chase after her.

Linden handed back the empty cup. "I've shared my worst fears with you in private. Please don't repeat any of them, especially to Reynier." Linden didn't have to say what they both knew to be true. Jayna and Reynier had few secrets between them. After recently completing the rites of binding, the newly married couple actually completed each other's sentences.

Jayna shook her head, her dark curls bouncing. "Of course not."

"Alright then, let's tell him I'm healed and ready to leave tomorrow as planned."

"I'll go talk to Reynier. There's someone else you need to have this conversation with, and you can't put it off any longer," said Jayna.

Linden lifted her shoulders in a half-shrug. "Fine. I'll try speaking with him, but I'm not convinced he's going to listen any better this time. Stubborn, obstinate man."

"Stubborn, obstinate man who saved your life, has his

hands overfull with clan duties, and has strong feelings for you. Which I'm convinced you reciprocate, but are too stubborn yourself to admit," said Jayna, packing up her healer's kit.

Stubbornness had nothing to do with it. Ever since Corbahn had brought Linden roses during her recovery and she'd kissed him, her head and heart warred with each other. Linden knew the prophecies about her and Corbahn—the Faymon Liege and Arrowood Chief—healing the rift between their clans through the rites of binding, a rift that had spawned a fifty-year civil war. She'd had her fill of old secrets and even older prophecies, and she would never agree to an arranged marriage, however attractive the clan chief.

Linden never asked to be the long-awaited Liege of Faynwood, inheriting the title, along with the duties and headaches, from her father's Faymon relatives. She wasn't about to let another prophecy rule her life, especially her love life, even if her resolve melted every time Corbahn looked at her with those sea green eyes of his.

Jayna parted the thin, translucent curtain separating Linden's private quarters from the remainder of her tent. "I'll see you later."

Linden gave her a quick hug. "Thank you, for all you've done to help me heal. And for listening."

"Of course. I just hope I haven't patched you up so you can head out and get yourself injured again or worse." Jayna left the tent, which served as the official gathering place for the Faymon Liege and other clan leaders whenever Linden traveled. A low table that could accommodate twenty guests occupied the far side of the public space, its purple and gold seat cushions scattered about the floor. The entire tent contained enough wall hangings and floor coverings to satisfy any head of state. Most days Linden felt as if she were a mage apprentice again, learning her spells for the first time, and definitely not the Liege or leader of anyone.

Linden smoothed her gown, a long swirl of silky blue artfully designed into a split skirt, allowing her the ability to ride her horse. All Linden's gowns followed the same formula of practical elegance. Grabbing a darker blue sweater from the trunk beside her bed, she squinted as she stepped out of the tent, the afternoon sunny, the air crisp and cool. She decided to walk instead of ride to Corbahn's tent inside the Arrowood enclave, giving herself more time to think.

The five Faymon clans had remained encamped through the summer, each clan setting up independent tent villages inside the large plain near the western border of Faynwood. Reunited after a long civil war, the clans worked together to repel repeated attacks from Glenbarra, their aggressive neighbors to the west. A second threat now emerged from the south, from occupied Valerra, overrun by the same Glenbarrans. Under the leadership of King Roi and Mordahn, the king's chief sorcerer, Linden's former homeland had become the stuff of nightmares.

Linden left her clan's campsite and crossed half the field, winding in and out of the colorful tent cities of two other clans along the way, skirting around open fire pits for communal cooking, waving back at children who called out to her by name. Before she knew it, she'd reached the Arrowood camp. One of the servants spotted her and ran ahead to Corbahn's tent to alert him. Another servant, an elderly woman, rose from stirring something inside her pot, the delicious scent filling the air around her. She bowed low. "M'Liege, may I walk with ye?"

Linden inclined her head. "Certainly." Although she didn't need anyone to escort her through the Arrowood site, she appreciated the servant's offer. Months earlier, her clan had been locked in combat with Arrowood, both sides unwilling to lay down arms to end the civil war.

The old woman tucked her white hair more firmly inside

her headscarf and fell into step beside Linden, neither of them in much of a hurry; Linden because of her pending argument with Corbahn, and the servant because of her age. "I was there, at yer crowning, m'Liege. And later, in the crowd to greet ye."

Linden arched an eyebrow. "How did you come to be at the ceremony? None of the Arrowood clan had been invited due to the civil war."

"Aye, but I was visiting my sister, who'd married into the Tanglewood clan a year before we took up arms against each other."

Linden's grandmother had fled from Tanglewood at the start of the civil war. Linden's ancestors—the long line of Faymon Lieges who'd come before her—had all belonged to the ruling Tanglewood clan. "Even so, I'm surprised you were able to travel so far from your home, through hostile territory, to visit your sister."

The servant grinned. "No one pays any mind to an old woman traveling by herself."

Linden smiled. "I suppose you're right. Perhaps we ought to employ older women as scouts and spies." They both chuckled as they approached Corbahn's tent, Linden sensing the woman had something more on her mind.

"When I greeted ye all those months ago, I grasped yer hand and saw much, m'Liege." The old woman stopped walking and looked at Linden through piercing amber eyes.

"You're a psychic, then?" Unlike seers, who had visions and dreams—Linden had plenty of those, often wishing she didn't have the gift of sight—psychics required physical touch to activate their ability. Their revelations tended to be more personal because they focused on a single individual.

"Aye, m'Liege. I've carried this with me fer months, waiting until this moment, when we came face-to-face."

Linden nodded slowly, uncertain she wanted to hear the psychic's revelation. "Very well, I'm listening."

"Ye have suffered much already in yer battles with Mordahn and his Fallow sorcery. But yer biggest test is yet to come. Ye will face him once more, alone. Ye must remember who ye are."

A cloud passed over the sun above, and the light autumn breeze kicked up, whipping Linden's skirts. She pulled her sweater more tightly around herself. "Anything else?" she whispered. *Can I defeat Mordahn this time?*

The woman reached out a gnarled hand to grip Linden's arm. "You and Chief are right for each other." The psychic nodded in the direction of Corbahn's tent. "But yer timing's all wrong."

Linden drew her brows together. "So does that mean..."

"I canna say for sure. Ye must let the future write itself, m'Liege." The old servant bowed again and shuffled toward her cooking fire.

"M'Liege!" The first servant, who'd scurried away to alert Corbahn, bowed before her. "Chief Corbahn awaits you."

Exhaling the breath she'd been holding, Linden nodded. "I know the way." She closed the distance to the chief's tent and paused at the entrance, hesitating. Corbahn always emerged from his tent to greet her. *Perhaps he's still angry.* She thought of the old psychic's words and called out, "Is this a bad time?"

His deep voice boomed from within the tent. "It's always good to see you, my Liege. Come inside. Please."

Linden pushed aside the tent flap and entered, her eyes taking a moment to adjust to the gloom. The unobtrusive interior, more suitable for a warrior than a clan chief, contained a cot, traveling trunk, and chair on one side of the tent, with an oval table and floor cushions on the other side. The tent's occupant, however, was anything but unobtrusive. Corbahn's larger-than-life presence and sheer physicality commanded attention. Broad chested, with muscled arms that maneuvered swords or bows with equal grace, he towered over her. Except at the moment, his leg wrapped in bandages, Corbahn sat propped up on his cot, a couple of pillows stacked behind his back. Gesturing at his leg, he said, "I'd stand to greet you, my Liege, but as you can see..."

Linden hurried over to his cot and unconsciously reached out her hand to touch him, inspect him, reassure herself that he was healthy overall. She let her hand drop to her side. She found his familiar scent, of wood smoke and leather, vaguely distracting. "What happened to your leg?"

Corbahn gave her a rueful smile and inclined his head at the chair. "Have a seat. I'm finding it difficult to be looking up all the time. I'm not used to it."

Pulling the chair up to his bed, Linden looked more closely at his leg, immobilized between a pair of wooden splints, and bound tightly all around with white strips of cloth. "Is it broken?"

"Aye, a clean break and plenty of bruising all around. My healer knit it together as best he could." He added, "But I'm not to put any weight on it for four weeks at least."

"How...and when?"

Corbahn ran a hand through the unruly mass of sandy brown hair grazing his shoulders. Although he wore it longer than customary among the clansmen, Linden liked the wildness of his hair, lightly salted with the bright blue highlights of his Faymon birthright. Even Linden, though only half-Faymon, had the same shade of bright blue streaking through her glossy black hair. "Yesterday, when I was breaking in a horse for my sister. That rowdy thing tossed me right from the saddle." He chuckled. "It'll be a marvelous mount when it's fully broken in."

"I wish someone had mentioned this to me."

"I'm not in the habit of reporting my injuries to the Faymon Liege," he grunted.

Linden rolled her eyes. "You know what I mean."

"I didn't think you cared." Corbahn squared his jaw. His

eyes, the same shade as the Pale Sea in summer, flashed deeper green.

He's definitely still angry. "Do we have to do this now?"

"Aye, we do. You're planning to enter occupied Valerra, search for your brother and other resistance fighters, if you can even find them, and enlist their support to defeat King Roi, Mordahn, and his Fallow sorcerers. You're going to do all this with Reynier, a handful of Valerran friends, and the few fays who've helped us in the past—"

"But that's only until we can make contact with the resistance fighters," explained Linden. "The other clans will be positioning warriors and mages all along the border with Valerra, ready to cross over when we give the word." She knew their odds of success were low but if they did nothing, the five Faymon clans—already decimated by fifty years of internal strife—would lose Faynwood, their home. Then the entire continent would fall under Glenbarra's boot, crushed by King Roi's brutal rule and Mordahn's dark magic.

Corbahn continued, ignoring her interruption. "You'll have several thousand Faymon warriors and mages, tops, to march all the way to the Valerran capital. And I'm supposed to remain here, defending our entire western border with less than a thousand trained fighters." Corbahn paused, his eyes boring into hers. "In the meantime, you'll not speak with me about...what happened, what we said to each other when we didn't think we'd make it back alive from our last battle with Mordahn." He scowled at her, folding his arms across his chest. Linden looked away to avoid being distracted by his biceps bulging beneath the thin fabric of his linen shirt.

"We discussed this. The Faymon chiefs and commanders debated it, and the clans agreed. Even the fays think this is the best plan. None of us made this decision lightly." She didn't add that Corbahn had been the only dissenter among the clan chiefs, objecting to the idea of a two-front war, voicing his opposition to being left behind to defend Faynwood's border instead of leading the charge into occupied Valerra. She knew it rankled him, but it also made the most sense militarily, since Faynwood's western border ran through his clan's territory.

She suspected he had personal reasons as well. More overprotective even than Reynier, he wanted to keep her in sight, defend her with his life if needed. Linden recognized the same tendency herself. She'd been secretly relieved when the other clans agreed to the plan. Corbahn would be safer defending Arrowood than at her side in another showdown with Mordahn.

Corbahn rubbed his beard, the same sandy brown as his hair. "You know the fays are already backtracking. Now they're saying they won't get involved until, or unless, you make it all the way to the Valerran capital in one piece."

Linden leaned forward in her chair. "But the fays agreed to the plan. Who told you this?"

"Pryl stopped in for a chat shortly before you arrived. He seemed in a particularly foul mood."

Pryl, Chief of the Fay Nation, was their most loyal supporter among the fays. If he'd changed his mind, then they didn't have a ghost of chance. "He's still coming, isn't he?"

"Aye, but the fay council stabbed him in the back again."

Linden shrugged. "Not for the first time. We'll have to proceed anyway, as we did before."

"Last time we went together." He waved his hand back and forth between them. "Now, you're leaving, and I'm staying behind."

"Is that what's bothering you?"

"Aye. Of course it's bothering me. I should be at your side. Now with this—" he flapped his hand impatiently at his broken leg "—I've no choice but to stay here with the rest of my clan, not knowing when, or if, I'll ever lay eyes on you again." His chest heaved as he took a deep breath, unable to continue.

Linden bit her bottom lip, wanting to wrap her arms around Corbahn, give some comfort to the large, gruff, impossible man, visibly struggling to check his emotions. She said, more softly, "We have to do what's in the best interests of Faynwood and the five clans, and the Valerrans too, for that matter. We can't make this about you and me."

"Even so, you've been avoiding any discussion about us, our future, ever since I brought you the roses and we kissed."

Linden looked at her hands in her lap because she'd lose her resolve if she continued to look at Corbahn. "I met an old psychic from your clan on my way over here today. She claims we are right for each other, but our timing is all wrong. I'm not sure what that means for our future, but she's absolutely right about the present. About our timing, I mean." Linden avoided mentioning the first part of the psychic's revelation, the part about her having to face Mordahn alone.

She glanced up, but Corbahn avoided making eye contact. He stared straight ahead, his mouth set in a firm line, and his arms still crossed. He spoke to the tent wall opposite him. "Liege Linden Arlyss of Tanglewood, may your magic serve in peace and lead through service. This is the true path." Corbahn had given her his formal farewell blessing; time for her to take her leave.

Linden rose from her seat and repeated the words of the blessing. "Chief Corbahn Erewin of Arrowood, may your magic serve in peace and lead through service." Her voice dropped to a whisper. "This is the true path." She stumbled out of his tent, swiping at her eyes to keep them from brimming over.

CHAPTER 2

"Shh! You'll raise the dead, and undead, with all the noise you're making!" Mara hissed, shaking her head, her wheat-colored ponytail swishing across her back. Mara and Linden had once been sworn enemies, pulling hair in grammar school, snubbing each other in junior high, and practicing avoidance in high school. That all changed after the Glenbarrans invaded Valerra, and they had no choice but to get along to survive. They learned to trust each other, their friendship blooming along the way.

"I can't help it," whined Remy. "I misplaced my jerky and I'm famished. We've been traveling all day and half the night." Linden sometimes wondered whether Remy had an extra stomach. Husky, with hazel eyes and curly hair, Remy had grown more subdued in recent months, more self-reflective. He still complained about being hungry all the time, but he'd outgrown his clownish schoolboy antics.

Mara's tone softened. She reached into her saddlebag and pulled out her jerky. "Here, have some of mine."

"Thanks," mumbled Remy, taking a bite. "How much longer, do you think?"

Linden ran her hand through Ashir's mane. Her stallion, sleek black with a white diamond above his eyes, whickered as if to reinforce Remy's question. They'd dismounted to rest their horses, but she didn't feel especially secure as night fell, standing in an unprotected spot near Valerra. After departing from their camp inside Arrowood, they'd been riding for four days, growing more cautious as they neared the Valerran border. "I'm not sure, but Reynier said to keep our horses saddled while he meets up with Pryl, so I'm thinking fairly soon."

"I don't like waiting in the dark, in the woods, without even a small fire to keep warm," grumbled Remy. Linden couldn't argue with him. The only reason they could see each other was the narrow shaft of moonlight filtering through the trees overhead.

Jayna said softly, "I miss him too."

"Sometimes I think I'll turn around and there he'll be, grinning, telling me it was all a joke." Remy shook his head, his voice catching.

Mara nodded. "I know. It feels so strange without him, four of us now, instead of five."

Linden's stomach clenched whenever she thought of Toz, killed during their last mission, stabbed through the chest by a Glenbarran guard. The five of them—Mara, Remy, Jayna, Linden, and Toz—had been classmates together, escaped from Valerra together, and faced the Glenbarrans together. She missed her mischievous, fun-loving friend, her grief still too deep, and the loss too raw.

"Toz would say something funny right now, to lighten our mood." Linden took a deep breath and exhaled. "I miss him terribly." What she didn't say, what none of them voiced, was the question on everyone's mind: how many more would they lose in this fight with Glenbarra? Linden's family had been either killed or scattered, or in the case of her brother, injured

LADY LIEGE

and now missing. Only after she fled from Valerra with her friends had she learned about her other family, her father's Faymon relatives, living inside Faynwood. She'd discovered the old prophecies as well, pointing toward her as the next Liege of Faynwood, and all the duties and obligations that came with the title.

"Did you hear that?" asked Jayna, peering over her shoulder. Everyone paused, listening to the wind whispering through the leaves. "It's horse hooves, striking the ground nearby."

Linden strained but didn't hear anything for a few more beats, and then she could make out the steady clip-clop of a horse or two. "Aye, coming from over there." As she pointed, a couple of shadows moved through the trees. She put her hand on the hilt of her sword.

"Who goes there?" Remy called out nervously.

"It's us," said Reynier. "Mount your horses; we found a good spot for the night." Reynier reminded Linden of her brother, same straight nose and strong chin, same dedication to duty and family. As her cousin and co-leader of the Faymon clans, Elder Reynier Arlyss had known little else but war his entire life. Even so, Reynier's face relaxed whenever he looked at Jayna. Linden's best friend had married well, becoming her cousin by marriage and securing Jayna's reputation as a well-respected healer among the Faymon clans.

They climbed a gentle rise and made camp inside a clearing, with several good-sized boulders to block the wind, and to scurry behind if necessary. When the sun rose, Linden figured they'd have a good view of the area and might be able to see into Valerra.

Sitting around the campfire, sharing a pot of stew Jayna had thrown together from their supplies, Linden felt almost normal. When she traveled on missions, she traveled like anyone else, no Liege's tent, no formalities, nothing to separate her from her friends, or from her old self, before the war changed everything. Everyone traveled with a pair of saddlebags, setting up their own pup tents, carrying their own supplies. They dressed simply in stretchy black tunics and leggings for the women, black trousers for the men, wearing padded leather jackets for extra warmth at night. She inhaled the smoke-scented air, waiting until Pryl had finished eating before she peppered him with questions.

"I hear the fay council is backtracking," said Linden, without preamble. She felt no need to tiptoe around the older fay. His slight build and thinning hair belied his true nature: a powerful, principled fay leader and master of Serving magic. Pryl had earned her trust and her friendship.

He scratched his blue beard, the same shade of vivid blue as his hair. Unlike the Faymons, with blue highlights running through their base hair color of black, brown, blonde, or red, the fays had bright, eye-catching blue hair through and through, except for their eyebrows, which were brown or blonde, or in Pryl's case, silver.

The fay chief sighed. "You heard correctly. I can't say I'm surprised by my fay friends, but disappointed? Aye. Very disappointed." Linden could only imagine how Pryl expressed his disappointment in the fay language, with a lot of buzzing and hissing and facial expressions.

"They don't seem to grasp the true nature of this conflict." Reynier waved his hands, his eyes glittering in the firelight. "King Roi and Mordahn have destroyed Serving magic inside Glenbarra. They're doing the same in Valera. Now Faynwood is next. If the fays don't help us, Fallow sorcery will rule over all."

Pryl nodded. "The fay council knows what's at stake. The problem is all the conflicting opinions and prophecies about how to defeat Fallow magic. Fays like certainty, and no one can say for sure how this will end—none of our seers agree—so they wait and see."

Linden recalled the old psychic's words about prophecies. "We need to make the best decisions we can right now and leave the future to write itself."

"Aye, well said." Pryl agreed. "But I'll confess even I'm flummoxed. I've consulted the oldest texts, the ancient scrolls, and spoken with every seer I can find. The only common denominator is you, my Liege."

"Me? How so?" Linden drew her brows together. *All these old seers and their prophecies, making predictions about me, interfering with my life. When will this end?*

As if reading her thoughts, and Linden wouldn't put it past the old fay chief, Pryl said, "This will end when we defeat Roi and Mordahn, and their Fallow ways, or they defeat us. And every seer agrees, the Faymon Liege is the central figure in this showdown, along with the Elder and a few trusted friends."

Remy leaned over to catch Pryl's attention. "But no one can see whether we win or lose?"

"I'm afraid not, son."

"What about our ensorcelled swords, from the Valerran Museum? Aren't they supposed to help?" asked Mara.

"The swords did help us when we snuck into Glenbarra. We used them to destroy that horrible crossbreeding equipment." Jayna shook her head and shuddered. "Those poor people."

"Which ones?" asked Mara. "The grihms or their families?" Linden and her friends, along with Corbahn, Reynier, Pryl, and a couple of fays had broken into a prison camp inside Glenbarra. They managed to destroy the crossbreeding equipment and set everyone free—the human prisoners, as well as the grihms—half-human, half-wolf crossbreeds. Linden witnessed the reunion of one family, the women still human, the men bred into grihms. Despite the horror, that family and others found a way to stay together. Linden often thought about the grandmother, with her daughter and granddaughter, leaving the prison with two male grihms loping alongside, overjoyed to have found each other again. Although gruesomely altered, they were alive and reunited.

"All of them," said Jayna. "I used to think all grihms were bad, but many of them helped us during the prison escape."

"It doesn't matter anymore, about the swords, I mean. After Toz died, only Corbahn could use his sword. But Corbahn stayed in Arrowood." Remy blinked rapidly at the mention of Toz's sword.

Linden closed her eyes, as a vision of the Weapons Room in the Valerran Museum came into focus. The Glenbarrans had broken through the city gates by then, but they were still fighting the marines in the streets of the Valerran capital. The Serving mages and apprentices hid themselves inside the museum, prepared to make their last stand. They laid all of the ancient fay-spelled weapons, swords and daggers mostly, on the museum floor. Every mage and apprentice walked around, picking up each weapon, waiting for a reaction. When Linden grasped her sword and matching dagger, the fay hieroglyphs along the blades pulsed green, a sure sign the weapons chose her. The same thing happened to Jayna, Mara, Remy, and Toz. The weapons did the choosing.

After Toz died inside that Glenbarran prison, Linden asked Corbahn to pick up the sword. Sure enough, Toz's sword responded to Corbahn's touch. Pryl had told her, before they'd entered the Glenbarran prison, they needed all five ensorcelled swords to break down the crossbreeding equipment. That had proven true then, but was that still the case? *Do we still need all five ensorcelled swords for our Valerran mission to succeed?*

The fay chief rose, went to his horse, and returned with a sword, which he held delicately between his fingers. He laid the sword on the ground. "Chief Corbahn gave me this sword before we left. He says it stopped responding to his touch. No longer lights up."

"Did he say when this happened? When the sword stopped

working for him?" Linden stared at the sword. The sight of Corbahn's weapon lying on the ground, as if fallen from his hand, cut her to the core.

"The day after the Faymon clans voted on the final war plan. You know how he stormed out of the meeting." Linden nodded at Pryl to continue. "When Corbahn returned to his tent he found the sword unsheathed, lying on the floor, not where he left it. He picked it up and nothing happened. The hieroglyphs remained dull gray. He tested it every day until the day before we left, when he gave it to me."

Linden thought of Corbahn, lying on the cot with a broken leg. He told her Pryl had been visiting. Corbahn must have handed over his sword just before she arrived. *What does it mean when a proud warrior and clan chief hands over his fay-spelled sword? When he looks away as he gives his Liege—the woman he loves—his farewell blessing?*

"Corbahn thinks he's going to be killed, fighting the Glenbarrans at the border, doesn't he?" Linden choked out the words, her heart constricting inside her chest. She believed Corbahn would be safer in Arrowood, far away from Mordahn and King Roi. Perhaps, instead, they had given Corbahn a death sentence.

"He didn't say that, nor should you." Pryl answered her sharply. "Didn't you just tell us to make the best decisions we could, in the moment? That's what Corbahn did. He handed over his sword, hoping we could use it on this mission."

Linden took a deep breath and nodded. She had to stay focused, not lose hope and fall into despair. "You're right." She thought about the weapons choosing their owners in the museum. "You've tried already, haven't you?"

Pryl shrugged. "Of course. The sword will choose another."

Linden glanced at Reynier. "Would you give it a try? You'll need to grip the sword firmly by the hilt."

Reynier reached over and picked up the sword. Nothing

happened, the blade remained gray, the hieroglyphs barely visible. "What do you think this means?"

"No idea. All we know for sure is the new owner isn't one of us." Linden narrowed her eyes, as if she could see the sword's owner just beyond the range of her vision, waiting for them somewhere in Valerra.

CHAPTER 3

"Ouch! Go away. I'm trying to sleep." Linden rolled over onto her side, but Kal kept pecking at her legs through her bedroll with his sharp beak. She flung back the covers and sat up, rubbing her eyes. Her miniature griffin had the face of an eagle, framed by a shaggy red mane, the compact body of a small lion, and a strong pair of wings that carried him across a field faster than Ashir could gallop.

Kal clicked his beak and poked her again. "What's up with you? It's still dark outside." Squawking, he flapped his wings. "You miss Zeena, don't you?" Linden had left her black and white cat, a gift from Corbahn, in the Tanglewood enclave with one of her servants. While Kal could hunt for his own food and make himself scarce if necessary, Linden couldn't very well sneak around Valerra looking for resistance fighters with a small cat following at her heels. Kal clicked his beak and walked over to the tent flap.

"Fine, I'm coming." Linden slipped into her leggings, pulled on her boots, and grabbing her jacket, followed Kal out of the tent. Kal padded around one of the boulders and faced south, toward Valerra, his former home. The first hints of pink and orange streaked the sky, the sun not yet above the horizon. Linden perched on one of the lower boulders, Kal climbing next to her and nestling against her side. "You want to watch the sunrise over Valerra?"

Linden buttoned up her black leather jacket and waited for the pink and orange bands to widen and spread as the sun peeked over the eastern ridge. Shafts of light spread across the plain below, casting a golden glow over the land. They'd traveled to the southern edge of Faynwood's densely wooded boundaries, where the towering sequoias, oaks, and maples started thinning out. Gently rolling green hills, farms, and woodlands crisscrossed most of Valerra's countryside. Although many hundreds of miles away, Linden imagined Bellaryss, the capital, sitting just beyond the eastern hills, its pink and gold marble buildings earning it the nickname of "Sunrise City."

She scanned the green valley below for any signs of troop movements or other Glenbarran activities, but everything looked surprisingly normal, peaceful even. She wondered whether the Glenbarrans had set up magical defenses along the border here, as they'd done elsewhere. Pryl would know; he had fay scouts everywhere.

"Will we find Matteo?" Linden said aloud. "Is he Tam, the resistance leader we keep hearing so much about?" Kal cocked his head and looked at her. "I keep hoping it's him, because if it's not, well." She stopped herself from considering the alternative, that her brother hadn't survived his injuries.

"Watching the sunrise, my Liege?" Pryl moved with quiet stealth, almost cat-like, something Linden noticed all fays had mastered. Was it their magic, she wondered, or just their fayness?

Linden pointed to a companion boulder nearby. "Care to join me?"

Pryl wore a short, hooded jacket with pointy sleeves over his dark trousers. He sat down on the flat surface of the boulder and waved his hand. "From this perspective, all looks well. Funny thing, perspective."

Linden arched an eyebrow, thinking perhaps Pryl was trying to tell her something. "Are we speaking about Valerra right now, or something else?"

Pryl lifted his shoulders in a half-shrug. "Generally speaking, I find that distance, and perspective, often help me resolve a situation or dilemma."

Linden glanced back over the land below. "A year ago my grandmother and I were preparing for my Teenth, my seventeenth birthday celebration. While I had qualms about my parents living so close to the border with Glenbarra, most of my concerns focused on what dress I should wear, which classmates to invite, and whether the queen would come."

She turned to look at Pryl. "Now here I am, having inherited the title of Faymon Liege and an entire nation to protect, but most days, I still want to be over there." She pointed toward the east and Bellaryss. "Home."

"Your Valerran home is buried in mists and magic."

"My grandmother's final spell, you mean?"

Pryl nodded. "Nari knew your heritage, of course, and ensured you wouldn't be able to return to your first home even if you wanted." Linden often dreamt of that home, tucked in the outskirts of Bellaryss: walking the lush gardens, picking fruit in the orchards, sipping tea with her grandmother in the library. She'd expected to miss her family, and she still worried whether her parents had made it to The Colonies after the Glenbarrans overran their border town. But she hadn't realized how much she could miss a place and time: Delavan Manor, before the war. Even the name evoked longing.

Linden pushed a chunk of black hair out of her eyes. "My grandmother used to tell me, toward the end, that I needed to find my second home. These days, nothing feels much like home."

Pryl muttered a phrase under his breath, a quick buzzing sound in the fay language. He seemed to be making up his mind about something. "What do you remember of Orion Arlyss?"

Linden shook her head. "My grandfather? He died when my father was just a boy. I've seen some images of him, a few grainy brown photographs and one family portrait hanging in my grandmother's sitting room, painted when my father was a toddler. Why, did you know him?"

Pryl answered her question with another of his own. "How do you think Nari came to live at Delavan Manor, as a young Faymon refugee?"

Linden had never given it any thought. "I figured my grandfather must have been wealthy, but he also fled from the Faymon civil war." She shrugged. "I don't know. Why?"

"I helped Nari escape from Faynwood." Pryl spread his hands out, indicating the green hills in the distance. "I accompanied her to Valerra and helped her make a new home."

Linden patted the fur on Kal's back, listening to him purr. She thought about Pryl's choice of words. He didn't say he helped Nari find a new home. *He helped her* make *a new home.* "Are you trying to tell me you conjured Delavan Manor? That it's all fake?"

Pryl drew his silver eyebrows together. "There is nothing 'fake' about Serving magic."

"You know what I mean. So you and Nari conjured Delavan?"

"You make us sound like two dark sorcerers, doing something illegal. I purchased the estate for her. It had been rundown, unlivable really. And together, we made the repairs."

"I didn't know fays use money," said Linden, trying to imagine her grandmother and Pryl magically repairing a rundown version of the manor.

"Fays have no need for money, but gold comes in handy when dealing with human landowners."

"So you fixed up Delavan Manor together, and then what? You left and she stayed in Valerra?" Linden tilted her head, trying to understand the timeline. "When did she meet my grandfather?"

Pryl ran a hand through his blue hair. Linden glanced at him, his shale gray eyes staring back at her. She'd never noticed Pryl's eye color before, the same shade of gray as her father's eyes, and Matteo's. And hers. She leaned back with a start, jolting Kal, who squawked and flapped his wings, flying off in search of breakfast. Pryl reached out a hand to grip hers. "I am your grandfather, my dear Linden. I have been watching over you since the moment of your birth."

CHAPTER 4

Linden wondered whether she was dreaming. How could the fay chief possibly be her grandfather? She gave her thigh a sharp pinch and winced. "I don't understand. Does that mean you're Orion Arlyss?"

Pryl noticed her wince and chose to ignore it. "My surname is Orion. When we entered Valerra, I dropped my first name of Pryl and took Nari's surname—I became Orion Arlyss. We let people assume we were distant cousins, originally from Faynwood."

"But why?" Linden was having a hard time reconciling Chief Pryl of the Fay Nation with her idea of a grandfather, someone who told exciting bedtime stories and played hide and seek all afternoon with his sons, two memories shared by her father about her grandfather. And who could have missed his shockingly blue hair and beard? She knew that fay scouts used glamour or dye to hide their hair color and blend in better with humans. Pryl must have done the same.

"We chose to hide my identity to protect the future generations, our children and grandchildren."

"Protect us from what?" asked Linden.

"From whom, you mean."

"Alright then," said Linden. "From whom?" Pryl looked at Linden steadily, waiting for her to catch on. She shaded her eyes from the rising sun, watching Kal glide over a nearby field. "From Mordahn?"

"Aye, but we were also concerned about the Fallow sorcerers among Mordahn's clan at the time. His father, a master sorcerer, started the civil war by killing Liege Ayala and her husband—Nari's parents. Although Mordahn's father died during the battle, we knew there were other dark sorcerers, Mordahn among them. His clan started their own version of a crossbreeding program before the war, creating the first grihms." Pryl paused and glanced out over the peaceful Valerran countryside. "We chose anonymity, until the appointed time."

Linden frowned, still struggling with the timelines. "What's the appointed time?"

Pryl spread his hands in front of him, palms upward. "Here and now. You and me sitting here, looking out over those green hills below, preparing for a final showdown—Serving magic versus Fallow sorcery—us against them."

"Did my father or Uncle Alban ever know they were half fay?"

Pryl shook his head. "We decided not to tell Ric and Alban when they were growing up. We thought it might be too tempting to brag about having a fay father, and we feared they might be ostracized. But then we had to fake my death to keep the truth from coming out. A servant spotted me one evening as I was arriving at Delavan Manor, emerging from my traveling mists. Nari and I realized we couldn't continue the fiction any longer and so I left."

The idea of two people who loved each other having to split up to keep their family safe made Linden feel incredibly sad. "Did you see my grandmother after that?"

"Whenever Nari traveled away from Delavan. We made the most of our time together." He paused, folding his hands in his lap. His voice sounded reedy, as if he had to force out the next words. "Now Nari and Alban are gone, and Ric has moved beyond my traveling mists."

Linden reached over and gripped his arm. "Would you know if my father was gone too, if he never made it to The Colonies with Mother?"

"With distance, and interference from the Barrens, the connection between us becomes more tenuous. But the answer is aye, I would know. I'm convinced your father and mother made it to The Colonies and are living somewhere beyond the Barrens."

Linden brought her hands to her heart and held them there for a moment, relief washing over her. "I've been worried about them for so long." She thought of her brother and asked, "What about Matteo?"

"After the base camp hospital where he was recovering fell to the Glenbarrans, I lost track of him."

Linden dropped her hands into her lap. "Matteo is gone?" She'd held onto her hope about Matteo for so long, and now this?

Pryl hastened to clarify. "Your brother is alive but hard to track, which tells me he's part of the resistance. Our challenge now is to find him. He's mastered the magic of remaining hidden, useful for avoiding the Glenbarrans, but difficult for us to make contact with him."

Linden nodded. "That makes sense. Matteo has always been good at protection charms and veiling spells. He would know how to conceal himself and those with him." She heard Remy say something about breakfast behind them, and she asked, "Who else knows about you and Nari?"

"No one else. This is a secret for your ears only. I understand how much you miss Valerra and your family; I miss them too. This is your home now, the Faymons and fays are your people, by magic and by blood. I'm proud of how well you've adjusted to your role as the Liege of Faynwood. I hope one day you'll be equally proud of yourself."

Linden's eyes welled and she sniffed. "Thank you for everything, for trusting me enough to tell me and for looking after me all these years. I'm glad to know the truth."

Remy called out to them, "I've made porridge, my mother's secret recipe. Are you coming?"

Pryl stood up and turned toward Remy's voice. "Of course. We wouldn't want to miss out on any secret recipes." Patting Linden's arm, he whispered. "We will find Matteo, and we will defeat the Glenbarrans. And afterward we'll come back home. There will be peace in Faynwood, and in Valerra as well."

"What are you two whispering about?" Reynier handed Pryl a mug of tea.

Pryl raised an eyebrow. "Secret recipes and world peace."

"If you have a secret recipe for peace, let's hear it."

"I'm afraid there's no secret recipe for defeating the Glenbarrans and their Fallow sorcery."

Linden sat down by the fire, cradling a mug of hot tea in her hands as a series of lightning-fast images came to her. She was back in her grandmother's study, trying to decipher *Collected Tales of the Fay Nation*. The ancient book, written in fay hieroglyphs, had chosen to reveal itself to Linden. However, since no one—not even Nari or Pryl—could decipher more than a few of the old fay hieroglyphs, the book had to be magically spelled for translation.

Linden had placed the open book beneath her grandmother's large crystal globe and uttered the incantation for translating. The book started decoding for Linden, pages flipping past, images scrolling so quickly she couldn't keep them straight. Those images were scrolling past her again, this time inside her head, and they were starting to weave a pattern she hadn't noticed before.

"Tunnels," said Linden.

"What about tunnels?" Mara leaned over and topped up Linden's mug with more hot water.

"That's the key to how the Valerran resistance has been evading the Glenbarrans. There are miles and miles of underground passages beneath the capital, a combination of limestone caves and old man-made tunnels that connect them. Some extend well beyond the gates of Bellaryss, and a couple lead to the Pale Sea." Linden put down her mug long enough to massage her temples. Her head usually ached after she expended a lot of magical energy, either interpreting visions or casting powerful spells.

"But the Glenbarrans would have figured that out by now," pointed out Remy.

"No one knows the tunnels better than the cadets at the Royal Marine Academy," said Jayna. She had dated Linden's brother in the months before the war. "I remember Matteo telling me how they had to memorize the main tunnel systems. No one could possibly memorize the entire layout. The marine instructors used to conduct practice drills with the cadets underground. I think the marines were the only ones who used those old tunnels anyway."

Linden nodded. "There would have been tunnels beneath the base camp headquarters as well, including the hospital. Once the Glenbarrans started attacking the base, Matteo and the other injured soldiers could have evacuated below ground."

"I've heard stories about those tunnels." Remy's eyes widened. "My mother used to tell me that little boys who wandered below ground disappeared, eaten by the tunnel witch."

Mara laughed. "She only told you that to keep you out of the tunnels. There's no such thing as a tunnel witch."

Remy shrugged. "Well it worked. I never set foot in one of them."

"Matteo did tell me there are a lot of unfinished tunnels and dead ends, so you could easily get lost," said Linden. "They can be dangerous if you don't know where the exits are located."

Pryl scratched his beard, thinking out loud. "If Matteo and other resistance fighters are using veils of drabness and immobility spells beneath the ground, only moving around when no one is in range, that would explain why my scouts haven't been able to make contact."

"But if that's the case, how are we supposed to find them?" asked Reynier.

"We go below ground as well, when the time comes." Linden didn't think Kal would be a fan, but she couldn't think of a better alternative.

"But you said there are a lot of dead ends, and it's easy to get lost," said Reynier. "How can we be sure we'll wind up anywhere near the resistance?"

Linden took a sip from her mug, her tea now tepid. "We have a lot of territory to cover above ground, before we're ready to search for them below ground. We'll go where the resistance has been creating the most trouble and either try to help them or hinder the Glenbarrans."

Pryl agreed. "We have a good idea where the resistance is most active, and it's at some of the bases and inside Bellaryss itself. It makes sense they're moving around underground."

"Why haven't the Glenbarrans tried smoking them out? Or blocking the tunnels?" asked Remy.

"I'm sure they've tried, but tunnels can be unblocked again, or different routes employed," replied Pryl.

Reynier wiped out his mug and stood up. "I suggest we pack up and keep moving. Although we can see Valerra, we'll be riding most of the day before we reach the border."

"Is the border heavily guarded?" Jayna began dousing the campfire.

"Or alarmed with defensive spells?" asked Mara.

Pryl rose from the ground and brushed off his trousers. "The Glenbarrans don't seem too concerned with guarding the Valerran border, at least not here. We'll have no trouble crossing over after dark."

CHAPTER 5

"What was that about having no trouble crossing over?" grumbled Remy, as a unit of Glenbarran troopers took up positions on the other side of the Valerran border within shouting distance. The last rays of the setting sun peeked through the trees.

"Could they have caught wind of our plans?" Linden whispered, worried everything they'd set in motion would backfire before they'd even gotten started.

Reynier shook his head. "I don't think so. This looks like a routine deployment of guards. The Glenbarrans move their units around to different locations along the border. We're not going to be able to cross here."

"Can't we use the traveling mists?" asked Mara. "They worked really well last time." Fays could conjure traveling mists when they wanted to move quickly from one location to another. Pryl and his fay scouts had used the mists during their last mission to transport the team in stages and avoid Glenbarran soldiers along the way.

Pryl shook his head. "It will take too long. The horses are so heavy I can only transfer two of us at a time."

"We're going to have to find another spot to cross over. I'll take point." Linden mounted Ashir and turned him around.

They backtracked farther into Faynwood territory and rode silently, single file, pausing periodically for Reynier or Pryl to dismount and slip through the trees to inspect the border. Each time they returned with a shake of the head, and the group crept forward, riding until the moon was high overhead.

Reynier returned from his latest border inspection. "All's quiet here, and I've confirmed there are no defensive shields up."

"How far are we from the rendezvous point?" asked Linden.

"About ten miles. We'll need to cross soon if we want to reach it before the sun rises," said Pryl, bringing his horse alongside Linden and Reynier. "Follow me, and no talking, hand signals only."

Linden rode directly behind Pryl, who held up his right hand and waved it back and forth when they reached the border. As Ashir crossed over, his front hooves in Valerra and rear hooves in Faynwood, Linden thought about stopping and putting a flag in the ground right there, to claim both sides of that border for herself. Earlier in the year, when she'd first learned about the long line of Faymon Lieges who'd come before her, she'd been surprised, shocked even. Discovering that Pryl, chief of the fays, was her grandfather Orion had left her feeling unmoored, wondering who she really was and where she belonged.

Linden wished she could retreat somewhere, away from clans and secrets and war, to dwell on all she'd learned, to get her head around the truth of her parentage and her heart around her jumbled feelings for Corbahn. However, she had no time to dwell on her own problems. She had to remain focused on finding the resistance and her brother, on fighting back against the Fallowness overtaking Valerra and threatening Faynwood.

"Someone's coming!" hissed Jayna, whose hearing abilities were second only to her healing skills.

Linden rode up to Pryl, who hadn't heard Jayna. "We need to cast a veil of drabness, now!"

Pryl's eyebrows rose, but he nodded. Linden and Pryl whispered the words of the incantation, "Drape us in a veil of gauze, hide us from inquiring eyes."

The others pulled up their horses, wondering why they'd stopped. The veil of drabness would blur their appearance, cloaking them in a blanket of grayness. No amount of magic could make them truly invisible, which Linden reflected would come in handy more times than she could count.

A pack of grihms howled nearby, raising the hairs on the back of Linden's neck. The crossbreeds, half-human and half-wolf, howled again, closer this time. Ashir neighed, Linden leaning over to pat his neck. She considered casting an immobility spell on the horses but decided they might need to gallop away in a hurry. She hoped the veil of drabness, coupled with the darkness, would be enough to hide them in plain sight. Kal, draped behind her saddle for a nap, let out a low, throaty hiss.

The lead grihm and his pack came into view, about a dozen of them, running hard. The veil of drabness worked better than Linden expected, the grihms charging toward them, unaware six horses blocked their path. Several of the horses neighed, Ashir among them. The lead grihm stopped, the others in his pack pausing, wary. He scratched his forehead with his front paw, a very human gesture. His yellow-amber eyes stared around wildly, as if he feared whatever was blocking his path. Rearing up on his wolfish hind legs, he sniffed the air with his long snout. Dropping down to all fours, he paced in front of the veil cast by Linden and Pryl, sensing their presence beyond the grayness. Baring his canines, the grihm yipped and turned toward the north, leading his pack around the strange impediment. Linden, who'd been holding her breath as the grihm stared into the veil, let it out in a soft sigh. She and Pryl waited a good five minutes before lifting the veil and soothing the horses, still spooked by the close encounter.

They rode a few more hours, even Remy subdued and not complaining of hunger pains, until Pryl pulled up his horse in front of a ridge, more of a mound than a hill. He dismounted and waved his right hand to indicate they should move forward, on foot, leading their horses directly into the mound. Linden couldn't make out any opening in its surface, but she trusted Pryl and walked ahead, leading Ashir by the reins while Kal plodded along beside her.

As Pryl and his horse passed through the wall of the mound, Kal sprinted ahead, tail high, and leapt into the wall. Linden knitted her eyebrows, still unable to see any opening, and ploughed forward. When she reached out to touch the wall, her hand fell through, its solidness turned to vaporous membrane.

"Come on in, it's spelled open." Pryl called from inside the compound.

Linden stepped through the membrane with Ashir, who nosed forward, probably smelling fresh hay and a bucket of oats on the other side. Linden squinted as light from dozens of oil lamps blazed cheerily, the oil lamps suspended from the ceiling of the mound, which arched overhead and stretched as far as Linden could see. They'd entered what appeared to be a great hall, with various passageways leading away from the center of the compound.

"Welcome to the oldest fay compound still in use today. Our ancestors constructed this over a millennia ago." Pryl pointed down the passage closest to the entrance. "Take care of your horses and then come find me."

Linden led Ashir to the stable area, triple the size of her uncle's stable at Delavan. Fresh hay lined one long wall of the stable, where several horses, including Pryl's, stared back at them. At the rear of the stable, water bubbled from beneath the ground, pooling in a semi-circular pond, an ever-present, continually refreshed watering trough. Large burlap sacks filled with oats and grains leaned against the third wall, with enough feed to satisfy their horses for the next few months. Linden removed Ashir's saddle and gave him a good brush-down. The others followed her into the stable, oohing and aahing at the accommodations for their horses. When Linden left Ashir, he was munching on some oats and nuzzling Hoff, Reynier's horse.

Linden returned to the great hall and followed the buzzing voices of Pryl and another fay, a woman. Linden went down a passageway that opened into a library, its shelves stocked floor to ceiling with old scrolls. A fire roared inside a large stone fireplace on one wall. Well-worn chairs and a few large tables were scattered about the room, with oil lamps suspended above them casting plenty of light for reading.

The fay scout wore her dyed-brown hair in a side braid, a few telltale blue highlights showing along her roots. When she spotted Linden, she smiled and bowed. "It's good to see you are fully recovered, my Liege."

"Wreyn! It's good to see you again." Linden walked over and gave the fay a hug. Sensing tension in the other woman, she stepped back. "What's wrong?"

Pryl nodded at Reynier and the others, who'd followed Linden into the library. "You may as well tell all of us, so we can plan accordingly."

Wreyn walked over to the fireplace, and turning to face them, folded her hands in front of her. "I stumbled across a handful of Glenbarran deserters fleeing from their guard unit the night before last. I offered them some food and a few gold coins in exchange for information. Their leader, a sergeant, told me they were all conscripts, taken from their farms to serve in the Glenbarran army. They were promised good pay, in return for a year of service. That was eighteen months ago. They've received no pay for months, and food rations are running low.

"Several weeks ago, they were reassigned to guard duty inside the largest and unruliest prison camp in Valerra. The camp commander forces Valerran prisoners to fight and kill each other, a contest of strength, in exchange for better food at regular intervals. At least, that's what the prisoners are being told. Many of the Valerrans are refusing and being killed outright. Those who fight and win are given one decent meal, before they're shipped off to the capital, to be crossbred into grihms." Wreyn paused, her dark eyes clouded. "Mordahn is working on creating a new race of grihms, super hunters, able to track down resistance fighters wherever they're hiding, above or below ground."

Linden rubbed her arms, a chill running down her spine. "How reliable were these deserters? They might have said anything, especially if they were hungry."

"I used a truth-saying spell on them. They were telling me the truth, as they understood it. Efram has heard similar accounts. He's gone to the capital to see for himself." Efram, along with Wreyn, were Pryl's most faithful scouts. They had accompanied Linden on their last mission inside Glenbarra, and she trusted them as much as she trusted her Valerran friends.

Pryl shook his head. "I specifically asked you and Efram to avoid the capital. It's too full of Fallow sorcerers. Mordahn has eyes and ears everywhere. I'll have to go after him."

"Aye, Chief, but I had a good lead." Efram stumbled out of his traveling mists, the foggy tendrils still wrapped around his legs. He fell forward onto the floor, bleeding from a gash on his forehead. His curly hair, dyed black, was damp with perspiration.

Wreyn ran over to him, touching his wound. "This wound's

infected with Fallow poison. He needs a fay healer, Chief, and soon."

"I'll take him now," said the chief, his brow furrowed, "but Efram might have been tracked back to the compound. Cast a defensive shield and wait for me." Pryl knelt beside Efram's still form, the vaporous mists wrapping themselves around the two of them, and then winking out as they both vanished.

Reynier looked at Linden and the others. "I don't think we have any time to waste. Are we ready to cast the shield?"

Nodding, Linden said, "I'll get us started." She uttered the incantation for the defensive shield, which everyone else repeated. "Conjure a shield around this spot, defend with strength against onslaught."

Unlike veils of drabness, useful for remaining hidden, defensive shields and charms provided physical protection from arrows, spears, or swords. However, they didn't offer protection against opposing magic. The right amount of Fallow magic could break down the shield if the Serving mages became too weak to reinforce it. Linden remembered her fellow mages collapsing as they battled against Mordahn's sorcery during the siege of the capital. In the end, the Serving mages were too few and too weakened to reinforce the defensive curtain of fog they'd spun up, and the fog evaporated. Fallow magic had defeated Serving magic that day, and many days since.

Reynier lifted his head and sniffed. "I smell something delicious."

"I almost forgot," said Wreyn, leading them out of the library and back into the great hall. "I made us dinner, or I guess its breakfast, but Efram and I mostly scout at night and sleep during the day, so my days and nights are all mixed up."

"I don't care what you call it; I'm beyond starved." Remy followed on Wreyn's heels. "If you need a taster, I volunteer."

Wreyn laughed and pointed at a long, low table, able to seat fifty or sixty, at the far end of the great hall. Floor cushions in bright hues of red, blue, yellow, and green, were scattered about the table, which had been set up in front of the largest fireplace Linden had ever seen. The different colored stones of the fireplace reflected the orange flames of the fire roaring inside the grate. "Have a seat, I've already laid the table."

Linden's stomach growled. She realized she hadn't eaten since breakfast that morning. They'd been too concerned with crossing the border and finding the fay compound to stop along the way.

Reynier poured out mugs of warm honeyed wine, while Wreyn served them a hearty soup, with chunks of brown bread and hard cheese on the side. Remy managed to put away three bowls before his head started nodding over his mug. Yawning, he said, "I don't think I'll be much use until I get a few hours of sleep. Can someone wake me when it's my turn to maintain the shield?"

"I'm not sleepy, so I'll take the first watch," said Linden.

"I'll sit up with you." Wreyn added some logs to the fire and pointed down a different passageway. "Sleeping nooks are that way."

"Alright," said Reynier, who gave Jayna a hand up from the floor cushion. "We could both use some rest. Jayna and I can take next watch."

Mara followed them down the hall. "That's good, because once I lay down my head, I may not wake up until morning, or evening. Whatever, you know what I mean."

Wreyn handed Linden a mug of coffee. "Here, I figured we could both use some."

"Good thinking, thanks." Linden inhaled the nutty aroma, taking small sips of the piping hot drink. She glanced at Wreyn, wondering whether her fay friend had noticed Pryl's face, just before he'd vanished into the mists with Efram.

Wreyn frowned into her mug. "Did you see the expression on Pryl's face, when he didn't think anyone was looking?"

Linden set her mug down on the table. "Pryl looked utterly defeated. I've never seen him that way before."

"Like we'd already lost the final battle in the final war against Fallow magic."

Linden tilted her head to one side, considering Wreyn's words. "You're talking about the complete destruction of Serving magic, aren't you?"

Wreyn nodded. "And all of us, along with it."

CHAPTER 6

"What did Pryl see that we didn't?" Linden picked up her mug and took another swallow. She didn't like the idea of a new breed of super-hunter grihms, but she didn't think that was it.

"The flesh around Efram's wound had turned putrid."

"What does that mean?"

Wreyn poured fresh coffee from an earthenware pitcher, topping up both their mugs. "That gash on Efram's forehead was caused by something Fallow and undead."

Linden stared at Wreyn, the implications sinking in. "Mordahn is both Fallow and undead, but if he injured Efram, then—"

"Then he probably tracked Efram back here," Wreyn concluded matter-of-factly.

Linden wanted to sound the alarm, immediately wake up her friends, but she forced herself to slow down and think. She stared into the fireplace, considering her previous encounters with Mordahn. Linden shook her head. "Mordahn prefers the element of surprise. He would have launched an attack before we spun up our shield. I'm certain it wasn't him."

Wreyn shrugged. "All I know is that someone like Mordahn, an undead Fallow mage, caused that injury."

Linden recalled something Mordahn had said to her during their first battle, which she repeated to Wreyn. "He once told me, 'There are others.' I thought he meant other Fallow sorcerers. But that's not it at all." Linden looked at Wreyn, her stomach feeling leaden all of a sudden. "Mordahn was talking about necromancers. If they could raise him, they could raise others like him."

"Which means King Roi's necromancers raised another sorcerer from the dead, someone like Mordahn. And that sorcerer got close enough to Efram to wound him," said Wreyn.

"How do you kill something that's already dead?" Linden wondered aloud.

"And multiplying?"

"No wonder Pryl looked so worried when he was leaving with Efram." Linden frowned and sipped her coffee. Neither of them spoke for a while.

Wreyn swirled the contents of her mug around, finally breaking the silence. "Tell me, what's going on with you and Corbahn? Why isn't he here?"

Linden thought of a dozen possible answers, all of them partially true. She opted for frankness. "I'm not sure what's going on between us, but it has nothing to do with why he remained behind in Arrowood. The clans decided we needed to split up our fighting forces and ensure the border with Glenbarra is protected. Since that border runs through Arrowood, Corbahn is charged with defending it."

"Something tells me he didn't like that plan very much. Corbahn isn't one to stay behind and defend. He'd much rather be out front, taking point."

Linden sighed. "You're right. He's unhappy staying behind

in Arrowood and angry I left without him. But then he broke his leg the day before we left, so he really had no choice."

"Ouch, I'm sorry to hear it." Wreyn hesitated before adding, "I'll say this just once, and because we're friends. You and Corbahn are more right together than any two people I know."

Linden shook her head. "What about Reynier and Jayna? They're perfect for each other."

Wreyn flapped her hand in the air dismissively. "They complement each other, a good melding of two like personalities. On the other hand, you and Corbahn are opposites. When you're in the same room, sparks fly. It's exciting to watch."

"That's exactly the problem. We spend more time arguing than not. Besides, I don't like the idea of a prophecy dictating my love life."

"I think you've hit on the real problem," said Wreyn.

"What's the real problem, then?"

"Knowing that some seers made a prediction about you and Corbahn is getting in the way of your true feelings. You're allowing the prophecy to rule your life. Set the seers and their predictions aside. When it comes to Corbahn, rule with your heart. You'll know what to do."

Linden thought about the number of prophecies that revolved around the Faymon Liege. "Easier said than done when you're the Liege. There seems to be a prophecy about everything."

Wreyn shrugged. "Unless there's something to be learned from the prophecies, such as how to defeat Mordahn, and I don't think there is, then ignore them. Live your life, write your own story as you go."

Wreyn's words echoed the old psychic's, good advice she shouldn't ignore. "Thanks, I'll do my best."

"Don't I know it. You always do your best." Wreyn picked

up the earthenware pitcher and their mugs and headed down the passageway to the left of the fireplace. Linden followed her, carrying the last remnants of their dinner into the kitchen. A large preparation table stood in the center of the room. Shelves, stocked with preserved vegetables and dried meats, lined one wall, and a hand pump stood between two deep basins for washing and rinsing. A fireplace darkened with age, and a large brick oven for baking bread, ran along the rear wall of the kitchen. Several pots of different sizes hung above the fire.

Linden wondered how many fays might have lived in the compound at one time and made a mental note to check out each passageway before she left. She knew the fays once occupied the entire continent, before the first man or woman had set foot in Faynwood or established outposts in Valerra or Glenbarra. Decimated by their own wars and internal strife in the past, the remaining fay population numbered a few thousand. According to Pryl, the fay council recently voted to leave Faynwood entirely, delaying their departure until after King Roi and Mordahn were defeated. The fays planned to find a new home, someplace where they would no longer be drawn into wars started by men.

Linden dried the dishes after Wreyn rinsed them. As she worked, Wreyn hummed a fay melody under her breath. Linden swayed, Wreyn's music nearly intoxicating in its sweetness. "Why Wreyn, you have a lovely voice. You should sing more often."

Wreyn blushed. "Nay, I'd rather sing for myself than others."

"But why?"

Wreyn rested her damp hands against the wash basin. "As a fay with perfect pitch and tone, I need to be careful about who hears me sing. You've heard it said that revealing your full name to someone gives them power over you?"

Linden nodded and Wreyn reached back into the soapy water to wash the last of the mugs. "It's the same with my voice. I must take care it doesn't fall into the wrong hands. Otherwise, my music could be misdirected."

"I'm finding it hard to imagine how music can be misused, but I'll take your word for it."

Wreyn glanced at Linden. "Music is one of the keys for accessing other realms. Music combined with dark sorcery could wreak havoc we'd be hard put to overcome."

Linden frowned as she considered Wreyn's words. The idea of music unlocking other realms confounded her. Although Linden was a master of Serving magic, she still had much to learn about fays and the world beyond her senses. She waited until Wreyn finished rinsing out the last mug using the hand pump. "It's about that time again. Let's reinforce the spell."

They repeated the words of the incantation, something they needed to do periodically to maintain the defensive shield in place. When they were done, Linden said, "There must be dozens, hundreds, of protection charms cast by fays over the years to protect this place. Do you think one more defensive spell is all that necessary?"

Wreyn started to answer, then pausing, cocked her head to one side. "Did you hear that? It sounds like rain, but the sky was clear earlier."

Linden listened. "I hear a pattering noise coming from outside. But I don't think it's rain." The pattering grew louder, sounding more like boots hitting the ground outside the compound. The oil lamps swayed above their heads. "Could the Glenbarrans have tracked us down?"

"Let's go check it out."

"How? It's too dangerous to leave the compound."

"We don't have to leave. Follow me." Wreyn scrambled out of the kitchen and crossed the great hall. Linden followed her down another passage that opened into a round room with a high, domed ceiling formed of clear panes of glass. Two scopes sat in the center of the observatory, a night scope for viewing constellations and planets, and a land scope that could be swiveled around in a complete circle and angled in any direction between ground and horizon.

Wreyn swung the land scope around to find the source of the noise. "Glenbarran troopers, lots of them. They're marching right past us. Here, take a look."

Linden peered through the eyepiece, adjusting the knobs on the side of the scope to bring the image into focus. Row after row of Glenbarran troopers, their boots pounding the ground, marched in formation toward the border. Linden's stomach seized when she realized their target wasn't the compound. Multiple units of soldiers and grihms, numbering in the thousands and heading northwest, could only mean one thing: the Glenbarrans were preparing to invade Arrowood. Corbahn's small army of warriors didn't stand a chance.

"We have to warn Corbahn." Linden stepped away from the scope, her mind made up. "And the other clan chiefs. The clans will need to focus on protecting Arrowood, and the rest of Faynwood, from invasion. We need a different plan, one that doesn't involve a reliance on the clans to help us in Valerra, at least for now."

"Jayna asked me to come check on you. She heard your voices, and some sort of commotion outside." Reynier rubbed the sleep out of his eyes, peering more closely at Linden. "What's going on?"

Linden quickly filled him in as he gazed through the scope. When Reynier straightened up and turned to face Linden, his face looked ashen. "I agree we need a new plan, one that leaves the clans in place to defend Faynwood for now. We need to let the other chiefs know what's going on."

Wreyn nodded. "I'm the only one who can leave here

unnoticed. I'll go find Pryl and explain about the change of plan. And I'll warn the others."

"What change of plan? Warn us about what?" Pryl emerged from the traveling mists, looking weary and a bit disheveled.

"Chief! How's Efram doing?"

"Efram will recover, but he needs complete rest for now, until the infection is leached out." Pryl walked over to the scope. Reynier swiveled the eyepiece around so the fay chief could peer out. After Pryl had taken a look, he stepped back, his mouth set in a firm line. "The clans will need to help Corbahn defend Faynwood. Wreyn and I will go warn the others."

"We'll wait until the troops move past and then we'll head east. We'll look to make contact with the resistance," said Linden.

Wreyn waved her hand in the direction of the great hall and library. "Efram and I made a map of resistance movements. It's in the library, along with our notes. That should give you some idea of where to start."

"Move only at night and avoid the villages and towns. Stick to the back roads. We'll find you after we've spoken with the clan chiefs." Vaporous tendrils wrapped themselves around Pryl and Wreyn. Pryl nodded at Linden, as if to reassure her all would be well, and then the mists came between them.

Linden watched as the last wisps of vapor dissipated, her thoughts with Corbahn, lying on his cot with a broken leg, unaware of the pending attack. "I don't like our odds."

"Which ones? The odds of us joining up with the resistance? Or the odds of Faynwood repelling the invasion?" asked Reynier.

"Both. But I was thinking about the survival of Serving magic. I sense defeat at every turn."

Reynier drew his brows together. "Have you seen a vision of our defeat?"

"It's not that." Linden shook her head. "I don't like admitting this to anyone else, but I can't see how we're going to win this."

"You're forgetting we had *some* good news from Wreyn. The Glenbarran war machine is running out of cash and food. In fact, I wouldn't be surprised if that sped up their timetable for the invasion."

Linden considered Wreyn's story of the Glenbarran deserters and agreed with Reynier—there was a small bit of good news amidst the gloom. "And Mordahn must be having trouble tracking down the resistance, if he's resorting to breeding better, faster super-grihms."

"Aye," said Reynier, "let's make it a point to find the resistance, and your brother, before the grihms do."

CHAPTER 7

When Linden finally crawled into her bedroll inside one of the sleeping nooks off the great hall, she expected to be lying awake for hours. Instead, she fell asleep immediately and dreamt of her brother. She and Matteo were staying with their grandmother at Delavan Manor while their parents took a trip. Matteo was about nine at the time, Linden two years younger, which meant Matteo chose what games they played. Invariably, he chose games he excelled in, such as hide and seek.

"...18, 19, 20, 21. Time's up, here I come!" called out Linden, opening her eyes and spinning around. She'd been standing in the corner of the front parlor, listening as Matteo scurried off to hide. Nari's bedroom and Uncle Alban's study were off-limits, but that left a lot of rooms for hiding and exploring. Linden started on the first floor looking for Matteo and worked her way up to the top of the manor, to the fourth floor where her grandmother kept her carrier pigeons. The pigeons cooed at Linden when she entered. Nari turned toward her.

"Looking for Matteo again? He isn't here." Nari smiled

sympathetically. "Have you ever noticed how he likes to hide in plain view?"

Linden shrugged and trudged down the stairs, mulling over Nari's question. Matteo could hide himself inside shrubbery, drapes, and wardrobes with ease, seeming to blend right in, without using veils of drabness or other magic, since that was against the rules. Somewhere below, she heard Matteo's muffled shout, "Give up yet?"

And she yelled back, "No!"

Retracing her steps, she barreled down to the second floor, into the gallery filled with portraits and sculptures. One of the sculptures, draped in a sheet, was being restored. She skidded on the polished wood floor, slid into the covered sculpture, and wrapped her arms around her brother. "Found you!"

Matteo whipped the sheet off his head, grinning. "But you overlooked me the first time you dashed through here." Pointing to a sculpture missing one of its arms, he added, "See, that's the one needing repair, and you ran right past it. You need to look more carefully. There are always clues if you're paying attention." He draped the sheet over the broken sculpture and took her hand. "Cook just made some chocolate biscuits, and I know where they're cooling. Let's go snatch some."

"But won't she get mad?"

Matteo shook his head. "Nah, she always makes extra. You worry too much."

The dream faded but Linden struggled to remain asleep, wanting to spend a few more moments with her memory of Matteo, playful and safe at Delavan Manor. She opened her eyes and stared at the ceiling of the sleeping nook. "You're out there somewhere in Valerra, hiding in plain view, and I'm going to find you."

Dressing quickly in her tunic and leggings, she crossed the great hall and entered the stable to feed Ashir. Kal padded over to her, clicking his beak in greeting. Linden leaned down to ruffle his mane. "So this is where you spent the night? Hanging with the horses?" Kal trotted away, tail held high, leading her to the food bins. He gave her boot a peck and then stepped back, waiting. "Coming right up."

Grabbing a sack of oats from the bin, she topped up all the feed buckets and pumped fresh water into the trough. She poured seeds from a second bin onto the ground for Kal. He normally hunted for his meals, but that wasn't an option while they were lying low inside the compound. Linden stepped back and counted off the horses, five in total. She didn't know when Pryl transported them, but the fays' horses were gone. "Five is a lonely number when you're riding into hostile territory."

Kal looked up from pecking the seeds and cocked his head at her. He gave a low rumble from his throat and went back to his seeds. Linden sat on one of the food bins, watching Kal and the horses munching their meal. As much as she wanted to find Matteo and join forces with the resistance, she wondered whether anything they did would change the course of the war. Fallow sorcerers had defeated Serving mages in battle after battle, their Fallowness creeping across Glenbarra, overtaking Valerra, and now threatening Faynwood.

Could they really save Faynwood and chase the Glenbarrans from Valerra? Without help from Pryl and the fays, they had no hope of overcoming King Roi and Mordahn.

When she had time to think about it, Linden struggled to reconcile the notion that Pryl Orion, fay chief, and Orion Arlyss, her grandfather, were one and the same. Fortunately, Pryl hadn't treated her any differently after she learned the truth about their blood tie. He'd always been politely deferential to her as the Liege of Faynwood, while at the same time offering his opinions as freely as any other person of his age and station. In other words, Pryl managed to act like both chief and grandfather.

"I wish Nari were here right now. I have a hundred questions for her."

Kal clicked his beak at Linden and flapped his wings, an offer to fly off and find her. "Thanks, but Nari has passed on. We have to do this without her advice, which means we're on our own." Kal tucked his head inside one wing. "I feel the same way." Her grandmother, the wisest woman and highest-ranking Serving mage in Valerra, died at the end of a Glenbarran sword. Linden missed her more as the months passed since her death, not less. Linden missed the simple things, sipping tea together in Nari's sitting room, or practicing magic under her watchful eye.

"Who are you talking to?" asked Mara, wandering into the stable.

"Myself, mostly, but Kal is a good listener."

Hearing his name, Kal padded over to Mara and rolled on his side, looking for a rub. Smiling, she bent down to pat his stomach. "Reynier thinks he found a clue, or more like several clues, to the whereabouts of the resistance. We're in the library."

Linden hopped off the bin. "I could use some good news."

Mara led the way out of the stable and down the hall to the library. "We need you to be the optimist. If you lose hope, then it's over."

Linden paused, placing her hand on Mara's arm. "Is that really true?"

Nodding, Mara patted her hand, and then tucked Linden's arm under her own. "We've been following you since the siege of Bellaryss, and you've been right at every turn."

Linden's eyes welled and she blinked rapidly. "But we lost Toz, and so many others."

"We all knew the risks, Toz included. Besides, Toz wasn't about to let you go into any fight alone." Mara's voice dropped low. "As I'm sure you figured out, he loved you."

Linden couldn't afford to dwell on Toz and their complicated relationship, or she'd completely break down. Toz had loved her deeply, unselfishly, and despite her strong feelings for him, she couldn't return his love the same way. She didn't have that heart-stomping, stomach-churning kind of reaction to Toz that Corbahn produced every time he looked at her with his sea green eyes. "I loved him too, but not that way."

"I know, and so did Toz. But let's focus on here and now, and what we're going to do next." They entered the library, Reynier and Jayna gathered in front of a map spread out on one of the tables.

Reynier waved her over. "I'm glad you're here. Take a look at this and tell me what you see."

Linden walked around the table, examining the map of Valerra, marked up with hand-drawn symbols in different colored inks. She saw no discernible patterns anywhere. "It's Valerra, but I'm not sure what all these markings mean, or the colors."

Using her index finger, Jayna traced the red triangles across the map. "Do you think these could be locations of the old marine bases?"

Linden peered closer, mentally trying to meld her father's Royal Marine map that hung on the wall of his office with the inked-up map on the table. She nodded slowly. "You may be on to something." Tapping the slightly larger triangle sitting west of Bellaryss on the map, she added, "That's about where base camp headquarters would have been. And these over here—" she pointed to a number of smaller triangles "—appear to be the forward base locations, closer to the border with Glenbarra."

Straightening up, Linden took another turn around the table, trying to decipher the remaining symbols: blue crosses, clustered mostly in Bellaryss and base camp headquarters, and green circles scattered about haphazardly, some of them intersecting a red triangle or blue cross. "Do you have a more detailed map of Bellaryss?"

Reynier walked to a stack of scrolls and brought over another map, unrolling it on top of the first map. "Look at this. The same symbols are drawn onto this map of the city. Mostly blue crosses, a few green circles, and one red triangle."

Mara placed her palms on the table and leaned over the two maps, comparing them. "That red triangle looks like the location of the Royal Marine Academy in Bellaryss."

Linden tilted her head, considering. "You're right. And over here is the Valerran Museum, with a blue cross on top, and there's the infirmary with another blue cross. But some of the other blue crosses seem to be random locations, like shops or offices. I wonder whether the green circles indicate some sort of activity?"

Shrugging, Reynier said, "I'm not sure. We'll need to search around here for the notes Wreyn mentioned. I'm hoping they can offer some clues."

Remy stepped into the library and joined them at the table. "I made pancakes with sausages for breakfast. Or dinner, I guess, since it's night time. Those fays really know how to stock a kitchen." Glancing down at the maps, he said, "What did you find out?"

Mara quickly filled him in, Remy's brows drawn together in concentration. "The blue crosses are probably entry points for the tunnels, since they run underneath all these buildings." Remy's finger hovered over the map. "Do you remember one of our escape routes out of the museum? It was the tunnel that ran below the road and opened into one of the shops."

"That makes a lot of sense," said Jayna. "The blue crosses aren't marking the buildings themselves, but the tunnel systems running beneath them."

Still frowning at the map, Remy added, "And I'll bet those green circles have something to do with the resistance, probably sightings or disruptions they've caused. Can we go eat now, while the food's hot?"

"Remy, you're brilliant." Linden smiled at him. "I think you've decoded the symbols for us." At her words of praise, Remy's face lit up in a wide grin. Linden thought she ought to offer praise more often, and not just to Remy. "Let's go eat your pancakes and then come back here. We have a lot of thinking to do."

"And planning," said Reynier. "We need to learn what Efram and Wreyn have already figured out: where and when the resistance is likely to show up, and hopefully, how to make contact with them."

CHAPTER 8

"According to Efram's notes—his handwriting is terrible, by the way—the Glenbarrans converted base camp headquarters into a prison camp, mostly for resistance fighters and anyone else who opposes the new regime. This lines up with what Wreyn was telling us, about food being withheld from prisoners, who are forced to fight each other to entertain the prison guards and commandant. The losers are killed outright, while the winners get to eat one decent meal before being sent to Bellaryss for crossbreeding." Reynier shook his head and continued. "Perhaps the worst part, anyone who exhibits Serving magic abilities is immediately executed."

"That's horrible." Jayna shuddered. "Do you think that's the same place Wreyn's deserters were from?"

"It sounds like it. However, according to Wreyn's journal, there are Glenbarran camps all over the place. Here, let me read this to you." Linden turned one of the thick pages, filled with Wreyn's neat script. "Here it is. 'The Glenbarrans have set up work camps next to Valerra's largest mines. Their troopers go through the villages, rounding up men, women, and children, pulling them from their homes, and herding them into the work camps. The Valerrans are compelled to turn over all their property, and then families are divided, men to one side of the camp, women and children to the other. They're forced to work in the mines, even the children, in twelve to fourteen-hour shifts. Anyone who falls sick is removed and not seen again.'" Linden stopped reading, overcome at the thought of anyone, especially children, being treated so cruelly. She put down the journal, tapping its cover closed with her finger.

"There's so much to do here, so many people who need our help." Jayna's dark eyes were moist.

"Who do we help first?" Mara wondered aloud. "Where do we even begin?"

"I'm not sure what we do first," Remy said, shaking his head. "But whatever it is, we need more than five of us to get it done."

"We need to focus on the goal, defeating King Roi and Mordahn. To do that, we need help from the resistance." Reynier stared down at the maps on the table, as if they could chart out the steps along the way.

"We need to find a way to set those resistance fighters free." Linden tapped the large red triangle on the map. "We have to break into base camp headquarters."

Reynier's eyebrows shot up. "Another prison break? But this time the guards aren't going to be so easily fooled."

Linden recalled the last prison break they orchestrated, when they had infiltrated a horrific prison in Glenbarra, dubbed "Hotel Zabor" by the inmates. They'd used a simple but effective ruse to enter that prison camp. Corbahn, wearing the uniform of a Glenbarran captain, had traveled to Zabor to deliver his "prisoners"—Linden, Wreyn, Pryl, and Efram—to the guards. Their team had managed to escape, free the inmates, and destroy the crossbreeding equipment inside, although not without casualties on all sides, Toz among them.

"True," Linden acknowledged, "but we'll have an element of surprise we didn't have before."

"What do you mean?"

"The tunnels running beneath base camp headquarters." Linden pointed to the blue crosses intersecting the red triangle on the map. "We'll take this fight underground."

Reynier rubbed the back of his neck, thinking. "If we can cause enough disruption ourselves, we have a shot at attracting the resistance leaders to us."

"My thoughts exactly," said Linden.

Reynier nodded. "Alright, then if that's our plan, let's leave the day after tomorrow. That will give all of us, including the horses, additional time to rest up while we plan our route."

"We'll also need to refresh our supplies for the trip. I volunteer to restock our saddlebags," said Remy.

"Good idea. I'll do the same with my healer's kit. I noticed the fays have some healing herbs I'm unfamiliar with." Jayna pointed to a row of scrolls. "And I have some reading to do about fay healing techniques, such as leaching out Fallow poison from a wound."

Linden turned to Mara. "Maybe you can help me brainstorm some ways to get into the base camp once we've arrived. Do we steal Glenbarran uniforms and some of us pretend to be guards, while others are the prisoners? It worked before, but I'd like some other ideas."

"I'll give it some thought. I also think we need to be prepared to fight grihms or super-grihms at that camp. We're going to need to be well armed," said Mara.

Linden pulled the map of Bellaryss toward her and tapped the blue cross over the Valerran Museum. "I'd like to spend some time learning more about ancient fay burial grounds. We know the museum was built over a royal burial site for fay kings and queens, and we know the old fay burial grounds produce huge amounts of magical energy that can be harnessed by mages, for good or ill."

Reynier nodded. "Which Mordahn and King Roi are using to power their crossbreeding equipment, creating super-grihms and anything else they can imagine."

"Given what we know about these places of power, we're going to need fay help neutralizing this one. Even so, let's find out what we can while we have access to this library."

"Either that, or we'll have to destroy everything, bring it all down," said Reynier.

Linden shook her head, the thought of destroying the Valerran Museum making her feel almost physically ill. "Only as a last resort. The museum houses the largest collection of ancient fay and Valerran artifacts in the known world, not to mention priceless scrolls and artwork. Countless Serving mages lost their lives defending that building, including my uncle."

Reynier waved his hand at the map of Valerra. "The loss of the museum would be a grave blow, but it pales in comparison to losing all of Faynwood to the Glenbarrans. Our primary goal is to stop the spread of Fallowness across this continent, and nothing can be off the table."

As much as it pained her, Linden knew Reynier was right. "Agreed. In the meantime, I'll leave no stone unturned in my search to find another way."

~

After rummaging through a roomful of discarded clothes, costumes, and a couple of partial Glenbarran uniforms, Linden and Mara couldn't find anything more suitable than the dark tunics and leggings they'd brought from Faynwood. Linden stood up from sorting through the last of the trunks and stretched her back. "Somehow, I don't think we'll be able to walk into that prison camp disguised as Glenbarran soldiers anyway."

Mara closed the lid on the trunk and rose to her feet. "We'll need to find another way into that prison camp, without attracting too much attention, at least until we're ready for the fight that's sure to come."

Linden pushed back a shank of hair. "We'll have to be careful with any magic we employ. If we use anything other than veils of drabness or immobility spells that aren't detectable by other mages, we risk tipping our hands too soon."

"Then it's swords and daggers, and the element of surprise." Mara paused. "If only we could appeal to their human side—of the grihms, I mean—ask them to help us, turn them against their masters. Now that would be something."

Linden blew out a puff of air, trying to imagine the possibilities, but soon gave up. Other than the handful of grihms who'd helped them at Zabor Prison because they'd been recently crossbred and still remembered their human families, she hadn't seen any evidence that grihms could be turned.

Closing her eyes, she recalled the grihms on the roof of the Valerran Museum, dropping their weapons and running when they saw her glowing green sword; the grihms fleeing during the battle of Arrowood, when Corbahn's father and so many others died, and returning to the fray only after their masters blew on whistles, the grihms yelping in fear and pain; on the Aurorialyss, the first time she faced Mordahn, the grihms fighting ferociously alongside him until they saw him fall, and then leaping to their own ship in full retreat.

"Some sort of Fallow magic binds the grihms to their masters. You've seen how the Glenbarrans use whistles and commands to control them. If we can find a way to disrupt that connection, the invisible chains that bind them, perhaps we may have a chance of turning the grihms."

A frown line formed between Mara's shapely eyebrows. "That's an interesting theory. I've often thought grihms seem so sad, not when they're coming at me with an ax, but when they're marching past, unaware of my existence. But I have no idea how to break down those chains."

"Perhaps Pryl will think of something," said Linden as they crossed the great hall. "I've been scouring the library for anything I can find on crossbreeding, necromancy, and ancient fay burial sites."

"What did you find?"

"Nothing much, other than admonitions against the unnatural practice of necromancy, calling it a perversion of magical law."

They entered the library, Mara sighing. "So no breakthrough clues?"

"No clues, period. Well, except maybe one. Let me show you." Linden opened a cabinet containing the oldest scrolls, their edges brittle and yellowed with age. She gingerly unrolled one of the scrolls, spreading it open on the nearest table. Mara handed her heavy books to anchor each corner of the scroll. "I can't read the fay hieroglyphs but look at these illustrations."

Mara examined the scroll and glanced at Linden. "A giant battle, a showdown really, between Serving magic and Fallow sorcery. Men, women, and fays against beasts and ghosts, or more accurately, crossbreeds and an undead army. "

Linden ran her finger over the illustration. "And the battle occurs inside this ring of hills, next to the sea."

"That must be Bellaryss. Least ways, it's the only location I can think of that fits, sitting at the edge of the Pale Sea and surrounded by hills."

Linden nodded. "I agree. And while the clans are busy defending Faynwood, the final battle lines are being drawn in Bellaryss. The Glenbarrans are breeding super-grihms and raising the dead, while we are distracted elsewhere."

"True," said Mara, "but we're not the only ones fighting a war on multiple fronts. So are the Glenbarrans, and they're stretched thin. We know they're running low on funds and supplies.

"We need to find their weakness and exploit it."

Mara shrugged. "King Roi and Mordahn are hungry for power and control. But I don't know how to turn that to our advantage."

Linden folded her arms. "I don't either, not yet, anyway. But our priority right now is to find the resistance. Everything hinges on them."

CHAPTER 9

They filed out of the compound two days later as the first stars twinkled in the dark sky above. After drawing and redrawing potential routes to base camp headquarters, Reynier had settled on one that skirted villages and towns, taking them through dense woods and across the low hills of central Valerra to avoid any population centers. Linden estimated they had four nights of travel ahead. Given the tension in the group, Remy jumping at every sound, she hoped Pryl would join them sooner than later.

Everyone, herself included, seemed less stressed when the fay chief formed a member of their party. Realizing she still thought of him first and foremost as the fay chief, and not as her grandfather, she tried to imagine Pryl and Nari as younger versions of themselves. She smiled to think of the sparks that flew when two powerful, headstrong mages, one Faymon, the other fay, clashed. Then she recalled Wreyn's comments about her and Corbahn, *"When you're in the same room, sparks fly. It's exciting to watch,"* and scowled at the comparison. She and Corbahn were nothing like her grandparents.

They evaded several smaller troop movements as they

traveled, casting veils of drabness each time. As the sky lightened toward the end of their fourth night of travel, they found an abandoned farm to shelter in. Kal immediately went to work ferreting out the rats that inhabited the barn and before long, they moved the horses into the stalls, gave them a good brushing, and unpacked their bedrolls. Mara and Jayna volunteered to make dinner while Linden and Reynier examined their maps to determine the best entry point into the tunnels. Remy had a slight head cold and decided to take a nap before dinner.

Linden estimated they were three miles from base camp headquarters. "Do you think we could do some reconnaissance during the daytime? Look at the pattern of troop movements and guard changes?"

"To confirm the tunnel entrance we're planning to use is still open?" asked Reynier.

Linden nodded. "I feel as if we're flying blind if we don't have some knowledge of the camp's current setup. And I'd like to look for any weaknesses that might help us."

Reynier drew his brows together, studying the map. "I don't like the idea of moving around during the day. It's simply too risky. But maybe we can do some spying at night. Any intelligence is better than none at all."

"Alright, I'll go tonight and take Mara with me."

Reynier's frown deepened. "I like that plan even less. The Faymon Liege should not be out and about, doing reconnaissance at night. I'll go, by myself."

Linden refrained from rolling her eyes at her cousin's overprotectiveness. Although it drove her crazy, she knew he was well intentioned. She also knew she wasn't going to listen, but life was easier if she could convince Reynier without descending into an argument about what the Liege should and shouldn't do. "I know the area better than anyone else. My father was stationed here for years, and I used to visit him with my mother and brother. And Mara's grandparents used to live near here, so she has a good general sense of the landmarks. On the other hand, this is your first time in Valerra. It's all unfamiliar to you."

Reynier lifted his shoulders, a reluctant half shrug. "Fine, I don't like it, but I can't argue with your logic. But I want you and Mara to take every possible precaution, don't get too close to the actual camp, and return before dawn."

"Of course, we'll leave after dark. But right now, I'm going to have something to eat. I'm famished and whatever Jayna and Mara are cooking up smells wonderful."

"You sound just like Remy."

Linden laughed. "Perhaps so. I know I enjoy sitting around the fire, sharing a meal together. It helps to fill the hollow place inside, and I'm not referring to my stomach."

Reynier's eyes softened. He put a hand on her shoulder. "Don't ever think I don't know what you've been through or can't appreciate the sacrifices you've had to make when you became our Liege. It's a difficult, lonely path, and I'm here for you. All of us are here for you."

Linden gave Reynier a swift nod and turned away before she became emotional. She'd learned to stop herself from dwelling on the past year, or she'd break down. Ever since leaving the forests of Faynwood behind, she set her face toward Bellaryss, where the final battle, if they made it that far, would take place. Nothing else mattered, not her past losses or her current challenges as Liege, and not her confused feelings for Corbahn and their uncertain future. Everything paled in comparison to the present moment and the need to rout Fallowness from their land and their lives.

Linden and Mara turned in early. Reynier and Jayna insisted they sleep until moonrise, volunteering to sit watch in alternate shifts while they slept. Linden was too exhausted to argue and curled up on her side, Kal settling down at her feet. She slept soundly and dreamt in a series of pleasant vignettes, of her parents, laughing together at something she'd said, and Nari, patiently showing her how to cast a protection charm, and Matteo, grinning at a silly joke. She woke up feeling rested for the first time in weeks and prepared for what lay ahead.

"Are we bringing our swords?" asked Mara. She pulled her long wheat-blonde hair back in a ponytail and tugged a dark cap down low over her forehead.

Linden buttoned up her leather jacket, which she layered over her tunic for extra warmth against the autumn chill. "No swords, it'll be too obvious we're up to no good if we're stopped. But I'm wearing a dagger on my belt and tucking a small knife inside my pocket."

Mara reached under her jacket to unstrap her sword and laid it on the ground near her bedroll. "Alright, I'm ready."

"Do you have a knife on you?"

Mara pointed to her boots. "I have a pair of daggers in my boots." She patted first her belt and then the pockets on her jacket. "Plus, brass knuckles, sharp arrowhead, pair of manacles, and an extra knife."

Linden arched an eyebrow. "Not taking any chances, are you?"

"This is just in case we run into trouble. I know we want to avoid using magic if possible."

"I think you would actually enjoy a rumble, so long as it doesn't interfere with our plans."

Mara rolled her shoulders. "Nothing wrong with being prepared."

"For two women traveling alone at night, I suppose you're right."

They said goodbye to Reynier, nervously pacing the barn as they got ready, and having second thoughts about their reconnaissance mission. "Look, I'll wake up Jayna and Remy, let them know I'm going with you."

Linden shook her head. "We'll be fine. I'll take Kal with me. He's better than any guard dog." When Kal heard his name, he trotted over to her, flicking his tail.

Reynier nodded reluctantly, then waved his hand at them. "Remember to keep a low profile and be back before daylight."

As they slipped out of the barn, Linden said to Kal, "Stay close by, and no flying unless I tell you to or there's trouble." Kal clicked his beak and flapped his wings once, an indication he understood. "That's a good griffin." She bent over to ruffle his mane.

Linden and Mara walked briskly along a little-used supply road leading to base camp headquarters. Although traveling on the main road leading into the camp would have been faster, they decided to avoid it for safety's sake. A nearly full moon cast enough light for their nighttime hike, and Linden found herself relaxing ever so slightly. After nearly an hour, Linden reached out and tapped Mara's shoulder. "We'll be coming up to the fork in the road soon," she whispered.

Mara nodded. "If memory serves me, it's around that bend up ahead."

"We should be able to see the entrance to the secondary tunnel Wreyn described in her journal. When she last visited, it was closed off, with no guards posted. Let's hope we're that lucky again." Linden dropped to one knee so she could be at eye level with Kal. "Can you fly up ahead and see if there's any movement on the road? Come right back."

Kal extended his wings and flapped them vigorously to gain enough speed to mount into the air. He circled once overhead and then flew around the bend. Mara and Linden waited, listening intently for any sounds other than the wind rustling through the trees lining the road. Mara pointed. "Here comes Kal."

Kal landed with a soft thud and padded over to Linden. He

rubbed his head against her legs, his body quivering. She knelt beside him. "What is it? What's wrong Kal?"

He clicked his beak and dipped his head under one wing. The fur along his back stood up, a ridge of prickly tufts. Linden frowned, trying to interpret. Something had frightened him, but what was it? She ran through the possibilities. "Did you see guards?" Kal didn't respond or raise his head, so she figured that was a no. "Did you see grihms up ahead?" He stood stock-still. While Kal wasn't a fan of Glenbarrans or grihms, Linden could tell something else had really spooked him.

"Whatever it is, I want to see for myself. I want to know numbers and whether they're simply passing through." Kal squawked and flapped his wings in alarm. Linden rubbed Kal's fur and said, "I'll be careful. But I need you to hang back from us now. If we get into trouble, fly back to Reynier and the others. Understand?" Kal clicked his beak several times.

Linden glanced at Mara, and they both started jogging toward the bend in the road, heading into the trees for extra cover. Mara grabbed Linden's arm and pushed her to the ground, tumbling down next to her. Linden peeked up from the underbrush and saw what had spooked poor Kal. Undead horses, their bones knit together with bits of sinew and scraps of skin, and their equally undead riders, wearing raggedy uniforms over their skeletal frames, milled about the tunnel entrance. The riders' moth-eaten jackets flapped loosely in the breeze, as the bones of their hands grasped imaginary reins. Linden smelled the odor of death all about them.

"Well, we have our answer," hissed Mara.

Linden grimaced. "Looks like they're searching for something."

"Or someone. The resistance perhaps?"

Linden canted her head to one side. "Or maybe an escaped prisoner, which I imagine they would like even less."

A guttural shout followed by a long, high-pitched whistle

came from somewhere farther up the road, and the undead riders took off in the direction of the whistle. Once they cleared out, Linden and Mara observed the tunnel entrance, which appeared to be well camouflaged and undisturbed. Linden saw no signs of guards stationed around the entrance. "Let's get back to Kal. We should check out the primary tunnel entrance and the guard situation around the camp's perimeter."

They retraced their steps around the bend, and Kal dashed over to Linden, clicking his beak. She patted the top of his head. "Those were undead riders. We've seen them before, but this is your first time. You'll get used to them. I expect we'll be seeing more of them."

At the fork in the road, they moved into the woods and picked their way more slowly in the direction of the camp buildings and other tunnel entrance. It was slow going, as they stopped and hid every time they heard a sound. "We're approaching the main road into the camp," whispered Linden. "We're going to lose this tree cover soon, and the moon is too full for us to get in much closer without being seen."

Mara nodded, reaching into one of her pockets to pull out a spyglass. "Here, take this. If I boost you up this tree over here, I think you'll be able to see into the compound."

"Good idea." Mara stood almost as tall as Reynier and Remy. While she could give Linden a boost, Linden would struggle to return the favor. Linden tucked the spyglass into her jacket pocket and reached up to grab a sturdy tree branch. She stepped into Mara's cupped hands, Mara bracing herself against the tree trunk to give her more leverage. After a few grunts, Linden managed to hoist herself onto the lowest branch. From there, she found it easier to climb up, since the branches grew together more closely. She climbed twenty feet and found a good place to perch, a V where the trunk had split.

Linden pulled out her spyglass and gazed into the compound,

her heart sinking. A horde of guards swarmed the grounds inside the prison camp, barking orders at the male prisoners, lined up in rows on one side of the yard. In an adjoining section stood the women and children, shivering in their thin prison garb. Makeshift gallows stood in the center of the yard, a noose around a young man's neck. Linden surmised he must have been an escaped prisoner who had the misfortune to be recaptured. She gasped as one of the guards kicked out the bench beneath the young prisoner. The hung man struggled for several minutes, his body eventually going limp. A woman wailed from the ranks of the prisoners and was swiftly silenced by a punch to her gut.

Linden tore her eyes away from the gruesome scene. Scanning the perimeter of the compound, she located the primary entrance into the tunnel system at the former base camp headquarters. Unfortunately, the entrance sat directly beneath the watchtower, which would be guarded around the clock. Linden secured the spyglass back in her pocket and shimmied down the tree. Mara took one look at her stony face and sighed. "I guess it's not great news."

Linden shook her head. "That tunnel entrance is too close to the watchtower to be of much use to us." Then she described the scene inside the prison compound, Mara wincing at her portrayal of the hanging, which even the young children were forced to watch.

When she finished, Mara glanced at the night sky. "We better start back if we want to make it before daylight. At least we have a better idea of what to expect inside the prison camp."

Linden nodded glumly. "Aye, and it rivals Hotel Zabor for its cruelty."

They retraced their steps to the supply road and arrived at the abandoned barn while the sky was still dark, the moon a cool white beacon overhead. As Kal scampered into the barn,

Linden heard Jayna exclaim. "Welcome back! I have a treat for you." Linden and Mara chuckled.

"Poor Kal," said Mara. "He was really scared tonight."

"I'm afraid he'll be seeing plenty to scare him before we're through," said Linden grimly.

Jayna ran out of the barn and hugged both her friends. "I'm glad you're back and safe. Wreyn is here with Efram, fully recovered. They brought us a guest."

"Who?"

"Come see. I won't spoil the surprise."

CHAPTER 10

Linden's heart turned over at the possibility it might be Corbahn, but she'd been gone from their home base in Faynwood a little over two weeks. His leg couldn't be healed this soon. Besides, Corbahn would never abandon his post as Arrowood Chief, regardless of his feelings for her. If he still had any feelings left, that is. Corbahn certainly had distanced himself from her by the time she departed with the others. Linden took a deep breath and followed Mara and Jayna into the barn.

Everyone stood up to greet the new arrivals. Linden gripped Efram's hand in both of hers. The scar on his forehead was a pale slash against his brown skin. She peered into the eyes of a fay who recognized he'd battled with death and defeated it this time, aware that even healthy young fays can't defeat death forever. "I'm so relieved to see you're healed from your ordeal." Efram smiled and thanked her.

A middle-aged man wearing a knit cap pulled low on his forehead, battered leather jacket open over a pilled sweater, and patched corduroy pants, hung back from the circle of friends surrounding Linden and Mara. His face and hands bore the scars of someone accustomed to hard fighting, and his dark eyes surveyed the new arrivals warily. Wreyn drew the man into their circle and introduced him. "This is Vas, one of our informants."

Vas gave a small bow to Mara and Linden. "An enemy of the current regime is a friend of mine."

Linden arched an eyebrow. "I appreciate the sentiment, Mr. Vas—"

"Just Vas, please," he interrupted with a smile that didn't reach his eyes. "My former life, with its rank and privileges, is gone. We do not use titles here."

"What 'we' are you referring to?" Linden felt as if she'd entered during Act Two of a drama. While Wreyn and Efram might trust the man, she had no intention of allowing him into their little circle without checking his bona fides, but she had no idea how to confirm he was a friend.

"All of us who oppose King Roi and the Fallowness overshadowing Valerra."

"Are you speaking of the resistance?"

Vas spread his hands. "The resistance is comprised of many different cells, some organized, others haphazardly aligned to a simple cause: overthrowing the Glenbarrans."

"Are you a member of one of the more organized cells?" Linden was in no mood to philosophize. She wanted to sit by the fire with a warm cup of tea and discuss options with Reynier, who was watching the exchange between her and Vas with interest. If she had her doubts about Vas, she figured Reynier was even more skeptical.

Reynier surprised Linden by touching her on the shoulder. "Vas was a Royal Marine officer before the occupation."

Linden turned to Reynier, confusion on her face. "And we know this to be true how?"

Vas smiled. "You are right to be skeptical. I served in the Royal Marines with Colonel Ric Arlyss, who saved my life twice during the border wars. My wife and I used to have dinner with him and his wife, Kamden. We saw them less often after the children came along, but I stopped by Ric and Kamden's home a few times when the children were quite small and met their young son and daughter. I met the boy again much later, as a Royal Marine himself. In fact, I was commanding officer at base camp headquarters where Corporal Matteo Arlyss attended training and later, where he was treated for his injuries. I used to visit him at the hospital."

Linden's brow cleared. Here was a man who knew her father and brother, who might know how to locate Matteo even now. But first, she wanted confirmation that Matteo was alive. Despite Pryl's assurances, Linden wanted proof from someone who had seen him since base camp headquarters was overrun. "Do you know whether my brother survived the invasion?"

Vas nodded. "Your brother is a fighter, in every sense of the word. Despite his injuries, he escaped during the attack on headquarters. I've seen him frequently since then."

Linden reached out and gripped Vas's arm. "Do you know where I can find him?" She tried recalling the name of the commanding officer at base camp headquarters—she was sure she would recognize it—but that was another time, another world, really, and the name escaped her.

Vas patted her hand, a comforting gesture. "I could get a message to your brother, but I'm not sure that's a good idea."

Linden withdrew her hand from the man's arm, scowling. "Why not?"

"I'm sorry, but this is no time for a family reunion. Many lives hang in the balance within Valerra."

Anger at this man's arrogance bubbled up inside her, acidic and bitter, like bile on the tongue. "And who are you to dictate such terms to me? I am his sister, here to provide assistance."

Vas waved his hand. "How can this small group, however motivated, assist us?"

Reynier cleared his throat. "You just said 'us.' Does this mean you are connected with the resistance movement? A member of one of the organized cells that you mentioned?"

"Aye. Although practically speaking, anyone who doesn't kowtow to King Roi and his puppets is a member of the resistance." Vas pointed at Wreyn. "I've been passing information along to your friend here for weeks. However, I confess to being surprised that my small bits of intelligence resulted in a group of you entering Valerra, with the purpose of contacting the resistance and offering assistance. I don't mean to offend, but I'll ask again, what sort of assistance can you offer? Isn't Faynwood struggling to fend off your own attacks?"

Linden, exasperated by Vas's non-answers, nodded at Reynier, who drew himself up and pulled back his shoulders, his Faymon warrior-chieftain posture. "Sir, while I recognize we are meeting under less-than-ordinary circumstances, I will ask that you treat the Liege of Faynwood with the same respect you would accord to any head of state."

Vas's dark eyebrows rose in a peak. "There hasn't been a Faymon Liege in over fifty years. I didn't think Liege Ayala had any survivors." He looked at each of the assembled group, his eyes coming to rest finally on Linden. Given the chaos of wartime Valerra, and the secretive nature of the Faymon clans, Linden wasn't surprised Vas knew nothing about recent events inside Faynwood. He might not even be aware the civil war was finally over, the five clans of Faynwood reunited after fifty years.

Reynier inclined his head. "Perhaps formal introductions are in order. I am Reynier Arlyss, Faymon Elder and Chief of the Tanglewood clan." Bowing first to Linden and then to Vas, he continued, "And this is Liege Linden Arlyss, a direct descendent of Liege Ayala, may she rest in love and peace.

Ayala had one child, a daughter, who escaped at the start of the civil war. You would have known her as Mage Nari Arlyss."

Vas stepped back and removed his knit cap, revealing dark brown hair, cropped short and threaded with blue highlights. Dropping to his knees in front of Linden, he bowed forward to expose the back of his neck. "I pledge my life, my home, and my mage's honor to Liege Linden Arlyss of Tanglewood and Valerra."

Linden glanced at Reynier, who shrugged. She arched an eyebrow, surprised Vas knew Faymon customs and was pledging allegiance to her. Although his hair color indicated Faymon lineage, he'd obviously been raised a Valerran. Linden proceeded with the Faymon protocols. "I accept your sworn allegiance, um...." She needed Vas's full name to complete the allegiance pledge.

Still kneeling, Vas supplied the missing information. "Colonel Martel Revas, at your service. My parents hailed from the Shorewood clan and escaped over the border with my sister and me during the civil war."

Linden started at the name, mentioned often with respect and even affection by her brother and his best friend, Stryker. Once upon a time, not so long ago, all she could think about was Stryker Soto, the man she'd pledged to marry at the start of the Valerran war with Glenbarra. So much had changed since then. "I accept your sworn allegiance, Colonel Martel Revas of Shorewood and Valerra. In return, I pledge my loyalty to you, your clan, and all of Faynwood—to fays and Faymons, to woodlands, streams, and all creatures therein." She amended the pledge to add, "And to all of Valerra."

Vas rose to his feet, holding his cap in his hands. "Thank you, Liege Linden."

She smiled. "Just Linden. We use no titles outside Faynwood's borders."

Reynier gripped Vas's hand. "I count many close friends

among the Shorewood clan, including several of your cousins. You must come visit."

Vas shook Reynier's hand. "I would like that very much." Vas turned to Linden and hesitated before saying, "I am sorry for your loss."

A small line formed between Linden's brows. "We have all suffered losses, Colonel—ah, I mean Vas. To which loss are you referring?"

"There was a young corporal, your brother's friend, whom I took a special interest in, Stryker Soto. I believe you were betrothed. We lost him during the battle at Wellan Pass last year."

Linden's face flushed. She recalled that Colonel Revas was practically a second father to Stryker, who'd lost his own father, a highly decorated marine, during the border wars. The colonel had bailed Stryker out of trouble more than once, helping him to stay in school at the Royal Marine Academy when Stryker was threatened with expulsion.

Reynier cleared his throat. "I will leave you and Vas to catch up a bit." Reynier and the others retreated to the far side of the barn, ostensibly to feed and water the horses, but Linden knew they wanted to give her privacy.

"I'm happy to report that Stryker survived the battle. He escaped with Sergeant Desi, and they eventually made their way to Faynwood," said Linden.

Vas brought his fist to his chest and heaved a sigh. "That is the single best piece of news I've had in a very long time. Where is he now?"

Linden folded her hands in front of her, knowing the colonel deserved an explanation. "Stryker and Sergeant Desi are serving with a Faymon ship called the Aurorialyss. Stryker and I are no longer betrothed."

"Ah, I see. Matters of the heart are best left to the individuals involved."

"Unfortunately, it's a bit more complicated than that. You see, Stryker misused his magic. He called down a horde of ravens, crows, and blackbirds on a crowd of Faymons during a celebration. Stryker was banished from Faynwood."

Stryker and Linden had become engaged quickly on impulse when he was called up for active duty. She'd been a senior in high school, he'd been a cadet at the Royal Marine Academy along with her brother. Those early, heady days of being in love were full of yearning and sweetness. Later, after they were reunited in Faynwood, as Linden was adapting to her new home and new role as the Faymon Liege, something shifted in their relationship. Stryker became moody, jealous of her friends, of her duties, and eventually, of Corbahn, whom Linden barely knew at the time.

When Stryker intentionally misused his magical gifts, wreaking havoc during the magic trials in Arrowood and nearly harming Corbahn, his sister Carissa, and a lot of bystanders, he lost Linden's respect, and her love. She broke off their engagement. As a kindness to her, Reynier secured Stryker a position on the Aurorialyss after he was banished from Faynwood, and Stryker's loyal sergeant went along with him.

Vas compressed his lips. "I'm sorry to hear that, but not entirely surprised. Stryker is a fine young man, with a fiery temper he needs to get under control. The shipboard discipline will do him good." Vas added, "Thank you for telling me the truth."

Remy called out to them. "Vas, Linden, come sit by the fire. The tea is ready and soon the porridge will be as well." They burned wood during daylight only, for breakfast and supper, when the campfire couldn't be spotted from miles away, pinpointing their location. As an extra precaution, Remy had cast a veil of drabness around the fire pit outside the barn.

Vas gave Linden his arm, as if formally escorting her to a marine function rather than through the doors of an old barn, and she looped her arm through his. The sun peeked over the horizon, casting the abandoned farmhouse and fields in a golden glow, as early morning mist rose from the ground.

Linden inhaled the crisp autumn air, suddenly hungry and for the first time in a long while, hopeful. Vas would help them. She was closer, much closer, to finding the resistance—and Matteo.

CHAPTER 11

Linden glanced over at Wreyn, sitting with her tea and porridge on the other side of the campfire. "Tell us the news from Faynwood. Are we able to hold the borders?"

Wreyn swallowed a spoonful of porridge and placed her bowl on the ground in front of her. "Aye, we're holding them. The Glenbarrans have broken through the line in several places, but our warriors and mages are repelling them, pushing them back to the perimeter. The fighting is fiercest in Arrowood."

Linden gripped her mug of tea, her knuckles turning white. She recalled the last time she saw Corbahn, that proud, larger-than-life man, his leg in a splint, lying on a cot inside his tent. She should never have left him without clearing the air between them. What would it have cost to brush her lips against his, a simple kiss goodbye? Or grip his hand and carry it to her heart, conveying without words her true feelings? *Too late*, she thought, *it's too late*. "And Corbahn? How does he fare?"

"He commands the Arrowood clan from a special chair he's had constructed, with wheels that enable him to maneuver around behind the lines, shouting orders to his warriors. He's even managed to fend off several attackers from his chair."

Linden's mouth went dry. *Corbahn is fighting from a chair? He's exposing himself to constant danger, practically inviting injury or worse.* "I can't imagine his healer is condoning this, or his mother for that matter."

Wreyn shrugged. "You know Corbahn. He will do what he will do. So far, it seems to be working. Despite their losses, Arrowood is standing firm."

"And the other clans? How are they managing?" asked Reynier.

"The other clans are fighting alongside Riverwood, given their long border with occupied Valerra. Glenbarrans are swarming the weakest spots with troopers and grihms, but they haven't broken through."

"That's a testament to Faymon unity," said Reynier.

"And our need to stand firm against an intruder. If an invasion of troopers and grihms couldn't rally Faymons to band together, I don't know what would." Linden asked the question on everyone's mind. "And what of fay support, in Faynwood and here in Valerra? Is that why Pryl is delayed?"

Wreyn flicked her braid, restored to its natural color of vivid blue, behind her shoulder. She sighed. "I don't know how Pryl does it, the debating and negotiating and cajoling. I wouldn't want to be chief of anything, with all the politics involved."

"Has it gotten any worse?" asked Mara.

"Aye, based on what I heard while I was recovering," said Efram, "it's much worse. I'm ashamed to admit it, but I think the fays on the council are afraid. They've never seen Fallow sorcery on this scale, and they don't know what to do. It's convenient to blame others when they should be looking inward."

Reynier placed his hands on his knees and leaned forward,

peering at Efram through the thin film of smoke rising from the fire pit. "Why do you say that? Are there fays connected in some way with Fallow magic?"

"Not now, but many of the ancient fay scrolls contain references to dark sorcery and necromancy, well before the first man or woman arrived on this continent. Fays planted the seeds of Fallowness, not humans, and fays must stamp it out."

Linden tucked a strand of hair behind her ears, considering. "And that's what Pryl is attempting to argue, and why he's meeting with such resistance. No one wants to be told they've caused such catastrophic misery. No wonder the fay council is trying to shift the blame."

Wreyn nodded sagely. "Exactly. Pryl is telling the fay council what they don't want to hear, and reminding them of our duty as fays, as the preservers of Serving magic."

"Did Pryl give any indication how much longer he'll be delayed?" asked Jayna.

Efram shook his head. "He told us to carry on and he would catch up as soon as possible."

Vas added more hot water to his mug and swirled it around. "Forgive me for asking, but what was your original plan? I'm still unclear how you were going to assist us."

Linden briefly outlined the plan. "Our goal when we left Faynwood was to find a way to contact the resistance and work together to bring down the Glenbarrans. While we were making our way to the resistance, four clans—Riverwood, Shorewood, Tanglewood, and Ridgewood—were positioning warriors and mages along our southern border with occupied Valerra, ready to cross over when we gave the word. We depended on the Arrowood clan to defend the western perimeter against Glenbarra. We figured with several thousand Faymon warriors and mages, ready to join up with your resistance, we might be able to march all the way to the Valerran capital. But as you heard, there's fighting along both the western and southern borders now, and all the clans are bogged down defending Faynwood."

"Don't forget the fay council had pledged fay mages and warriors as well," added Wreyn. "But now they're backtracking."

Vas took a sip from his mug and frowned. "I appreciate what you're trying to do for us. While we could use all the help we can get, I'm not sure your plan would have worked even under the best of circumstances."

"Why not?" asked Reynier.

"Your warriors would never have made it through Wellan Pass."

Reynier looked confused, so Linden explained. "As you know, Bellaryss sits on the shore of the Pale Sea. A ring of hills surrounds Bellaryss on its other three sides, forming a natural boundary all the way around. Wellan Pass is the only viable passage through those hills for a large troop movement. The other passes are narrow, rocky, and able to accommodate a single rider at a time. It's one of the reasons Bellaryss was never taken by an invader, until now."

Vas stroked his beard with one hand, cradling his tea with the other. "Unfortunately for us, the Glenbarrans have that pass well-fortified, with troops, grihms, and Fallow magic. We won't be able to storm Bellaryss without crossing over Wellan Pass, and even with several thousand Faymons to help us try to take the pass, we're still vastly outnumbered. The Glenbarrans would obliterate us."

Linden refused to become discouraged; they'd come too far to turn back now. There had to be a way into the capital. "We know there's an extensive tunnel system in and around Bellaryss. We figured we could divert our best mages to the underground passages and put them to work disabling the Fallow defensive spells surrounding the city, including at Wellan Pass."

"How do you know about Mordahn's defensive spells?"

Linden shrugged. "A matter of deduction. We're assuming Mordahn will deploy everything at his disposal to defend Bellaryss from attack. Our best option is to sneak in through a back door, find a way to disrupt the Glenbarrans' defenses from inside the city."

"And that's where our fay friends come in," said Reynier. "We're depending on them to help us slip into Bellaryss, secure several safe routes into the city, and take the capital by surprise."

Vas pursed his lips. "But you're saying the fays aren't going to help us."

"Our chief is working on it, and the fay council will come through in the end. In the meantime, we're here to help." Efram pointed to himself and Wreyn.

Vas's eyebrows rose. "While I appreciate the offer, I'm not sure how much damage two young fays can do to Mordahn's defensive spells."

Linden and Wreyn glanced at each other and smiled. Linden answered for them. "Alone, we can do very little. But together, we've already freed the captives in Glenbarra's Zabor Prison and destroyed Glendin Palace, damaging King Roi's crossbreeding equipment beyond repair."

Vas sat up straighter. "You're telling me this small group of —" he paused to count them "—seven slipped into Glenbarra and accomplished all that?"

Reynier cleared his throat. "We started our last mission with ten of us, a group comprised of Faymons, Valerrans, and fays."

"And now you're down to seven?"

Remy spoke up. "We lost my friend Toz, bringing our current number to nine. Chief Pryl was a member of our team, and so was Chief Corbahn of Arrowood. Pryl will join us soon, and the other clans will help us too once they can secure Faynwood's border."

"Although we started our last mission with ten of us, in the end, it was just Linden and Corbahn who managed to destroy Glendin Palace," added Mara. "And Corbahn said he was unconscious during most of it, so really it was Linden who brought down the palace."

Vas's brow furrowed and he shook his head. "I don't mean any disrespect, but that doesn't seem possible, even for a master mage."

"There was so much Fallow magical energy swirling about that I managed to create a sort of chain reaction, an eruption, by infusing Serving magic into the mix. The combination caused an earthquake that brought down the palace." Linden didn't go into the details, not wanting to dwell on the fact that Mordahn had come perilously close to turning her and Corbahn into crossbreeds.

"And you escaped unscathed?" asked Vas.

"Not at all," said Jayna. "Linden was severely injured. If it hadn't been for Corbahn—"

Linden interrupted, shifting the focus to their present troubles. They had more pressing concerns than telling stories, especially stories centered on her. "So the point is, we're here to help. Mara and I just surveyed the prison camp at base camp headquarters, and we've confirmed a few things." She described what she'd observed from the top of the tree and nodded at Mara to report what they'd seen on the ground.

"While the primary entrance into the tunnel is too close to the watchtower to be useful to us, the alternate entrance appears to be open. We saw no guards stationed at the secondary tunnel." Mara hesitated and added, "Although undead riders do patrol the perimeter of the camp. They were pursuing someone, probably the escaped prisoner they later hanged."

"I hate those undead riders. They're relentless and nearly impossible to shake off." Jayna shivered slightly, although the sun was warming the spot where they sat. It promised to be a perfect early fall day, bright blue sky and the first leaves beginning to change, turning yellow, orange, and auburn. Later in the fall, as the leaves become more brittle, their colors shifted again, into metallic shades of gold, bronze, and copper.

When she was younger, Linden's father would wake her at midnight once a year, at the end of the season, and bundle her into her coat. They would dash outside and stand under the moonlit sky, their breath forming frosty puffs. Linden would slip her hand into her father's and watch as the gilded and bronzed leaves shimmered in the moonlight, and then fell to the frozen ground. Linden sighed, tucking away the memory of her dad and forcing her attention back to the discussion around the campfire.

Vas said, "The guards didn't hang the escaped prisoner, but it was a close call. They hung someone they thought was an accomplice."

Reynier's head snapped up. "And you know that how?"

"I was there myself and helped the prisoner escape. He's safe for now."

"How did he escape from those riders and guards?" asked Mara.

Vas smiled. "There are some underground passages the Glenbarrans haven't discovered yet, partial tunnels systems that were started and never completed. We're repurposing them, digging additional passages as well as more escape hatches away from the tunnels, into houses, shops, and so forth. We've been busy." He paused and then added, "Of course, now that we've had a successful prison break, the Glenbarrans will be scouring the area. They'll no doubt discover some of the additional tunnels."

"The Glenbarrans put a lot of effort into finding that particular prisoner," observed Linden. "Why?"

Vas shrugged. "There are rarely any escapes, and rarer still, successful ones. This was the first time they used undead riders though. "

"Who escaped from that prison camp last night?"

Vas looked directly at Linden, his eyes locking on hers. "A key leader in the resistance who goes by the name of Tam."

She sat up straighter, leaning toward Vas. "What name did Tam call himself before the war?"

"A lifetime ago, he was known as Matteo Arlyss."

CHAPTER 12

"So Tam is Matteo, or actually, Matteo is Tam? He's really here?" Jayna babbled, and then slipped her hand into Reynier's, who was sitting next to her. Reynier gripped her hand, and Jayna exhaled.

Linden blinked rapidly to keep her damp eyes from spilling over. Her reaction wasn't much different than Jayna's, who'd mourned for Matteo nearly as much as Linden. It was Linden who'd encouraged her friend to move on, to explore her feelings for Reynier without feeling guilty about Matteo. "When will it be safe for me to see my brother?" She swept her hand around her circle of friends. "For all of us to meet him and the other resistance leaders?"

Vas steepled his fingers in front of his chest, which in Linden's experience usually meant someone was going to launch into a long explanation for why she couldn't get what she wanted. She braced herself and tried to listen with an open mind. "I'm afraid it's not the best time to see your brother, for several reasons."

Before Vas could list the reasons, Linden opened her mouth to object. Vas raised his hand, palm outward, and said, "Please, hear me out." Linden closed her mouth and tried to temper her impatience.

"First, we're moving Tam to a safe location where he will have to lay low, very, very low, for a while, at least until the search for him becomes less intensive. Any visits could potentially blow his cover. There will be ample opportunity to meet up with Tam soon, just not now.

"Second, I'm very concerned about the mistreatment of prisoners at base camp headquarters, many of whom are resistance members. All of my attention is focused on those prisoners at the moment. I'm working on a prison break, the largest I've ever attempted.

"Finally, consider yourselves an adjunct arm of the Valerran resistance. In other words, I could really use your help coming up with a plan to free those prisoners. I figure it can't be much more difficult than your actions at Zabor Prison." Vas paused to sip from his mug of tea.

"Base camp headquarters is huge. How many prisoners are housed there?" asked Remy.

"Close to five hundred, about double the size of Zabor Prison, if my calculations are accurate."

Mara tossed her head, her blonde ponytail swishing behind her. "Let me get this straight. You want us to find a way to free five hundred prisoners, who are guarded by troopers, grihms, and an army of undead soldiers?"

Vas nodded. "That's about right."

Mara arched her eyebrow and glanced at Remy. Together they replied, "Count us in."

"Of course we want to help," said Reynier, who waved his hand to indicate himself and Jayna as she nodded her agreement.

Wreyn and Efram glanced at each other and Wreyn replied, "So do we."

Everyone looked at Linden expectantly. She knew this was

the right thing to do, and yet she also knew this could go horribly, irrevocably wrong. If they couldn't pull this off, there was little chance of any of them surviving long enough to rally support from the clans or find a way to slip into Bellaryss to face Mordahn. But she couldn't turn her back on what was happening inside that prison camp, not after what she'd glimpsed from her perch in the tree earlier that night. Linden nodded. "Let's do it. Let's free those prisoners."

"Welcome to the rebellion!" Vas smiled, momentarily transforming his sad, craggy face. Linden could imagine him as a younger marine officer, joking around with her father, falling in love about the same time, planning his future without trepidation, not knowing how much his world, their world, would be cleaved apart. He brought his hands together. "Thank you, all of you. I know what I'm asking, and I also know we will have one chance to get this right." Vas noticed Mara yawning and said, "Perhaps we ought to get some rest and pick up this conversation later?"

~

Using a sharp stick, Vas etched a map of the prison camp in the hard-packed soil of the barn floor, pointing out the sections where the most "dangerous" prisoners were housed. These were the prisoners with suspected ties to the resistance. "You mentioned they're being mistreated. What is their condition? Are the prisoners able to walk without assistance?" asked Jayna, the master healer of their group.

"Their conditions vary. Most should be able to walk out of there, although some will need to be carried."

"We're going to need to deploy some serious Serving magic in order to pull this off, and that much magic is going to draw Mordahn's attention. Are you prepared for that?" Reynier rubbed his beard, looking at the map Vas had drawn.

Vas shrugged. "What choice do we have? I can't see any other way to free the prisoners without a heavy reliance on magic."

"My thoughts exactly," said Linden. "Last time, we tricked the guards and walked into Zabor Prison. A few of us entered as 'prisoners' and were tossed into the cells, while the rest served as our 'guards' and milled about the prison, gaining intelligence until we were ready to break out. Given the fact there was a recent, successful prison break at this camp, that plan won't work. The guards will be immediately suspicious. Using magic to disrupt their defenses and confuse them will be our best option."

"Our timing has to be perfect. We won't get any do-overs," said Wreyn. "Are we planning on entering through the secondary tunnel?"

Vas drew four *X*s on the ground, roughly at each corner of the map. "We can't use the tunnel to enter because it's blocked from the inside. That's why the alternate entrance wasn't guarded. Instead, we're going to position ourselves here, here, and here—" Vas pointed at three of the *X*s "—and at our pre-arranged signal, we'll cast dissolving spells. We'll use magic to eat away at the wood perimeter fencing during the final evening roll call, when the guards line up all the prisoners, except for those in the special high-security wing, to count them off and make sure none have escaped."

"What happens at that last *X*?" Wreyn pointed at the map.

"That's where we'll stage a major distraction, right in front of the watchtower to draw off the attention of a lot of the guards. We'll set that off first, before we cast the dissolving spells."

"What sort of a distraction do you have in mind?" asked Linden.

"I'm not sure. I could really use your help figuring out this part of the plan."

Reynier summarized. "So we create some sort of a distraction, coupled with dissolving spells, and enter the prison camp...how? Through the main gate?"

Vas drew circles around the three Xs where they'd be casting dissolving spells. "When we melt down the wood fencing, we're counting on the inmates inside the prison yard to help us stage a coup right then and there. We have a lot of good friends, resistance fighters and former marines, who've been imprisoned. While some will escape immediately—and I wouldn't blame them—most will tackle the guards, and we'll race inside to free the remaining prisoners."

"The Glenbarrans must have defensive wards around that prison. Are you sure the dissolving spells will work?" asked Linden.

"I've been testing various spells for weeks on those wooden fences. Whatever wards they're using to repel attacks at the prison camp don't stand up to a simple dissolving spell."

"I'm surprised you haven't been caught."

Vas grinned. "I've had some close calls, but I've been casting very low-grade spells in the middle of the night."

"And how about our exit? Whatever we do, there will still be guards or grihms coming after us—" Remy swallowed hard "—or those creepy undead riders. How do we escape without being pursued?"

"Actually, we don't," replied Vas. "We want the guards to pursue us, or rather, some of us, to draw them away from the bulk of the prisoners, who are going to need time to escape."

Mara folded her arms and frowned. "So you want to use some of us as bait to draw the guards away from the prison?"

Vas held out his hands, palms up. "I know it's asking a lot, but you won't be alone. I've recruited four other resistance fighters for this mission, all highly skilled, all completely trustworthy. Even so, we're small in number, and it's going to take some time for five hundred prisoners to escape."

'Time, a foolproof plan, and a lot of magic." Linden bit her bottom lip, thinking about how to pull off a prison break on this scale. "Are any of the guards sympathetic to our cause?"

Vas nodded. "Aye, there are several who are actively helping us, and a few more who will look the other way when the time comes. But most will perform their sworn duty out of fear of punishment."

Linden pointed at the fourth X on the map, where they needed a major distraction. "Remy, how large of a fireball could you conjure?" Remy's pyro gift, while an odd magical ability, came in handy from time to time. He didn't need to shapeshift something to create the fire or cast a spell to call up fire. He simply snapped his fingers.

Remy shrugged. "Without fuel, about six feet high or so. With fuel, the sky's the limit, so to speak."

"So you're a pyro?" asked Vas.

Remy nodded. Vas clapped him on the shoulder. "Excellent! The camp's watchtower is made entirely of wood. Would that do for fuel?"

Remy grinned. "I'd say the sky's the limit."

CHAPTER 13

Four nights later, Linden and her friends crept along the route to base camp headquarters. This time they traveled with their swords and daggers strapped firmly at their sides, in plain view, prepared for a fight. They'd planned to leave sooner, but first they had to wait out two days of intermittent showers, since Remy needed dry wood to fuel the huge fireball he planned to start. Then they had to wait out the full moon, deciding it was almost too bright for their plans. When they finally left the barn, having removed all evidence of their stay, the waning moon was visible through a partially cloudy sky, the evening air crisp but not too cold.

The day before they left, Wreyn and Efram used their traveling mists to transport their horses some twenty miles away, to the stable of a wealthy farmer who "cooperated" with the authorities but in fact served the resistance. Linden and Reynier had made the call to move the horses, figuring if they didn't make it out of the prison camp, at least the animals would be well cared for. And if they did make it to the farmer's stable, then the horses would be well rested and ready for the next leg of their journey east, to Bellaryss.

Before Efram had led Ashir away, Linden threw her arms around his neck, leaning against his solidness, and promised she'd find him again. He whickered softly. Kal circled around them, clicking his beak rapidly as if sending Ashir a coded message. Linden had briefly considered asking the farmer to look after Kal as well, but she knew Kal would be miserable. So instead, she gave Kal strict orders. He had to stay well out of sight throughout the prison break, and if something went horribly wrong, he needed to return to Faynwood and find Pryl.

"Base camp is about half a mile away, around the bend up ahead," whispered Mara, who'd taken point.

"We're approaching the rendezvous with Vas. In fact, I think that's him over there, hiding in those trees." Linden pointed at a copse of trees near the fork in the supply road leading to headquarters.

"Wait here, I'll confirm it's Vas," said Reynier.

Efram placed his hand on his sword belt and nodded toward the trees. "I'll keep you company."

Reynier and Efram returned a short while later with Vas and four others, two men and two women, all dressed in dark clothes to blend into the night. Vas introduced each resistance member, all of whom had served with Vas in the marines: Burr, who looked about Reynier's age, Dunn, who seemed closer to thirty, Gem, a small, dark woman who moved with the grace of a cat, and Nahn, a tall woman with a commanding air.

After Vas introduced his team, he added, "Nahn was one of my senior officers at base camp headquarters and knows the layout better than anyone. She will team up with me and Linden and lead us to the high security area, to ensure we release those prisoners, many of whom are friends from the resistance." Nahn, dressed in tunic and tights, her hair firmly tucked under a knit cap, nodded to the group.

"Glad to meet you. I'm Linden." She introduced her friends, using first names only, leaving Kal for last. "And this is my miniature griffin. Kal will wait out here for us. If we don't return, he'll fly back to Faynwood to alert our clan leaders there." Kal had been licking one of his paws and yawned when his name was mentioned.

Nahn knelt down and offered her hand to Kal. He placed his paw in her palm and she shook it solemnly. Kal purred and she rubbed his mane. Linden's eyebrows rose. "He's usually very reserved with strangers."

Nahn smiled. "My mother was a healer, but strictly of animals. I was her assistant growing up. I suppose I inherited her way of communicating with them."

Vas quickly recapped the plan: Gem, Wreyn, and Efram would cast the dissolving spell on the southern side of the prison, while Burr, Reynier and Jayna would take the northern side. Dunn would accompany Remy and Mara to the watchtower, on the prison's western side. That left the eastern side of the prison, where the high-security wing was housed, for Linden, Vas, and Nahn.

Reynier asked, "Remy, are you ready?" When he nodded, Reynier turned to Vas. "Looks like we're all set."

Vas nodded briskly. "Right then. Everyone knows the signal to initiate the dissolving spells—Remy's fireball. We immediately begin casting. When the fencing is dissolved, Burr's team is going to encourage an uprising inside that prison yard, Gem's team is going to locate the women and children and lead them out, and once the watchtower is burning nicely without magical support, Dunn's team is going to lead as many guards as possible on a merry chase away from the compound. Meanwhile, Nahn, Linden, and I will be freeing prisoners in the high-security wing. We're counting on speed, the element of surprise, and the ensuing chaos to help us pull this off. Questions?"

Since they'd reviewed this plan countless times, no one had any questions left. Linden shifted from one foot to the other, anxious to get started, and at the same time, wishing it was already over. She worried about her friends and prayed everyone would make it back safely.

"Alright," said Vas, "let's move out. Good luck, everyone."

Linden thought of her grandmother, who recited the Serving mage's mantra whenever something important was about to occur. "May your magic serve in peace and lead through service. This is the true path."

Everyone solemnly repeated, "This is the true path."

Vas gave a firm head nod. "We'll see each other in two days' time at the checkpoint."

∼

Linden swallowed hard, her senses on high alert, every muscle poised for action. Nahn crouched low on her right side, Vas on her left, leaning against the wooden perimeter fencing. They'd crawled on their bellies the last fifty yards, crossing the wide-open lawn surrounding the prison. Linden hated leaving the tree cover behind them, but base camp headquarters sat in a clearing, making it very hard for any intruders to sneak up unannounced.

Nahn voiced her concern. "What's taking so long? Remy should have started that fire by now."

"It's not Remy. He can snap his fingers and poof, there's a fireball. Something else is holding them up," said Linden.

Vas shrugged. "Don't forget, they have to sneak in under that watchtower, no easy feat. Dunn is probably waiting it out in the woods until they have a clear approach. They'll get started soon enough."

Vas no sooner finished speaking when they heard a loud whoosh and then shouting. The three of them backed away from the fence just far enough to confirm it: Remy's fireball lit up the western side of the camp. "Let's do this!" whispered

Linden. She reached out to grasp Vas's hand and Nahn's, their physical connection helping to reinforce the spell, and started the incantation. The three of them murmured the spell in unison, a low mumble barely audible even to their own ears. "Dissolve fence and defense in this place, make an opening in this space."

Meanwhile, Linden registered commotion on the other side of the camp, where Remy's fireball was eating away at the watchtower. Inside the prison yard, Linden heard guards shouting at inmates to stay in line, and a lot of grumbling among the prisoners trying to figure out what was happening. She focused on the fence directly in front of her, which didn't seem to be responding to the spell. Vas had warned them not to let appearances deceive them. The fence's defensive wards included a masking mechanism, which hid any visible damage to the naked eye, at least until the fence and its defenses collapsed. Linden squinted in concentration, beads of sweat breaking out beneath her wool cap. Her hands felt clammy inside her gloves. *What if this doesn't work? What if the Glenbarran commander changed his defensive wards since the last time Vas checked? Then we're all sitting ducks, waiting to be picked off.*

"Step back," hissed Vas, who dropped her hand and charged the fencing. At the last moment he spun around in a flying kick that made contact with the fence. His boot went right through the wood, which splintered into a heap of broken planks. Now the roar of the fire competed with the shouts of the guards and their captives.

"Come on!" said Nahn, drawing her sword and charging after Vas.

Linden pulled her sword from her scabbard, and the blade pulsed green, lighting up the ancient fay hieroglyphs. She ran alongside Nahn, expecting an immediate assault, but the guards were more concerned with securing the prisoners than attacking the intruders. One of the guards finally took notice of her and Nahn. Shouting, he ran at Linden, the point of his blade aimed at her throat. Linden brought her sword up, checked his blade, and then ducked under his arm, jabbing her sword into his side. Howling, the guard turned toward her, as another, much larger guard came to his aid.

The two guards closed in on her, the tips of their swords surrounding Linden in a tight circle. Nahn and Vas had disappeared, presumably to find the inmates hidden away in the special wing. *So much for either one of them having my flank*, thought Linden grimly. *Or am I being unfair?* Vas had been very clear about their mission. Releasing the prisoners was the top priority. Still, Linden wouldn't leave anyone behind in a fight.

The large guard charged her first. Linden sidestepped left, swinging her blade up with both hands. Their blades collided in a spray of sparks, Linden parrying every one of his lunges. She sensed the wounded guard behind her, preparing to run her through with his sword while his large friend kept her occupied. Screaming "Evakunouz!" an ancient fay war cry that basically meant "Retreat or die," she charged the large guard, dropping to the ground at the last minute. Sliding past his right leg, she drew her sword across his calf muscle. He yelped and slashed out at her, nicking her left arm.

Gritting her teeth at the sharp pain, Linden jumped to her feet and turned to face her opponents. The large guard favored his injured calf, the other guard clutched his side. She raised her sword, waiting for them to make the next move. The two guards looked at each other, shrugged, and charged past her, not even attempting to make contact. Linden whipped around, thinking they were trying to run around and catch her from behind, but the men kept running, right out of the opening in the fence and toward the woods. They weren't the only ones running; many of the prisoners were running alongside them.

Linden turned back to the chaos inside the prison yard, with prisoners and guards fighting hand-to-hand. The watchtower, completely engulfed in flames, leaned precariously to one side. It crashed suddenly with a loud boom, showering burning wood and sparks over the yard. This was the signal for Remy, Mara, and Dunn to lead the guards on a chase through the woods, away from the prison camp. Linden hoped they were fast enough, and wily enough, to escape from the guards pursuing them.

Although the large buildings in the center of the complex blocked her view, she knew Reynier and Jayna were off to her right somewhere, and Wreyn and Efram were off to her left, on the other side of the prison grounds. Collecting herself, Linden ran past the melee in the yard, four to five prisoners tackling each guard, some guards gaining the upper hand because of their weapons, but mostly the prisoners were winning.

Linden needed to find the others and help release the prisoners in the special wing. Nahn had told her to enter the building closest to their entry point and take a series of left turns, beginning with the first corridor. Linden slipped into the building, leading with her sword. The bodies of three guards lay sprawled around the entrance. Clearly, she was in the right place, and Vas and Nahn had passed through ahead of her. Linden jogged down the second corridor and almost tripped over two guards slumped on the tiled floor. She expected to be charged by more guards, but at every turn, she found more felled guards, their weapons lying useless on the floor nearby. She was surprised by Vas and Nahn's deadly efficiency but reminded herself they'd been highly trained marine officers before becoming resistance fighters.

As she turned into the next corridor, Linden noticed a flicker on the whitewashed wall, and then another, until the entire wall pulsed, as if small white lights were flashing on and off. Everything began to blur and waver before her eyes and she stopped running, recognizing the start of a powerful vision, one that was coming on her full force. Feeling panicky now, because this was no ordinary vision, she found a supply closet filled with buckets, mops, and cleaning supplies. Linden pulled the door firmly shut as sharp stabs of pain struck inside her head. Sliding to the floor, she put her sword down next to her right leg and leaned her head against the wall, relieved to be safe for the moment, hidden in the darkness of the closet. At least the white flickering lights had stopped.

Images came at her, lightning fast, so many she felt dizzy with their speed as they flashed past. She'd been an apprentice the first time she experienced powerful visions, and she hadn't known how to focus and control the flow of information coming at her. Linden reminded herself she was a master mage now, and she had to get a grip. Taking deep breaths, she forced her mind to slow down, to capture each image, however faint, bending the vision to her will. She felt certain there was an important message embedded within the images if she could sort them out and actually "see" them.

The spinning inside her head, which had been making her nauseous, slowed down and finally stopped. Linden was in control now, as one image after another entered the frame she'd opened up in her mind. Now that she could see them clearly, she frowned, unable to interpret the "what, where, and when" of the images. In her vision, she descended an endless staircase that wound around and around, passing willowy shadows on each level. Linden tried to sharpen her focus on the shadows, thinking there was some message within, but she couldn't see beyond a thin gauze of film blocking her view. She found herself pausing on each landing of the winding staircase and weeping as she gazed at whatever moved just beyond her line of sight. The images faded away. Linden wiped her damp cheeks, feeling as if some unseen force had plunged a knife deep into her soul and twisted the blade.

Linden picked up her sword and rose from the floor. Her left arm throbbed where the guard's sword had made contact.

She tried lifting that arm and stifled a scream. Jayna would give her another lecture. She wondered how Jayna, Reynier, and the others were faring and hoped their resistance friends hadn't entirely abandoned them the first chance they got. Linden had expected more from Vas, but she was beginning to think he saw her and her friends as expendable, despite his show of fealty to her as the Liege. Had that been all show? She didn't know, but she didn't like how quickly Vas and Nahn had disappeared and left her to fend for herself. Friends had each other's backs, especially when fighting with swords and daggers. She'd have to have a word with him, that is, if they got out of there with their lives. Putting her ear to the door, she listened before opening it a crack.

She heard footsteps now, and shouting, people running and shuffling. "Hurry, this way now!" urged Nahn. "What are you slowing down for?"

"But my wife, they've got her here somewhere," cried a man, "I'm not leaving without her."

"We have friends on that side of the prison, freeing her right now," replied Nahn. "Now go!"

Released prisoners shuffled past, many stooped over and being assisted by others. Linden spotted Vas, a nasty cut on his forehead, running up the corridor toward Nahn. Linden decided to eavesdrop before showing herself. She needed to know if they could be trusted.

"Have you seen her?" he asked Nahn, his voice urgent.

"Not yet."

"Queen's Crown, where could she have gone? And why didn't you stay with her?"

Nahn shrugged. "Because I decided to save your sorry butt first. When I turned around again, she was gone."

"Tam will never forgive me if we've lost his sister, or worse, if she's been captured."

Nahn yelled at several prisoners who had slowed down.

"Keep moving, out into the yard and through the fence. We're right behind you."

Linden stepped out of the supply closet and closed the door behind her. Vas's face lit up when he saw her. "We've been looking for you. We feared maybe you'd been captured."

He seemed genuinely relieved to see her, which Linden took as an encouraging sign. "I ran into a couple of guards and then came here but couldn't find anyone."

Nodding, Vas noticed her injured left arm. "Glad to see you're in one piece, more or less."

Nahn pointed down the corridor. "We've cleared this section, so I think it's time we high-tailed it out of here."

Linden fell into step beside them, jogging along behind the last of the prisoners. One of the guards must have triggered an alarm, because claxons were blaring from every direction, the noise so loud Linden's ears were ringing. They ran to the main entrance and paused, the freed prisoners massing inside the lobby.

"What's going on?" barked Vas. "Why aren't you moving out?"

Nahn tapped his shoulder. "Take a look outside."

Linden glanced through the window, her blood freezing in her veins. Grihms milled about the prison yard, swinging axes at anyone who moved. They'd already mowed down several dozen of the freed prisoners. Linden's headache, which had lifted, came back with a vengeance. She worried about her friends, trying to release the women and children, hoping they'd been able to escape before the grihms were released from their cages to wreak their havoc.

Taking a deep breath, she shouted above the blaring, "We need to cast a spell to protect these prisoners and get them to safety."

"Got anything in mind?" yelled Vas.

Linden mentally ran through the possibilities from *Timely Spells,* a birthday gift from her grandmother that had been in her family for generations. Written in fay hieroglyphs that no one could read anymore, the book decided which set of spells to reveal, and when, translating them for the current owner. Although she'd left the book back in Faynwood, Linden had memorized every incantation, including a couple of new spells. "A spell to temporarily freeze anything canine for ninety seconds. We'll have to remain here to cast it while the prisoners escape, and then try to bind it on our way out. We won't have much time."

Vas shouted at the prisoners pressed up against the doors and windows. "We're going to immobilize those grihms with magic. You'll have ninety seconds to get out of here. Now get ready!" He turned back to Linden and nodded.

She used her commanding voice to conjure the magic needed to stop the grihms' killing spree, at least temporarily. "Canine foes or friends now stand still, for ninety seconds bend to our will." It took three repetitions before she noticed the grihms slowing down, another two repetitions before the grihms could no longer raise their axes or swords. On the seventh repetition, the grihms were frozen in place, still breathing but unable to lift even one leg.

"Run as if your lives depended on it, because they do!" yelled Vas. The prisoners burst through the doors, running, hobbling, shuffling. Those needing assistance were half-carried, half-dragged by their friends.

Linden, Vas, and Nahn continued repeating the incantation as they weaved their way out of the prison building and across the yard, stepping over the bodies of guards and prisoners, and skirting around the frozen grihms. When they reached the hole in the fence, they turned around for a last look. Since Linden couldn't see beyond the buildings to the other side of the sprawling camp, she had no idea whether her friends had managed to free the prisoners and were running for safety at that very moment.

Nodding at Vas and Nahn, she led them in a binding incantation. "Bind this spell that we have spun, magic stay sharp until we're done." Binding spells reinforced the existing magic, but it was anyone's guess how long the original spell would stay bound. At most, she'd bought them another couple of minutes.

Linden shouted, "And now we run!"

CHAPTER 14

Linden sprinted behind Vas and Nahn across the open field, straining to keep up with them, their longer legs taking them farther away with each stride. Nahn and Vas slowed enough to keep pace with her. They were halfway across the field when she heard a scream that could curdle fresh milk.

"Undead riders," yelled Nahn, "coming up behind us. Don't look back. We need to make it to the woods before they're on us."

Nahn gripped Linden's right arm, Vas grasped her left arm, and they half-lifted her as they dashed to the woods. She groaned at the searing pain in her arm, but they didn't let go. They scrambled into the heaviest undergrowth they could find as the undead riders clambered into the forest. Their rank odor assaulted Linden's nostrils, and she had to clamp her mouth shut to keep from gagging.

She whispered, "Don't move. I'm casting a veil of drabness over us." Linden silently incanted the spell, repeating over and over in her head, "Drape us in a veil of gauze, hide us from inquiring eyes!" The undead horses nosed about the woods, but they didn't have an active sense of smell anymore. Their equally undead riders, their eye sockets open holes, decaying flesh hanging from their skeletal faces and bodies, scanned the woods.

They eventually retreated back to the open meadow, joined by the now unfrozen grihms and the guards who'd survived the prison break. The guards blew high-pitched whistles as the grihms regrouped and awaited their orders.

"Now what?" hissed Nahn.

"We need to give those prisoners more time to escape," said Vas grimly.

Linden figured by now, her friends were probably in a similar predicament, hunkering down somewhere, trying to figure out how to overcome superior forces. While she could freeze the grihms again, that wouldn't be enough. She needed a spell that made it difficult for the grihms to follow them. With their superior sense of smell, grihms could track them for miles, unless Linden could throw the crossbreeds off the scent. "We need a good rainstorm, with lots of lightning and thunder."

"Grihms can still track in wet weather," Nahn pointed out.

Vas shrugged. "True, but the lightning and thunder will scare them and slow them down."

Linden said, "If we can slow them down long enough so the prisoners can make it across a stream or tributary—and there are lots of them in this part of Valerra—they ought to be able to throw the grihms off their scent."

Vas nodded. "It's worth a try."

"I've got this," Linden incanted one of her favorite water-douser spells, but she added a twist. "Thunderclap and stormy cloud, drench this ground with your power. Send upon us lightning strikes, hit with force the man-made spires." Lightning would hit the buildings or towers in the area, but not natural fixtures such as mountains or trees. As she incanted, storm clouds obscured the moon and stars overhead. Thunder boomed in the distance, and lightening began forking across the sky. A bolt of lightning struck the main prison building, followed by several more. The building caught on fire, and half the guards turned around to see to the fire.

The clouds burst open, and large drops of rain streamed down on the open field and the woods where Linden, Vas, and Nahn were hiding. Her hair plastered to her head, she continued incanting until Vas said, "Looks like pandemonium on that field. The grihms and riders are definitely off the scent. Can you bind that spell now, give us time to slip away?"

Nodding, Linden switched the incantation in her head, binding the water-douser spell in place. "It should hold for a couple of minutes, maybe a bit longer if we're lucky."

The three of them crept through the woods until they were out of earshot and then ran as quickly as they could in the dark. They jogged around fallen tree trunks, trying to avoid taking a tumble as the ground grew wet and slippery beneath their boots. Linden's legs had cramped up while they were crouched down, and it felt good to stretch them.

"I hear howling behind us," yelled Nahn.

Linden glanced up at the moon emerging from the clouds. "The spell has wound down. How much farther?"

She and Nahn followed Vas, who waved them onward. "There's a stream over there, through these trees."

Linden heard a blare of whistles and yowling, grihms trained on their scent, and the ghastly screeching the riders made when the wind passed through what used to be their mouths. She put on her last burst of speed, her pulse pounding, her temples throbbing from the hard running and the energy expended from conjuring so many spells in a row. Her legs ached as she clutched a stitch in her side. Linden stumbled, but Nahn gripped her right elbow and hissed, "Come on, we're so close."

Linden pushed herself to keep pace with Nahn, even as the yelping and screaming told her the grihms and riders were on their heels. Linden knew better than to look back. "Jump!" shouted Nahn, pushing Linden in front of her. Linden tumbled down an embankment, landing in the running water. Vas pulled her up and the three of them waded across the stream, the grihms yowling as they dashed to the water's edge, the riders opening the hinges of their jaws and howling, a strange chorus that sent chills down Linden's spine.

Linden figured she could cast one more spell without rest, but she wouldn't be able to maintain it for long, her magical energy nearly spent. "If I cast a curtain of impenetrable fog along this stretch of water, can the two of you sustain it?" Vas and Nahn nodded. Linden repeated the incantation she'd used to help defend Bellaryss from Mordahn's Fallow magic. "Raise impenetrable fog with this charm, protect those within from outside harm." They'd been able to hold the city for eight days before the last of the Serving mages collapsed at their posts, their magic all but expended. She only needed to hold those grihms and riders back long enough for them to give up the search.

Linden cast the spell and her legs gave out. She crumpled in a heap on the ground, letting Vas and Nahn carry on without her. After the yelping and yelling faded, the grihms and riders having moved downstream, Vas and Nahn bound the foggy shield. Vas knelt down beside Linden. "Do you think you can move now? We need to get to some shelter before daybreak."

"So long as I don't have to run, I'll be fine." Vas gave her a hand up and the three of them headed along the stream, in the opposite direction as the grihms and riders, until they felt they'd lost them. They climbed a low ridge and Vas pointed. "A little farther along, we'll find a cave I've used in the past."

"That's good, because I feel like I can sleep for a year," mumbled Linden, her legs leaden, her left arm pulsing with pain. She had a headache behind her eyes that made her want to squint at the pale light of the moon, as if even that much light was too much for her to handle.

Vas pulled out his sword. "What the blazes is that clicking noise?"

Linden pushed his sword down. "Wait, I think that's Kal." Her miniature griffin chose that moment to dive bomb from the sky and hurl himself into her chest, sending her tumbling backward. "You found us! That's a good griffin." She rubbed his mane and he purred as he burrowed into her neck. Linden realized he'd been scared. She patted his back. "We're safe, but you need to get off me now." Kal clicked his beak and hopped off her chest. He flapped his wings once and waited for her to stand up. She brushed herself off, although she needn't have bothered. Her leather jacket and leggings were soaked through and spattered with mud.

"Where did he come from?" asked Vas.

"I told Kal to stay out of sight until we'd escaped and then to come find us. He's been tracking us from the air."

"It's a good thing griffins are so rare, otherwise the Glenbarrans would be using them instead of wolves in their crossbreeding programs."

"Perish the thought," muttered Nahn. "Dorihms are bad enough." Linden agreed; she'd encountered the condor-human crossbreeds only once before, on her last mission inside Glenbarra, and she had no interest in repeating the experience.

Vas's hideout was warm, dry, and stocked with basic supplies: nuts, dried berries, several jugs of water, a few bottles of ale, and blankets. Linden's teeth were chattering by the time she removed her wet clothing, wrapping herself in one of the blankets. Nahn dressed the wound on her arm and forced some water on Linden, who fell asleep before Nahn had finished, Kal curled up at her feet.

She stirred twice, each time when Nahn checked her arm

and applied a new dressing. Linden woke at dusk, dreaming of coffee, scones, and eggs. Instead, Nahn brought her a handful of nuts and a drink of water. She left Linden's clothes, stiff with dirt but thoroughly dry, on the ground next to her. Linden dressed quickly and joined Vas and Nahn at the mouth of the cave, Kal softly snoring on her blanket. Her left arm still ached, but it no longer throbbed with every movement. She noticed the gash on Vas's forehead had been cleaned and a bandage applied.

"Where are we, and when will it be safe for us to move on?" Linden ran her fingers through her tangled hair, yearning for a warm bath to soothe her aching muscles and wash off the grime. She used a long strand of hair to wrap around her unruly layers, pulling them back out of her face.

"About three miles southeast of the prison camp. I've scouted the area, and we've lost the guards and grihms," said Nahn.

"Or they found a richer target in some of those injured prisoners and rounded them up again." Vas shook his head wearily.

"Unless we destroyed the prison, which we couldn't do without confirming everyone was out of there and accounted for, I'm afraid it's only natural some of the prisoners might be recaptured." Linden thought they'd managed remarkably well, given the size of their team, and the fact they were short one very powerful fay and one highly skilled warrior chief. She wondered how Pryl was faring with the fay council and whether Corbahn's leg was healed. She found herself thinking about Corbahn more as the days passed, rather than less. Jayna would say that was a sure sign she was in love. Frowning, Linden concentrated on what Vas was saying.

"We need to make our way to the checkpoint without being followed, which means a bob and weave sort of an approach."

"Bob and weave?"

Nahn explained. "We do a lot of backtracking as we go, to confuse anyone who may be tailing us."

"And we position ourselves outside the farm where the horses are stabled, watching for any signs we've been compromised," added Vas.

"I thought you trusted the farmer enough to leave our horses with him," said Linden.

Vas lifted his shoulders in a half-shrug. "I trust him to look after the horses. I'm not going to trust him with our lives without confirming he hasn't betrayed us."

"How likely do you think that is?" asked Linden.

"I'd say fifty-fifty."

"You couldn't find anyone more trustworthy than that?"

Vas gave Linden a tight smile. "When you're a resistance leader, you become accustomed to betrayal. Why do you think we have such small numbers? Other than Nahn here, and Dunn, Burr, and Gem—as well as your brother and a couple of other close friends—I don't trust too many other allies when it comes to face-to-face meetings. We contact most of our network through a series of intermediaries. It's not a guarantee of safety, but it does cut down on the deadly backstabbing."

"But you trusted me and my friends," Linden pointed out.

Vas waved his hands. "You're the Liege of Faynwood, traveling with the Faymon Elder, some quirky Valerrans, and a couple of fays. Your story is so unlikely that once I confirmed who you were, it made sense to trust you. Who else would be crazy enough to sneak into occupied Valerra and offer us help?"

Linden gave Vas a half-smile. "Thanks, I think."

Nahn nodded at Linden. "Do you feel up to moving out, or do you need some more rest? I know you expended a lot of magical energy last night."

"I won't be able to do much running, but I'll be fine walking. Let me go rouse Kal."

They zigzagged their way across hills, fields, and woods, ensuring they weren't being tracked. The first night, they slept in an abandoned hunter's cabin, each of them taking turns sitting watch. They reached the checkpoint sometime after midnight on the second night. Linden kept hoping they'd run into the others as they neared their contact's thriving farm, but there was no sign of her friends. She hoped that meant they were being equally cautious about their approach to the checkpoint and nothing more ominous.

They stared across the farmer's extensive fields, the soil tilled, the crops already harvested. Vas pulled a spyglass from his jacket and peered through it, scanning the farmhouse and outer buildings, including the stable. He handed the spyglass to Linden. "I don't see anything amiss, but no sign of our friends, either. I'm not inclined to just waltz up to the house without doing a bit of reconnaissance."

"I think you're being paranoid," said Nahn.

"Paranoid or not, I want a closer look. You two stay here." Vas slipped away quietly.

Nahn sat on the ground, leaned against a tree trunk, and yawned. "I'm going to catch some dreams." Kal curled up next to Nahn, purring in his sleep.

"Traitor," Linden whispered at Kal, shaking her head. She sat watch, leaning against another tree across from Nahn. After an hour passed with no sign of Vas, Linden started to worry. When another hour passed, she couldn't stand the waiting any longer. She poked Nahn in the leg. Nahn came to in an instant, her dagger drawn. "I'm worried. Vas has been gone too long."

Nahn returned her dagger to the inside of her boot and stood up, stretching. She glanced at the moon's position and held out her hand for the spyglass. Scanning the area, she adjusted the focus several times and then paused, peering straight ahead. "He's coming back, and he's not alone. Looks like your fay friends are with him."

"That's great news!"

Nahn scowled. "Maybe not so great news. None of them look too happy, and Gem's not with them."

Linden ran over to Wreyn and Efram as they approached. "What's happened? Have you seen the others?"

Wreyn blew out a puff of air. "Gem sent us on to the checkpoint. She's going to stay with the women and children for the time being. Gem will lead them in small groups to several different safe houses set up by the resistance. We got every last woman and child out of that wretched place."

Efram added, "We were lucky, other than some scrapes and a few cuts, we're fine."

Linden sensed the "but" and waited for Vas to explain.

Vas compressed his lips. "Reynier and Jayna managed to reach the checkpoint first." He paused and shook his head. "We overheard several of the stable hands talking. We've been double-crossed. Our contact handed them over to the local Glenbarran authorities, claiming they had something to do with the resistance."

"What? We have to rescue them!" Linden folded her arms, her brows drawn together in an angry scowl.

"But what about Burr? Was he arrested too?" asked Nahn.

Vas glanced down at his scuffed boots. "The lads were talking about a beautiful, brown-skinned woman and her husband, with the blue streaks in his hair." He raised his head and looked directly at Nahn. "I'm sorry, lass. They made no mention of a second man in the group."

Nahn stifled a cry and turned away. Linden hadn't realized there was more than friendship between Burr and Nahn. Her heart went out to the tall female warrior. She sensed that Nahn did not share her affections easily.

Efram waved his hand. "If Burr has been injured and captured, we can attempt to retrieve him later."

Nahn turned toward Efram, shaking her head as tears streamed down her cheeks. "Even if Burr survived his initial injuries, he's long gone by now. The Glenbarrans would have seen to that." Nahn stumbled toward the nearest tree and leaned against it for support, cradling her head in the crook of her arm.

Linden glanced at Vas. "I'm very sorry to hear about Burr. I know he was a trusted friend to all of you, and this is a heavy blow. Unfortunately, we haven't much time. We have to figure out where Reynier and Jayna were taken, so we can help them."

Vas agreed. "Aye, but we need to wait for Dunn, Remy, and Mara, who haven't shown up yet."

Wreyn and Efram looked at one another and nodded. Efram spoke first. "I'll go search the area for Mara, Remy, and the resistance fighter."

Wreyn said, "And I'll see what I can learn about where Reynier and Jayna were taken. We overheard one of the stable hands talking about the local jailhouse." Vaporous tendrils curled around Efram and Wreyn's legs, rising higher until the mists obscured them entirely, and they were gone.

Vas walked over to Nahn, and clapping a hand on her shoulder, spoke in low, soothing tones. Linden heard Nahn crying softly. Kal rubbed his head against Linden's legs and then padded over to Nahn. He clicked his beak and flapped his wings half-heartedly. Nahn swiped her eyes with the sleeve of her jacket and bent down to run her hands through Kal's mane, the miniature griffin purring deep in his throat. Linden never ceased to be amazed by how well tuned Kal was to his surroundings and to the people he cared about, which now also included Nahn.

Three-quarters of an hour later, they heard a rustling sound coming from the thicket of trees behind them. Nahn, Vas, and

LADY LIEGE

Linden jumped up from the ground, withdrew their blades, and waited. Linden noticed the traveling mists first and re-sheathed her sword. "Stand down. It looks like either Wreyn or Efram, coming back to us."

Linden waited impatiently to see who would be emerging from the mists first. She broke into a smile when she spotted a slender woman sporting a blonde ponytail. "Mara!" Linden ran over to give her friend a quick hug. "How did you make out?" She pointed to a cut above Mara's eye. "Are you okay?"

Mara nodded. "Looks worse than it is. I'm fine."

Remy came alongside Mara and added, "We managed to lead a good number of guards away from the prison, and they're still searching for us—in the wrong direction. Turns out Dunn here is a master of deception, in a good way."

Dunn stepped up and gave a half-shrug. "A bit of magic combined with a lot of field training." He noticed Nahn's swollen eyes and looked over at Vas, who shook his head. Dunn set his mouth in a firm line, walked over to Nahn, and placed his hands on her shoulders. "I'm sorry to hear about Burr. He was a good man." Nahn nodded wordlessly and sniffled.

"Where are Reynier and Jayna?" asked Mara. Linden pulled Remy and Mara aside and quickly told them about the farmer's betrayal. As she was speaking, she heard Efram call out, "Wreyn's coming back."

Everyone gathered around as the young fay woman walked out of the foggy wisps encircling her. Linden's heart sank at the grim look on Wreyn's face. "Well?"

Wreyn pointed behind her. "I picked up their trail a few miles down the road and followed them into town. They're spending the night in the local jail and will be moved in the morning."

"Can you use your traveling mists to whisk them out of there?" asked Linden.

Wreyn shook her head. "We can get inside the building, but

the bars and walls of their cell are reinforced with twisted steel, blocking our magic."

"How many guards do they have at the local jail?" asked Dunn, who had wandered over to join the conversation.

"I counted six," said Wreyn. "But I didn't stick around very long. There are probably more during the daytime."

"You said they're going to be moved in the morning, which means they'll be transferred out of that cell," said Linden. "That's when we'll have the best chance to snatch them back."

Vas nodded. "Makes sense. Wreyn, can you lead us back to the jail? I want to get a lay of the land, see the roads in and out. Let's come up with a plan and be ready to act when we need to."

"What about our horses?" asked Remy.

Vas frowned. "In all the commotion, I forgot to tell you the other bad news. Our contact has sold the animals."

Nahn's head snapped up and she stepped forward. "That traitor sold the horses? When I get my hands on him, he'll wish he never laid eyes on the lot of us."

Linden had promised Ashir she'd be back for him. She felt sick to her stomach; first Burr, then Reynier and Jayna, and now the horses. This mission of theirs was going downhill fast.

Efram held up his hands. "We have a little time yet. The horses have been sold, but they're still over there for now. We overheard the stable hands say the new owner will pick them up tomorrow."

Linden looked at Vas. "We need to split up into two teams. One team to rescue Reynier and Jayna, and the other to retrieve our horses."

"Or we grab the horses right now and beat feet out of here," said Dunn.

"But won't that create more fuss than we want? We won't exactly be able to sneak around with 'stolen' horses," said Mara.

Linden ran a hand through her hair and thought about her

grandmother. Surely Nari would come up with a solution. She would find a way to turn the farmer's greed against him somehow, save their horses, and spring Reynier and Jayna. "Does the farmer have the usual protection charms about his property?" Wreyn and Efram nodded. "Anything out of the ordinary?" They shook their heads.

"What are you thinking?" said Vas. "Another dissolving spell?"

"I think it would take too long, and the building might collapse first, injuring the horses. No, I'm thinking about a shapeshifting spell."

"You mean shapeshift the stable into something else entirely? Like what?"

Linden nodded. "I'm still working out the details, but shapeshifting the horses' stalls and either end of the building into piles of feathers or pillars of salt, something like that. We could set all the horses free at once. That stable is large enough to shelter thirty horses, maybe more. Everyone will be so busy chasing down the farmer's prized horses they won't notice when a few go missing, and then a few more."

She waved her hand at Wreyn and Efram. "I know the two of you can use the traveling mists to transport two horses apiece. A couple of trips, and we'll have our horses back. We can ride to the outskirts of town, wait for Reynier and Jayna to be transferred, and make our next move."

Vas turned to the two fays. "If we open up that stable, do you think the two of you could snatch those horses back for us?"

Wreyn grinned. "Aye, we'd be happy to oblige."

CHAPTER 15

Linden crept through a small apple orchard and stood behind a tree, giving her a good view of the stable, about fifty yards away. While she could have cast the spell from a safer distance, she worried about precision, since live animals were involved. Vas insisted on accompanying her and positioned himself at an adjacent tree. He nodded. "Ready when you are."

Linden started the incantation, softly murmuring the words to the spell in case anyone from the household was wandering about. "Shift stalls and doors on either side, from solid wood to dusty piles."

She visualized the individual stalls inside the stable, and the two opposing ends of the stable building, and focused with all her attention. Despite the chilly air, beads of sweat broke out on her forehead. She cycled through the incantation six times before she heard it: a gentle whoosh followed by horses neighing. A few of the more adventurous horses wandered out of the stable into the yard. One of the stable lads started shouting, which had the opposite effect on the remaining horses; they bolted out of the stable and milled about the yard and adjoining field.

"Well done!" said Vas, bringing up his spyglass for a closer look. "What did you wind up shifting the building ends and stalls into? I don't see feathers or salt piles or anything."

"Dust."

"Dust?" Vas grinned. "Brilliant."

They slipped away from the orchard and retreated to the edge of the farmer's property, where Mara, Remy, Nahn, and Dunn waited. Wreyn and Efram wasted no time, having already left to retrieve their horses. Minutes later, Linden heard the sound of hooves hitting the ground nearby. Wreyn and Efram emerged from their traveling mists, dismounted, and handed the reins over to Remy and Mara. It took them less than fifteen minutes to round up their horses. Linden could hear the farmer shouting at his stable hands as they rode away, Ashir tossing his head in response.

They holed up in a wooded area outside the village where Reynier and Jayna were spending the night. "Are you sure they're going to have to pass this way when they're transferred in the morning?" Linden handed the spyglass back to Vas. She figured they had about two hours before sunrise. Her stomach grumbled with hunger pains, but she forced herself to ignore it.

Vas nodded. "The guards will be under orders to transport them to Bellaryss for questioning and a sham trial."

"What happens at the trial?"

"If we don't rescue them, they'll be found guilty of crimes against the state and promptly executed."

Linden shuddered. She would never allow that to happen to Jayna and Reynier.

Mara leaned over and said, "Why don't you catch some sleep while you can? I'll sit watch." Linden thanked her and curled on her side, Kal snuggling at her feet. The next thing she knew, Mara was shaking her awake. "They're coming this way!"

Linden bolted upright, rubbing the sleep from her eyes. Kal flapped his wings, squawking, and Linden ordered him to fly into one of the trees and stay out of sight. He clicked his beak a few times, objecting to his interrupted sleep, before retreating to a sturdy tree branch. She heard the horses' hooves before she saw them: a small unit of a dozen guards, surrounding two figures huddled over on borrowed horses.

Vas and Nahn dashed down the road toward the guards, dropping down into a ditch to hide. Dunn slung his bow and quiver over his shoulder and scaled one of the trees behind them. Everyone else stayed put, waiting until the lead horse was twenty yards away.

Linden started the incantation, murmuring the words to an illusion spell. "Appearing before these horses' eyes, a wall of stone ten feet high!"

The lead horse neighed and slowed down. The others slowed down behind him, creating a jam. "What's going on?" shouted the captain of the guard, riding to the front.

"I don't know, sir, but something's spooked him."

"Well get him moving again. We have a long ride to the capital."

"Aye, Captain."

The guard snapped his horse's reins, but the stallion moved even slower, finally stopping in front of what he perceived to be a ten-foot-high stone wall. The other horses clogged up the road behind him, despite their riders' attempts to spur them on. All of the horses "saw" the wall, but to the guards, the road ahead was clear.

The captain dismounted to investigate, followed by most of the guards. Vas and Nahn nipped around to the rear of the guard unit, daggers drawn, zeroing in on the last two guards. Before they could make a move, arrows started flying. Linden frowned, confused why the arrows were coming from the trees on the other side of the road. She quickly bound the illusion spell and unsheathed her sword. Vas and Nahn clamped their hands over the two rear guards' mouths, drawing their blades across their throats.

"What the—" The captain's words were lost as one of Dunn's arrows caught him in the chest.

Linden, Mara, and Remy charged from the woods, swords in their hands, while Wreyn and Efram used their traveling mists to transport the two horses carrying Reynier and Jayna up the road and out of danger. Linden still had to find a way to free them from their twisted steel bonds, but they were safe for the moment.

More arrows, this time from Dunn as well as the unknown stranger who was helping them, picked off a few more of the guards. The sounds of clanging metal and grunting men and women filled the air. At some point the illusion spell faded, and the horses began to bolt. A skinny guard covered in chainmail came after Linden, slicing through the air with his sword. Linden parried his first lunge, then his second, looking for any weakness in his chainmail. He looked to be covered in the stuff from neck to boot and must have invested half his pay in his body armor, a man motivated to stay alive at all costs.

The guard lunged at her several more times, but Linden easily avoided the tip of his blade, his armor slowing down his reflexes. However, he could swing his sword at her all morning, and Linden had friends to rescue. She deflected the next thrust of his sword, ducked under his fighting arm, and jumped up behind him. Performing a double flying kick, she took careful aim at the back of his knees. The man's legs crumpled beneath him, and he dropped like a stone to his knees. Linden brought her blade to the side of his neck.

"Don't kill me!" he cried out, dropping his weapon and

raising his hands. "I can help you free those prisoners. I carry the keys to their manacles."

"Hand them over and make no false moves."

The man reached down to his belt and detached a ring of keys. "Here, now let me go."

"How do I know they're the right keys?" Linden kept the pressure on his neck.

"Take me with you and you'll see—" An arrow pierced through the man's throat, and he tumbled forward onto the ground.

Linden tucked the keys inside her leather jacket and spun around to see who needed help subduing the remainder of the guards, but the Glenbarrans were down on the ground and most of the horses had run off.

Vas shouted, "Let's get our horses and move! We haven't long before we'll have someone on our tails."

Linden jogged next to him. "Looks like someone has been helping us. Any idea who it could be?"

He shook his head. "No idea, but an enemy of my enemy is my friend."

One of the keys on the ring from the chainmail-covered guard worked, and the twisted steel manacles fell from Jayna and Reynier's wrists. Linden threw her arms around her friend, who wept in relief. Reynier nodded first at Linden, then the others. "Thank you, all of you. I prefer to be heading to Bellaryss in the company of my friends."

"At least you didn't have any grihms or undead escorts," said Remy.

"They save those for the escaped prisoners and to intermingle with the troops," said Dunn.

Remy paled. "So they'll be coming after us any time now?"

Vas nodded. "Aye, soon enough, so let's mount up and be on our way."

Reynier and Jayna transferred to their own horses, which

Wreyn had snatched for them from the farmer's field. They rode as hard as they could, crossing two streams to throw off any trackers. Jayna nodded off a few times, and even Reynier's head bobbed once or twice as he struggled to remain alert.

By late afternoon, the sun ducked behind a bank of clouds and the wind shifted, bringing much cooler air. Linden worried Jayna might topple off her horse if they didn't find a place to stop soon. Vas must have been thinking along the same lines. He pointed to a small cottage perched on the side of a green hill, overlooking the farms in the valley below. "We'll be safe there for a night or two."

"Are you sure? You thought we'd be safe at the last place," grumbled Remy.

"I can guarantee we will be safe there."

"How can you be so sure?" Remy pressed him.

Vas sighed. "That's my sister's house."

"But will it be safe for her if we stay?" asked Jayna.

Linden appreciated Jayna's unselfish concern for others, but now was not the time to turn down the gift of a safe haven. They needed to get out of the open and lay low for a while, and they needed some rest. "Thank you, Vas, we appreciate it. Will we be able to stable our horses somewhere?" She saw no outer buildings, not even a small barn or tool shed, and had no idea where they could shelter their horses.

Vas grinned. "Aye, she has plenty of room for the horses. Follow me."

Linden's eyebrows rose but she said nothing, following Vas up the hill to the modest stone cottage. He led them past the cottage and kept walking, right into the side of the hill. Vas's sister's home sat at the entrance of a large cave that seemed to stretch all the way to the other side of the hill. The main cave split off into smaller caverns on either side of the entrance. Iron torch holders had been hammered into the cave walls at regular intervals, the torches flickering slightly as they walked past.

The larger cavern to the right was the stable area for horses and a few dairy cows. It contained bales of fresh hay, a trough of water, and several sacks of oats. Extra hay bales were stacked at the back of the room, where the cave wall seemed to bend around into another passage. The cavern to the left contained the winter pantry and storage area for food, barrels of water and wine, and various tools. Linden thought she heard some movement in the storage room, but Kal distracted her. He dashed on ahead of her into the stable area and made himself a bed out of some fresh hay. Turning around a few times, Kal settled in for a nap with a contented purr.

After everyone had brushed down the horses, checked and cleaned their hooves, and fed and watered them, Vas led them back to the other side of the cave, through the storage area, and into a sleeping room. Someone else was sharing the space with them; a bedroll and knapsack occupied the far corner, and several stacks of clothes sat on a shelf inside the room. Vas pointed down another passageway. "There's an underground spring that feeds into a small pond through there. Ladies, please go ahead. When you're finished, the men can have a bath."

Nahn pointed at their mud-caked clothes. "Can we rustle up something else to wear while we launder these?"

Vas nodded. "The clothes on that shelf over there are for the taking. You ought to find something suitable until your own stuff dries out."

The only thing better than tumbling right into her bedroll, thought Linden, was having a bath first. She sorted through the clothing and found a white ruffled top, not her usual style, and a pair of boy's trousers made of brown corduroy that looked like they'd fit. Following the flickering torches down the damp corridor, she slipped on the slick floor of the cave. Righting herself, she gasped. Vas's description didn't do justice to the "small pond," which was more of a freshwater pool tucked inside a limestone alcove. The grotto was large enough for eight or nine women to bathe in at once.

Nahn was already in the water and called out, "There are pieces of soap over on that ledge, and clean rags to use for towels." Linden grabbed a sliver of soap and a rag, then stripped off her clothes and waded into the pond.

The water temperature was just right, neither too warm nor too cold. Linden scrubbed every inch of herself and washed her hair four times, before she was satisfied she'd gotten out all of the dirt. She leaned against the rock wall at the edge of the water and closed her eyes. "I could stay here all day."

Wreyn chuckled. "I think you've got another five minutes, and then the guys will be hollering for their turn."

Nahn splashed water on her face, smoothed back her hair, and turned to Jayna. "Can you tell me what happened to Burr back at the prison?"

Jayna's eyes clouded over, and she bit her bottom lip. "Everything happened so fast. We were helping the inmates escape through the opening in the wall and holding off a group of guards. A huge grihm came out of nowhere and charged me, swinging his ax. Burr pushed me down, taking the killing blow. Reynier finished off the grihm, but there was nothing we could do for Burr. I'm so sorry, Nahn."

Nahn wiped away a stray tear and sniffed. "Thanks for telling me how it went down. Burr died a hero's death, which was what he always wanted. I just wish we could've had more time together first."

Remy called out to them from the other room, reminding them their time was about up. Linden climbed out of the water, dried herself off, and changed into the borrowed clothes. She carried her balled-up wad of dripping-wet tunic and leggings into the main cave. Someone had thoughtfully strung a clothesline along the wall behind the fire pit, where a roaring fire blazed. A few narrow slits in the rock face overhead allowed the smoke to escape. Linden draped her clothes over the line and sat by the fire. Staring into the flames, she finger-combed her wet hair and thought about Corbahn.

A vision came to her, of Corbahn charging through one of the forested bluffs of Arrowood, his sword drawn, a slight limp the only sign of his injured leg. His broad back was to her as he shouted commands to the men and women fighting alongside him. Linden watched as he dispatched several grihms in rapid succession. There was a pause in the fighting. Corbahn turned around, as if sensing her presence, and looked her full in the face. The corners of his mouth turned up in a tender smile, and he nodded. Linden leaned closer to his image, so close Mara yanked her back. "Snap out of it before you singe your hair!" Linden quickly pulled her hair away from the fire, as Corbahn turned back to the battle and the image faded.

"Does that happen to her often?" Nahn winced a few times as she attempted to untangle her hair with an old comb.

"Aye, too often," answered Jayna and Mara in unison. They looked at one another and then at Linden, and chuckled. Jayna said, "But we're kind of used to it by now."

"Did you see anything useful?" asked Wreyn.

Linden shook her head. "It was more of a personal thing."

"Ooh, do tell. Was it Corbahn?" Jayna wiggled her eyebrows at Linden. Mara and Wreyn laughed.

Linden rolled her eyes. "It was nothing. Besides, he's many hundreds of miles away, defending Faynwood. He has no time to think about me, and vice versa."

"But you just were," said Mara. "You were just thinking about him."

Linden shrugged. "I was wondering how Arrowood was faring in their border war with Glenbarra. My thoughts naturally turned to the Arrowood chief."

Jayna grinned. "You can tell yourself that's all it is, but I have eyes."

"So how is Arrowood coping with the Glenbarrans?" said Mara.

"They seem to be holding their own. Corbahn is back in the thick of battle, his leg healed well enough."

"And now you're worrying about him."

Linden nodded. "We had words before I left. He was very angry with me."

Jayna shook her head. "The two of you always have words; it's the way you communicate. And Corbahn's anger never lasts long. I have a feeling you'll be seeing him sooner than you think."

Linden tilted her head. "Why do you say that?"

"I had a dream, a really vivid dream that was more like a vision."

"*You* had a vision?"

Jayna pursed her full lips. "Don't look so surprised. Anyone can have a vision once in a while."

"You're right; I'm just surprised since you've never mentioned them before. So what was your dream?" said Linden.

Jayna shrugged. "You and Corbahn were in the woods near Delavan Manor, and his arms were around you. You both seemed happy. Not much of a vision, I guess, but it seemed very real."

"Whether it comes to pass or not, it's a lovely image," smiled Linden.

Vas's sister invited all of them into her cottage, where several tables had been pushed together in her parlor to accommodate her guests. The aromas of meat and root vegetable stew, fresh-baked bread, and fruit pies cooling on the counter filled the small house. Linden's stomach growled in anticipation. She heard voices in the kitchen, and one voice stopped her cold. *It couldn't be him, could it?*

And then the owner of the voice walked into the parlor, and Linden stood rock-still, rooted in place. The man had her shale gray eyes, and the same strong chin as their father. But the left side of his face and neck were badly scarred, the skin pinkish and puckered, from what looked like a fire. His hair was long, much longer than he'd ever worn it before.

Linden took a step toward the man. "Matteo?"

CHAPTER 16

"Linden? How did you find me?"

Linden ran the last few steps and hurled herself into her brother's chest, tears flowing freely down her face. Her much larger brother wrapped his arms around her and rubbed her back, the way he used to do when she'd fallen down as a child and had run to him for comfort. Linden's head swirled as she recalled the dark days after she learned Matteo had been severely injured, and then later, when the hospital where he'd been recovering was attacked. She often wondered whether they would ever see each other again.

Linden pulled herself back long enough to ask, "Why are you here? We thought you were in a safe house somewhere."

Matteo smiled. "This is a safe house, operated by Vas's sister and her husband, whom you've already met." Matteo turned her around so she could see the rest of the room. Dunn was locked in an embrace with a pretty woman, her light brown hair streaked with blue. "That's Ameliah, Vas's sister, who is married to Dunn. And those are their children, as you've probably guessed." Two young boys and two girls ran into the room to greet their father. "Dunn always cleans up first, before entering the house. He doesn't want Ameliah or the children to see any signs of battle on his face or hands or clothes."

Jayna took a few tentative steps toward Matteo, her hand inside Reynier's. "Matteo, it's so good to see you again."

"It's Tam now. I don't use my old name anymore. That was another time and place."

Jayna nodded and cleared her throat. "Tam, I'd like you to meet my husband, Reynier Arlyss, a cousin of yours and Chief of the Tanglewood clan."

Tam gave Reynier a small bow, which Reynier returned. "Congratulations on your marriage; you're a lucky man. There were a number of cadets at the academy who wanted to court Jayna, myself included."

Reynier smiled and draped his arm around Jayna's waist. "I count myself very fortunate indeed. I'd like to hear more about you and the academy, and what Valerra was like before the war. Perhaps later this evening?"

Tam nodded. "Of course, anytime. And I'd like to learn more about Tanglewood, my grandmother's clan." Vas and the others made their way over to Tam, everyone speaking at once, telling about the prison break and the loss of Burr. Tam went over to Nahn and gripped both her hands in his. "I'm sorry to hear about Burr. He was a good man." Nahn nodded and murmured her thanks, her eyes moist.

Vas described their rescue of Reynier and Jayna, and the mysterious archer who aided them. Tam grinned. "How many resistance fighters do you know who possess that level of skill with a bow and arrow?"

Vas rubbed his beard, considering. "I can name them on one hand. Why?" As Tam continued grinning at him, Vas said, "Wait a minute, that was you?"

Tam nodded and Vas clapped him on the shoulder. "Thanks for the extra hand. We needed it. But how did you come to be there?"

Tam shrugged. "I overheard a couple of Glenbarran thugs talking about a Faymon chief who'd been arrested for his part in the prison break. The mention of a Faymon chief this far south, here to aid the resistance, struck me as curious. I decided to check it out."

"I'm glad you came along when you did. I take it you haven't been here very long yourself?" said Vas.

"I arrived less than an hour before you did."

Linden half-listened to their exchange, but her mind was miles away. *Does Matteo know Nari and Uncle Alban died at the start of the war? Has he heard any news of our parents? And what about Pryl, should I explain about our fay grandfather? Then there's my story, my journey toward becoming a master mage and being crowned the Faymon Liege, and everything since.*

Dinner was a lively affair, with Dunn sitting at one end of the long table and Ameliah at the opposite end, and everyone in between talking at once. The children had their supper earlier and were sent upstairs to bed, but Linden noticed they'd slipped back down the stairs and listened to the conversations around the table. She smiled to herself, remembering how she and Matteo used to do the same thing when their parents had "important" guests over to dinner. Although she sat next to her brother, they couldn't manage to string together more than a sentence or two between them, before someone interrupted to ask a question or tell another story.

After coffee and three-berry pie, Linden and Tam volunteered to wash and dry the dishes, giving them some time alone in the kitchen. "You've changed a lot, Linden. You've really matured since I saw you last. Tell me everything."

Linden smiled. "Everything? Have you got all night?"

"I do, actually, and I want to hear it all."

Linden took a deep breath and started to talk, beginning with the siege of Bellaryss. She described those last days, defending the city walls with magic against the darker magic of

Mordahn and his sorcerers, how the Serving mages, one by one, collapsed and were carried away. Linden told him about losing Nari and Uncle Alban, and the bleak days following their deaths.

"What about Mother and Dad? I've been so worried about everyone in Quorne. Any news?"

"They left the border with the elder aunties, and Cousin Boreus and his family, paying for passage with a traveling merchant caravan through the Barrens. I haven't heard from Mother and Dad directly, but I've been assured they arrived safely in The Colonies."

"What kind of assurances? Who told you this?"

Linden blew out a puff of air. "Do you remember the stories Dad used to tell us, of his father, who'd died when he was just a boy?"

Tam nodded. "Aye, about Grandfather Orion. I remember. Why?"

"I've met Orion Arlyss, our grandfather. He's alive and well —and wipe those storm clouds off your face—he didn't abandon his family. He left because he knew if he didn't, Nari and his sons would be in constant danger."

"Huh?"

"Our grandfather isn't Faymon after all. He is a powerful fay who helped Nari escape from Faynwood at the start of the civil war. His real name is Pryl, and he is Chief of the Fay Nation. He has this extrasensory ability to know whether anyone he's connected to is alive and well, or not. Pryl is the one who assured me you were alive, as well as Mother and Dad."

Tam pushed a chunk of brown and blue hair out of his eyes. "Are you sure about all of this? It's a lot to take in."

"I'm positive. And there's more." Linden reminded him of the Faymon history they'd learned from Nari, about the civil war, which started when Mordahn's father, then Chief of

Arrowood, killed Liege Ayala of Tanglewood. Faynwood had been without a Liege for fifty years, until very recently.

"That's interesting, but I don't understand what the new Faymon Liege has to do with us," said Tam.

Linden looked at her brother, and he saw something in her eyes that caused him to shake his head and mouth the words "no way." Linden nodded. "I spent months on Sanrellyss Island, studying to become a master mage. Afterward I traveled to Faynwood, where Reynier has been giving me a crash course in how to be the Faymon Liege ever since."

Tam hung up the damp kitchen towel he'd been using to dry dishes, pulled out a stool, and sat down. "Is there anything else? What you've shared is enough to fill two volumes, but I have a feeling there's more."

"You haven't asked me about Stryker yet. The good news is he survived the battle at Wellan Pass."

"That's great news. I heard about what happened at Wellan Pass, and I'm amazed he made it through. Where is he now? Or is that your bad news?"

Linden pulled up a stool next to Tam, wondering how he would react when he found out she was no longer engaged to his best friend. "Stryker is serving on a Faymon ship in the Pale Sea. We're no longer together. I broke it off with him."

"Do you want to talk about it?"

Linden shook her head. "Not really, but you should know he's been banned from Faynwood. He made a lot of mistakes, but the worst was when he misused his magic."

Tam whistled. "Stryker always had a temper. I'm glad he survived, and frankly, I'm glad you're no longer betrothed to him. He was a true friend to me, but I was never convinced he would be the right husband for you."

"I was worried you might be upset about our breakup."

"Of course not. You're my little sister. I want what's best

for you." Tam punched her arm lightly like he used to do, and Linden felt transported back to earlier days, happier times.

"You haven't told me about you, your injuries, and how you survived."

Tam shrugged. "There isn't much to tell, and it's not nearly as interesting as your story. The Glenbarrans completely overwhelmed us at Ravyn's Gate, with both their Fallow magic and their weaponry. They used some sort of catapult to hurl capsules of fire at us, which was how I got this." Tam pointed at his face. "I was knocked unconscious, with burns over most of my left side. The next thing I remember was waking up in base camp hospital, screaming my head off, convinced I was still on fire. If it weren't for the healers there, I'd never have survived. They helped heal both my body and my mind." Tam dropped his gaze and said more softly, "The only thing that got me through those dark days was realizing this war would be over one day, and then I could go home again.

"Anyway, one crisp autumn morning, the kind that always reminds me of Delavan Manor during the harvest, all the claxons at the base started going off. The staff hustled us into the underground tunnels, and told us to start walking, or in most cases, hobbling, shuffling, and even crawling, in the direction of Bellaryss. I turned down one of the side passages and dragged myself along, leaning on a walking stick one of the healers handed me. My left side was still bandaged, and I could only see out of the right eye, so it was slow going. I heard a commotion behind me, a lot of yelling and grunting, but I kept shuffling along. I figured it was my duty to survive to fight another day. Eventually, I collapsed, and Vas found me. We managed to escape and over time, formed the core of the resistance. And here we are." Frowning, he looked at Linden. "But I still don't know why you're here, in Valerra."

Linden brought him up to speed on developments in Faynwood, and their plans to join forces with the resistance to take down King Roi, Mordahn, and their Fallow sorcerers. Tam gave her a rueful smile. "You may be the Liege of Faynwood now, little sister, but without a lot more warriors and mages behind us, we don't stand a fighting chance."

"Agreed. Unfortunately, the Glenbarrans have been ahead of us at every turn, sending troops and grihms to Faynwood's southern and western borders. Until we're sure we can hold the borders against a sustained assault, we can't afford to detach several thousand warriors and send them into Valerra."

"Do you have any updates on your border wars?"

Linden nodded. "Based on what we're hearing, there's still a lot of heavy fighting. So far, we've been able to thwart most of the attacks. But we're not out of the woods yet."

Tam scratched his beard. "So what are your plans now?"

Linden teased her brother. "I can't believe my ears. Matteo 'Tam' Arlyss, the model marine and famous resistance leader, is asking about *my* plans."

Grinning, Tam waved his hand at her. "You're the Faymon Liege with several thousand warriors at your disposal. I have less than a hundred reliable resistance fighters. I'll take all the help you can give me."

Linden smiled and then gave her brother a business-like nod, returning to the main topic of discussion: how to defeat the Glenbarrans and their Fallow ways. "We're planning on continuing to head east, all the way to Bellaryss. Even if our Faymon warriors are still engaged in fighting inside Faynwood, we have one more ally who has promised to—er—possibly help us."

Tam arched an eyebrow. "Please don't tell me you're thinking of relying on any help from the fays."

"Why not?"

Tam hopped off the stool and paced around the small kitchen. "The Fay Nation can't be trusted. Fays say one thing and do another, always recasting whatever they committed to doing and then haggling about every detail. And they think they're better than everyone else."

Linden flapped her hand at him. "Hush! Keep your voice down. Wreyn and Efram are fays, and they've proven themselves as trustworthy as anyone. And Pryl is constantly advocating for the human race at the fay council meetings."

"I don't mean to cast aspersions on your fay friends, and I'm glad they are by your side, because fays have some real skills. But the fay council is another matter. The fact the fay chief has to advocate for us with his own council just makes my point."

Linden couldn't deny what Tam was saying, because it wasn't any different from what Wreyn and Efram had said about the fay council. "However we manage it, we have to get inside the Valerran Museum and neutralize the energy source powering Mordahn's Fallow activities, shutting down, or at least slowing down, his crossbreeding and necromantic programs."

"The museum? Are you sure about this? It's more heavily guarded than the palace."

Linden looked at Tam and waited for him to catch on. He scowled. "I've always wondered why the Glenbarrans wanted that museum and posted so many guards around it. So there's some kind of a power source inside?"

"Did you hear about what happened to Glendin Palace, where King Roi used to reside?"

"You mean the earthquake? I hear there's nothing but rubble where the palace once stood."

Linden tilted her head. "An earthquake? I supposed that's the official story line."

"Wait a minute—that was you?"

Linden nodded. "We slipped into Glenbarra with the goal of destroying their places of power."

"You said 'places of power.' What exactly are they?"

Linden gave Tam a quick run-down of her last mission, explaining that places of power were actually synonymous with ancient fay burial sites. Before funeral pyres became commonplace among the fays and Faymons, and bodies were cremated, fays used to bury the dead in large caves that served as underground mausoleums. Their latent magic went unclaimed, buried with them in their crypts for a millennia or more, an amazingly potent source of magical power to anyone who could summon and use it.

Unfortunately, Fallow sorcerers were the first to stumble upon the mystery of these places of power and learn how to funnel the energy sources. Linden and her friends had found a way to neutralize the place of power inside the infamous Zabor Prison and later, Glendin Palace. However, things went sideways at the palace. Linden wound up creating a chain reaction inside the place of power located underneath the palace, causing a very localized earthquake. Glendin Palace tumbled to the ground, but not before King Roi, Mordahn, and most of his Fallow sorcerers had fled.

"And you're telling me there's a place of power beneath the Valerran Museum?"

"Not just any place of power," said Linden. "The museum was constructed over a royal fay burial site. We're talking about a massive amount of latent magical energy."

"So we have to figure out a way to get you and your friends into that museum?"

Linden nodded. "That's the plan. Destroying the place of power will seriously damage King Roi's war machine, but we know it won't be enough. We'll have to defeat the Glenbarrans on the battlefield as well, if we want to kick them out of Valerra."

"And to do that, we're going to need help from your clansmen in Faynwood."

"You mean *our* clansmen," said Linden. "You're as much Faymon as I am."

Tam shrugged. "Fine. But even if you can stop their crossbreeding programs, a few thousand Faymon warriors won't be enough to overthrow the Glenbarrans at this point. Look at what happened to Valerra's military; we were outmaneuvered at every turn, despite the fact we had superior equipment and better-trained marines. Plus, Mordahn has bred himself a new generation of super-grihms, and his necromancers have raised an entire army of undead soldiers that guard the capital."

"That's why we need Pryl and the fays to help us rid Valerra of Fallowness once and for all. Without fay help, the most we can hope for is to carry on with the resistance movement."

"Until they stomp out every last one of us," said Tam grimly.

Linden folded her arms and frowned. "When did you become such a morose pessimist? That was always my territory."

"Since this happened." Tam pointed at his damaged face. "And since I lost my country, my home, and most of my family and friends."

"At least you haven't lost hope."

"What makes you say that?"

"You wouldn't be leading the resistance otherwise."

Tam chuckled. "You got me there. Guess I'm an optimist after all."

"A gnarly, grouchy sort of an optimist." Linden smiled. "My favorite kind."

CHAPTER 17

Linden had no trouble falling asleep as soon as she laid her head down on the bedroll. She dreamt of Corbahn again. He was leaning toward her, their lips nearly touching, her heart racing in anticipation.

"The Glenbarran guards have tracked us here! They're crossing the valley and will be at our doorstep any minute. You need to leave now, before anyone's the wiser!" Dunn shouted into the sleeping room.

Linden had no idea what time it was or how long she'd been resting. The sweet dream of Corbahn faded, and she found herself feeling lonelier than ever, almost bereft. Linden came fully awake, rubbing the sleep out of her eyes. "But what about you and Ameliah? Will your family be safe?"

"If you and your horses are gone before they arrive, we'll be fine. Take your gear—leave nothing behind—and follow me."

Mara groaned as she scrambled out of her bedroll and ran over to Remy's huddled form. She shook him hard until he finally opened his eyes. Everyone else stumbled around the cavern, half asleep, grabbing bedrolls and saddlebags.

"Follow me," hissed Dunn. "Hurry!"

Linden and the others jogged behind Dunn, who led them through the main cavern where they grabbed their clothes off the line and then dashed into the stable area. "Take your horses and go through here. Vas knows the way." Dunn removed large bales of hay stacked against the rear of the stable room to reveal yet another passageway, dark and uninviting. Linden tossed Ashir's saddle onto his back and carried her gear, falling in line behind Vas. The dark, narrow passageway had a low ceiling, too low for them to sit on top of their horses.

The only light came from a torch Dunn handed Vas as they left, and a small fireball Remy conjured by snapping his fingers. When the last of their horses had passed through the opening, Dunn re-stacked the bales of hay to conceal the passageway once again. Linden heard him cast a veil of drabness over the hay bales, another precaution to prevent prying eyes from discovering the obvious escape route.

They walked single file, the damp, chilly walls of the passage barely wide enough for the horses to squeeze through. Linden whispered encouragements to Ashir and Kal, who padded silently along behind her.

When they'd crawled along half a mile or so, the cramped passageway widened again, opening into another cavern just large enough to gather their horses together in one space. Vas spoke softly. "Let's saddle up our horses properly, stow the gear, and get ready to ride like the wind. If they tracked us to Ameliah's place, they're not stopping there."

Linden could tell he was worried about his sister and her family. "Perhaps we could help Ameliah and Dunn first?"

"The best way to help them is what we just did, a disappearing act."

Tam glanced at his sister. "I think Linden has something else in mind."

Vas frowned. "Such as?"

Linden thought about her last evening at Delavan Manor. Although Linden didn't realize it at the time, Nari had cast a powerful spell that effectively made Delavan Manor "disappear" from view; it also meant Linden and Matteo couldn't return there for the next five years. Linden had been studying *Timely Spells* before she left Arrowood and came across a version of the spell.

"I'd like to cast a powerful protection charm around your sister's home. However, when I'm through, you won't be able to visit again, for six months at least, maybe longer."

Vas's eyebrows shot up. Tam found his voice first. "Can you really do that?"

Linden explained about Nari's spell at Delavan Manor. "I think so. I can set it for a shorter time span, say half a year instead of five, but I'm fairly certain I've worked out the spell." She glanced at Vas. "What do you say?"

Vas nodded. "Do it. I can't bear the thought of anyone harming Ameliah or the children."

"It does mean that Dunn will need to stay put, along with the family, until the spell wears off."

"That's a small price to pay for their safety."

"Alright then." Turning to Wreyn, Linden said, "Can you give me a lift on your traveling mists? We'll slip back to Ameliah's house and cast the spell."

"What if the guards are already there?" asked Vas.

Efram stepped forward. "I'll go with you. Wreyn and I can confuse the guards. We can transport them somewhere else without their horses. Perhaps dunk them in the river while we're at it."

"Let me ride along with Efram," said Tam. "Just in case those guards cause you trouble."

"Absolutely not. We just sprang you out of prison. You are a wanted man. I'll go," said Vas.

"You're just as wanted as Tam is. I'll go. At least my face

isn't plastered all about on bounty posters." Nahn stepped forward, strapping her sword around her waist.

Reynier nodded at Linden. "You know how I feel about you placing yourself in harm's way, but I'm going to save my breath. Be careful and whatever you do, don't get caught!"

Linden glanced at the group. "Time to leave. We'll catch up with you later—one of the advantages of travel by fay mist." Linden stepped between Wreyn and Efram, and Nahn joined them. Foggy tendrils wound up their legs and curled around their waists. The mists enveloped them in a slightly damp, but highly effective, translocation cocoon.

Wreyn and Efram dropped them down on the hillside overlooking the back of Ameliah's cottage. The cave complex was directly below them. The sky was beginning to lighten. Linden figured they had less than an hour before the sun peeked over the hills, and then they'd be running in broad daylight.

Five horses were gathered in front of the cottage, with two guards waiting outside. That left three guards inside the house. Linden whispered, "We need to create a distraction and get those other guards outside. But first, can we take those two and drop them somewhere else?"

Wreyn nodded. "Sure, I can slip up behind them and transport them on my mists."

"Can they attack you while you're moving them?"

Wreyn shook her head. "Nah. They won't know what's happening. It'll be over before they know it. Most Glenbarrans have never even met a fay, let alone know about our traveling mists. Just say the word and I'll go."

Nahn turned to Efram. "Can you drop me down about ten yards in front of the house? I have an idea."

Efram said, "Sure, what's the plan?"

Nahn slid her sword belt around, so her blade was tucked behind her. "I'm going to sing."

"What? Are you crazy?" Everyone hissed at once.

Nahn grinned. "Relax. I'm going to create so much noise the other guards are going to have to check it out. When they dash outside, Efram can take their sorry butts and drop them somewhere else."

"What if they don't all come out?"

Nahn shrugged. "Then we take the action inside. Dunn and Ameliah can handle themselves. It's those children I want to keep out of the way. Hopefully, they're still in bed."

Everyone looked at Linden, who nodded. "Once we have the guards squared away, I'll slip into the house and explain about the spell to Dunn and Ameliah. They need to understand how it works before I cast it."

Wreyn's mist rose up around her and she emerged moments later behind the two guards, who were sharing a smoke between them. As the fog swirled around their legs, one of the guards shouted, "What the..." before his voice was swallowed up in the mist.

Moments later, Efram deposited Nahn on the cobbled pathway leading to the front of the stone cottage. She stumbled up to the house, singing at the top of her lungs, by all appearances a woman who'd downed one too many brews. Two guards ran out of the cottage, their hands on their sword hilts. The shorter of the two yelled at Nahn, "What're ye squalling about? Be gone with ye!"

They surrounded Nahn, who slipped her hand behind her back and came out with her sword. The shorter guard put his hands in the air, while the other man spat out an oath and reached for his blade. Efram crept up behind them, capturing the two guards and Nahn in his traveling mists. Linden heard one of the men shouting about the "strange fog and stranger woman" before disappearing in a vaporous plume. That left one guard inside the house still unaccounted for.

Linden scrambled down the low hill and crept up to the

rear of the stone cottage. She stooped low and peeked through the window. Several candles flickered on the table, casting nightmarish shadows against the wall of the parlor. A nasty-looking Glenbarran held the tip of his dagger against the throat of Leah, Ameliah's oldest daughter, a sweet child of eight whose eyes were wide in terror. Dunn and Ameliah held their hands in the air as they pleaded with the man not to harm their little girl. Linden's blood boiled, but she took a breath to steady her nerves before casting a shapeshifting spell. "Soften that knife, make it stop, shift from blade to bunny hops."

The man's dagger turned into a cuddly, cotton-tailed rabbit. Ameliah's daughter giggled when the rabbit grazed her throat. The man dropped the rabbit, yelling something about "crazy sorcery." Leah caught the bunny in her arms as her mother grabbed at the child and held her close. Meanwhile, Dunn tackled the startled guard to the ground, twisting the man's arms behind his back.

Linden ran into the house. "We've removed the other guards. This is the last one."

"Linden, what are you doing here? Is everyone alright?" asked Ameliah.

"We're fine, but we haven't much time."

Wreyn emerged from the mists into the center of the room. "I'll take care of this one and then we'll move their horses. Be ready to go in five."

Linden nodded as the traveling mists encircled the guard's prone form and Dunn found himself kneeling on the floorboards instead of the man's back. He shook his head. "Maybe you can explain what's going on?"

Linden knelt down next to Leah. "I need to speak with your mommy and daddy now. Can you take your bunny into the kitchen and wait for them there?" Leah nodded and cradling the rabbit in her arms, scurried into the adjoining room.

Linden gave a quick run-down of their plan to transport the

guards away from their cottage and to move the horses in a completely different direction.

"But won't they just come back here, angrier than ever?" asked Ameliah.

"They will, but they won't be able to find you," said Linden. "With your permission, I'd like to cast a spell my grandmother used on our estate in Bellaryss. Your home, grounds, and even your cave will vanish from view. No one outside of your family will be able to see them, but inside, your life will go on as before."

"Sounds too good to be true," said Dunn. "What's the catch?"

"There are two. First, none of you will be able to leave the premises for the duration of the spell. Dunn, that means you're here for the time being with Ameliah and your family."

Dunn glanced at Ameliah and smiled. "That's easy enough. What else?"

"The duration of the spell is a bit trickier. I'm going to aim for six months, but it could be more like nine months or even a year. Do you have enough provisions to last you that long?"

Ameliah nodded. "Between our kitchen garden, the dried and preserved food in storage, and our cows and chickens, we'll be fine."

"Alright then, I'm going outside and will walk down the road a bit before casting the spell. Good luck!" Linden turned to leave, but not before Ameliah rushed over to hug her. "Thank you for saving our daughter just now."

Dunn gripped Linden's hands in his, reciting the Serving mage's blessing. Linden repeated the blessing, adding, "Be safe and well."

She walked down the cobbled pathway and waited until she reached a stand of trees before casting the spell. "Protect family and creatures living inside, hide land and home from prying eyes. Grant no access for half a year, when all will as before appear."

She repeated the incantation until the house, the grounds, and the low hill containing the cave vanished from sight. Linden thought about her grandmother, casting her spell over Delavan Manor last year. Nari had strong premonitions about where Linden and Matteo would find themselves, as well as foreknowledge that her own life would be cut off too soon. She'd done what she could to preserve the estate for them, however far in the future it seemed at the time.

"Are you ready?" asked Wreyn quietly. "We didn't want to disturb you while you were incanting." Efram and Nahn waited nearby.

Linden stifled a yawn and rubbed her temples. Casting powerful spells took a tremendous amount of energy and focus; she wished for a long nap in a warm bed, but that wasn't something she could conjure up. "More than ready. Let's get back to the group."

CHAPTER 18

Although the most direct route into Bellaryss was through Wellan Pass and then due east to the city gates, Vas confirmed both the pass and gates were heavily guarded and nearly impenetrable. Instead, they rode northeast in a wide arc around the city and hills surrounding it. Tam knew of an abandoned tunnel north of the city, near the Pale Sea, which wound its way back into Bellaryss and would deposit them inside the city gates.

"How can you be sure this tunnel is still usable?" Linden rode alongside her brother. Night had fallen, with a bright moon overhead. They were riding on a horse trail she and Tam used to take when traveling between Delavan Manor and some of the other estates in the area. Linden found it hard to believe Delavan was a few miles to the north, and yet completely hidden by Nari's spell.

"Or not overrun with grihms by now?" grumbled Remy, whose rapidly declining mood was in direct proportion to the deteriorating quality of the meals they'd been eating. Breakfast was nonexistent, and dinner the evening before had been a sliver of salted pork and a stale crust of bread.

"I used this tunnel some months ago. It hasn't been maintained in years but seems structurally sound. As for grihms and patrols, King Roi and his army are focusing on the western wall of the city. The Glenbarrans aren't too worried about an old tunnel near the beach."

Linden sat up straighter in her saddle. Something Tam said triggered a memory of her and Corbahn standing together on a similar beach, staring out at the Pale Sea. Except Corbahn had never visited the Pale Sea, and the image had been more precognition than memory. Even so, the same vision had recurred in her dreams and appeared to her again, just now: she and Corbahn, standing side-by-side, and looking at the sea. They were holding hands and when Corbahn turned to her, a smile playing on his lips, his blue-green eyes were the same color as the sea itself. Each time he turned to look at her with those remarkable eyes of his, her heart stuttered inside her chest.

Linden couldn't understand why this vision kept recurring, but she'd learned from her grandmother that repetition was often as important as the image itself. The more occurrences, the more seriously she needed to examine the vision. The words of the old psychic at the Arrowood camp came back to her, insisting she and Corbahn were meant for each other, if they could only overcome their poor timing. Perhaps, but there was something more here, just beyond her grasp. Then it came to her. *Why was Corbahn standing on the shores of the Pale Sea, when he was Chief of the Arrowood clan, which occupied the westernmost portion of Faynwood? Why travel from west to east, unless Corbahn had turned the tide of the border wars, and he was in Bellaryss to help her defeat the Glenbarrans?*

Linden glanced over at Tam. "You mentioned the Glenbarrans aren't so focused on defending the eastern perimeter of the city."

Tam shrugged. "It makes sense. Valerra had a small navy,

which Uncle Alban used to evacuate the queen and a contingent of the population from Bellaryss. Why would the Glenbarrans bother with the eastern side of the city, when there are no obvious threats?"

"They wouldn't, but perhaps we could exploit it to our advantage," said Linden.

"Other than checking out that old tunnel on the beach, what else is there?"

"The Glenbarrans aren't factoring in the Faymon clans, and our close proximity to Shorewood."

Tam frowned. "Tell me more."

Linden guided Ashir around a fallen tree branch on the trail, mulling over the possibilities in her head. "All the clans, including Shorewood, have standing armies. Until recently, they'd been engaged in fighting each other, but with the end to the civil war, the clans are defending the border against the Glenbarrans, and they're prepared to help us rid Valerra of the Fallow curse.

"I've been assuming our clansmen would have to storm Wellan Pass, which we know is heavily guarded. We'd risk losing large numbers of warriors, without any guarantee we would defeat the Glenbarrans. What if, instead, we invade Bellaryss from the east, from the beaches?"

Tam ran a hand through his blue-streaked brown hair. "Are you suggesting the clans march down the coast from Shorewood and gather on the beaches here?"

Linden nodded. "The beach is certainly wide enough. And you said yourself that King Roi's attention is focused elsewhere."

"The beach is wide enough, but I'm not sure how many troops we could gather along the shoreline without alerting Mordahn and King Roi."

Linden compressed her lips, deep in thought. Then an idea came to her, a potentially crazy idea, but she figured *why not?*

"Faymons are naturally more magical than Valerrans, which means even a young warrior is able to cast simple spells with ease."

"So you're suggesting we'd use Serving magic somehow? But Mordahn will detect the magic and be on your warriors in no time."

"He can detect active magic, but inactivating spells won't draw his attention. We could instruct the mages and warriors, and even the Faymon ships, to cast veils of drabness. I've used them a few times now with the Glenbarrans, and we've escaped their notice."

Tam blew out a puff of air. "That's the craziest invasion plan I've ever heard."

"Too crazy to work?"

"Just the opposite—crazy enough to just possibly work."

~

Before they reached the beach, they took a detour off the horse trail and visited one of Tam's childhood friends, who owned a stable for boarding horses. They wouldn't be needing their horses inside the underground tunnel, or in downtown Bellaryss for that matter. Tam's friend asked them no questions when they arrived. Instead, he walked down to the stable yard himself and roused a couple of his stable hands to help them. Linden ran her fingers along Ashir's coat and assured him she would see him again. Ashir nuzzled her hair in reply.

As they trudged along the trail after dropping off their horses, Linden fell into step with Wreyn. "Don't you think Pryl should have joined us by now?"

Wreyn shrugged. "I got the impression Chief wasn't going to leave until he'd convinced the fay council to support us in this war."

"But they might never support us. Won't he eventually give up and come help us?"

"He's helping us now; it's just that we can't see it. Convincing those fusty old councilors to get off their duffs and support us is the best way he can help us at the moment."

Linden adjusted the straps of her knapsack. "Let's hope Pryl can convince them before we make it to the museum. He's the only one who knows the fay incantations for neutralizing a place of power."

Wreyn gave her a wry smile. "You did just fine without Pryl when you brought down Glendin Palace. You managed to neutralize that place of power on your own."

"I completely demolished it, which isn't the same thing. The Valerran Museum is quite a different matter, and it would break my heart to destroy it."

"You may have to, if that's the only way to stop Mordahn."

Linden drew her brows together, unwilling to seriously consider destroying the museum unless it was the very last resort. "I want to speak with Pryl before we attempt anything at the museum."

Wreyn nodded. "If he doesn't show up soon, I'll go find him."

"Thanks." Linden had another reason for wanting to see Pryl before she faced Mordahn again. She knew this would be the final showdown; one of them wouldn't be walking away. She had to finish off the undead version of Mordahn or die herself in the attempt. But first, she wanted the chance to introduce Tam to their grandfather. In case the worst happened, they deserved the opportunity to meet each other at least once. Linden knew her brother had a lot of unanswered questions for their long-lost fay grandfather.

They approached the beach, the wind whipping off the sea coating their clothes and hair in a fine mist. The rain had held off the past few days, but the air was thick with moisture.

Linden buttoned her leather jacket closed and picked up her pace, hoping to make it to the tunnel entrance before the clouds opened up and she was soaked.

The first large raindrops pelted Linden's head and shoulders as she dashed into the dark tunnel behind Tam. The entrance smelled of damp soil, moldy stones, and animal droppings. Tam felt along the ground until he found a half-used torch. "Anyone have something we can use to light this?"

"Here, allow me." Remy snapped his fingers, and a small fireball appeared between his thumb and index finger.

Tam grinned. "Yours is a very convenient gift, my friend."

Remy chuckled. "It's funny my teachers never thought so."

"That's because you kept starting fires in class," drawled Mara. "You even yanked out some of my hair in grade school and demonstrated how fast it flared up."

"Oh yeah, I forgot about that."

Tam waved the torch at the crumbling passageway behind them. "Looks the same as the last time I visited. There's no sign of any Glenbarran activity. They haven't bothered to secure the entrance or block access to the tunnel. We ought to be able to take this all the way to the cemetery on High Street."

"Then what?" asked Nahn.

"This section doesn't connect to the rest of the tunnel system running beneath Bellaryss. The city authorities ran out of funding and never finished this portion of the project. We'll have to come out into the open and then make our way to the Valerran Museum."

"How far away is the next nearest tunnel entrance from the cemetery?" Remy peered down the dark passage anxiously, the small fireball still burning brightly in his hand.

"The nearest entrance is three blocks to the south, but it's right under the fire brigade building, which is heavily guarded. We may find it's easier to creep along on street-level to the museum and then figure out how to slip inside." Tam pointed to his dark jacket and trousers. "We're dressed like any other civilians."

"Minus the sword, knapsack, and your bow and arrow," pointed out Vas.

"Alright, we may need to steal some uniforms if we're going to travel above ground," conceded Tam.

"We barely escaped from the museum with our lives, and now we're going to try to break into it." Remy shook his head. "That place is going to be crawling with Glenbarrans and grihms."

"Aye, it's crawling alright," grunted Vas, "with guards, super-grihms, and undead sorcerers, Mordahn among them—a real mishmash of Fallowness."

"Given what you've just shared, this sounds like a good time to get some rest and regroup, find out what's happening inside Faynwood before we go any further," said Reynier.

Linden nodded. "My thoughts exactly. Before we take on Mordahn directly, we need to know what sort of support we'll have from the clans and the fays."

"And if we're on our own, what then?" asked Mara.

"Then we're no worse off than we are right now." Linden tucked a strand of damp hair behind her ear. "When we planned this operation back in Faynwood, we knew the odds were never good. Nothing's changed. But what choice do we have? If we wait for help that might never come, then we lose all hope of defeating the Glenbarrans. Serving magic will disappear into the dustbin of history. We'll be surrounded on every side by Fallow sorcery and misery. However—" Linden paused long enough to glance at every individual standing inside the tunnel "—any one of us can back out right now, no hard feelings, no questions asked. We've already accomplished so much more than we could have imagined. I mean, come on, we actually performed a drama for King Roi and Mordahn at

Glendin Palace and lived to tell about it!" A few of them chuckled at the memory. "And we freed hundreds of prisoners—twice, I might add—inside Glenbarra and at base camp prison. We have a lot to be proud of."

"Look, I may grumble a lot and I'm scared to death of what we'll be facing at the other end of this tunnel, but Toz didn't die for nothing." Remy's voice cracked. "I'm in this until the end. My end or Mordahn's."

"Aye, so am I," said Mara and Jayna.

Reynier nodded. "This is the only way to rid ourselves of Fallowness." Everyone else agreed with head nods and ayes.

"In that case," said Linden. "I agree with Reynier. We need to get some rest and regroup with our Faymon and fay friends."

Efram glanced at Wreyn, who stepped forward. "Efram and I can easily travel to Faynwood and bring one or two of you with us. We can find out what's happening and let the clan chiefs and fay council know we met up with the Valerran resistance and have made it to Bellaryss."

"You may not want to mention that we only have three members of the resistance here with us. That won't help our case," pointed out Jayna.

Vas cleared his throat. "Actually, after the base camp prison break, we activated our network. We have about a hundred resistance fighters inside the city who are ready to fight when we give the signal."

Linden noticed Reynier put his arm around Jayna, who leaned against him. Jayna's capture, prison stay, and days on the road had taken their toll. Linden didn't think Jayna would be able to make it to the museum in her current condition. Although she carried one of the ensorcelled swords, they'd have to manage without her, at least until she felt better. "Reynier, since you're the Faymon Elder, it makes sense for you to return to Faynwood and meet up with the other chiefs."

"But you're the Liege, why not you?"

Linden shook her head. "You know the chiefs are more likely to listen to you than to me, especially when it comes to war councils. Besides, Jayna could use some rest."

Jayna started to object, but Linden looked directly at her friend. "You're always telling me that healing takes time, and I'll say the same to you right now. You look exhausted and will be no good to anyone until you've had complete rest, which means no traipsing through tunnels and sneaking around Bellaryss at night." Jayna bit her bottom lip but didn't respond.

Linden turned back to Reynier. "The two of you can travel with Efram to Shorewood and speak with the clansmen there, let them know what we're thinking. I'd like to ask Wreyn to find Pryl and ask him to join us or at least meet with us right away. I also have a message for Chief Corbahn that Wreyn can deliver for me." Everyone looked at her expectantly. She rolled her eyes. "A private message."

Linden figured the best way to win over Reynier was planting the notion that he could take Jayna back to Faynwood with him. Reynier rubbed his beard, thinking. Linden knew better than to rush him. He finally grunted. "Alright. Jayna and I will go with Efram and speak to the Shorewood clan. From there, we'll locate the other clan chiefs and determine how many warriors we can peel away from our borders to march down the beach from Shorewood. Wreyn, please locate Pryl and send him back here, at least for a quick meet-up. Since you'll be carrying a message to Corbahn, why don't you also explain our plan to him and find out if Arrowood can contribute warriors."

Linden and Jayna locked eyes and her friend gave her a little smile. Linden had not only convinced Reynier of the plan, but now he owned it. There was one more thing Linden wanted to clarify, which she knew Reynier wasn't going to like. "It's going to take you and Jayna some time to travel to the different clan chiefs and rally enough Faymon warriors for the march down from Shorewood. I think this is where our group needs to split up in order to accomplish our goal. I suggest we wait here until tomorrow evening, rest up and hopefully confer with Pryl, and then we move out."

Reynier protested. "But it's far too dangerous for the Liege to—"

Tam clapped Reynier on the shoulder. "I'll look after my sister the best I can, although given her skills, it may be the other way around. That said, the longer we delay, the likelier it is the Glenbarrans will track us down and we'll fail before we've begun."

Reynier heaved a sigh. "Fine, I don't like it, but I can see it's the best course of action." He said to Jayna, "Are you ready?"

Jayna hugged Linden first, and then Mara and Remy. When she reached Tam, she put her hand on the broken side of his face. "I am glad to have seen you again. Now make sure you take care of Linden and my friends, and don't get yourself killed. Got it?"

Tam smiled and gave her a quick hug back. Reynier and Jayna nodded at everyone else and then turned to Efram. "Ready when you are," said Reynier, taking Jayna's hand. Efram summoned the traveling mists, the vaporous wisps rising up to envelope the three of them. Jayna waved goodbye before she disappeared.

Wreyn stepped into the empty spot occupied by Efram moments earlier. "I'd better be going as well." She arched an eyebrow at Linden. "You had a message for Corbahn?"

Linden took Wreyn by the elbow and guided her farther into the tunnel, out of earshot of everyone else. "Um, could you let him know he's in my thoughts?"

Wreyn put her finger into her mouth and pretended to be gagging. "You've got to be kidding me. Is that the best you can do? You may never see the man again, and you want me to tell him you're thinking of him?"

Linden blew out a puff of air. "Fine. You're right, of course." She leaned in and whispered. "Tell Corbahn I'm sorry and I can't wait to see him again. Tell him he has to stay safe because I don't know what I'll do if—" Her voice broke just a little. "Well you get the idea." Linden flapped her hand at Wreyn, who grinned.

"That's more like it. Alright, I'm leaving now. I'll send Pryl here and will deliver your message to Corbahn personally." Wreyn called out her goodbyes to the rest of the group and left in a cloud of mist.

"Do you think we could make a small fire and rustle up something to eat? I'm starving," said Remy.

Vas chortled. "I think we've all earned a final meal, so to speak."

Remy's face paled. "Aw, why did you have to put it that way? You've gone and spoiled my appetite."

CHAPTER 19

Linden curled up tighter in her bedroll, listening to the waves lapping the beach, the sound lulling her back to sleep. Then she smelled fresh coffee brewing somewhere nearby and inhaled the intoxicating aroma. *But we ran out of coffee days ago, so where has it come from? Or more importantly, who's brought it?* Linden sat up, rubbing the sleep out of her eyes.

Pryl sat next to the fire Remy had started at the mouth of the tunnel, holding a pot over the flames. He must have sensed she was awake, because he whispered, "Linden, come join me. We'll let the others sleep a bit longer."

Wrapping herself in her blanket, Linden stepped over Mara's sleeping form. Nahn slept sitting up; she'd been last to sit watch, but she was out cold. "Did you cast a sleeping spell over Nahn?"

Pryl shrugged. "I thought the lass could do with some rest, and since I was wide awake, why not? Besides, I wanted to speak to you without rousing the others."

Linden sat down next to Pryl. She thought about hugging him—after all, he was her grandfather—but settled for gripping his hand instead. He gave hers a firm squeeze and then went back to swishing coffee grounds and hot water around inside the pot. He pulled two battered mugs and a piece of mesh out of a sack on the ground by his feet. He poured the coffee, using the square of mesh to filter out most of the grounds. Pryl handed Linden one of the mugs. "I know you prefer tea in the morning, but this was all I had at hand."

Linden took a sip. Delicious. "This is just what I needed. Thanks." She noticed the lines around Pryl's eyes and mouth were more deeply etched. "I take it things haven't been going well with the fay council?"

"Why would you say that?"

"You look...tired, weary I guess."

Pryl cradled the mug in his hands. "It's true I'm weary of politics and endless debates, but I bring good news. Even the last holdouts on the council have agreed we must stop King Roi and Mordahn from destroying Serving magic. The council has even reconsidered leaving Faynwood."

"Well that's great news! Why the change of heart about leaving?"

"I'd appointed three of the most vocal council members to lead the search committee for a new home for the Fay Nation. After months of extensive travel across every continent, the committee has recommended we remain in Faynwood. They discovered the problems with humanity are the same everywhere, and as it turns out, Faynwood is the best of the lot. The committee was appalled to learn Serving magic had died out elsewhere. They helped convince the rest of the fay council we had to defeat Fallow sorcery and restore magical order inside Valerra. We're coordinating with the clans and finalizing battle plans now."

"Does that mean you can stay here and help me neutralize the place of power inside the Valerran Museum?"

Pryl took a long swallow from his mug and then shook his

head. "The fays have agreed to take on Wellan Pass, a tricky proposition at the best of times, but with all of the Fallow sorcery swirling about the pass, we're heading into a dangerous battle, one that could turn the tide of the war. As Chief of the Fay Nation, my place is leading the fay army on the battlefield."

Linden scowled at her grandfather. *How could he possibly expect me to neutralize the place of power without him? Besides, isn't he too old to be commanding the fay army?*

As if reading her thoughts, Pryl arched an eyebrow. "If you're thinking I'm too old to be a battlefield commander, I'll have you know your great-grandfather, Archipryllius Orion the Thirteenth, led the fay army to victory against the notorious rebel commander, Sonarryius the Tenth. Dad was one hundred and eight at the time."

"Archipryllius Orion the Thirteenth? Does that make you Archipryllius Orion the Fourteenth?"

When Pryl nodded, Linden snorted. "I'm glad you didn't name my dad 'Archipryllius Orion the Fifteenth.' Talk about a mouthful."

"It's a fay name with a lot of rich history, one to be proud of, I might add."

Linden decided to bring the conversation back to the most pressing problem at the moment. "You're the only one who knows the fay incantations for rebalancing the magical energy inside the museum. How are we supposed to perform the cleansing ceremony without you?"

"That's why I wanted to speak with you before anyone else was awake." Pryl placed his mug down on the ground and held out his hand toward Linden. She placed her hand in his. "I'm going to cast a transference spell that will implant the incantation inside your head. You'll be able to neutralize the royal burial chamber without me present."

Linden quickly withdrew her hand. This sounded too similar to what Nari had done shortly before she died: she'd gripped Linden's hand and transferred over her latent magic, which enabled Linden to become a master mage in record time. Linden still had worked incredibly hard under Mage Mother Pawllah's tutelage to achieve master status, but she couldn't have made such rapid progress without Nari's gift. "I don't want to lose you too."

Pryl stared at Linden, his frown lines deepening between his brows. "What are you talking about?"

Linden explained how Nari had transferred her latent magic shortly before she died, and Pryl's frown lines relaxed. "I'm going to transfer over one very complicated spell in the ancient fay tongue, and its translation, not all of my magic. I intend to be walking around in this realm for many years to come. But—" Pryl stopped abruptly and looked away, toward the sea.

"But what?" prompted Linden.

He took a deep breath and exhaled. "I've had disturbing dreams lately, of your final showdown with Mordahn. I think you already know you will need to meet him alone—the Lady Liege of Faynwood against the Commander-in-Chief of the Undead—a master of Serving magic versus a master of Fallow sorcery."

"I get the feeling I don't want to hear how it ends." The wind whipped up small eddies of surf on the shore, sending sprays of water into the air. Linden shivered, drawing her blanket more firmly around herself.

Pryl glanced out at the rough sea again and then returned his gaze to her. "Sometimes you overcome Mordahn, and sometimes you don't."

Linden took another swallow of hot coffee to ward off the chill she felt inside. She wasn't afraid of dying, so much as she was afraid of what Mordahn could do to her while she still lived. He'd tried turning her into a crossbreed the last time they met, and he'd nearly succeeded. "Did these dreams of yours provide any clues as to how I can defeat him? What did I do differently when I won?"

"You didn't do anything differently at all. There was no change in the action. My dreams so confounded me that I made a side trip to Sanrellyss Island to consult with Pawllah."

"What did Mage Mother say?"

"She said the difference comes down to focus."

"I should have known," grumbled Linden. "All my magic teachers used to repeat the same phrase: 'Focus, Funnel, Find, Flow.' Which means you have to focus your magic, funnel your energy, and find the spell's flow."

"That's correct, although according to Pawllah, there's one more vital ingredient. She said you also must have hope—hope in the future of Serving magic—and hope in your own future, as Liege of Faynwood. Without hope, your ability to focus will suffer in the end."

Linden slowly nodded. "That makes sense, I suppose. Although hope isn't something I can conjure up for myself."

"No, but it starts with believing in the power of love, which creates the foundation for hope to thrive in our lives. Love builds bridges over a multitude of obstacles, hurts, and sorrows. Love of family and friends, love of duty and Serving magic. Love of your young man."

"*My young man?*" Linden's eyebrows rose. She wondered whether Pryl had read romantic stories when he was growing up. No one talked like that anymore. "Who did you have in mind?"

Pryl waved his hand. "Come now, it doesn't take a fay chief to see the attraction between you and Corbahn Erewin."

"So what are you saying? That I need to believe in Corbahn in order to have hope in my own future? And that's going to help me defeat Mordahn?"

Now it was Pryl's turn to scowl at her. "You're not taking

this seriously. You know very well what I mean. You and Corbahn left on a sour note and it's been eating at you inside."

"It hasn't been eating at me. Not exactly."

"But you admit you left with a lot of unresolved feelings."

Linden sighed. "True enough. I asked Wreyn to tell Corbahn I'm sorry, and to give him a message from me."

Pryl's face lit up. "That's all I can ask. I want you to have a clear head and unblocked heart. Nothing to hold back the flow of your magic when you face Mordahn."

Linden mumbled into her coffee mug, and Pryl asked her to repeat herself. "What if Corbahn has moved on?"

Pryl chortled. "Have no worries on that score, lass. He's stuck on you."

Linden looked up and grinned. "Really?"

Pryl said briskly, "I'm not going to sit here like a schoolgirl and gossip about the Chief of Arrowood. Now give me your hand so I can transfer the incantation." Pryl began murmuring softly. Linden's hand tingled, like small needles puncturing her skin. The tingling spread up her arm and into her chest.

When Pryl released her hand, Linden asked, "Do I need a keyword to release the spell?"

He shook his head. "When you're ready to neutralize the place of power, simply open your mouth and the spell will begin." Pryl nodded toward the sleeping forms inside the tunnel. "I see Tam is stirring. I'd like to have a word with my grandson."

Linden decided she better come clean with her grandfather. "I wound up telling Tam about you. It didn't seem right that he didn't know the truth. I hope you don't mind."

"I'd expected as much, and I'm glad he knows."

Linden cleaned out her coffee mug with some sand and then rinsed it with water from Pryl's canteen. She handed him the mug and leaned over to kiss his cheek. "Thank you, for everything, for looking out for me and my family all these years, and for leaving us so we could be safe."

Pryl patted her arm. "Of course, my dear. You and your family are my family."

Linden rose, gathered her blanket, and passed Tam as he shuffled toward the fire and Pryl. "I thought I smelled fresh coffee."

"Pryl will brew you some. He'd like a word with you."

Tam nodded. "Good. I have some questions for him."

"I think you'll find he has the answers, or at least most of the answers, to what you're looking for."

∾

Remy discovered the fixings for breakfast inside Pryl's sack and wound up scrambling together eggs, bacon, onions, and potatoes for everyone to share. Afterward, Pryl said, "I've been thinking about the best way for you to enter the museum."

"All ideas are welcome." Vas topped up his mug with more coffee. "We know the tunnels and streets are patrolled, and the museum itself is completely locked down and guarded."

Pryl nodded. "That's why I brought along some uniforms for you. You may not be able to pass for Glenbarran guards in front of Mordahn, but they might help you get through the door of the museum." Linden never ceased to be amazed at how Pryl could get his hands on costumes, uniforms, pretty much anything they might need, even fresh coffee and breakfast. Having a fay for a grandfather definitely had its advantages.

Reaching into Pryl's sack, Mara pulled out the uniforms and stacked them on the ground. "Looks like we're one short."

"Check again. The last one is more of a costume than a uniform."

Mara's eyebrows rose as she pulled out a large bundle

covered in gray fur. She unfurled the hairy-looking outfit. "It sort of looks like a deflated grihm."

Pryl smiled. "Exactly." Pointing at Remy, he added, "I believe I know just the man to pull it off too."

Remy scratched his head. "You're wanting me to dress up like a grihm? How come? I'd prefer one of the uniforms. They're much smarter."

Pryl hesitated before he explained. "You're the largest man in the group and will be able to carry off this disguise." Linden realized Pryl was trying to be diplomatic about Remy's size, although he needn't have bothered. Remy was comfortable with his husky build and would be the first to admit he enjoyed his meals. Pryl continued, "Besides, Glenbarran guards always patrol with at least one grihm. You'll blend in better if you have a grihm alongside you."

"But I have no idea how to behave like a grihm."

"All you need to do is grunt, growl, and hunch over a bit when you walk. Nothing to it," said Tam. Linden could tell her brother was trying hard not to laugh out loud. It was obvious Remy wasn't keen to run around Bellaryss dressed like a grihm, and she couldn't really blame him.

"Fine, if it helps us get into the museum, I'll do it. But I still think I'd be a better guard than a grihm." Remy shook out the costume, which was constructed from wolf fur. The human parts—the forehead and eyes with tiny slits for seeing, and the grizzled front hands—were made from a realistic-looking rubbery material. When the costume was filled out by Remy's bulk, he would definitely pass as a grihm.

Before he left, Pryl wished everyone good luck and promised the fays would come through for them. Pryl gripped Tam's hand and said something only Tam could hear. Her brother nodded solemnly. Then Pryl turned to Linden, who gave him a hug. Pryl patted her back and whispered, "Remember what I said about the final ingredient."

Linden nodded. "Focus, Funnel, Find, Flow, and Hope. It doesn't have quite the same ring, but I understand why it's important." She took a step back and then remembered Corbahn's ensorcelled sword. "Oh, could you wait please? I have something for you to take back to Faynwood." Linden retrieved the sword, which had stopped working for Corbahn. Unfortunately, the fay-spelled sword didn't respond to anyone else's touch either. She'd asked Tam to grip the sword's hilt, and the blade had remained a dull gray. Vas and Nahn had tried too, with the same results. She thought Pryl ought to return it to Corbahn for safekeeping; perhaps the ancient magic might start working again for him one day.

Gathering his sack, Pryl gently pushed the sword back into Linden's outstretched hand. As the cloud of mist enveloped him, Pryl looked at her and winked. "Give that sword back to Corbahn when you see him."

"But I don't know when I'll see—" Linden started to say, but she found herself staring at the empty spot where Pryl had been standing. *What is Pryl talking about? He's more likely to see Corbahn before I will.*

Mara handed out the uniforms, leaving the furry costume for last. Remy took it from her with a grunt. "Next time we have to go undercover, someone else can dress like a grihm."

Vas clapped Remy on the shoulder. "Let's hope we survive this, and there *is* a next time."

CHAPTER 20

Linden layered the bronzed chainmail over the dark-gray tunic and pants of her Glenbarran uniform. She positioned the peaked cap to hide the blue streaks in her hair. Her trousers fit well, but the tunic was a bit loose. She tightened the belt around her waist, adjusting her ensorcelled sword and dagger in their scabbards. She'd asked Remy to carry Corbahn's sword along with his own. Without horses and saddlebags, they were down to carting around everything they owned in small leather belt pouches or strapped to their sides. Even their bedrolls and knapsacks had to be left behind.

Tam led the way through the abandoned tunnel, pausing periodically to listen for any activity up ahead. Remy walked alongside him, a surprisingly realistic-looking grihm, except for the small fireball blazing in his right hand. As the light from the fireball brightened each consecutive section of tunnel, Linden heard a lot of skittering from the native rats and mice, dashing into their crevices and holes.

Vas fell into step beside Linden. "I understand from Tam that Pryl gave you some sort of spell you'll be able to use to neutralize the place of power beneath the museum. How long does it take to incant the spell?"

Linden tapped the side of her head. "Pryl used transference, which means I know the spell instinctively, but I'm not sure how long it will take to perform the actual ceremony. When we cleansed the burial chamber at Zabor Prison, Pryl incanted a phrase, and we repeated it. We mimicked everything he did, including his hand motions. I think it must have taken us half an hour or so, but it felt like forever. Pryl spun a defensive shield around us while we cleansed the site, since we were surrounded by guards trying to interrupt the ceremony."

Vas rubbed his beard. "Trying to stave off guards and grihms inside the museum for thirty minutes is going to be a feat in and of itself. That's *after* we gain access to the building and royal burial chamber underneath."

"The chamber will be located beneath the oldest part of the museum. There are a lot of passageways and at least one hidden staircase that I'm aware of. Once we're inside the building, so long as the grihms haven't picked up our trail, we should be able to sneak into the basement."

"But that kind of magic is sure to rouse Mordahn and every one of his Fallow sorcerers. They'll be on us in no time."

Linden nodded. "Aye. That's why I was hoping we'd have Pryl to help us out. I'm afraid it's going to be just the six of us, which—"

Kal flapped his wings and clicked his beak rapidly, interrupting Linden. She reached down to scratch his mane. She'd obviously insulted her miniature griffin. "Sorry about that. We have seven, including Kal here."

Vas smiled at Kal. "He's a smart one; I'll grant you that."

Tam held up his right fist to signal they should stop. At first Linden heard nothing, but then she picked up the faintest sounds of grunts and snorts up ahead. Remy quickly doused his fireball, and they were plunged into complete darkness. "Sounds like grihms up ahead," whispered Nahn.

Tam agreed. "Aye. We don't know how many or whether they'll buy our disguises."

"Or even why they're here. I thought this was an abandoned tunnel," said Vas.

"It's abandoned and doesn't connect up with the rest of the underground system, so the fact there are a group of them up ahead feels off to me," hissed Tam.

"Could they be on to us somehow?" asked Linden.

"I don't see how," said Tam. "Let's play this out and see how it goes. Consider this our dress rehearsal."

"That's just great," mumbled Remy. "How am I supposed to pull this off in front of a lot of other grihms?"

Linden had a thought. "If they get too nosy about you, Tam can tell them you've been recently bred and are still disoriented."

"Good idea," said Tam. "Alright, let's move out. Remy, we're going to need your fireball."

"But isn't that going to look strange, a grihm walking around with a fireball in his front paw?"

"If anyone asks, I'll tell them you retained your gift from the human you were bred with."

Remy snapped his fingers and the fireball appeared once more. Linden put her hand out in the center of their circle, and Tam nodded at her to indicate he got the message: their small team needed a mighty dose of inspiration at the moment. Tam put his hand on top of hers. Mara followed suit, and then Vas and Nahn. Remy put his non-fireball hand on top.

Linden spoke softly. "None of us could have imagined that a year ago, Valerra would be overrun with Glenbarrans, grihms, and Fallowness at every turn. Each of us has suffered hardships and losses, too many and too painful to name. But here we are, the last remnant, the few men and women left standing, and it's up to us to put a stop to the Fallow crossbreeding and necromancy. If we don't make it all the way, or if only a few of us see this through, so be it. This is our moment, this is for Serving magic, for Valerra and Faynwood, and for all we've suffered and lost. This is the true path."

Linden's stomach was in knots by the time she stopped. Although Linden still didn't like making speeches and was filled with self-doubt about saying the right things at the right time, she'd had a lot more practice since becoming Liege. She nodded at Tam, who recited the mage's blessing over them, but with a twist. "May our magic serve in peace, lead through service, and rise up, steady and true, to rout Fallow sorcery from our land. This is the true path."

"This is the true path," whispered the group, and lifting their hands, they each formed a fist and pounded the center of their chests, to represent they'd taken the words and blessing to heart.

They resumed walking along the tunnel, pausing periodically to listen as the grunts got louder. "This is it," whispered Tam as he rounded a bend. "Show time."

"What's going on here?" he shouted, sniffing the air. "I smell strong spirits. Is this some kind of party? Get up and salute your superior officer!" The air inside the tunnel reeked of animal fur and whiskey, not a pleasing combination. One of the grihms belched.

Vas thrust out his chest and marched into the center of half a dozen inebriated grihms. "Look alive, soldiers! Get up now, before I send ye all to base camp prison for another round of breeding. How'd you like it if I asked Mordahn to pay you a personal visit? Hmm?"

Whimpering, the super-sized grihms rose unsteadily on their feet, their tails between their legs. Linden had no idea grihms liked to drink spirits and had to bite her lip to keep from laughing out loud. In their current condition, they were about as threatening as a litter of puppies, very large, unsteady puppies. One huge grihm, larger than the rest, managed to grunt out a few words. Linden reckoned some crossbreeds retained the capacity for speech, which was perhaps not all that surprising, since they were still part human. The grihm was difficult to understand through his wolfish snout, and so he repeated himself. "No more hurt, please."

Tam walked over to the huge grihm, put a hand on its shoulder, and peered into its eyes. "Farleigh? Is that you?"

The super-grihm burst into howls and sobs. Dropping to all fours, he leaned against Tam's shins and cried, "Aye, aye, Farleigh."

Tam looked around at the group and shrugged. He patted Farleigh's mangy fur. "There, there, man. I'm sorry to see you in this state, but glad that you're alive."

Farleigh sobbed harder. The other grihms dropped down to all fours again and resumed their howling. Tam raised his hand and shouted, "Silence! I want to hear what Farleigh has to say." The grihms quieted down, letting out an occasional whine. Linden found herself feeling sorrier for them by the minute.

Tam explained he and Farleigh had been in the same class at the Royal Marine Academy. They'd both joined the resistance after Valerra fell. Farleigh told his story, his speech badly garbled. Tam seemed able to understand Farleigh better than the rest of them and at times translated for the grihm. "I captured few weeks ago. Not know why. But think Mordahn want me 'cause I'm over six feet. He want big men to make big grihms."

Here Farleigh broke down and wept. The other grihms hiccupped and whimpered along with him. "I not fight other prisoners in stupid game, so was punished. Commander pick me to make grihm. We all sent to Bellaryss together." He waved his front paw at the others, who whined. "They bred us.

Hurt terrible. We now horrible, sad creatures." Farleigh raised his head and howled, the other grihms howling along with him.

Tam asked, "How did you wind up here?"

Farleigh sighed. "We run from museum during fire, small one. Machine broke and made fire. Caretaker opened cages. She let us go. Didn't want us trapped. We ran and ran 'til reach tunnel. Then you find us."

"How did you manage to get the spirits?"

Farleigh hung his shaggy head. "Stole from pub. Barman not argue with big grihms."

Tam rolled his eyes. "What are your plans? Are you going to sit around here, drinking and wallowing, or are you going to exact your revenge?"

Farleigh's large head snapped up. "Revenge? How?"

Linden stepped forward. "We hold the key to reversing the energy flow Mordahn is using to power his crossbreeding program. If we can get into the basement of the museum, we'll cast a fay spell that will cleanse the chamber so he can't power up his equipment again."

Farleigh grunted. "Smash equipment too."

"Smash, smash!" echoed the other grihms.

"Of course. Once we neutralize the basement chamber, then you can destroy all of Mordahn's crossbreeding machines," said Vas. "Can you help us get into the museum?"

Farleigh shrugged his muscular wolfish shoulders. "Dress like guards. Enter during shift change. They not check papers and badges. Unless you act suspicious."

"Like what?" asked Remy.

Farleigh yipped with something like laughter. "Like grihm with fireball in paw." The other grihms yipped along with him. He waved one meaty, fur-covered hand in Remy's direction. "You be fine. You trick me. But no fireball when leave tunnel."

"So will you help us?" asked Tam. "We could use some extra

muscle once we're inside the museum. The spell takes a while to perform."

Farleigh glanced at his friends, who one by one, gave a head nod. "We afraid. Afraid to go back to bad place. But we will go. We help stop Mordahn. Stop him so no more grihms."

Tam nodded. "Alright then, let's go. We're not far from the exit."

Remy's fireball bounced along at the head of the line, casting a yellowish light across the heads and shoulders of Tam, Farleigh, and the others. Linden smiled at the image. They formed the strangest resistance team in the history of warfare: six super-grihms, two men, three women, and one fake grihm carrying a ball of flames. Strange was fine with her, so long as they were effective. They had no choice. They couldn't afford to fail.

CHAPTER 21

Emerging from the tunnel's crumbling staircase, Linden stepped onto a grassy expanse of lawn within the grounds of the Bellaryss City Cemetery. She inhaled deeply, grateful for the fresh air above ground. Farleigh and the other grihms milled about, one of them knocking a heavy gravestone awry. "Hey, guys," hissed Tam. "I know you're still getting used to your bodies, but you have to be more careful." What Tam didn't say was they were still somewhat inebriated and needed to sober up fast.

"Sorry," grunted the smallest of the super-grihms. He and Farleigh shoved the gravestone back in place.

"When's the next shift change at the museum?" asked Vas.

Farleigh pointed to the clock tower atop the government building across the road. "Midnight."

"Then we better move along briskly." Vas turned to Linden. "Let's take point together, seeing how familiar you are with the museum."

They sprinted out of the cemetery gates and turned left, heading up High Street. Although gaslights lined the street on either side, about every third lamp was lit, whether due to negligence or lack of supplies, Linden didn't know, but she suspected the latter. One of the functioning gaslights illuminated the area just beyond the cemetery gates. Linden inhaled sharply, unable to believe what she was seeing.

Burnt-out shells of locomobiles lined the sides of the road, abandoned by their owners. Across the street, the opera house was a blackened ruin, nothing left of its former elegance but rubble. Next door, the government building was unscathed. The mayor's official residence seemed intact, but on the other side of the stately home, all that remained from Madame Zostra's dress shop was the rear wall. Block after block told the same story, some buildings undamaged, others gone, replaced by charred bricks and ashes.

"This is worse than I imagined." As Linden jogged alongside Vas, she felt a sharp pang of loss over the once-magnificent city, so much of it reduced to ruin.

"Aye, and the outer districts are even worse. The Glenbarrans used catapults to toss fiery projectiles throughout the city, to break the will of the people."

Fresh anger simmered in Linden's gut at the destruction wrought by King Roi, Mordahn, and their Fallow troopers. She took a deep breath to clear her head, knowing she had to stay sharp and centered on her mission. Holding onto her anger would make it that much harder to tap into her Serving magic when she really needed it.

Linden slowed down as they neared the sprawling museum, which covered three city blocks. Huge stone columns soared into the air on all sides of the imposing building, which was capped on top with a large dome. The walnut doors at the main entrance were covered in ancient fay hieroglyphs, and the same hieroglyphs were etched at the tops of each of the columns. She called back to Farleigh, "Which entrance is used for the shift changes?"

Farleigh grunted. "Around back, old section."

"That's a small bit of luck." Linden peeled off to the right and headed behind the museum complex, Vas keeping pace with her.

"What's so lucky about that entrance?"

"We'll be entering the original building, where the fay artifacts and scrolls are housed. It stands to reason the oldest part of the museum would have been constructed above the royal burial chamber. At least, I hope so."

"Let's hope you're right. I get the feeling we're not going to have a lot of time for exploring."

Kal clicked his beak next to Linden. She ordered him up to the roof of the museum. "Stay hidden until we come out. And if we don't, fly to Faynwood and Pryl. He'll know what to do." Kal squawked as if admonishing her, and then flapping his wings, took off for the roof.

A pair of bored-looking guards stood at the entrance. Linden and Vas joined the motley assortment of troopers and grihms standing in line, the rest of their group falling in behind them. The trooper in front of Linden, a wide man with a snub nose, turned around to give her and Vas the once over. Hooking his thumb at the super-grihms in their group, he said, "What's with all those grihms?"

"What do you mean?" Vas indicated the grihms standing in front of the trooper. "You've got several in your patrol group."

"Aye, but I have the standard crossbreed. You've got all super-grihms, except for that one funny-looking grihm. What makes you so special?"

"Because we know how to handle them. You said so yourself, we're special." Crossing her arms, Linden decided to shut down this line of inquiry. She didn't want the man getting any more curious or provoking Remy. "Now maybe you can mind your own business?" The trooper muttered something under his breath about cheeky females and turned back around.

LADY LIEGE

Linden's palms grew sweaty as she neared the entrance. The troopers and grihms in front of her nodded at the guards and passed through. One of the guards glanced their way. He arched an eyebrow at the super-grihms queuing up and then shrugged. The group walked past the two guards and entered a drab hallway, its dull gray stone floors and scuffed walls clearly designed for staff use. Flickering gas lamps, many of them sputtering, hung from the ceiling at regular intervals, punctuating the gloom. The troopers and grihms in front of them were dispersing, heading toward their various posts inside the museum. Linden kept walking along the staff hallway until they were alone and then turned to Farleigh, "Where's the crossbreeding suite?"

Farleigh pointed a paw to indicate the floor. "Down there."

"Aye, but how do we get there?"

Farleigh barked, "Jerdahn."

The smallest of the super-grihms, the clumsy one who'd knocked the gravestone off-kilter in the cemetery, scampered over to them. Farleigh grunted, "Take us to basement."

Jerdahn yipped. "This way!" He loped down the long hallway, rounded one corner, then another, and paused in front of a heavy wooden door. Panting slightly, he waited for everyone else to catch up.

Linden estimated they were near the section of the museum where the ancient scrolls and illuminated manuscripts were archived. She used to volunteer in the Scrolls Collection room and often felt a humming sort of vibration no one else seemed to notice. She wondered now whether she might have been picking up traces of the latent fay magic buried deep beneath the museum. She'd find out soon enough.

Tam joined Linden in front of the door, his hand on the hilt of his sword. Linden glanced at Mara, Nahn, Vas, and Remy, still wearing his grihm's costume, and brought her hands together in a silent thank you for all they'd managed to accomplish together. Turning to Farleigh and his grihm friends, she nodded to acknowledge them and their help. She whispered, "For Serving magic!"

Tam flung open the door. A set of steep stairs led down into a dark, musty space. A single lantern, dangling overhead, gave off the only light. Once Linden's eyes adjusted to the gloom, she could just make out Tam's peaked cap as he crept down the steps in front of her. She heard what sounded like squeaky gears turning and heavy objects thumping the ground. Some sort of machinery whirred in the background. Straining her ears, she thought she detected yips and howls.

They reached the bottom of the stairs and Farleigh grunted, "Cages this way!" The six super-grihms lumbered past Linden, heading off to the right.

"Wait. We need to stick together!" hissed Linden, but the crossbreeds had already disappeared.

"I think there's another level below us," whispered Mara. "Listen."

The whirring machines and squeaking gears seemed to be located under Linden's feet. Then she felt it: the humming vibration she used to feel whenever she worked around the old scrolls and manuscripts.

"Whatever we're doing, let's do it fast and get out of here," grumbled Remy.

Tam nodded. "Remy's right. We're here to perform the cleansing ritual. So let's find that burial chamber before Farleigh and the others tip our hand."

"We've got to go down farther, to the lowest level of the foundation," said Linden. "There's a vibration down below us I'm going to follow. Come on." She headed off to the right, since she reasoned the cages would be near the crossbreeding equipment, which would be somewhere in the vicinity of the burial chamber. Another overhead lantern cast a dull yellowish light about midway down the passage.

As she jogged in the same direction Farleigh headed, she discovered the floor sloped in a downward spiral, the angle so gradual she didn't immediately register their descent. Linden continued peering around, looking for another set of steps to take down to the lower floors. It wasn't until she heard the same sounds as before but louder now—machinery squeaking and clanking, wolves yipping—that she realized they'd almost reached the foundation-level. Linden sensed the latent magical energy in the air, vibrating with fay power.

An ear-splitting shriek rent the air, followed by wailing and screaming, as if someone were being torn apart. Linden recognized the anguished cries. Somewhere inside that vast complex another poor soul was being crossbred. Her heart raced, her vision blurred as memories flooded her head. She was strapped to a table, screaming and arching her back as wave after wave of evil magic coursed through her body; Mordahn's plan had been to turn her into a meek doe crossbreed, so the panther-man crossbreed Corbahn was becoming could rip her to shreds.

"Linden, are you alright?" Tam shook her arm, peering into her eyes.

Linden blinked away the horror in her mind's eye and exhaled, willing her heart to slow down to its normal, steady beat. She shuddered. "We need to stop that crossbreeding."

"That's what we're here to do," said Tam.

Linden knew they couldn't simply charge into the operating suite, at least not before they'd neutralized the place of power, although that's what she wanted to do: charge ahead and smash the equipment. She understood where Farleigh and the other grihms were coming from. "I can feel the energy here, so we're close, but we need to find the actual burial chamber without being spotted." She had an idea. "I'm going to cast a veil of drabness over us."

"But we're going to keep moving. It's not like we'll be invisible or anything," said Vas.

"Not invisible, but in this dim lighting, if no one's looking for trouble, it might be enough." Linden incanted the spell and a gauzy drabness blurred their appearance. Nodding, she whispered, "Let's go."

They reached the bottommost level and stepped into a large, low-ceilinged room that was part cave and part basement. The limestone walls were reinforced with wooden beams to keep the rocks from tumbling onto the hard-packed dirt floor. Wooden room dividers screened off portions of the basement. Behind one of the panels they heard whimpering, the crossbreeding nearly complete.

Off to the left, a pair of guards chatted about the weather, sharing a cigarette between them. Linden forced herself to focus on the humming vibrations, which seemed to fill the air all around them. She crept deeper into the basement, past the guards, and approached another set of wooden dividers at the opposite end of the room. Listening carefully, she didn't hear any activity or voices coming from the other side of the screens. She slipped around the set of dividers and gasped.

"What is it?" hissed Tam, who was behind her, on the other side of the wooden screens.

"Come see for yourselves," breathed Linden, stepping out of the way so the rest of the group could step into the ancient burial chamber, reserved for fay kings and queens. Similar to the set up at Zabor Prison, the limestone sarcophagi were stacked one on top of the other, six high and six deep, and arranged in neat rows. The ancient fays had organized their dead into orderly columns, with not a single stone coffin out of alignment with the one above or below it. Linden estimated three hundred royal fays had been entombed in the chamber. Ancient hieroglyphs covered the walls and each sarcophagus. The symbols, once gilded but now dull and tarnished, were barely visible in the flickering light of torches rimming the chamber. The coffins were arranged in a semi-circle around an underground lake, the water murky and dark.

Fearful they might alert one of the guards nearby, Linden kept her voice low. "Everyone, except for Tam, will need to hold hands throughout the incantation. Under no circumstances can we break the connection between us. I'll cast each portion of the spell twice, first in fay, and then the translation. Repeat the translation word for word and follow my hand motions. Once we start, there's no going back. Every Fallow sorcerer in the place will know we're here. Basically, we'll be leaving our magical calling card out for all to see." Glancing at Tam, she said, "The defensive shield is going to be down to you. I'll need everyone else to help me cleanse this place of power. Let me know when you're ready."

"I'm ready," nodded Tam. He started the defensive spell, whispering the incantation in a continual loop. "Conjure a shield around this spot, defend with strength against onslaught." He cast the shield around the six of them, the underground lake, and the rows of sarcophagi. A thin silvery film formed over their heads, the air outside their protective dome shimmering slightly. Tam would need to maintain the shield throughout the cleansing ceremony, while the rest of the group focused on neutralizing the latent magical power inside the burial chamber.

With the shield firmly in place, Linden took a deep breath and blinked. *You've got to really focus here, Linden!* She thought about Pryl and Nari, their fractured family life, and about all the fractures, before and since, caused by Fallow sorcery and evil men. She squeezed Nahn's hand, on her left, and Mara's hand, on her right, a signal she was ready to begin. Remy stood next to Mara, gripping her hand, with Vas on the other side of Nahn. Just five of them, none of them fays, were attempting to restore magical equity to a royal fay burial site. *Would this even work?* Time to find out.

Linden opened her mouth, willing the incantation Pryl had transferred to begin to flow. The words to the spell tumbled out, first in the buzzing language of the fays, which Reynier had been slowly teaching Linden. She had a long way to go and could only understand a few of the words as she spoke them. After the fay portion of the spell came the translation, line for line.

"Oh Kings and queens and royal fays
Unwind the Fallowness in this place.
Cleanse evil sorcery from this site.
Restore Serving magic with strength and might.
Permit balance and order to prevail.
Stop magical abuse once and for all."

As she incanted the cleansing ritual, Linden raised her hands up and down in a rhythmic motion that swayed with the beat of the incantation. The rest of the group copied her every movement, repeating each line of the spell in a continuous cycle. Time seemed to expand like a rubber band, stretched almost to breaking, as she looped through the words of the spell, over and over, waiting for something to happen. Linden ignored the throbbing in her temples, all her thoughts centered on completing the ritual.

A white dot appeared over the lake. As Linden focused on the dot, it grew larger, transforming into a bolt of lightning that repeatedly struck the lake's center. Sparks of bright light flashed across the burial chamber until every sarcophagus was bathed in a white glow. Perspiration beaded on Linden's brow and dribbled into her eyes, stinging them, but she couldn't free her hands to wipe away the sweat. She focused with all her mental energy on the incantation, raising her voice so it echoed across the lake, her hands moving faster now, keeping time with the beat and intensity of the spell.

Linden heard hobnailed boots pounding the ground nearby as Glenbarran guards poured into the chamber, shouting at them to stop. The guards punched the shield with their fists and attempted to poke through with the tips of their daggers, but the shield held. Although Linden could sense Tam tiring, she couldn't stop the incantation to help him. Linden worried his magical energy might be nearly spent by the time they finished the ritual, but she trusted her brother and his magic. She knew Tam would hold on to the very end. Her head heavy and aching with the effort to cleanse the chamber, Linden felt something trickling onto her upper lip and realized her nose was bleeding. She didn't have much more time before she collapsed in a heap on the ground.

Tam dropped to his knees first but continued incanting the spell to protect them. The silvery shield started thinning out; instead of providing a solid film of protection, it grew splotchy. Holes began opening and closing in the shield. A guard managed to poke through one of the holes with his dagger, but the hole closed back up and his weapon clattered harmlessly to the ground.

The tempo of the spell changed, and Linden realized she was nearing the end of the ritual. She raised her voice, shouting the final incantation and wondering whether it worked.

"In peace and harmony, or enmity and war,
In readiness for future years
And remembrance of what's past,
We consecrate this royal place
To Serving magic at long last."

"I'm so cold," whispered Linden through chattering teeth. She started to convulse, her legs shaking beneath her, and reached her hand out to Tam. Nahn and Mara gripped her arms on either side, holding her upright. "Help my brother."

Vas ran over to Tam and knelt beside him on the ground. Vas took Tam's hand and together they uttered the defensive spell, although Vas's voice wavered, the exhaustion evident on his face. More holes opened in the filmy shield surrounding them. The holes stayed open longer, while others didn't quite close down all the way.

Nahn glanced at Mara, both of them still holding tight to Linden. "I'm sorry, but I have to sit down. Can you take her?" Mara nodded and Nahn slid to the floor, dropping her head between her knees.

Remy yelled, "This shield isn't going to hold much longer!"

Mara was struggling to keep Linden from falling over. "Then do something about it!"

"Like what? My magic is down to nothing."

"I don't know, something with fire maybe."

Shrugging, Remy snapped his fingers and began tossing fireballs through the holes in the shield. His fireballs were smaller than usual, little bits of flame, but they were enough. The guards shouted, confused by the "fire-grihm." After several guards caught a fireball in the arm or chest, they pulled back, swatting at the flames. The rest of the guards retreated from the shield, swords drawn and ready. They'd reached a standoff: Linden and the group, stuck in the basement of the museum completely surrounded, and the Glenbarran guards, waiting until the shield finally collapsed before they charged.

Linden brought her hand up to her nose and it came away bloody. Mara said, "If you can hold on, I'll reach into my pocket for a handkerchief."

Linden swayed and shook her head. "Don't bother. I don't think I can stand without support." All she wanted was to curl up under a thick blanket and sleep for a month. She knew her chills and aches were due to expending so much magical energy on the cleansing ritual, but she wondered how long it would take her and her friends to return to full strength. They had virtually no magical reserves left to fight off Mordahn and his sorcerers.

Linden closed her eyes and the room started spinning, so she quickly opened them again. Linden couldn't detect any difference inside the chamber. *Has the spell even worked?* She tried to remember how long the spell had taken inside Zabor Prison but soon gave up. Pryl had led the incantation to cleanse the last place of power. He was a powerful fay chief, and she was a half Faymon, half Valerran girl who couldn't possibly have pulled off such a complicated fay ritual. Then she remembered she was also part fay. Even so, there was no way the spell worked. Something should have happened by now. She'd been a fool for even trying, and now Tam, Mara, and the rest of them would die because of her stupidity.

A pinprick of light appeared over the lake, and Linden wondered whether another bolt of lightning would strike the water. Instead, the dot grew larger, changing shape until it took on the form of a woman, her dark brown skin glistening with dew. The woman's hair flowed in translucent blue wisps all around her head, as if blown by some invisible wind. She hovered above the water, her silver gown cinched at the waist and billowing around her legs. Something about the fay woman struck Linden as familiar, as if she'd met her before.

The woman held a small round object cupped inside her hands. Raising the globe aloft, she tossed it into the air. The globe floated across the lake and came to rest in front of Linden, who frowned, not knowing what to make of the globe or the woman, who seemed to be waiting for her to do something. Linden reached out her hand to grasp the clear globe, which Linden saw had multiple facets, like cut crystal. The woman smiled at her, and recognition dawned.

"Mage Mother Pawllah?" Linden's fay tutor had been

ancient, far older than her grandmother, but Linden would know that smile anywhere. The woman nodded.

Linden frowned. "You look so...young...and beautiful." Then it dawned on Linden that Pawllah must have passed into the realms of the dead. No other explanation made sense. Still smiling, the fay's form began to slowly fade. "Wait, don't go yet." Linden watched as Pawllah's image dissolved in a puff of white light.

"Was that really Mage Mother Pawllah?" whispered Mara.

Linden nodded slowly, a tear trickling down her cheek. "She's passed on."

"Are you sure?"

"I'm positive." Linden opened her palm wider and stared at the crystal globe. Her teeth stopped chattering from the cold, and she no longer felt like she'd fall to her knees any moment.

"What is that thing?"

Linden shook her head. "I have no idea. But I do feel a little bit stronger."

Nahn rose slowly to her feet. "Now you mention it, so do I."

Tam blew out a puff of air. "Me too, I'm feeling better." He and Vas helped each other stand up.

Tossing fireballs through the holes in the shield to keep the guards at bay, Remy glanced over at the globe in Linden's hand. He turned back toward the guards, lobbing slightly larger fireballs at them. "That's funny."

"What's funny?"

"I've seen that before," said Remy. "I remember now. It used to be in the room on the second floor, the one that displayed the old fay artifacts."

Linden stared at the small crystal globe, about the size of a lime, in her hand. She remembered the Ancient Fay Historical Collection, but where had this artifact been displayed? "Remy, you're brilliant!"

"Huh?"

She opened her palm wider so everyone could see the crystal. "This looks like the Sollareus crystal, which was supposed to have powerful healing properties. According to the old fay tales, this once belonged to Hanalorah, a fay princess who made the mistake of falling in love with a local Faymon clan chief. When she announced her plans to marry the man, the fay king disowned her. She eloped with the clan chief, taking nothing from her father's household, except this crystal. She became known as Lady Liege Hanalorah, the first Liege of Faynwood."

"Forget the history lesson," said Nahn. "Let's figure out if that crystal can help us fight off the guards. They just keep coming."

Linden remembered something else from the old stories about Liege Hanalorah and the Sollareus. Whenever Hanalorah blew on the crystal, its healing properties increased twenty-fold. *Maybe the Sollareus holds the secret to completely cleansing the royal burial chamber?* Linden cupped the Sollareus in her hands and blew on the crystal, which started to glow.

Slender shafts of light erupted from every facet, dancing across the ceiling and water, multiplying until the entire chamber burst into silvery light. The gilded fay hieroglyphs on the sarcophagi and walls seemed to catch fire, each sparkling like a small sun. A small eddy swirled in the center of the lake and expanded outward, cleansing the water until it looked clean and clear, reflecting the silver light inside the chamber.

The protective film of their shield strengthened, the holes closing up. Linden felt the healing magic coursing through every muscle, healing her aches, restoring her magical energy, and finally, cleansing away the cobwebs of fear and doubt inside her head. She glanced at Tam, who flexed his leg muscles and nodded at her. Everyone looked fit, stronger than when they'd started the ritual.

"Let's keep that in a safe place," said Tam.

"Good point." Although the crystal was no longer emitting light beams, an afterglow remained inside the chamber, every surface glistening and cleansed. Linden placed the Sollareus carefully inside her belt pouch.

Linden took one final look at the gilded walls and sparkling lake, wanting to know the story behind each sarcophagus, each life lived. Another time, perhaps, when the war was over, she could sit with her fay grandfather and learn more about the history of his people, who were her people too.

"What now?" asked Remy, staring at the guards, prepared to send more fireballs their way if the holes opened up in the shield again. The guards, for their part, hadn't seemed to notice the light show. Or if they did notice, it had no effect on them. They remained with their swords drawn, waiting for something. Or someone.

Linden turned away from the semi-circle of sarcophagi, ready to face what came next. She didn't have long to wait. She heard his roar of frustration, a shrieking wail of pure hatred aimed at her and her friends. Mordahn was in the building. She'd sensed his presence the moment they entered the museum. And he wasn't alone.

The shrieking continued, growing louder, Linden fighting the urge to cover her ears and cower. Instead she withdrew her sword, its blade bright with green hieroglyphs, and shouted, "Swords up! Let's maintain the defensive shield as long as we can, incanting together."

Tam yelled, "Conjure a shield around this spot, defend with strength against onslaught!" Everyone chanted the words out loud, the spell becoming a mantra of sorts as they withdrew their swords and waited.

The wailing intensified until Linden couldn't hear herself think. A single long screech filled the chamber, blowing out the torches and plunging them into darkness.

CHAPTER 22

Tam and the others faltered, the shield thinning and dissolving around them. "Don't lose focus!" Linden shouted, "Maintain the shield." She poured every ounce of concentration into the shield, strengthening it again. The torches relit themselves, the burial chamber glowing even brighter than before.

"Spawn of Tanglewood, I've come for you." Mordahn spat out the words as he entered the chamber. He wore a long black and silver robe, his hem and cuffs embroidered with runes Linden didn't recognize. She was convinced they had something to do with necromancy.

Mordahn threw back his hood. Linden grimaced at the sight of his face, the skin hanging in strips, his mouth a gaping hole full of pointy teeth, his nose two narrow slits. His eyes burned orange inside their sockets. Four more Fallow sorcerers flanked him, two on either side. They wore plain black robes, except for a row of runes embroidered in blood-red thread along their hems. *Mordahn is taking no chances this time,* thought Linden. *He's brought undead reinforcements.*

Mordahn and the sorcerers started chanting a counterspell,

their voices low and guttural. Every syllable and word wrapped itself around Linden's heart, and each lilt of the incantation seemed to drive twisted steel nails into all her organs. She gave an anguished moan, the pain searing every fiber of her being, as her magic fought against Mordahn's sorcerous invasion.

The defensive shield collapsed in a whoosh, but the chamber remained brightly lit, the walls and coffins gilded and cleansed. Despite the loss of the shield, Linden felt a small bubble of satisfaction. *Whatever happens here, Mordahn won't be able to pervert the magic in the royal burial chamber again. This place of power has been consecrated to Serving magic.*

Waving his hands, Mordahn signaled to the guards and shouted, "Leave the girl with the green sword for me. Kill the others."

Linden's stomach churned at Mordahn's words, but her first priority was to protect Tam and her friends. She stepped out in front, gritting her teeth against the heavy aching in her limbs. She raised her sword at the charging guards, her arm shaking with the effort. Tam came alongside her. "I'm not letting him take you."

"Me neither," grunted Mara, who stepped up to her other side. Nahn, Remy, and Vas lined up as well, legs flexed and swords up defensively. Linden blinked back tears of gratitude. Inhaling, she felt stronger than she had moments earlier, as if her friends' loyalty had fortified her against Mordahn's spell.

The guards surrounded them, swinging their blades, attempting to slip behind their group to subdue them. "Watch your backs!" shouted Vas.

A short, muscular guard with five gold hoops in one ear spat at Linden as he stabbed the air in front of her with his sword. She couldn't remember his name, but she'd know that cruel mug of his anywhere. He'd killed Nari and nearly choked Linden to death when the queen's demented brother was briefly in charge at the Valerran palace.

Linden shouted, "Evakunouz!" and centered herself, focused not on revenge but on protecting her friends and herself. She parried the guard's powerful blows, defending each lunge of his sword.

Another guard, large enough to be a super-grihm, joined the guard with the gold hoops. Together they attempted to separate Linden from the group. She refused to give any ground, her green blade countering every thrust of their swords, left to right, right to left, the sound of metal clanging and blades swishing filled the air, along with grunts and yells when someone caught the tip of a sword. Linden couldn't take her eyes off the two guards in front of her, but she heard Tam hiss in pain and wondered how long they could defend themselves against this onslaught.

Then she heard a surprisingly welcome sound: a chorus of yips and howls. The howling grew louder, and Linden heard the grihms' garbled chant: "Smash! Smash!" She saw a flicker of fear in the muscular guard's eyes. Farleigh, Jerdahn, and their friends surged into the basement, accompanied by another twenty super-sized grihms. Linden figured Farleigh must have freed the other grihms from their cages.

Mordahn shouted at the guards, "Stop messing with that lot and subdue these grihms! We need them back in their cages now!"

Mordahn raised his hands, preparing to cast a spell. Linden suspected he was about to use magic against the grihms. She had to act fast. "Freeze all magic swirling about, stop our spells 'til the hour runs out!" She'd just evened up the odds, freezing both Fallow and Serving magic for an hour, more than enough time for Farleigh and his friends to rout the guards.

Mordahn opened his mouth to screech in frustration, his lower jaw coming partially unhinged, turning Linden's stomach. A couple of grihms turned toward the old sorcerer. Mordahn flung his long, bony arms in the air and fled, retreating up the passageway with his undead cohort scurrying behind him. Farleigh and the grihms took care of the remaining guards. No one was left standing when they were through, including the short, nasty man with the five gold hoops.

Meanwhile, Nahn fashioned a tourniquet around Tam's left arm, punctured during the fighting and bleeding heavily, the sleeve of his uniform already soaked through. Everyone else had sustained cuts and scratches fending off the guards, except for Remy, who'd been protected by his furry grihm costume.

Farleigh loped over to Linden, panting. "Smashed bad machines. Opened cages. What next?"

Sheathing her sword, Linden pointed at the dead guards sprawled about the chamber. "Can you help tidy up the room? We need to leave this chamber cleansed of all flesh and blood. And maybe clear a path for us upstairs so we can get out of the museum unnoticed?"

"Aye," yipped Farleigh. He barked at the other grihms, who began dragging bodies out of the chamber, grunting and snorting all the way up the passage. Farleigh remained behind after the room had cleared. Waving his paw, he said, "We want to help. Can stay...with you?" Farleigh bowed his head, waiting for her reply

Moved by the giant crossbreed's offer, Linden nodded. Although she couldn't exactly sneak around Bellaryss with Farleigh and his friends in tow, she wasn't about to turn away any offers of help. Besides, having six super-grihms as an escort couldn't hurt. "Thank you. We can use all the help we can get. Do you want to gather up your group and wait for us at the next level? We need to finish up down here."

Farleigh yipped in agreement. Glancing at Remy, he said, "Follow me. Find you better uniform. Unless you want keep that fur blanket?"

Remy practically hugged Farleigh then thought better of it.

Turning back to Linden and Mara, he said, "See you upstairs then?"

"Be careful!" Mara called after Remy.

Linden pulled the Sollareus out of her belt pouch. Holding it in the palm of her hand, she spoke half to the crystal, half to herself. "Since I froze all magic for the hour, I wonder whether your healing magic will work now. We need to rid this site of all blood stains and gore."

The Sollareus vibrated slightly, a low humming sensation, almost as if it heard and understood. Linden blew on the crystal. The facets glowed more gently than before, emitting sparkly particles rather than bright shafts of light. The sparkles danced around the room, scrubbing away the stained ground and spattered walls. When the chamber was cleansed and whole once again, the crystal stopped vibrating and the sparkles faded away.

"Look at my arm!" Tam pulled away the tourniquet, his puncture wound closing as they watched. Even the sleeve of his uniform looked fresh and clean.

Still holding the Sollareus, Linden arched an eyebrow. "This artifact has been on display for centuries. I'm amazed no one has stumbled across its power." She felt healed again, her limbs and head no longer aching. Securing the crystal in her belt pouch, she said, "I trust our grihm friends have caused enough mayhem upstairs by now. Are we ready?"

"Aye, more than ready. I'm not a fan of basements," said Nahn with a shiver. "Too many spiders." Linden shook her head, chuckling. Nahn had faced undead riders, grihms, necromancers, and sorcerers without flinching, but she shuddered at spiders.

Nahn raised her eyebrows. "What? Spiders are creepy crawly things. They're disgusting."

"Speaking of disgusting things, how should we track Mordahn and his undead friends?" asked Mara.

"I say we leave him be for now," said Tam. "Escape while Mordahn's magic is still useless. I figure we have about twenty minutes before that spell wears off. He'll come after us again. I'd prefer to face him on the battlefield."

Vas nodded. "Agreed. We'll be better off connecting up with some reinforcements."

Linden said, "Then let's make our way back to the beach. Wreyn and Efram should be returning soon with news from the clans."

They jogged up the passageway, making faster progress than when they'd descended, and ran into a grinning Remy at the top level of the basement. "What do you think?" He pointed at his uniform.

"Lovely, but we have fifteen minutes to get out of here before Mordahn's magic is back to full strength," said Mara.

Remy's eyes widened. "What are we waiting for?"

Farleigh and Jerdahn came alongside them. "Others outside already."

"Are we going out the same way we entered, or do you have another exit in mind?" asked Linden.

Jerdahn yipped and dashed up the steps to the first floor. Pausing to listen, he waved his paw and scrambled to his left. Linden heard sounds of fighting, growling grihms and shouting guards, down the hallway to the right. She closed the distance between herself and Jerdahn, the rest of their group running behind them. Jerdahn flung open a set of double doors that opened onto a deserted platform, used for loading and unloading deliveries.

They stepped outside cautiously and then trotted along the back of the museum to the opposite side street they'd used earlier. Linden was surprised to see it was still dark; she felt as if she'd been inside the museum for days. She jumped at the sound of breaking glass behind her. The fight that began in the museum between the freed grihms and the guards had spilled outside, the guards and grihms brawling in the road behind the museum.

"This way, hurry!" hissed Farleigh, jogging alongside Linden. One of his grihm friends was waiting for them at the corner. He waved his paw and turned to dash down the side street. Linden and the others rounded the bend, colliding with Farleigh's four friends, who yipped happily.

Linden glanced up at the museum's roof. She whistled and moments later a projectile of fur, beak, and wings hurled into her chest. Linden hugged Kal, who clicked his beak at her. She noticed he was trembling slightly, a sign he'd been frightened waiting for her alone on the roof.

As Linden put Kal down on the ground, Tam said, "We need to get off the street before daybreak, which is less than an hour away."

"There's a shop a few blocks over that will do nicely," Vas pointed across the street.

"Huh?" asked Remy. "What kind of shop is open at this hour?"

"They'll open for us." Glancing at Farleigh, he added, "Well, some of us. We'll have to explain about our grihm friends."

"The 'freeze' spell will unwind itself any minute. When it does, I'll cast a veil of drabness over us," said Linden.

They picked up their pace, Vas taking the lead. Two blocks from the museum, Linden sensed her power return and hastily cast a veil of drabness over the group. She needn't have bothered, since they encountered no one, except a stray dog, whose guard hairs rose along his back when they ran past him. The dog turned tail and fled in the opposite direction, whimpering.

"Wait here for me." Vas unwound himself from the veil of drabness, slipped down an alley, and knocked on a door. Linden had no idea what sort of a shop it might be, since they were facing an alley that ran behind a row of shops on either side.

The door opened and Vas stepped into the building. Moments later the door opened again. Vas stuck his head out and waved them through.

Linden waited until everyone had crossed the threshold before allowing the veil of drabness to evaporate. They were jammed into the shop's rear entrance, the super-grihms taking up most of the space. Boxes and crates full of tiny gears, shafts, and cranks were stacked floor to ceiling on either side of them. Linden couldn't imagine why anyone would need that many mechanical parts, especially in such small sizes.

Vas opened a door and pointed down a set of wood-plank steps. "Farleigh, you and your friends will sleep down below. Our host will bring you some food and water shortly. The rest of us will head through the shop." Farleigh yipped twice and the huge grihms lumbered into the basement, tails wagging. Linden figured the mention of food brought on the wagging tails.

Linden was curious about their host, wondering whether he belonged to the resistance network Vas had activated. Why else would a shopkeeper risk hiding a group of grihms and resistance fighters on the run?

A curtain separated the rear alley entrance from the rest of the shop. Linden stepped beyond the curtain, passed through a narrow office with more tiny mechanical parts scattered about a worktable, and entered a roomful of clockwork toys: wind-up cats with glittering green eyes, mechanical dogs in a variety of breeds, from small poodles to mastiffs, dancing ballerinas, and miniature locomobiles.

"Well, well, a motley crew if I ever saw one." A slender woman wearing a blue-and-gold striped blouse, slim-fitting gold slacks, and a blue turban around her head, stood in the center of the shop, her hands on her hips. She looked about sixty, with a strong chin, aquiline nose, and dark brown eyes that missed nothing. "What've you dragged through my door now, Vas? Six massive grihms in my basement and fake Glenbarran guards cluttering up my shop. The grihms alone will eat me out of house and home."

"It's good to see you too, Katrine," laughed Vas, giving the older woman a hug.

She pushed him away with a grin. "I've always been a sucker for a man in a uniform." Waving her hand at his clothes, she added, "Though not these Glenbarran rags you're wearing. We'll get you sorted out soon enough."

Tam gave Katrine a lopsided smile. "What about me? I thought I was your favorite!" Katrine shook her head at Tam and patted his scarred cheek. "You're a bit on the young side, lad, but you'll do in a pinch."

Tam chuckled as she turned away. Katrine went over to Nahn and wrapped her in a bear hug. "I heard about Burr. I'm so sorry, lass." Nahn stepped back, her eyes moist.

Vas started to introduce the rest of the group, but Kal interrupted them with a loud squawk. He poked his beak at a small clockwork griffin. The mechanical griffin opened its wings and clicked its beak, causing Kal to scurry backward, knocking over a metallic cat. Kal shook his head and sat down, infatuated with the toy griffin. Katrine and the others laughed. The woman bent down and solemnly shook Kal's paw. "Welcome, Companion of Protectors."

Linden tilted her head at Katrine, surprised by her choice of words. Only one other woman had ever greeted Kal that way; Mage Mother Pawllah, the first time Linden and Kal had visited her residence on Sanrellyss Island. Linden glanced at the blue turban wrapped around Katrine's head. That vivid blue was the same shade as Pryl's hair, and Pawllah's, and every other fay she'd ever known, even Wreyn and Efram when they weren't dying their hair for their undercover work. *Is Katrine a fay? And if so, why is she hiding her identity? Is it fear of the Glenbarrans, or something to do with her work in the resistance?*

Vas introduced Remy, Mara, and then finally Linden. He used first names only and didn't mention Linden's title. Apparently, he didn't have to because Katrine seemed to know. She bowed. "Welcome, Protector of Serving magic."

Linden answered, "Well met, Protector of Serving magic, and thank you." Then she asked, "How?"

The woman shrugged. "Rumors abound, lass, about the Liege of Faynwood working with the Valerran resistance. I'm not a genius, but I have eyes. You have bright blue streaks in your hair, a miniature griffin as a pet, and an aura of magic about you." Linden reached up and touched the top of her head. Somewhere between the museum and the shop, she'd lost her peaked cap.

Linden nodded at the woman's turban. "And you're a fay?" Katrine removed her turban to reveal short blue curls. Linden asked, "Why cover up your hair?"

Katrine glanced at the shuttered shop windows, frowning. "Valerra is a lovely country—or it was before the occupation—but some are not so welcoming of outsiders, whether Faymons or fays. When I left Sanrellyss Island forty years ago, as a young lass about your age, my mentor advised me to hide my blue hair. Sometimes I rely on a glamour spell, other times I simply use a head covering."

"Your mentor wouldn't happen to have been Mage Mother Pawllah, by any chance?" asked Linden.

Katrine arched her straight eyebrows. "She was Sister Pawllah in those days, and she was my mentor and best friend. I've been meaning to pop over to Sanrellyss to have a spot of tea with her. But with these Fallow sorcerers running amok, I've not had the chance."

Linden placed her hand on Katrine's arm. "Pawllah has passed on. I'm sorry. She was my mentor too."

"Oh." Katrine bowed her head and closed her eyes. When she opened them, they glistened with unshed tears. "I suppose

I shouldn't be surprised, given her age. But now I'll never get to say a proper goodbye."

After waiting a respectful silence, Tam cleared his throat. "I'm afraid if we don't get some food and water bowls down to the basement soon, we'll have a pack of howling grihms to contend with. If you would show me where the supplies are kept, I'll sort something out for them."

"I'll help you," said Remy. Linden suspected Remy's motives might not be purely altruistic, given his love of food.

"Aye, follow me, lads. You too, Vas. We'll get the grihms their grub and then we can have our breakfast in peace."

After they left the shop floor, Mara picked up a clockwork ballerina and examined it. "I suppose these mechanical toys work so long as there's not too much magic in the nursery." Mara was stating what every mage learned at an early age. Powerful magic interfered with the functioning of anything mechanical—which was why marines carried swords into battle along with their pistols—and why master mages like Nari had preferred carrier pigeons to telegrams, and horses to locomobiles.

Nahn shrugged. "Even the children of master mages don't come into their gifts until they're teenagers. Anyway, this shop's been around for decades, so Katrine has figured out how to make a go of it."

Linden pointed to a sign by the door and read it aloud. "Use of magic around these toys will impede their proper functioning. I will repair non-functioning toys for up to ninety days from purchase at no charge." Linden read from a second sign, hand lettered and hanging below the first one. "There's no need to save receipts because I know when every toy was purchased. No one fools Katrine."

Nahn chuckled. "Katrine's one of a kind, that's for certain." Lowering her voice, she added. "Katrine and Vas run the resistance network inside Bellaryss. Like the sign says, nothing gets past her."

After the grihms were fed, Katrine invited everyone to the second floor, where she lived above the shop. She opened a tall wooden wardrobe just inside the door. "You can place your swords in here. They're easy enough to take up if we need them, but we shouldn't. My place is warded with protection charms and masking spells." Katrine's eyes flickered when she noticed the old, polished leather scabbards and jeweled hilts that Linden, Remy, and Mara dropped inside the wardrobe. "Where did you get these fay weapons?"

Linden told her about the retreat to the Valerran Museum during the siege of Bellaryss. She described the Weapons Room, and how the weapons chose their new owners from among the mages and apprentices who were present.

Katrine shook her head. "I've always regretted not being on hand to help during the siege of Bellaryss. I was visiting an ill friend outside the city when the attack started. By the time I returned home, Glenbarran thugs were ransacking buildings and swarming the streets."

She pointed to Linden's sword and scabbard. "But these weapons shouldn't be lighting up for anyone other than their rightful owners, which would have been fays. And yet you're saying these swords chose you?" When Linden and the others nodded, the fay looked thoughtful. "There is an old fay legend about the Swords of Five. After we've eaten, let me see if I can find the reference among my books."

CHAPTER 23

Katrine's apartment consisted of an eat-in kitchen with a large oak table and eight chairs, a parlor with a sofa and couple of stuffed chairs, and books everywhere else. Bookshelves lined every wall of the parlor, one wall of the kitchen, and the narrow hallway leading to the bedroom and bath. Katrine's reading tastes ran from history, literature, and science, to healing and magic.

Linden's eyes were drawn to a thick, tattered book covered in fay hieroglyphs. She followed the shopkeeper into the kitchen, where Katrine handed Linden a wheel of cheese and a knife. Katrine picked up another knife and started slicing a loaf of bread. Linden cut chunks of cheese off the wheel and stacked them neatly on a platter on the table. "Can you read the ancient fay hieroglyphs?"

Katrine shook her head. "Other than a few symbols here and there, not at all. But there are spells of translating and revealing, which I suspect you're familiar with."

Linden nodded. "My grandmother had a crystal globe in her office that worked well with those spells. But I didn't notice any crystals in your parlor."

"Crystals and other such artifacts help channel magical energy, but you don't need them to perform the spells."

"Not even to read the hieroglyphs?"

"Especially to read the hieroglyphs," said Katrine.

"Have you come across any incantations for reversing the effects of necromancy?"

Katrine snorted. "You mean for sending Mordahn and his undead pals back to their graves?" She pulled a basket out of the cupboard, lined it with a linen napkin, and laid out the sliced bread. "Well of course there's a way, but it's not so simple as incanting a spell."

Linden almost cut herself with the knife in her excitement. Here, finally, was someone with the answers. "How does it work? What do we need to do?"

Katrine pulled a sausage out of her larder and cut it into bite-sized pieces. "It's mighty complicated, and it's not like anyone has experience with this sort of thing. We haven't actually had to deal with a bunch of Fallow undead in at least a hundred years, maybe longer."

"So theoretically it can be done, but it's not like anyone has a lot of practical experience dealing with the undead."

"Aye. Not only that, it's also dangerous, very, very dangerous. You could wind up sending yourself into the realms of the dead, permanently." Katrine gave a small shudder. "It's not somewhere I'd want to visit again."

Linden put down the knife before she did serious damage to herself or the cheese wheel. "You've been there? To the realms of the dead?"

Katrine shook her blue curls. "Not exactly. I've stood on the edge of the realms of the dead and peeked inside. It was after my mum passed. I got it in my head that maybe I could see her one last time. Not bring her back, mind you, but tell her I loved her. What a mistake."

"What happened?"

"My mum wasn't anywhere near the edge, even though she'd recently passed. In hindsight, I realize she'd already moved on. But what I saw, gathered there at the edge of the realms? Well, let's just say it's the stuff of nightmares and leave it at that." Katrine shuddered again.

Linden thought about the implications. "But you're saying there is a way to send Mordahn back to the realms of the dead?"

"Aye, there's a way. But first, you have to be close enough to lasso him with an ensorcelled rope. Then you have to escort him to the realms of the dead and drag him to the center of the river in the lowest realm. And you have to be sure nothing nasty follows you out when you leave."

Linden had a sinking feeling that what Katrine just described was what Pryl had "seen" in his visions of her final showdown with Mordahn. It would explain why her grandfather found the sneak peek into the future so disturbing. In his visions, sometimes Linden won the final battle in the realms of the dead, and other times Mordahn won.

Linden tucked a lock of hair behind her ear, determined not to dwell on what would happen if she lost the battle. "Do we have to lasso all the undead riders and sorcerers he's raised and drag them back to the realms of the dead?"

Katrine shook her head. "Not exactly. The undead minions, the horses and their riders, are tied to Mordahn by an invisible thread. It's Mordahn's power that's driving them. If we take him out, the minions will follow him into the realms."

"What about the undead sorcerers? How do we send them back to the realms?"

"How many did you see?"

"There were four of them with Mordahn."

"Did they stick close to his side, arriving and departing at the same time?"

When Linden nodded, Katrine asked, "Have you gotten a

good look at the other sorcerers? Did any of them drop their hoods?"

"No. If anything, they were even more shrouded than Mordahn. "

Katrine sighed. "Well, that further complicates things."

"What do you mean?"

"While they look like sorcerers, they're not. They're even worse."

Linden blew out a puff of air, trying to imagine what could be worse than undead sorcerers. "What are they?"

Katrine pulled a few apples toward her and started slicing them. "They're called protectors and they do one thing really well: they protect the necromancer who brought them back from the dead. Basically, Mordahn has raised undead bodyguards for himself. We'll have to send the protectors back to the realms of the dead along with Mordahn. And protectors are especially talented at eluding capture."

"Do we need to capture all of them?"

"Aye, we'll need to lasso the lot of them and send them back to the realms of the dead. If you leave even one protector free, he would be able to raise Mordahn again. Protectors are engineered for necromancy."

Linden's head was spinning with questions, but she asked the most important one. "Where do we find this special ensorcelled rope? It sounds like we're going to need a lot of it."

Katrine arranged the apples on another platter and grabbed some plates from her cupboard. She poured out mugs of tea, which she'd been brewing on top of her stove, and stepped back to survey her table. "We'll have to make a small side trip to gather enough fay-spelled rope, but let's eat first." Katrine stepped into the parlor and waved the group into the kitchen. Remy managed to arrive first at the table, his face lighting up when he spotted the platter of sliced cheese and sausages.

When their plates were empty and they were on their

second mugs of tea, Katrine asked, "How much help will the Faymons be able to provide us? And what about the fays?"

Linden nodded at Vas, who put down his mug of tea to explain the plan. "The Faymon clans are going to free up as many troops as they're able to provide, without compromising their own borders. They'll march down from Shorewood in the north, hiding under veils of drabness on the beach until we give them the signal to swarm into Bellaryss. Meanwhile, Pryl and his fay army will be assembling in the hills west of Bellaryss, ready for the assault on Wellan Pass. Once the fays retake the pass—assuming they retake it—the fay and Faymon armies will squeeze the Glenbarrans between them. It's a classic pincer move."

"With poor Bellaryss caught in the crosshairs," said Remy.

"Even if we defeat the Glenbarrans, that still leaves Mordahn. He can keep bringing back more undead troops. He's a menace to any sort of lasting peace," said Mara.

Linden explained what Katrine had told her about Mordahn and his protectors, Katrine filling in the details. The reality of what needed to happen next shifted the mood around the table, from something approaching optimism after escaping the museum, to the opposite.

"It's almost as if we have a three-front war we're waging: at Wellan Pass to the west, on Bellaryss Beach to the east, and in the realms of the dead," said Tam. "I have a feeling the third battle is going to be the toughest of all."

"Now may be a good time for me to tell you about the Swords of Five. It's in one of my old books." Katrine walked into the parlor. Mumbling as she ran her fingers along a shelf of leather-bound books, their bindings cracked with age, Katrine pulled down one tome after another, finally uttering, "Ah, here it is."

Returning to the table, she nodded at the teapot. "Top up

your mugs, this is a bit of a tale. But I think there may be some clues within here."

"A long time ago," began Katrine, "during a very difficult year in Havynweal, filled with wars and plagues and dark sorceries, a young fay girl named Sollara closed the door to her cottage and walked into the woods at the edge of her family's property. She intended to pick some wild truffles for her grandmother and return home right away, but every time she bent down to pluck a truffle from the soft undergrowth, the mushroom turned to fay dust in her hands.

"Now Sollara was well accustomed to magic, so this didn't scare her or cause her to consider perhaps she'd wandered too far. Instead, she trundled deeper into those enchanted woods, plucking more mushrooms that turned into more fay dust. To her delight, the dust itself seemed spelled, because it blossomed into a rainbow of colors in her hand, sometimes green, other times gold, or purple, or red, or blue. Since she was a smart young fay, she realized this magical dust must have special significance, and rather than sprinkling it on the ground, she carefully deposited all the dust she collected into her basket.

"By the time Sollara had filled her basket to the brim with fay dust, she realized two things. The sun was setting, and she was utterly lost. Unfortunately, Sollara hadn't yet learned how to travel on the mists, and she'd wandered so far, she could no longer sense her cottage in the woods. While many young fays in her predicament might have sat down on the forest floor and cried, not Sollara. She spotted a flickering light in the distance and walked toward it. 'There must be someone over there who can help me get back home,' she reasoned.

"Sollara pushed aside some tree branches and stood still, wondering whether she should seek help elsewhere. A pall of gloom hung about the spot and she felt distinctly uncomfortable, and perhaps, if she were completely honest, she was frightened, as well. Sollara had discovered the source of the flickering light. A massive blacksmith's forge sat in a clearing in the forest, the flames of the fire glowing in the twilight. Standing over his anvil, pounding away with his mighty hammer, was the tallest, broadest giant imaginable. Sollara made her decision. She turned to flee back into the woods, but at the exact moment the giant raised his beefy arm for another strike at his anvil, Sollara stepped on a twig that crackled loudly in the sudden silence.

"The giant dropped his hammer and turned his coal-black eyes on her. He wore patched breeches, a stained brown leather apron, and a fierce expression on his dreadful face. 'What's this? A wee fay girl, wandering into my realm?' he boomed.

"Sollara found her voice, though her knees were quaking. 'Aye, Sir Giant, I apologize for disturbing your important work, however, I have become lost in these woods. Can you please help me get back home?'

"The giant guffawed, a loud, unpleasant snorting noise. 'I am far too busy, lass. And since ye have wandered so far that ye are lost, I may as well keep ye as a pet. 'Tis lonely here, making weapons for the fay king, and I need someone to talk to.' With that, the giant snapped his fingers and a golden cage descended over Sollara's head. A little cot and a round table with bread, cheese, and a pitcher of water sat inside the cage.

"Sollara was a practical young fay and knew better than to turn down a meal, even one conjured by a giant. Shrugging, she sat down to eat. She was concerned, of course, about finding a way home, but she was also hungry and thirsty, and she didn't think the giant intended her any harm if he wanted her for a pet.

"After she'd eaten, Sollara's eyes grew heavy. She'd walked many, many miles that day and decided the little cot looked quite inviting. 'I'll just take a short nap and then I'll see about how to get home,' she whispered to herself. Sollara stretched out and fell asleep instantly. She awoke hours later and rubbed her eyes, thinking perhaps it was morning already. But it was the full moon overhead that lit up the clearing, as well as the giant at work in his forge, stoking the fires even hotter, the flames licking high into the sky.

"Suddenly, the giant tossed his hammer onto the ground and dropped to his knees. 'Woe is me,' he sobbed to the moon and stars above. 'Giant magic is too weak. The fay king has set me to an impossible task. I will never be able to forge swords to defeat the darker powers. The king shall have my head.' The giant threw himself on top of his anvil and wept bitter tears.

"Sollara took pity on the giant. 'Sir Giant, perhaps I can help. After all, I am a fay girl with my own special magic.'

"The giant guffawed again, and Sollara winced at his braying laughter. 'What can a wee young fay do that a handsome giant like myself can't accomplish?'

" 'I have a basketful of fay dust, here inside this cage. If you free me, I'll sprinkle the dust over the swords you've made, and they'll grow the stronger for it. Your fine blacksmithing skills, combined with my magic dust, ought to be sufficient against any dark powers.'

"The giant drew his black brows together. 'Give me your basket of dust, and if the magic is as you say, then I'll free you.'

"Now Sollara's grandmother had warned her about giants. The young fay knew they couldn't be trusted to keep their word. As she lifted the basket from the table, she reached inside and grasped a handful of the fay dust. She hid her fist full of dust in the pocket of her jacket. Handing her basket to the giant through the bars of her cage, she said, 'Here is the dust. Now sprinkle it over the blade of each sword. When you see the colors of the rainbow burst over the weapons, you will know the magic is working. And then you will free me.'

" 'Aye, lass, of course,' mumbled the giant. He took her

basket and lumbered over to the five swords laid out on his stone hearth. The giant dumped the basket of dust over the weapons. In an explosion of greens, golds, purples, reds, and blues, the dust coated each sword, etching hieroglyphs filled with magic into every blade. When the dust had settled, the blades thrummed with pure Serving magic. The giant reached down to pick up the hilt of one of the swords, and he screamed in pain. One by one, each sword rejected him.

"His anger burned as hot as the fires of his forge, and he turned on Sollara. 'What have ye done, lass? These weapons may be spelled, but now I can't even touch them. I'll not be able to bring them to the fay king, and he will still have my head. Ye have tricked me!'

" 'I haven't tricked you,' said Sollara. 'Those swords are designed to fight against the darker powers, whether living or dead. You are obviously not a very nice giant, and so the swords have rejected you.'

" 'How dare you insult me, you spiteful guttersnipe!' The giant reached through the roof of Sollara's cage and grabbing her legs in his meaty hand, he dangled her, headfirst, above his mouth. Sollara struggled and screamed, realizing the evil giant intended to eat her. As the giant suspended Sollara over his open jaws, she wracked her brain for a way to stop him. Then she remembered the fistful of fay dust in her pocket, which she hastily withdrew and rammed into the giant's throat.

"With a loud screech, the giant dropped Sollara, who tumbled onto a bed of moss on the forest floor. The giant stumbled backward, his hands over his face. Swirls of dancing light, in the colors of the rainbow, burst out of his mouth and eyes and ears. The giant crumbled to the ground, hollering, as the colorful rays of light swirled around him. When the fay dust had finished working its magic, nothing was left of the giant, except for a clear, multi-faceted crystal, about the size of

Sollara's palm. Sollara wiped her streaming eyes and scooped the crystal off the ground.

"Sollara, dear child, where are you?" called Sollara's father from deep inside the woods.

"Sollara cried out, 'Father, I'm over here! I've been held prisoner by a giant!' Her father burst into the clearing, followed by her five older brothers and her grandmother. Sollara threw herself into her father's arms and told him about the truffles and the fay dust, and the evil giant and the swords. Her father patted her vivid blue hair and praised her, promising the king himself would hear of her bravery. He ordered her brothers to take the magic swords and the crystal to the fay king and to offer themselves in his service.

"And so Sollara's brothers became the first reapers, wielding the Swords of Five against the darker powers within the fay realms and beyond, wherever Fallow sorcery had taken root. They quickly learned the magic of the swords multiplied when used together, and so they always fought as one unit.

"The fay king named the crystal Sollareus in honor of the girl who'd forged it. He gave the crystal to his daughter, Princess Hanalorah, on her fifteenth birthday. There are many stories about Hanalorah, the first Lady Liege of Faynwood, and so we will not repeat them here. But what of the young fay girl who forged the healing crystal and magicked the swords?

"Young Sollara grew up to become a famous bard. She traveled across the seven seasons of Havynweal, singing of ensorcelled swords and dark sorcery, of evil giants and magic dust. Some fays claim even to this day, on a full-moon night, when the wind whips through the trees in Havynweal, you can still hear Sollara's soft voice, humming a warning to all who turn to Fallow ways."

Katrine put down the book. Mara and Remy looked at Linden, who said, "We are going to need Jayna and Corbahn to help us wrestle Mordahn and his protectors back to the realms of the dead."

"But Jayna is in Shorewood, and Corbahn's sword stopped working for him before we left Arrowood." Remy turned toward Linden. "Although sometimes I think the reason Corbahn's sword stopped glowing might have been due to his feelings at the time. He was pretty upset about you leaving without him. Maybe our attitudes have as much to do with the magic as anything."

Mara drew her brows together and asked Katrine, "Could Remy be right?"

"You mean the reason why someone's sword would stop responding? Of course the lad's right. For an ensorcelled object to function, the mage must channel the magical energy within. If he's not able to focus properly, the magic will go awry, or cease altogether."

Linden sipped from her mug, her thoughts swirling. Corbahn's loyalties, and if she were being completely honest with herself, probably his heart too, had been divided. As clan chief, Corbahn had a duty to defend Arrowood, but he also wanted to accompany her into Valerra and fight alongside her. No one can be in two places at once. His inner conflict must have interfered with his ability to channel the magic in his sword. "Remy, you're brilliant!"

Remy grinned. "Maybe so, but how are we supposed to get Corbahn and his sword back together? And what about Jayna? She wasn't feeling well, which is the only reason she agreed to leave with Reynier."

"Jayna was exhausted when she left, and perhaps dispirited too. She's the gentle one of our group." Linden added, more for Mara's benefit, "No offense."

Mara shrugged. "None taken. And you're right. Of all of us who could have been hauled off to that village prison by those stupid goons, Jayna would have been the most vulnerable, even with Reynier there along with her." Mara explained to Katrine, "Jayna is a master healer; her mother was head of the Royal Healer's Guild before the war. Jayna would much rather be brewing healing potions and seeing patients than on the battlefield. However, she is the owner of one of the swords, and she's masterful with it too. We'll need her to make this work."

"And Corbahn is a force all his own," said Remy. "The man's nearly indestructible. If we're going to have to take Mordahn and those four protectors back to the realms of the dead, I want Corbahn fighting by my side."

Katrine turned to Linden. "Well, lass, it sounds as if you need to make some amends with the Chief of Arrowood, and you'll need to determine whether your friend Jayna will be up to the fight."

Linden compressed her lips. "I have complete faith in Jayna. With some rest, she will be more than ready. Corbahn, on the other hand, is more problematic. He won't abandon his duties to his clan."

"Then you'll need to convince him that helping us in this fight *is* his duty. He'll be keeping his clan safe from Mordahn's Fallow influences, and he'll be protecting you. Sounds like something that ought to appeal to the man, based on what you've told me."

Linden swallowed the last of her tea and placed her mug on the table. Squinting at her host, she said, "And how am I supposed to do that?"

Katrine waved her hand at Linden. "Queen's Crown! You're the Faymon Liege, the ruler of the five clans of Faynwood. You have position, magic, and beauty. Use them!"

Linden's face turned red. "Ah, um, well...." Nahn sniggered first, and then Mara giggled. The men chortled, winking and grinning. Linden rolled her eyes. "We'll see how Corbahn reacts when Wreyn delivers my message."

Katrine's face broke into a wide smile. "Why didn't you say so? You've already got the ball rolling, so to speak."

Linden opened and closed her mouth, deciding it was time to move onto another topic. She'd sent the message to Corbahn because she wanted him to know how she felt, not because she was trying to get him to join them for their showdown with Mordahn. On the other hand, she really, really wanted to see Corbahn again. And she'd feel much better about the idea of wrestling the undead Mordahn and his sorcerer friends back to the realms of the dead with Corbahn by her side.

Tam cleared his throat. "Whatever happens between Linden and Corbahn is up to them. We need to coordinate with Reynier and the clans who will be riding down from Shorewood, as well as with Pryl and his fay army. And we need to determine how and when to make our move on Mordahn and his undead minions." Glancing at Katrine, he said, "I know you and Vas have activated the network inside Bellaryss. I'm assuming they're waiting for a signal of some sort from one of you."

Vas and Katrine nodded in unison. Vas said, "Everyone's on alert, and the signal is simple: when the fighting starts, move against your assigned targets."

"So you've assigned targets to the network?" asked Remy. "What are they?"

Katrine topped up the hot water in everyone's mugs. "Vas and I have split up the districts within Bellaryss and each taken half. We've parsed out the assignments to several of our next-level resistance leaders, who have in turn communicated with their cells. The end result is that no one knows the entire resistance plan inside Bellaryss. It's much safer that way. If one network member, or even one cell, is compromised, they can't tell the Glenbarrans our plans for the rest of the city."

"Smart move," agreed Remy, as he helped himself to the last

of the sausage and cheese on the platter, which had somehow come to rest in front of his plate. The others chatted about various strategies, Linden remaining quiet as she turned over each strategy in her head.

Tam arched an eyebrow at Linden. "You're unusually quiet. Are you having a vision?"

Linden shook her head. "I've been mulling over how we're going to coordinate among the Faymon clans marching down from the north, the fays gathering at Wellan Pass, and deal with Mordahn at the same time. We need a final meet-up somewhere to make all this work."

"That shouldn't be too difficult to pull off." Katrine shrugged. "We know Pryl is leading the fay army. And didn't you say fay scouts were traveling to the various clan chiefs?" When Linden nodded, Katrine continued, "Then we can meet in Hayvnweal."

Linden's eyebrows rose. "But I thought Hayvnweal was just some fictional fay land in the old story books. It's not a real place, is it?" She looked at her brother.

"I majored in geography before the war, and I've never come across an actual Havynweal anywhere on the continent," said Tam.

"I'm not surprised," said Katrine. "Hayvnweal is another name for the fays' homeland—you know it as the Fay Nation. Hayvnweal is located within Faynwood, but you won't find Havynweal on any map."

"So are you saying it's located in a different dimension of sorts?" Remy grabbed the last apple slice from the fruit platter that had migrated in front of him and popped it in his mouth.

"That's about right. Havynweal is magically tethered to Faynwood, but it's accessible only to fays."

"Then how are we supposed to get there?"

"*We* won't be going there. No human can enter Havynweal, or for that matter leave, without a fay escort." Katrine inclined her head toward Linden. "I will take one of you. And since the fays recognize the Liege here as the head of state for the Faymon clans, then it should be Linden. Once we're in Havynweal, I will summon Pryl and the fay scouts."

Tam ran a hand through his blue-and-brown hair and grunted. "How long will all this take? I don't think we have much time. Protective wards are only going to last for so long against Mordahn." Linden could tell he wasn't happy about the idea of her traveling to Havynweal. She wasn't sure how she felt about the idea, but if it was the fastest, surest way of bringing together Pryl, Wreyn, Efram, and the clans, it was worth a try.

Vas said, "Tam's right. We can't afford to stay put for long. We'll need to move after dark."

Katrine nodded. "Agreed. But for now, get some rest. I have bedrolls and pillows in the wardrobe down the hall. When we leave, I'll cast a forgotten spell over the shop. Anyone who tries to enter the shop today will get confused and forget all about it."

"I've never come across a forgotten spell in any of my books," said Linden, wondering how it worked and thinking of a few times such a spell would have come in handy.

"I'm sure you'll come across it the next time you read *Timely Spells*." Katrine waved her hand vaguely in the air.

Linden drew her brows together in surprise. "My grandmother gave *Timely Spells* to me on my sixteenth birthday. How do you know about it?"

In typical fay fashion, Katrine didn't answer her. She stood up and carried her empty plate and mug over to the sink. Everyone else followed suit, scraping their chairs against the wooden floor, clearing away the dishes, platters, and mugs. Remy filled the sink with soapy water and began washing the dishes. Vas picked up a towel to dry the mugs and platters, while Mara and Nahn went in search of the bedrolls down the hall.

Tam gave Katrine a swift nod. "Take good care of my sister."

"I can take care of myself, thank you very much," grinned Linden. Tam gave her a peck on the cheek and stepped back.

Katrine pointed to the tall wardrobe and said, "Tam, would you fetch me the clan chief's sword. A quick trip to Havynweal will do that weapon a world of good." Tam returned with the sword, a perplexed look on his face. He glanced at Linden and they both shrugged. Linden had no idea what Katrine had in mind. She barely knew the fay resistance leader, but Linden trusted her nonetheless. Vaporous tendrils curled around Katrine and Linden's ankles, snaked up their legs and arms, and enveloped them in the traveling mists.

CHAPTER 24

In the final moments before they left the flat, Katrine hastily cast the forgotten spell. Linden concentrated, trying hard to memorize it, but as soon as Katrine had finished, Linden realized she couldn't recall a single word she heard. She was determined to learn more about the spell, as well as how Katrine knew about *Timely Spells*.

They landed with a soft thud, their feet touching down on a grassy expanse of lawn. Many varieties of flowers, some Linden recognized, but others completely foreign to her, rose on either side of them. The flowers waved in a soft summer breeze, casting a rainbow of colors—yellow, pink, red, purple, and also lime green, bright orange, and the same vivid blue as Katrine's short curls. Large red and orange hummingbirds, the size of Linden's fist, flitted about the flowers, feeding from the nectar.

"It's summer here, but it's autumn back in Valerra," said Linden, stating the obvious. "Is it always summer in Havynweal?"

"It depends on where you decide to set down. We have seven seasons occurring simultaneously, but this is my favorite, so I nearly always come here when I'm visiting Havynweal."

"Seven seasons?"

Katrine grinned. "Of course. You have them too, but you don't have names for them all. They're dead of winter, chilled spring, gentle spring, sweet summer—that's where we are now—auburn summer, harvest fall, and frosty fall."

Linden ran a hand through her blue-streaked black hair. "My grandmother did have a book called *Seven Spells for Seven Seasons*, but I thought it was just a play on words. You know, alliteration. But I guess not."

"Did you ever read it?"

"I never got the chance."

They were interrupted by the arrival of a miniature griffin, which skimmed the tops of the tallest sunflowers before dropping down to the ground in front of them. The griffin folded in its wings, cocked its head to one side, and rapidly clicked its beak. The clicking echoed around them, or more like behind them, and something brushed past Linden's legs with a loud squawk. "Kal? But how—"

Katrine laughed, a tinkling sound not unlike Mage Mother Pawllah's laugh. "Your little griffin hitched a ride with us. He wanted to visit Gloria, his mother."

The two griffins clicked furiously and flapped their wings in what looked almost like a hug. "His mother? You mean Kal was born here, in Havynweal?"

"Aye. Griffins are magical creatures, and like all magical creatures, they have their roots in Havynweal. But Kal chose to attach himself to you. So his mother transported him to that nest in Quorne where you found him two years ago."

Linden shook her head. "I had no idea Kal chose me. I thought I'd rescued him."

Katrine nodded at the two griffins, which were now rubbing their heads together and purring. "Every Liege has a mini-griffin as a companion. Liege Ayala's griffin had injured his wing the day before Ayala left Tanglewood for the last time.

When Ayala's griffin heard the Liege had been assassinated, he died shortly afterward, most believe of a broken heart."

"But how did Kal even know about me?"

"Everyone in Havynweal has known about you since before you were born. Gloria was convinced one of her offspring would become your companion. She flew to Valerra with each of her children and observed how they responded to the future Liege. Apparently Kal nearly hopped off her back when you came into view, clicking his beak and squeaking. Gloria knew right then that Kal had chosen to be your griffin, and so she left him in the nest for you to find."

Linden walked over to Kal and his mother and dropped to her knees. She put her arms around the two griffins, giving them a hug before rising to her feet. "Thank you, Kal, for choosing me. You've been such a comfort to me, and such a loyal friend. And thank you, Gloria, for allowing your son to come live with me."

Kal tucked his head shyly beneath one wing. Gloria gave a small bow and opened her beak and clicked. As she clicked, Linden realized she could understand what the griffin was saying. Her head spun as Kal's mother addressed her. Linden forced herself to concentrate on the words coming out of the elder griffin's beak. "You are welcome, Lady Liege. I am honored my youngest son has chosen to be your companion. He serves in the household of the Liege of all Faynwood, the protector of fays, Faymons, woodlands, streams, and all creatures therein."

"That's, well it's, um...that's amazing." Linden wasn't usually tongue-tied, but she was having trouble coming to grips with the whole idea of talking to a griffin. "I didn't realize griffins could speak."

Gloria nodded. "Aye. It is a function of where we are standing, as it were. Animals can speak in Havynweal if they wish." Gloria gently pecked Kal's mane and said, "It was good to see you again, my son. I will not interrupt your important business here any longer. Good day to you, Lady Liege, Lady Katrinareus." Gloria flapped her wings and soared into the sky. Kal watched until Gloria was no more than a tiny speck, and then he nestled against Linden's knees. She bent down to rub his mane.

"I'm so glad to have met your mother. She is quite dignified."

Kal opened his beak. He clicked and sputtered a few times and finally croaked out his first words spoken to Linden. "Mother has always been a stickler for formality, concerned about upholding the family name and all. I hope we can come again and have a longer visit." He glanced up at Katrine. "And now shouldn't we meet the others and find us some ensorcelled rope?"

"Aye," Katrine sighed. "There's nothing like a loyal griffin to keep us focused on our mission. But first, we're going to need something warmer to wear." She clapped her hands, and Linden found herself covered in a fleece-lined black trench coat, a pair of sturdy boots on her feet. Katrine wore a matching coat and pulled on some gloves. Nodding at Linden's coat pockets, Katrine said, "Best get those gloves on, lass. We'll be traveling to dead of winter. 'Tis the season for conducting war councils, for speaking of Fallow sorcery and how to defeat it."

Katrine snapped her fingers. Havynweal seemed to revolve around them, a kaleidoscope of colors, smells, sounds, and seasons, and then the world snapped into place once again. They stood in a snow-covered valley, dotted with dark green fir trees and holly bushes with bright red berries. Towering mountains surrounded them, their icy peaks sharp and jagged like pointy teeth. A pair of white squirrels scurried up the nearest tree, chattering at the interruption. Kal dashed after them, calling out, "Don't worry, I won't hurt them. I just need to stretch my legs. And I love the dead of winter!"

Linden squinted as the sun peeked out from a cloud, lighting up the valley and mountains in a blaze of white. In the center of the valley stood a large gazebo, wide enough to accommodate twenty people or more. The gazebo seemed to be formed from cut crystal, its roof and pillars gleaming brightly, reflecting points of light from every facet. She pointed, "Look, I see someone waiting over there."

Linden and Katrine trudged through the snow toward the gazebo, their boots crunching as they walked. As they neared the crystal building, Linden saw the person waiting inside was bundled in a long fur coat with the hood pulled up. Given his size and bulk, she thought the person was probably a man. His back was turned, and he faced the other side of the valley, as if searching for something or someone.

When they were twenty paces from the gazebo, Katrine stopped walking and nodded toward the man. "Go on ahead, you need to have this conversation alone." Linden tilted her head at Katrine and then looked at the man again. Although he was wrapped in furs and still had his back turned, there was something familiar in his stance. He shifted a bit and she noticed he favored one leg. Linden's heart thudded in her chest and she took a ragged breath. She picked up her pace, jogging toward the man in the gazebo. He heard her boots hitting the snow and turned toward her, a smile lighting up his face. She ran up the steps and into his outstretched arms.

Corbahn drew her close and whispered into her hair. "Am I really holding you? Or is this another of my dreams, and when I wake, I'll be clutching at the air instead?"

Linden nestled deeper into his broad chest. Standing in this frozen valley, Corbahn's arms around her, she felt as if she'd come home. If she could blink away all her worries and responsibilities in that moment, she would, and she'd keep right on blinking if only she could stay rooted with Corbahn in this spot. She smiled. "This is real, or at least, as real as anything else in Havynweal."

Corbahn pulled back just enough to tilt her face upward, his eyes the color of the Pale Sea locked onto hers, waiting. She knew he was waiting for her consent, not for this one kiss but for so much more. She nodded with a certainty that surprised her. *Hang all the prophecies and all the battles still to be fought and won. I long to be with this man, this stubborn, argumentative clan chief, this leader of the most troublesome clan in Faynwood.*

Their lips touched, their kiss slow and tentative at first, and then quickening into a searching, deepening expression of everything they meant to one another and never said aloud. Corbahn wound his hands through Linden's hair, sending shivers down her spine that had nothing to do with the frosty air. Linden decided a kiss could convey feelings so much better than words.

Corbahn pulled away with a shaky sigh. "We'll have company soon enough, so let me say this here and now. I don't care a fay's breath about seers and psychics and whether our timing is wrong or right. I know only that I love you, Linden Arlyss of Tanglewood. When we've defeated my crazy clansman and sent him back to the realms of the dead, and when we've freed Valerra from the grip of Fallowness and the boot of Glenbarra, well then..." He paused and took a deep breath. "Well then, I want no more half-life, no mere dreams of you in my arms. I want to wake up each morning to the reality of you in my arms. When this war is over, will you join me in the rites of binding?"

Linden's pulse quickened, the butterflies in her stomach performing joyful somersaults. She stood on her tiptoes and placed her palms on each side of his face. She kissed him full on the lips. "Aye, Corbahn Erewin of Arrowood," she said, her eyes unexpectedly damp. She laughed through her tears and repeated more softly, "Aye." Laughing along with her, Corbahn wrapped her in a bear hug and kissed the top of her head.

Linden heard some throat clearing nearby and stepped back with a sigh. *So much for staying rooted in this spot, without a care for anyone or anything beyond Corbahn and me.* She turned around, Corbahn draping an arm around her waist. Katrine stood at the entrance to the gazebo, smiling broadly at them. Kal skittered to a stop next to Katrine, looking slightly guilty. Linden hoped he hadn't been teasing those lovely white squirrels.

Katrine bowed to Corbahn, a twinkle in her eyes. "Well met, Chief Corbahn Erewin. It's a pleasure to meet the head of the Arrowood clan. I'm Katrinareus the Fifteenth, though my friends call me Katrine."

Linden arched her brows when her fay friend introduced herself as Katrinareus the Fifteenth. She wondered whether all fays had unusually long names that they shortened when dealing with humans. Pryl had told her his full name was Archipryllius Orion the Fourteenth, although technically he was Chief of the Fay Nation, so perhaps only fays in government positions had such long official-sounding names. If that were true, what did that make Katrine? She certainly seemed to have a lot of power. Maybe any fay could snap her fingers and have the world revolve around to a new season, but Linden doubted it.

Corbahn returned the bow. "Well met, Katrine. I believe you are responsible for this brief interlude, so Linden and I could meet in private?" When Katrine nodded, Corbahn continued, "Then I thank you with all the gratitude I possess."

Katrine crossed the glass floor of the gazebo as she spoke. "It does my heart good to see two people who love each other have the chance to declare their feelings. However, a fay's motives are never straightforward." Katrine stood before them and withdrew Corbahn's sword from the scabbard at her waist. She laid the sword lengthwise across both her palms, and bowing slightly, presented the sword to Corbahn. "I believe this is your property, Chief Corbahn."

Now it was Corbahn's turn to clear his throat. "While I briefly owned this sword, it stopped working for me months ago. I gave it to Pryl before he left Arrowood." He cocked his head to the side. "How did you..."

"It's a bit of a long story," said Linden. "However, Katrine believes this sword is yours and only yours. It's not responded to anyone else's touch." She nodded at Katrine's outstretched hands. "Could you try again?"

Shrugging, Corbahn reached over and wrapped his calloused hand around the hilt of the sword. He raised the sword up, as if leading a battle charge, and gold hieroglyphs lit up along the blade. "It's working again! But I don't understand—how did you repair it?"

Katrine laughed. "I merely helped to repair the rift between the two of you. I brought you together in this brief interlude, as you called it. You did the rest."

Linden put her hand over Corbahn's, and the sword glowed a deeper gold. They looked at one another in surprise. Linden explained, "It's your magic, working with the fay magic in the sword, which causes it to light up with power. Katrine believed your magic was blocked because of how things were left between us."

Katrine handed Corbahn his scabbard. Sheathing his sword, he strapped his scabbard around his waist and reached out to grip Linden's gloved hands in his own. "So by healing my heart, you've unblocked my magic as well? What sort of spell is this, my Liege?"

A cloud of traveling mists interrupted them. Efram, Reynier, and Jayna emerged from the vapors. A grinning Reynier said, "We thought we were here to discuss battle plans. Did we make a wrong turn somewhere?"

Corbahn and Linden laughed as they greeted the new

arrivals and introduced Katrine. Efram bowed low to Katrine and seemed almost shy around the older fay. Jayna wrapped her arms around both Linden and Corbahn. The gazebo filled again with traveling mists, and more voices emerged from the vapors. Wreyn and Pryl arrived, and traveling with them were Chief Serai of Shorewood, Chief Hemma of Ridgewood, and Chief Orlaf of Riverwood. With the exception of Katrine, everyone was well acquainted with another, some old friends, others former enemies who'd become allies during the past year. After initial greetings and bows of acknowledgement were exchanged, the group inside the gazebo grew silent.

Katrine was standing off to the side and approached Pryl. Bowing low, she said, "Well met, Chief Archipryllius Orion the Fourteenth. It's been a long time."

Pryl returned the bow and said quietly, his voice catching, "Well met, Lady Katrinareus Orion the Fifteenth. It's been a long time indeed. Too long." Pryl took a tentative step toward Katrine, his arms outstretched. Katrine closed the gap between them, and they hugged each other.

Linden's eyes widened; she noticed Pryl used the same surname for Katrine as his own. She glanced at Wreyn, standing nearby. Her fay friend sidled closer and whispered, "Katrine is Pryl's half-sister. Rumor has it they haven't spoken in years. As you've probably guessed by now, fays are even more stubborn than humans."

"Half-sister?" Linden stared at Katrine, who apparently was her great-aunt—although Linden couldn't imagine calling her anything other than Katrine, never Auntie Katrinareus—and she looked for any family resemblance. Linden and Pryl shared the same shale gray eye color, while Katrine's eyes were dark brown. Katrine and Pryl were the same height, tall for a woman and certainly taller than Linden, but then again nearly everyone was taller than Linden.

Ah, thought Linden, *it's her nose*. Katrine and Pryl had the same proud aquiline nose as Linden's father. Linden had inherited her mother's smaller, straight nose, for which she'd always thanked her lucky stars.

"Aye," nodded Wreyn. "Pryl's mother passed on when he was a small child, and his dad remarried. Katrine is quite a bit younger. Pryl has always been more of a second father to her. He became her legal guardian when she was still underage, after both parents died."

"Katrine told me she grew up on Sanrellyss Island, living and studying with the sisterhood."

"It makes sense Pryl's father would have sent her to the Sanrellyss Sisters for her formal education," said Wreyn. "After Pryl became fay chief—and a very young fay chief at that—he would have wanted her to continue her education without interruption. Besides, he wouldn't have had the time to raise Katrine properly, who by all accounts was quite a handful."

Pryl glanced at the group standing about and said, "I suppose we could use some chairs."

"Here, allow me." Katrine snapped her fingers. A round glass table with eleven white chairs appeared off to one side of the gazebo. She snapped her fingers again, conjuring a white marble fireplace with a cheery fire inside.

"Thank you, Katrinareus. The fireplace is a nice touch." Pryl headed over to the table and sat in one of the chairs with a sigh. Linden thought he looked weary, as if the weight of the world—or at least their continent—rested on his shoulders. The rest of the group gathered around the table and pulled out the chairs, which slid across the surface of the crystalline floor without making a sound.

When everyone was seated, Pryl nodded at Chief Orlaf, who spoke into the silence that had descended around the table, "After suffering heavy losses, which would have been far heavier had the other clans not contributed warriors—" Orlaf paused, giving each of the chiefs a bow before continuing "—I can report Riverwood is holding the border with occupied Valerra. In fact, we've pushed the Glenbarrans back across our perimeter wherever they had broken through. However, we will need to hold fast to our positions, which means I'll not be able to contribute any warriors to retaking Valerra." Linden was disappointed but not surprised, given Riverwood's location, stretching across the northern boundary with Valerra. She wondered whether Arrowood, which shared a common border with Glenbarra to the west, was likewise too bogged down to help. She didn't have long to wait for her answer.

Corbahn's deep voice echoed off the crystal ceiling and pillars of the gazebo. He thanked the other clans for contributing warriors and mages to the defense of Arrowood and then went on to explain that like Riverwood, his clan was able to hold their positions; in fact, they'd driven any would-be invaders back across the Windrun River, into Glenbarran territory.

"It's no surprise to any here that we're in a similar position to Riverwood. Although we're unable to contribute a company of warriors, I will accompany the Liege back to Valerra." He stood up and withdrew his sword, the blade pulsing gold. "We will face Mordahn again, and this time, we will defeat him." Linden wondered whether Corbahn would feel as confident about defeating Mordahn once he realized they'd have to send him back to the realms of the dead. On the other hand, Corbahn had been raised on the old fay stories and prophecies, so perhaps he already suspected as much.

"Who is leading the clan in your absence?" Chief Hemma frowned.

Corbahn re-sheathed his sword and took his seat once again. "My mother is now leading the clan—temporarily, I hope. I trust that no one needs reminding of her credentials." He smiled, but his sea-green eyes remained steely.

Hemma shook her head. "We all know Beryl was clan

commander for many years, until your brother Riordahn came of age. But it's been a long time, and we can't take chances with the western border of Faynwood. If Arrowood falls, every clan will be at risk."

Linden sensed Corbahn tensing next to her, and she put a hand on his arm. He took a deep breath, and then another, before replying. "Commander Beryl has been fighting in the forests of Arrowood for these past few months, training my sister Carissa and serving as my number two. I can assure you, she is more than capable."

Pryl rose from his seat and leaned on the table for emphasis. "I have full confidence in Commander Beryl and the Arrowood clan. They will hold the border. We must focus on defeating Mordahn, and freeing Valerra from the boot of Glenbarra. Otherwise, Faynwood will fall, and with it, Serving Magic." His shale gray eyes bored into Hemma's, and when she nodded in agreement, he continued. "Now that's settled, I trust that Ridgewood and Shorewood will be contributing men and women to the fight?"

Chief Serai remained seated and spoke quietly but firmly, "Shorewood will contribute half our clan's warriors and mages. We would contribute more, but all the rest are in Riverwood and Arrowood, helping to secure the borders."

"Thank you, Chief Serai," Pryl bowed before taking his seat. "Future generations will sing of the generosity of the Shorewood clan."

Chief Hemma stood up, waving her hand in Pryl's direction. "Aye, 'tis a generous offer, and one the Ridgewood clan matches. We will contribute half our fighting force. You have my word."

Pryl thanked Hemma for her generosity and praised the fighting skills of the Ridgewood clan, considered the best archers among the clans. Clearly mollified by Pryl's words, the clan chief sat back down with a satisfied nod. Linden found herself impressed with her grandfather's political skills, despite the fact she knew he negotiated all the time as fay chief. She didn't think she'd ever be half so accomplished, and she didn't really want to be either.

Reynier cleared his throat and ran his hand through his blue-streaked hair. "Tanglewood has already contributed half our clan to the border wars. I will lead our remaining warriors and mages into Valerra. We'll march down from the north and snake our way along the beaches until we reach Bellaryss. Fighting alongside the Shorewood and Ridgewood clans, we will defeat the Glenbarrans. Frankly, we have no choice."

After Pryl thanked Reynier and the Tanglewood clan, he said, "As all of you know, the fay army is preparing to retake Wellan Pass and march all the way to Bellaryss. It won't be easy. King Roi is a formidable military leader, and he'll be commanding the Glenbarran army. Even so, we believe we will win the battle on the ground." Pryl hesitated and glanced over at Linden.

"I sense there's a 'but' in there somewhere. What is it?" asked Linden.

Pryl's hesitations usually meant bad news was about to be delivered. "I think it's time you tell us about what happened in the museum and how you intend to defeat Mordahn. I believe this last part is where my sister has a role to play."

Linden blew out a puff of air, and staring into the fire, told them about meeting the super-grihms in the tunnel and how the grihms helped get them into the museum. Corbahn gripped her hand harder as she spoke. She described how they had to fight off Glenbarrans, grihms, and Mordahn and his undead protectors. Wiping at a tear that rolled down her cheek, she told them how Mage Mother Pawllah came to them across the lake and handed her the Sollareus crystal, which Linden used to complete the cleansing ceremony. She stopped speaking and turned to Katrine, "Perhaps you should tell the rest of the story, and about our plan to send Mordahn back to the realms of the dead."

Katrine picked up the thread of the story, from the time Vas and the rest of the group showed up at her shop, and then she told them about the Swords of Five. When she was finished, Reynier spoke first. "But that's just an old myth. You don't really believe the fay-spelled swords from the Valerran Museum are part of this legend, do you?" He placed a gloved hand on Jayna's shoulder, as if protecting her from the need to take up her sword again. Linden felt sorry for Reynier, but she knew her best friend. If they needed Jayna to fight Mordahn again, nothing and no one could prevent her from joining them.

Corbahn leaned forward and addressed Reynier across the table. "This is more than an old myth, my friend." He glanced around at the other chiefs and continued. "I know most of you believe Arrowood to be the most troublesome of the Faymon clans, and the one most likely to run toward dark magic. Unfortunately, Great-Uncle Mordahn is living proof of our less than stellar reputation. And because we understand how easily one can turn from light to dark, from good to bad, from Serving magic to Fallow sorcery, we study the old scrolls, prophecies, and legends. I'm familiar with this story, and I believe Katrine is right—we must send Mordahn and his protectors back to the realms of the dead—and we will need the five ensorcelled swords and a length of fay-spelled rope to do this."

Jayna gently removed Reynier's hand from her shoulder and threaded her gloved fingers through his. Looking into his eyes, she said, "No one else can wield my sword. I need to do this. Nay, I *want* to do this. We'll never have peace until we've defeated Mordahn."

Reynier raised her hand to his lips for a kiss and sighed. He turned back to Corbahn and the other chiefs gathered around the table. "Jayna, Linden, and Corbahn, along with Mara and Remy, own the Five Swords, which means they need to be the ones to capture Mordahn and his protectors. But where can we find the fay-spelled rope mentioned in the legend? And who will lasso these undead creatures?"

Katrine asked Pryl, "Is Mother's rope still in the back of my wardrobe?" Pryl nodded slowly, worry lines creasing his brow. Katrine ran a hand through her short blue curls. "My mother was a reaper, but a special kind." There was a sharp intake of breath, and she held up her hand to explain. "Mother sent the undead back to where they belonged. I come from a long line of such reapers—known as extractors—women and men whose job is to ensure the dead stay that way."

"But Katrinareus has never been formally trained," said Pryl, "And this particular extraction would test the mettle of any reaper."

"That's not exactly true."

"What do you mean?"

"That I haven't been formally trained," said Katrine. "There was an elder on Sanrellyss Island, a distant cousin of Mother's, who trained me. We used to perform extractions together."

Pryl's eyebrows rose at the news. Linden sensed he had a lot of questions about Katrine's years with the Sanrellyss Sisterhood, but he cleared his throat and asked, "Have you performed any extractions since you left the island?"

Katrine said, "The dead have stayed dead in Valerra, at least until recently. It was one of the things that I liked particularly well about living there."

"So in other words, you haven't lassoed anyone in nearly forty years."

"I didn't say that. It's true I haven't lassoed any undead since leaving the island. But lassoing is a useful skill, and I've kept up my practice using normal rope. I help out at a few horse farms in Bellaryss. When there's an especially stubborn horse that needs training, the breeders call me. I've even taught some of the stable lads over the years how to lasso."

"Sending Mordahn and four protectors back to the realms of the dead will require more than one reaper." Pryl shook his head. "I don't see how you're going to be able to do that on your own, regardless of your skills."

"Katrine won't be alone. She'll have us with her." Linden waved her hand to indicate herself, Corbahn, and Jayna. "We can keep Mordahn and his minions busy while Katrine works her extraction magic."

"But Katrine trained with an elder and they worked as a team. Her mother never worked solo, until that last time." Pryl paused and then said more softly, addressing Katrine, "I'm not a fan of history repeating itself. I loved her too, you know."

Katrine looked down at the crystal-clear table and bit her bottom lip. "It's true. Mother always worked with at least one other reaper, except for the one time. A nasty fay sorcerer had been raised, and she decided to take him on herself, since her partner was away visiting his brother. Mother's golden lasso turned up a few days later, in the spot where she was last seen. That's when we knew she'd been pulled into the realms of the dead, along with the dark sorcerer." Despite her layers of warm clothing and the roaring fire, Linden felt goosebumps rise on her arms and a tingling at the back of her neck. She couldn't imagine being drawn into the realms of the dead while still alive.

Wreyn had been listening intently, watching the exchange between Pryl and Katrine. She said, "I'll go with you. I may not know how to use a lasso, but I can hold the rope for you."

"Aye, I can help too," piped up Efram.

"I appreciate the offer," said Katrine, "but it's the lassoing where I'll need the help. Besides, I think your talent as scouts and messengers will be in more demand than ever once the fighting starts."

Pryl nodded, "Katrinareus is right. We need the two of you to keep all of us informed, so we can coordinate on the battlefield. Our timing has to be precise."

Something had been nagging at Linden, and she suddenly realized what it was. She turned to Katrine. "You mentioned you trained stable lads over the years. Any chance one or two of them can lend us a hand?"

Katrine shook her head. "All the lads have gone off to war." She paused and said more slowly, "Although Vas's father trained horses for a living, and Vas himself is a fair hand with the lasso. We've had our share of lassoing competitions, mostly using string and bottles of lager, but nonetheless, Vas has come close to beating me once or twice."

"Alright then," said Reynier. "It sounds as if Katrine will have a partner to help her lasso Mordahn and the protectors. We have a plan of sorts. Let's talk about timing."

Pryl and the chiefs discussed how long it would take the clans to march from Shorewood down along the shoreline toward Bellaryss. They'd cast veils of drabness along the way and remain undercover until it was time to charge into the capital. The entire fay army could materialize in minutes, using traveling mists once they received the go-ahead. They would line up in their fighting formations inside Havynweal, on a field beyond the mountains for just such a purpose.

Pryl recommended that Efram and Wreyn travel with the Faymon clans, carrying messages and aiding with communication among the chiefs. Once they arrived on the beach outside Bellaryss, the fay scouts would travel back to Havynweal to inform Pryl the clans were in position.

As soon as the fays materialized on the plain below Wellan Pass, Wreyn would rejoin the Faymon clans on the beach, and the fighting would begin. Efram would remain with Pryl as his envoy, carrying messages to the other fay leaders on the ground. Wreyn would serve in the same capacity with the

Faymon clans on the beach. Inside Bellaryss, the resistance was already primed to take out their targets as soon as the battle was underway, which would quickly become obvious to every resident of the city.

Meanwhile, Linden, Corbahn, Katrine, and the rest of the group would draw Mordahn out somehow and capture him. That part of the plan was still the fuzziest, but Linden knew Mordahn wouldn't be able to resist an opportunity to capture or kill her. If it came down to it, Linden would serve herself up as the bait.

CHAPTER 25

While the chiefs debated the finer points of the battle plan, Pryl conjured up steaming mugs of mulled wine and platters of cheese, nuts, and dried fruits. Katrine left to retrieve her mother's rope and returned fifteen minutes later with the golden cords looped crosswise over her left shoulder, coming to rest on her right hip. Linden thought Katrine's eyes looked slightly misty, but she didn't remark on it.

Kal positioned himself between Linden and Corbahn, pecking at her chair. She bent down to pet his mane. "What is it, Kal?"

"We'll be leaving soon," he chirped. "And, well, I won't be able to speak once we're back in Valerra."

Corbahn's eyes widened. "Do all animals speak here in Havynweal?"

Kal cocked his head. "If they choose to speak, they have the ability. But some animals stick to their own language, while others prefer to hibernate and not speak to anyone for long stretches." Kal paused and addressed Linden again. "I just want you to know I'm happy being your griffin. That's all I wanted to say."

Linden kissed the top of his fuzzy head. "You are the best griffin ever. Love you." Kal leaned into her leg and clicked happily.

Orlaf, Hemma, and Serai rose from the table first. Wreyn would be transporting the chiefs back to their clans in Faynwood. She turned to Linden and said, "The next time I see you, the fighting will have started. All this planning, and we're almost there. Now be sure you don't get yourself killed or anything!"

Linden chuckled and told her to not do anything she wouldn't do. Wreyn gave her a sly wink and waved goodbye to the rest of the group. As Wreyn's cloud of traveling mists wrapped around the clan chiefs, she could be heard humming a delicate fay melody in her pitch-perfect voice.

Jayna and Reynier walked to the opposite side of the gazebo and shared a private goodbye. Linden waited until they finished embracing before giving her cousin a quick hug and wishing him good luck. As he left with Efram, Reynier brought his fist to his chest in a silent salute to them all.

Pryl clapped his hands and the table, chairs, and cozy fire vanished. As the cold settled in around them, Linden drew her coat collar more firmly closed. Pryl approached Katrine, taking her hands in his, and spoke quietly to her. She nodded and stepped back, swiping at her cheek. Linden didn't think Katrine was the type of woman to tear up twice in one day; she wondered whether Katrine expected a similar fate to her mother's.

Pryl shared a few private words first with Jayna, and then with Corbahn, before approaching Linden. He gripped her gloved hands and said, "We've reached the point where our present lives have outpaced the prophecies. My dreams and visions are a befuddled mess. It's as it should be. None of us can truly know the future. I don't know whether we will meet again, so let me say this: no one could be prouder of his granddaughter than I am of you." Pryl kissed her forehead and took a few steps back. The mists enveloped him before Linden could do anything more than whisper goodbye, her throat thick, her heart heavy inside her chest.

"Are we ready to leave?" asked Katrine. The others nodded, and the traveling vapors twined around their legs. Linden felt a sudden chill and glancing down through the misty fog surrounding them, she saw their heavy layers of winter clothing had vanished. They arrived in Katrine's darkened kitchen in her flat above the shop. Linden had no idea how long they'd been gone, but the sound of snores coming from the book-lined parlor told her everyone was asleep. Just as well, she thought, stifling a yawn. She needed some rest before Tam and the others started peppering her with questions.

Katrine handed Corbahn a bedroll and pointed him in the direction of the snoring. "Stretch out with the other lads and try to sleep." Corbahn nodded and gave Linden a peck on her cheek before heading into the parlor.

Linden and Jayna followed Katrine down the hall to the bedroom. She handed them pillows and blankets, and they found space on the floor to lie down. Kal nestled in near Linden's feet. Before Linden drifted off to sleep, she heard Jayna softly whisper, "Happy birthday. Or belated birthday, I should say."

Linden opened one eye. "Huh?"

"The autumn solstice passed by weeks ago, along with your birthday, which I totally forgot. One year ago we were dancing at your Teenth."

The Teenth was a special Valerran celebration, commemorating a young woman's official coming of age at seventeen. Linden's Teenth had started out rough, when she learned her parents wouldn't make it in time, due to troop movements and road closures. Despite that disappointment, her Teenth party had been a lovely affair until the end. Disaster struck when her old boyfriend, Stryker, started a fight with Ian, another guest. They knocked over some lanterns during their scuffle, causing a fire to spread around an outdoor patio. Linden had used a water douser spell to put out the fire, but not before drenching herself and ruining her own party. So many people who'd attended that party were now gone, including Toz, Uncle Alban, Nari, and even Ian.

Linden yawned again and tried not to dwell on the sadness that threatened to overwhelm her whenever she thought about all she had lost. "That was another lifetime ago. But thanks for remembering."

"I just hope we're both around to celebrate your next birthday."

"Me too."

Linden had no sooner closed her eyes than Mara was shaking her awake. "Time to get up. Katrine and Remy are in the kitchen fixing us a snack, and then we're moving out."

Linden yawned and rose from the floor, stretching her back. Then she remembered Corbahn was in the flat somewhere, and she brought a hand up to her hair, which was a snarly mess. "I'll be along in a few minutes. Is Corbahn up yet?"

Mara grinned. "Aye, he's not only up, but Remy has introduced him to everyone. Last I saw, Corbahn and Tam were having a bit of a talk, just the two of them. I wonder who they might be chatting about?"

Linden groaned. "Well that sure motivates me to get a move on. Be right out." Linden slipped into the bathroom, splashed water on her face, ran a comb through her tangled hair, and gagged as she rinsed out her mouth with some of Katrine's homemade mouthwash. She looked at the mirror and shook her head. She was wearing clothes she'd borrowed the previous day from Katrine, when she changed out of the guard uniform—a black and silver belted tunic and black leggings—and yet, her clothes looked as fresh as if she'd just donned them. Katrine and her crazy fay magic, she thought. She's even found a way to freshen up clothes.

Linden heard chairs scraping in the kitchen and cautiously opened the door. She didn't think she was ready yet for Corbahn and Tam together, in the same room, overprotective boyfriend and overprotective brother. She took a steadying breath and headed down the hallway. When she entered the crowded kitchen, Corbahn glanced away from Tam and turned the full force of his gaze on her. He smiled, causing her pulse to quicken, and she smiled back. *Get a grip, Linden, we have work to do, seriously important work. The fate of Serving magic depends on it.*

She squeezed into a chair wedged between Corbahn and Jayna. Tam sat across from her, Nahn on one side and Mara on the other. Vas and Katrine took chairs at opposite ends of the table. Remy elected to sit at a stool near the stove, where he could serve the food, snag the leftovers, and listen to everything going on. Linden hadn't realized she was hungry, but her stomach rumbled as Remy placed a steaming bowl of cheddar-bacon soup in front of her. As she ate, the talk resumed around the table, with Katrine filling in Vas and the others about the meeting.

"What I can't get my head around is how we're going to capture Mordahn and his protectors," said Remy as he sat back down on his stool. Nahn and Tam offered up some opinions and everyone else joined the debate.

Linden listened as she slowly ate her soup, knowing deep in the pit of her belly there was only one way to lure Mordahn into a trap. During a lull in the conversation, Mara said, "Linden, you've been noticeably silent on this topic. What are you thinking?"

Linden pushed her empty bowl away. "Who does Mordahn hate, above all others?"

"Serving families," said Jayna.

Nahn added, "He hates Valerra, our prosperity and technology, even our way of life."

"Faynwood too, especially now our civil war is over, and the clans are reunited," said Corbahn.

"Mordahn hates anything he can't get his grasping hands around and control for himself," replied Vas. Mara and Remy nodded in agreement.

Tam cleared his throat. "Those are all true statements. But I think what my sister is getting at is a deeper, almost elemental kind of hatred. Mordahn despises the Arlyss family of the Tanglewood clan with a particular ferocity." An uneasy silence descended around the table. Tam continued, "And he hates Linden most of all. He's been targeting her specifically for more than a year, since the first border raid at Quorne, when her school and our home were attacked."

Corbahn reached over and placed his hand over hers, a gesture both comforting and protective. Linden wished she could curl up in his arms right then and there and forget about the fight ahead of them. She bit her bottom lip and focused. "Tam's right. Mordahn and I have a rare gift—or a curse, depending on your perspective—we're revelators, both mages and seers in equal balance. Liege Ayala, my great-grandmother, was the last Faymon known to possess this powerful gift." She looked at Tam. "Perhaps it's time to tell them the rest. I know Pryl spoke with you at the beach."

"I'll do my best. Fill in whatever I might miss or misinterpret." Tam took a sip of coffee from his mug before continuing. "Linden and I never met our grandfather, Orion Arlyss, because he'd died when our father and uncle were still boys. We knew only what we'd been told, that Orion and Nari had been Faymon refugees, distant cousins from the same clan who escaped from Faynwood at the start of the civil war. But the truth was more complicated and potentially more dangerous if it fell into the wrong hands. Our grandfather wasn't Faymon at all, but fay, and he wasn't just any fay, but Chief of the Fay Nation."

There was a collective gasp from everyone, except Katrine and Linden. Mara asked, "Wait a minute. Are you saying Chief Pryl is your grandfather, and Linden's?"

Tam nodded. "Aye, that's exactly what I'm saying."

"Then why did Pryl leave and let everyone think he was dead? Did Nari know he was alive all along?" Jayna shook her head, a thin line forming between her brows. "I don't understand."

"Pryl and Nari planned everything together, knowing that faking his death was the only way to keep others from learning the truth. They did it to protect their sons. Pryl told me he saw our grandmother whenever she traveled away from Delavan Manor. Most of the time, they met up at Sanrellyss Island," said Tam.

Katrine met Linden's eyes and gave a small smile. "There's perhaps one more piece of the family puzzle that I can fill in here." She turned to Tam and said, "I'm Pryl's half-sister, which makes me your great-aunt."

Tam arched his undamaged eyebrow. "I always knew there was something I liked about you, Katrine."

She waved her hand at him. "Hah! Aren't you the charmer? But wait until you hear the rest before you decide how you feel about me being part of your family tree." She explained about being an extractor, a special type of fay reaper, and described what it would entail to capture Mordahn and his protectors.

Silence descended around the table as everyone processed what they'd just learned. Remy popped a cracker in his mouth and crunched it loudly. "So let me see if I've got this straight. We need to lure Mordahn into the open somehow—probably by using Linden as bait, given how much he hates her. While Katrine is busy lassoing Mordahn and his protectors with the golden rope, the five of us with the ensorcelled swords are fighting off his minions—his Glenbarran guards and grihms. Is that about, right?"

"We're not using Linden as bait!" Corbahn, his voice a low growl, reached behind her chair and draped his arm around her shoulders. "It's far too dangerous."

"It's out of the question," agreed Tam. "We need a different plan."

"If Mordahn thinks he can capture me, or worse, he won't be able to resist. It's the only way we'll be able to get Mordahn to come to us," said Linden matter-of-factly, knowing her brother and Corbahn would come around. Ever since Pryl told her about his vision, or nightmare, of her final showdown with Mordahn, when she'd have to face him alone, she'd been wondering how it would go down. This must have been what Pryl had foreseen all along.

Katrine leaned back in her chair. "Linden is right. Mordahn won't be able to resist. He'll also be expecting a trap, which means he'll have plenty of reinforcements."

Vas sighed. "I don't like the idea of using Linden as bait either, but I'm not sure we have much choice. I also don't see how Katrine is going to be able to lasso all those protectors, and Mordahn, by herself—even with ensorcelled rope."

"I wasn't planning on working solo. Reapers work in pairs." Katrine waggled her eyebrows at Vas. "Fancy putting your lassoing skills to work, doing something more useful than snagging bottles of lager?"

Vas ran a hand through his beard. "Of course I'll help you, Katrine. But first, I'd like to practice on something larger than a beer bottle." Everyone laughed, which helped to break up the tension around the table.

"Where do we come in?" asked Nahn, waving her hand to indicate Tam and herself. "I can't lasso, but I can sure use a sword."

"Or bow and arrow, lance, dagger, pretty much any other weapon," said Tam. "If Mordahn is expecting a trap, you're going to need help."

"Let's not forget the most important weapon of all." Linden looked steadily at her brother.

He frowned in confusion, and then his brow cleared when he realized what she was saying. "You're going to need me to conjure a defensive shield."

Linden nodded. "A very special shield. It needs to keep anyone we capture inside, and anyone else—like Glenbarran troopers, grihms, and undead riders—outside."

"The shield will also need to keep out anyone attempting to emerge from the realms of the dead," said Katrine.

Tam whistled. "I'm going to need some help constructing the incantation."

Katrine left the table and returned moments later with a slender volume, which she handed to Tam. "Take this spell book along with you and study it. We'll work on the incantation together."

"It's bad enough fighting the living. I don't like the idea of being attacked by the dead too. It's creepy." Remy shuddered.

"I wouldn't worry too much about it if I were you," said Vas. "You'll be so busy fighting, you won't notice whether the hand holding the sword is living flesh and blood, or decaying bone and sinew."

"That's not very comforting," grumbled Remy.

Linden remembered the super-grihms in the shop's basement. "What about Farleigh and the others? Can they help us somehow?"

Katrine explained that while they'd been in Havynweal, Vas and Tam had recruited the grihms into the actual resistance network. They'd already left to prepare for their mission.

"Oh, I wanted to thank them for all of their help," said

Linden. "Maybe you could let them know if you're meeting them again?"

"If all goes well, you'll be seeing them soon enough and can thank them yourself." Katrine busied herself by starting to clear up the table. Everyone else pitched in, washing dishes, folding up bedrolls, and generally tidying up the apartment.

Katrine surveyed her flat, adjusted the books on her coffee table in the parlor, and went over to the tall wardrobe where Linden and the others stored their swords. Instead of opening the right side of the wardrobe and retrieving their weapons, Katrine opened the left side, which was filled with coats and jackets of various sizes and lengths. A separate shelf contained hats, scarves, and gloves. "Have a look and pick out whatever fits. Without those ugly Glenbarran uniforms, you'll need something to ward off the autumn chill."

Linden pulled out a black leather, hip-length jacket that fit her perfectly. She looped a soft gray scarf around her neck, pulled on a pair of black leather gloves, and belted on her sword and dagger. Linden transferred the lime-sized Sollareus crystal from the bottom of the wardrobe, where she'd stashed it for safekeeping, to the inside pocket of her jacket.

Corbahn found a dark brown leather jacket that made his shoulders look even wider, if that were possible, and matching leather gloves. Jayna, Mara, and the rest each found equally attractive jackets and accessories, all of which fit as if tailor made. Linden was beginning to recognize Katrine's special brand of fay magic, between the always-fresh looking tunics and slacks to the fitted leather outerwear. Katrine was a fashion-conscious fay, in addition to being a reaper and leader of the resistance. Linden decided her newfound fay aunt was pretty amazing.

Katrine opened the front door. "Go on down below, but don't turn on any lamps. I need to lock up tighter than usual." Linden took that to mean she would be casting another one of her forgotten spells, and probably boosting the protection wards around her home and shop. Vas led them down the stairs, everyone feeling the walls on either side of themselves to keep from tripping in the dark.

They waited for Katrine in the storage area at the back of the shop, near the entrance to the alley. Vas went to a large trunk wedged between stacks of boxes and supplies and lifted the lid. "Help yourselves to one of the backpacks. They contain a basic healer's kit, food rations, and a canteen of water. We always keep a ready supply in here." Linden looped the straps of one of the lightweight backpacks over her shoulders and stepped aside, wondering where exactly Katrine and Vas were taking them. Every time Linden asked about their destination, the conversation seemed to veer into another direction.

Katrine came down the stairs. She wore a navy leather jacket and had tucked her blue hair into a navy headscarf. The golden rope was slung over her left shoulder, and two swords hung from her belt. Grabbing one of the backpacks from the trunk, Katrine pointed to the doorway leading to the basement. "Let's stay below ground." Vas nodded and opening the door, led them down to the lower level. The room smelled like dog fur and bacon, a lingering reminder of the grihms who'd been holed up there.

Vas wound his way past shelves lined with boxes, broken toys, tools, nuts, bolts, and wire, to the back of the basement. He pushed aside several large crates to reveal a narrow door, about four feet high. "You'll have to duck, but once we're outside the building, you'll be able to stand up."

"Is it dry in there?" asked Mara, wrinkling her nose. Linden wondered the same thing, no doubt a flashback to the previous year, when the queen's demented half-brother had tossed them in the palace dungeon. They'd wound up using an underground passage filled with raw sewage to escape.

Vas drew his brows together. "It leaks a bit in the rain, but otherwise it's dry. Is there a problem?"

Mara flapped her hand. "No, I want to be prepared, that's all." Poor Mara hadn't been able to stomach the smell of the queen's sewers, retching periodically as they'd run through the sludge. Linden nearly chuckled at the memory, which somehow didn't seem appropriate given they were heading toward a final showdown with Mordahn.

Vas grabbed a couple of oil-filled lanterns hanging near the exit, which Remy lit with a snap of his fingers. Vas took one of the lanterns and passed the other to Nahn before going through the door. The rest of the group followed, Kal sticking close to Linden, the fur on his back standing up. Katrine closed and bolted the door, and then cast a softly mumbled spell in the fay language. All Linden could make out was a series of hisses and buzzes. Katrine's voice echoed in the tunnel. "Alright, let's move. The sooner we can stand again, the better. My sciatica is acting up. And no talking for the time being; our voices will carry upward and give us away."

Vas crabbed along and soon they were able to stand upright, although barely. They maintained a good pace, something between a walk and a trot, until they came to a three-way intersection. Linden figured they'd covered four or five miles by then, but she couldn't summon her internal compass this far below ground and had no sense of direction. Vas and Nahn held up their lanterns, casting light on what looked like a pile of rubble. As Linden moved closer, she realized the stack of rocks was actually a cairn.

Katrine skirted around the group and knelt down to examine the cairn. She picked up a stone and placed it on top. With a nod she pointed straight ahead, down the narrowest and least inviting of the three passages. Not that any looked particularly inviting. But Linden noticed a giant spider's web strung across the entrance, its intricate lacework a testament to how seldom that particular tunnel was used. She unwound her scarf and wrapped it around her head, copying Katrine's head covering. Vas removed a cap from his pocket and thrust it on his head. "Try to duck under the web," whispered Vas. "If anyone's on our trail, we don't want them to see the area's been disturbed."

"You don't have to worry about that," hissed Mara, taking the cap Remy offered her and plunging it on her head. "I'll do my best to give it a miss."

Jayna nudged Linden, pointing to a cute little beret perched on top of her head. Her dark curly hair flounced out all around her face, practically a magnet for spider webs. "This is all I've got."

Linden squinted at the large web and decided Jayna's hair needs were greater than her own. She unwound the scarf from her head and handed it to her best friend. "Here, let's trade."

Jayna accepted the scarf and handed over the beret. "Thanks. I owe you one."

Linden twisted her hair into a low ponytail, which she tucked inside the collar of her jacket. She pulled the beret down as far as it would go, figuring at least the top of her head would be bug-and-spider-free. "Don't mention it. I owe you a lot more than you owe me."

Linden glanced over at Corbahn, whose longish blue-streaked brown hair was tucked under a wool cap. He grinned, sending off another flurry of butterflies in her stomach. *Get a grip, Linden. You have to focus on Mordahn right now, not on how gorgeous Corbahn looks in his brown leather, and how his jacket is straining across his chest and shoulders.* She smiled at him and then quickly bent down to pet Kal's mane.

"Are we ready?" asked Vas. Everyone gave half-hearted shrugs as he ducked under the massive spider web.

CHAPTER 26

Tam and Vas took turns on point, periodically calling out warnings where the tunnel was crumbling and the footing uncertain. Cobwebs were numerous, and every so often, someone would screech when they walked straight into one.

The farther along they went, the more debris and loose rocks they encountered. Corbahn stopped abruptly in front of Linden, who bumped into his back. "Sorry," she whispered. "Why are we stopping?"

"It looks like the way is blocked up ahead."

"Katrine, I need your opinion here," hissed Tam.

Katrine wound her way from the back of the line to the front, while everyone else clustered behind her in the tight space. The tunnel had caved in ahead of them, forming a wall of rocks and rubble they couldn't possibly climb over. Tam and Nahn held the flickering lanterns high, their oil nearly spent, as Katrine stood with her hands on her hips surveying the damaged tunnel.

"What do you think? Try to move enough of this aside manually so we can pass or use magic?" asked Vas.

Katrine removed her glove to touch the debris and then pulled away her hand quickly. "This cave-in was caused by Fallow magic."

"So Mordahn is onto us then?" asked Remy, his voice half an octave higher than usual.

Katrine shrugged. "Not necessarily—and this doesn't have his magical signature. A Fallow mage of average abilities caused this damage. My guess is that every passage in this part of the tunnel system has damage. It's just one more tactic to thwart the resistance."

"And if we use magic to clear away the debris, then they'll know we've been here," said Nahn.

"True enough," Katrine said, "but we don't have the time to sift through this mess manually, so magic it is."

Linden adjusted her beret, deep in thought. "You mentioned something about Mordahn having a magical signature. Does everyone have a magical signature?"

Katrine turned to Linden. "Every mage has a basic signature to indicate level of proficiency and type of magic—Serving or Fallow. Master mages, though, have individualized signatures. So when I use magic, for example, another fay can tell it's me who's casting the spell."

"Is this something only another fay can detect? asked Linden.

"With practice, I can teach a master mage such as yourself how to read the signatures."

"And what about Mordahn, does he know how to read signatures?" asked Corbahn.

"Aye, somewhere along the way, he's learned that skill," agreed Katrine.

Corbahn narrowed his eyes at Katrine. "That's part of your plan then, isn't it? Have Linden cast a spell that would lure Mordahn directly to her."

Linden put her hand on Corbahn's arm. "This is no time for

a debate, and you know as well as anyone Mordahn is going to be difficult to capture. We need to use every tool at our disposal, and if that includes my magical signature, then so be it." Linden stepped forward. "Should I clear this away so Mordahn can track me down?"

Katrine shook her head. "Not here, lass. This is neither the time nor place to pick a fight. I'd do it myself, but I don't want to reveal myself just yet."

"You mean because you're a fay member of the resistance?"

"Not just that. I don't want him putting two and two together and realizing I'm the reaper who's come to haul his sorry, undead butt back where it belongs."

"I'll do it," said Tam, raising his hands.

"Not you, either." Katrine gently pushed his hands away. "We can't have anyone who was in the museum casting this spell—they'll be onto us in no time. That leaves Corbahn and Jayna."

"But Corbahn is Mordahn's great-nephew and Chief of Arrowood," pointed out Linden.

"I guess that leaves me." Jayna stepped around the fallen rocks to join Katrine in front of the wall of rubble. "But I'm going to need help."

"If I channel some of my magic into Jayna, and help her cast the spell, would that work?" asked Linden

Katrine nodded. "Basically, you'll be casting the spell together, but only Jayna's signature will show up."

"And since I'm not on anyone's radar, we shouldn't raise any alarms with Mordahn."

"That's the theory," said Katrine. "Alright, stand back everyone!"

Linden conferred with Jayna about which spell to use. When Jayna nodded to indicate she was ready, Linden stood directly behind her. Placing a hand on Jayna's shoulder, Linden furrowed her forehead in concentration, silently channeling her magic into Jayna as her friend incanted the spell.

"Remove this wall of rock and debris, restack this mess so we can pass!" shouted Jayna. The wall imploded in a plume of dust, the rocks and stones shifting themselves to one side of the tunnel. Jayna continued incanting until the spell had run its course, and the tunnel had a neat ledge comprised of rocks and stones that extended for a good twelve feet along the right side.

"Well done," Katrine pulled on her glove. "And now we'd better move ahead at double time. I want to be well clear of these tunnels before daybreak."

They jogged the rest of the way through the tunnel, stumbling occasionally over loose stones. Rats and other underground creatures chittered angrily at them before scurrying into their holes. Linden noticed Kal remained by her side, clearly not inclined to chase down any of the rodents in such a dank, dark hole of a passage. About the time Linden thought her legs were going to give out from under her, Tam slowed down to a normal pace. Linden peered around Corbahn and saw the floor of the tunnel sloped gently upward.

They cautiously climbed up the incline. Linden smelled fresh air ahead; they'd finally reached the end of the tunnel. Tam held up his fist to indicate everyone else should wait. Withdrawing his sword, he stepped out of the mouth of the tunnel, quickly scanned the area, and then sheathed his sword.

Linden stepped clear of the tunnel and took a few cleansing breaths, grateful she was no longer inhaling the stale, fetid underground air. It was still dark, though Linden could make out the barest band of midnight blue in the sky toward the east. Dawn would be coming soon, which didn't give them much time to find a good hiding spot. Linden listened and thought she heard the sound of the surf pounding the beach below them, some distance away. A strong gust of wind nearly blew the beret off her head. She pulled off the hat and stuffed it in a pocket. Something wailed nearby, sending shivers down her spine. The wailing grew louder as the wind picked up.

"Is that a wild animal?" Corbahn stopped in his tracks, his hand on the hilt of his sword.

Linden put her hand over his. "Wait, I think we must be near the Howling Cliffs. Is that where we're heading?" Although Linden had never visited the cliffs before, every resident of Bellaryss had heard of them. The cliffs, located south of the city, seemed to moan whenever the wind whipped through them, which happened pretty much all the time. The Howling Cliffs hugged the rim of the Pale Sea, a long shelf of limestone bluffs and caves that were buffeted by the wind all year round.

"Aye," said Katrine, "let's keep moving."

Linden waved her hand in the direction of the moaning. "Whenever the wind picks up, there's something about the formation of these cliffs and caves that causes the sound."

"It sounds unnatural to me," said Corbahn.

"The cliffs and caves are natural enough," replied Katrine. "For the time being, we're going to call them home."

Linden could sense Corbahn shifting uneasily next to her. She couldn't really blame him; living inside the Howling Cliffs sounded about as appealing as taking a holiday in Glenbarra. There was an eerie quality to the howling and wailing that seemed to be caused by more than just the wind. She wondered whether they'd find something not quite natural once they were inside.

Tam waved Remy over. "Can you cast a fireball to give us more light? The oil in my lantern's almost gone." Remy snapped his fingers, and a ball of bright orange light appeared inside his palm.

Katrine stood next to Remy and scanned the area around the tunnel. "There's another cairn around here we need to find." Remy enlarged the fireball and held it aloft. He rotated slowly in a circle while everyone fanned out, looking for the cairn.

"What about those rocks over there?" Jayna pointed to a stack of stones perched twenty feet from where they stood.

Katrine knelt down to study the cairn in the light of Remy's fireball. Nodding, she placed a stone on top of the cairn and rose to her feet. "We need to walk along the cliffs until we find the right cave entrance. Watch your step." Katrine and Remy took point together, the rest of the group falling in behind them.

The cliffs seemed a solid mass from a distance, without any entry points, but as they neared them, Linden could make out gaps and indentations. Sometimes the sound of the sea crashing onto the shore was loud, and other times it was more muffled. They picked their way slowly, careful to avoid slipping into a hole or tripping over a boulder. Katrine stopped in front of a thin slit in the rock face and dragged a reluctant Remy inside. She popped her head out a few moments later. "What are you waiting for? We've found it."

Linden and the others followed Katrine into a narrow, damp, howling alcove.

"Of all the places for us to hide out, why here?" asked Remy.

"I've been wondering the same thing," said Corbahn. "I figured it must have special significance."

Mara shrugged. "The only thing special about this place, as far as I can tell, is the enormous racket the wind makes as it whistles through the cliffs."

Katrine walked through the narrow alcove and headed into another cave, dragging Remy along with her. "Reserve your judgment for now. This is only the outer chamber."

They entered a second, larger chamber. Katrine asked Remy to light a couple of torches hanging in sconces on the rear wall. Linden arched her eyebrows, surprised to see someone had thoughtfully supplied torches inside the remote cave.

As the cavern filled with flickering light, "oohs" of surprise escaped from Linden and the others. They were standing on a wide limestone ledge, overlooking a crystal-clear underground river that emerged from the floor of the cavern. The river ran beneath their feet and flowed into the Pale Sea. The sea crashed against the outer wall of the cave, which had window-like openings in the rock face where the elements had worn down the hard surface of the stone. Linden could feel the spray from the river gushing into the sea, and the sea slapping up against the rocks.

The howling of the cliffs sounded different inside the chamber, taking on a more musical quality as the wind whipped through the porous rock face and swirled around the stalactites suspended from the ceiling above them. Something about the chamber seemed other-worldly, a place where nature and magic came together in perfect harmony.

"It's beautiful," breathed Linden. "I can feel the magical energy flowing through here. Is this another fay place of power?" Linden glanced around but didn't see anything that looked even remotely like a burial chamber, but something about the energy felt pure to her, almost elemental.

Katrine shook her head. "This magic is ancient, older than any of our ancestors, fay or human."

Jayna knelt down and dipped her hand in the clear river water. "There's strong healing energy here too."

Nahn furrowed her brow. "How about a hint, Katrine. What should we know about this place that you haven't told us?"

Katrine stared out at the Pale Sea, watching as the sky lightened from deep blue to orange-gold. "Keep looking out there. A few more minutes, and you'll see it for yourselves." She pointed to the outer wall of the cave, where the river water met the sea.

The bronze orb of the sun peeked above the horizon and the entire cavern filled with golden light. The air shimmered and separated, as if someone had pulled back a gauzy curtain. Instead of a crystal-clear river, the water on the other side of the curtain was dark and murky. Translucent figures gathered on the north shore of that other river, their faces tilted upward to the light. They sang a poignant melody in an unknown language, harmonizing with the wind as it whistled through the cave. The music filled the cavern and seemed to thrum with its own special energy.

Rowboats made of gray weathered wood lined the southern shore, as far as the eye could see. Men, women, and a few children, all as translucent as the willowy figures opposite them, entered the boats. The boats seemed to move of their own volition and crossed the river without anyone needing to take up the oars. A shout of joy went up as each boatful of passengers arrived. The new arrivals mingled with the figures on the other side, raising their voices together in song. When the last of them finished crossing, everyone faded from view.

Linden thought that must be the end of the vision, but she heard splashing and shouting as late arrivals struggled to enter the remaining boats on the southern shore. Fistfights broke out, as men and women raced to board the boats, pushing each other out of the way. Meanwhile, the river's current became rough and choppy. The boats entered the inky water, their passengers rowing furiously to cross to the other side. More fights broke out on the boats, with men falling or being tossed overboard, their screeches filling the cave as they thrashed in the water and were sucked under by the current.

A few of the boats capsized, tossing the passengers into the swirling, foaming river, which drew them down into its depths. Finally, just one boat remained; a dozen or so powerful strokes of the oar, and that boat would reach the opposite shore. Linden wondered what would happen when the boat arrived. *Would anyone be on hand to greet them? Were these tardy arrivals even welcome?* She didn't have long to wait for an answer. An eddy of water engulfed the boat, which spun inside the swirling current. Faster and faster the boat whipped around, the passengers screaming and cursing, some of them leaping out of the boat and trying to swim ashore. The watery vortex widened, grabbing swimmers, boat, and remaining passengers in one mighty wave and pulling them all under. The river seemed to let out a sigh, its currents calmed again, and the gauzy curtain closed. Linden found herself staring at the crystal-clear river again, as it coursed its way to the Pale Sea.

"What was that?" asked Remy, rubbing his eyes. "Was it even real?"

Katrine answered with a question of her own. "What do you think?" She glanced at the rest of them. "What does your gut tell you?"

Tam shrugged. "That was about as real as anything I've ever seen. But it was also a vision, because I'm looking at that same river right now, and it's nothing like that other place."

Katrine looked at Linden with raised eyebrows, waiting for her interpretation. "I agree with Tam," said Linden. "What we saw was very real, but also not of this world."

Katrine nodded. "As you've probably guessed, you caught a glimpse into the realms of the dead, or more precisely, the lowest realm, where The Crossing occurs."

Corbahn scratched his beard. "So is it safe to assume that everyone wants to get to the far shore, but not everyone is found worthy?"

"Aye, that's true enough."

Nahn asked, "What happens to those who don't make it to the other side?"

"I have no idea since it's not for the living to know these

things. But based on what I've seen, I don't think it's very pleasant."

"Let's take this a bit further," Linden frowned, thinking aloud. "Mordahn and his protectors would have been brought back here from the near shore. They never could have crossed over, given their unsavory natures."

"Aye. It's a safe assumption," said Katrine.

"When we send Mordahn back," said Linden, knowing there was a big "if" but plowing ahead anyway, "is there some way we can seal him in, so that no necromancer, no matter how powerful, will be able to raise him again?"

Katrine looked away and wouldn't meet Linden's eyes when she replied. "Possibly. There's a scrap of fay prophecy about it anyway."

Everyone groaned and stared at Linden, who raised her hands, palms out. "What? This prophecy business isn't my fault, you know." She waited for Katrine to explain.

Katrine waved her hand at some boulders. "Grab a seat." After everyone found seats, Katrine continued, "I know you're all familiar with the history of the fifty-year war in Faynwood, which began when Mordahn's father killed Linden and Tam's great-grandmother, the powerful Liege Ayala. Many seers predicted the Faymons would need to wait until the third generation for their new Liege to emerge and unite the clans."

She nodded at Linden. "Many seers claim we'll not be able to stop the spread of Fallow magic overtaking our land, that it will spread across the continent. But one seer predicts we will be able to stop the darkness, or at least limit its spread and influence. According to the prophecy, a small band of warrior-mages, led by the Liege, will capture the undead and return them where they belong. There is one exception, however."

Katrine looked directly at Linden, who picked a piece of imaginary lint off her leather jacket. This felt like a repeat of her conversations with Pryl, and Linden didn't want to go there again, and definitely not with Corbahn and Tam, the overprotective duo, staring at her. The silence lengthened until Linden said, "Except for Mordahn. I'm guessing this is the part where the seer said I'll need to face Mordahn myself."

Katrine nodded but didn't elaborate, so Linden finished the prophecy for her. "And even the seer can't accurately predict who will win in the end. Sometimes Mordahn defeats me, and other times I defeat him."

"I get the impression you've heard this all before," said Katrine.

Linden shrugged. "Pryl told me about it."

"Well this is news to me, and it's pure nonsense. There's no way you're going to face Mordahn alone," huffed Corbahn, folding his arms across his chest.

Tam agreed with him. "Corbahn's right. You're not facing him alone, no matter what. Besides, nothing about the future is set in stone."

"True enough, but just in case I do have to face Mordahn by myself, I'd like to have an inkling how to confine him to the realms of the dead." Linden stared into the river, hoping for a clue to emerge from the depths of the water.

Katrine removed her scarf and ran a hand through her short blue hair. "There's one clue, which unfortunately isn't very helpful. The seer says you will have everything you need to overcome Mordahn, but you need to believe."

Linden rolled her eyes. "Sounds like the kind of advice I'd get from my grandfather. Oh, wait, that's what he did tell me, more or less. Although to be fair, Pryl was quoting Mage Mother Pawllah, and what she said was I needed to have hope."

"Do you?" asked Jayna.

Linden drew her brows together. "Do I what?"

"Do you have hope?"

Linden kicked a rock with the toe of her boot. When she glanced up, her eyes met Corbahn's. He gave her a lopsided smile. She bit her bottom lip and returned his smile. "Aye," said Linden, her voice husky. She cleared her throat and repeated, "Aye. I have hope, and I have friends, and I have my ensorcelled sword. It's all good."

Katrine rose from her boulder. "On that note, I suggest we move to more comfortable accommodations, set up a watch, and get some shut-eye."

"Do these accommodations include something to eat? All this talk about Mordahn makes me hungry." Remy managed to rub his belly and stifle a yawn at the same time.

"Everything makes you hungry, lad," grumbled Vas.

Katrine chuckled. "I think we can rustle something up."

CHAPTER 27

Katrine led them down a passage into a spacious chamber. She directed Remy to light the torches on either side of the room. A fire pit had been set up at the far end of the chamber, where the porous limestone formed a natural vent for the smoke to waft out toward the sea. A cauldron sat above a neat stack of wood inside the fire pit, ready to use.

Along the left wall stood a row of barrels, which Remy immediately explored. The first three barrels contained root vegetables, onions, potatoes, and carrots. The fourth barrel held pickled eggs, the fifth barrel contained salt, and the last two barrels were filled with fresh water. Above the barrels, set into a ledge in the wall, were mugs, bowls, spoons and forks, as well as a few canisters, which Linden hoped contained coffee and tea. Dried strips of beef and pork jerky hung from hooks next to the barrels.

The right side of the room was set up for sleeping, complete with a stack of bedrolls and pillows. Linden suspected Katrine had made multiple trips using her traveling mists to ensure the room was well supplied. "Thanks for arranging all of this for us." Linden waved her hand. "This is a great place to hole up for a while."

Katrine shrugged. "I can't take full credit. These cliffs were often used as a stopover for merchant caravans, traveling between Valerra and The Colonies. The fire pit was already here, and so were the barrels, although they were empty. It was fast work to resupply the room."

"Though no one is making the trip these days," said Tam. "Not since the occupation." Linden thought of their parents, who'd made the arduous trip with their elderly aunts, fleeing south to The Colonies at the start of the war. Neither she nor Tam had heard from them since they'd left. While Pryl was convinced they'd arrived safely, due to his nearly infallible fay sixth sense, Linden would give anything to see them again.

"How did you know we'd need to use this cave as a hideout?" asked Mara.

"We set up a couple of other hideouts in and around Bellaryss," said Vas. "Partly in case we needed a place to stay for a night or two, and partly as a delaying tactic to throw the Glenbarrans off our trail. However, we knew we'd wind up at the Howling Cliffs in the end."

"I know you explained it, sort of, but I'm still not sure why we were able to see that vision at all," said Nahn.

Katrine waved her hand. "These cliffs were not forged by fay or human hands, but by earth and wind and water. The magic within these limestone caves is elemental, a force of energy that can be tapped by anyone with the know-how, by Serving mage or Fallow sorcerer. Elemental magic takes no sides, has no preferences; no one sings ballads about earth magic or wind magic; there are no scrolls to tell tales of magic so ancient as this. But every master mage, sooner or later, comes to recognize that the source of our magic is far older, deeper, and more mysterious than can ever be captured in song or scroll or tapestry. When that happens, the mage must make a decision: do I revere what I do not understand, or do I exploit it?"

Nahn frowned. "So are you saying Mordahn has found a way to exploit elemental magic to his advantage?"

"Not yet. There would be almost no stopping him if he does. But I believe he's been searching for a way to tap into elemental magic. His search will become more frantic now that we've destroyed the last place of power inside the museum."

"And that's what this is?" Tam rubbed his beard. "A portal that provides access to elemental magic and opens briefly at sunrise each day?"

"The portal opens at sunrise for four consecutive days—every fifty years. This morning was the first day of its opening."

Corbahn narrowed his eyes. "So the last time this opened was during the Faymon civil war?"

"According to my calculations, this portal opened about two weeks before Mordahn's father killed Liege Ayala, which sparked the civil war."

"Who else knows about this place?" asked Tam.

"Mage Mother Pawllah told me about the Howling Cliffs when I was preparing to leave the sisterhood years ago. While reapers can access the lower realms when escorting the newly departed—or recapturing an escaped spirit—Pawllah believed the portal inside these cliffs held a special power. She feared if this power fell into the wrong hands, it would spell the end of Serving magic. To my knowledge, she told no one else. I mentioned the portal to Pryl before leaving Havynweal. He knew nothing about it, although he wasn't surprised that one existed."

Linden tried to pull together the various threads of what Katrine was really saying. "So do you believe Mordahn's father found this portal, drew upon the ancient magic, and that enabled him to overcome Liege Ayala and her husband, both of whom were formidable warriors and mages?"

"Aye."

"If that's the case, then are we here to guard this portal or to use it to trap Mordahn?" asked Linden.

"Both, actually. We're here to guard this portal for the next three days. We won't do anything to attract Mordahn's attention until this portal closes up for another fifty years," said Katrine. "Afterward we'll make our move, let Mordahn think there's something in these cliffs worth exploring."

"What sort of a move do you have in mind?" said Corbahn.

Rather than answering Corbahn's question, Katrine glanced at Linden, who worried her bottom lip between her teeth, knowing there would be no going back. "The next move will be mine. I'll have to expose myself by casting a powerful enough spell to catch Mordahn's attention."

Corbahn shook his head. "I don't like it, not at all."

Tam grunted. "I don't like it either. But sooner or later we're going to have to do something dramatic if we want to capture Mordahn. I'd prefer to choose our timing and have the element of surprise on our side."

"What happens if he finds this place before the portal closes again?" said Jayna softly, asking the question on everyone's mind.

"Then it won't matter how many warriors and mages and fays we throw into the fight. Mordahn will be able to call up legions from the realms of the dead, an endless supply of undead soldiers, to do his bidding. Serving magic will be wiped out, and every last mage along with it."

Linden's stomach turned to lead at Katrine's words. She couldn't think about it anymore. She was too tired to sit and discuss Mordahn and what was to come. Linden covered her mouth to hide a yawn, but Vas noticed. "I'll take first watch. I wasn't traveling half the night to see Pryl and the clan chiefs. Why don't the rest of you grab a sleeping roll and get some rest."

"I'll join you," said Tam. "I'm not tired at the moment."

Remy, who was munching on a couple of pickled eggs, nodded. "I'll take second watch. That way I can cook up my mother's famous stew for our lunch. I guess I'll have to make do without tomatoes though."

Katrine pointed to the ledge above the barrels. "I think you'll find dried tomatoes in one of those canisters."

Remy's eyes lit up and he rubbed his hands together. "Then Mother's stew it is!"

"I'll join Remy on second watch," said Mara. "Besides, the aroma from his good cooking usually wakes me up."

Remy laughed. "It's true. Mara always manages to wake up when the meal is ready."

Linden didn't think anything, even the scent of Remy's mother's famous stew recipe, would be enough to wake her up. She spread out one of the bedrolls, removed her weapons, jacket, and boots, and laid her head on the pillow with a sigh. Kal circled around her feet a few times and then burrowed in. Corbahn dropped his bedroll nearby, pulled off his boots, and placed his sword within arm's reach. He whispered goodnight and rolled onto his side. Linden listened to his steady breathing, surprised at how quickly he'd fallen asleep. Of course, Corbahn's day had been as eventful as hers. She started to count backward from a hundred, drifting off before she reached seventy.

Linden dreamt of the river and Mordahn, the two of them locked in a deadly battle. She fought with everything she had, her sword, her magic, her wits, but never won. Every time, Mordahn overpowered her, pushing her head under the swift current until she sank into the depths of the water, and all she saw was the dark void beneath the waves.

Linden opened her eyes, fully awake in an instant. She smelled Remy's stew bubbling over the fire and heard the low rumble of his voice punctuated by the soft murmur of Mara's.

She felt discouraged and out of sorts, wishing for just once during her sleep she'd managed to vanquish Mordahn.

"Are you awake?" whispered Corbahn. He reclined on his side, leaning on his elbow as he waited for her reply.

Linden rolled onto her side so she could face him. "Aye. Slowly waking, more like." Corbahn's biceps bulged beneath the fabric of his shirt, and he looked refreshed after a halfway decent bout of sleep. She immediately regretted not having a comb handy to run through her tangled waves.

"I heard you last night. You must have been having a nightmare."

Linden winced, wondering how much Corbahn had heard. "Sorry about that. I hope I wasn't too loud."

He shook his head. "I only heard you hiss Mordahn's name a few times, and then what sounded like whimpering. That's why I figured whatever you were dreaming wasn't very pleasant."

Linden rubbed the sleep out of her eyes. "Aye. I'd like to forget my dream entirely."

"That bad, huh?"

"Let's just say I could take no comfort from it."

Corbahn's face softened, and he lowered his voice. "You're not alone, no matter what the vision might lead you to believe. I'll never abandon you to Mordahn." He waved his hand at the rest of the group behind him. "None of us will."

Linden pressed her lips together to keep them from quivering. "I know," she whispered, "that's what scares me the most."

Corbahn brought his brows together, momentarily confused. He realized the meaning behind her words and grunted, "Don't let him get inside your head. You've defeated him twice before. You can do it again. *We* can do it again."

Linden sighed. "I saw some things...this is going to be different, harder. And we know the stakes are higher."

"Do you want to talk about it?"

"I don't think it'll do any good, but perhaps someone else will be able to make something of it. Maybe it's best if I tell everyone at the same time." She shuddered.

"Based on the scents coming from Remy's cooking pot over there, I don't think you'll have long to wait."

"I never cease to be amazed by his skills with a cooking pot and the simplest of ingredients."

"That boy can cook; I'll grant him that. But he has some depth to him. Remy's not the fool he pretends to be."

Linden smiled wistfully. "He and Toz were very much alike in that respect. Always goofing off, in school and outside of it. Toz especially—he really was such a serious person—but he never showed that side of himself, until you'd gained his trust. Most people never saw him as anything other than a clown."

"You miss him, don't you?"

"Very much. He was my oldest friend." Linden still couldn't think of Toz's final moments without an ache in her chest.

"We've both suffered losses, heavy losses, thanks in part to Mordahn. The Glenbarrans could never have defeated Valerra without the aid of Mordahn's dark sorcery."

Linden knew he was thinking of his father, Haydahn, who'd been killed by Glenbarran archers while protecting her. "True enough. But we're reaching the end of it all, or at least, the end of our efforts to defeat him. Either we win this next round, or Mordahn wins. There will be no do-overs."

"Aye, in this game, winner takes all." Corbahn sat up and stretched. "Let's have some stew and mull over that vision of yours together."

After everyone had a mug of coffee and a bowl of stew, or in Remy's case, a bowl or three, Linden told them about her nightmare. Since she couldn't predict which aspects might prove useful later, she told them everything she could recall about how Mordahn defeated her. Or almost everything; she couldn't bring herself to describe the blackness at the very end, when she'd lost her life and sank into the river.

Linden stared into her mug, waiting for someone to break the silence. Corbahn reached over and grasped her hand firmly, demonstrating his feelings through touch rather than words.

Tam cleared his throat. "It's a sobering dream, but not a surprising one. Pryl had a similar vision, which he shared with me before we left the beach."

Linden recalled the part of Pryl's vision he'd shared with her, which basically came down to the showdown between Mordahn and her. No one could "see" the outcome. Linden wondered whether there'd been more to Pryl's vision than what he'd told her. "How similar was Pryl's vision?"

"It's hard to say, since Pryl described the final battle for Bellaryss and our battle with Mordahn at the same time. They all kind of blurred together, between the fay army fighting for Wellan Pass, the clans attacking from the beach, and the rest of us taking on Mordahn and his protectors," said Tam.

"When did the clan chiefs say they'd be in position on the beach?" asked Nahn.

Katrine pulled a log from a stack of wood in the corner of the room and tossed it onto the fire. She watched as it started to burn before retaking her seat. "The clans should start arriving on the beach, under a veil of drabness, tomorrow. It'll be another couple of days before most of them are in position."

Vas scratched his beard. "Three days of moving that many troops onto the beach and trying to keep it all on the down low is a challenge. The risk of exposure grows with each day. One false move, one mage who forgets and uses active magic anywhere near Bellaryss, and Mordahn will be all over them before they even have a chance. It'll be a bloodbath—not even the fays will be able to stop it in time."

Remy waved his spoon in the air. "And the portal is open for another three days?" When Katrine nodded, he continued.

"Too bad we can't distract Mordahn sooner than later, make him notice us so he doesn't notice the clans moving toward Bellaryss."

Katrine folded her arms. "I've been thinking the same thing, but we have no choice. We have to sit tight until the portal closes. Let's just hope the clans can keep themselves under wraps in the meantime."

Linden nodded, more to herself than anyone else. She decided a short respite from everything related to Mordahn would be just fine. In fact, it was exactly what all of them needed, a few days of normalcy before they had to face the end of everything, or the end of Mordahn. Either way, there would be an ending. She stood up, extending her hand down to Corbahn, who rose from the ground. He gripped her hand in his, a questioning smile on his face.

She addressed the group. "It seems to me we have a few days, at most, to relax before our showdown with Mordahn. I intend to make the most of this time." Smiling up at Corbahn, she said, "Are you up for a walk along the shore of the Pale Sea?" He nodded, his smile broadening as he followed her out of the chamber.

Katrine called after them, "The protection charms extend to the beach below the cliffs, so don't wander too far beyond that."

"And cast a veil of drabness while you're walking about, just in case," suggested Tam. Linden raised her hand and waved to acknowledge her anxious relatives. As she and Corbahn headed out, she heard Mara suggest to Remy and Jayna that they explore the cave a bit more. *Good, this is exactly what we need, the calm before the storm.*

Linden and Corbahn followed a gravel trail down from the bluff and cliffs overlooking the sea, until their boots hit the soft white sand of the beach. Hand-in-hand, they sauntered along the shoreline until they reached the mouth of the underground river as it coursed into the sea. The sun shone brightly overhead, the sky a clear blue. Linden pointed at the Pale Sea, its waves rolling toward the beach where they stood. "The sun is so bright today; it feels more like summer than fall. And look at the color of the sea—it's the same blue-green as your eyes."

Corbahn quirked an eyebrow at her. "My Liege, when did you first notice the color of my eyes and compare it to this beautiful sea?"

Linden knew he was teasing, but she wanted to answer him honestly. Who knew how much time either of them had left? "The first time we met, at the Arrowood longhouse. I'd just overheard you complaining to your father, telling him you didn't want to meet the new little Liege. I must confess I was quite angry with you at the time."

Corbahn had the good sense to look sheepish. He took her hand in his and peeled off her leather glove. He kissed her palm, slowly and delicately, sending shivers through her that nearly brought her to her knees. "I apologize for my boorish behavior. Of course, that was before I ever laid eyes on you. After our first meeting, you must admit my tune changed rather quickly."

Linden chuckled. "Aye. I suspect your solicitous attentions may have caused my ex-fiancé some heartburn."

Corbahn's brow furrowed. "Linden, I never meant to come between you and Stryker. I hope you know that."

Linden put a finger to his lips. "Hush. Stryker and I were already heading toward a breakup. He couldn't adjust to my new role as the Faymon Liege. Then he misused his magic, almost injuring you and your sister. Stryker's actions drove us apart—you have nothing to apologize for."

Corbahn swept Linden into his arms, holding her close against his chest. She inhaled his delicious scent of wood smoke and leather, and wished, hoped, prayed, that she'd be able to complete the rites of binding with this large, gruff, impossibly handsome man. Corbahn brushed his lips against her hair and whispered, "I will not allow Mordahn to destroy what we have—we will defeat him this time, together."

Linden wrapped her arms around his broad back and nodded. "Aye, together." She knew this was more wishful thinking than strategic planning, but she meant it with all her heart.

CHAPTER 28

"Any minute now," said Corbahn, peering over his shoulder. Linden nodded but didn't turn around, afraid she'd miss her final glimpse of the portal when the sun peeked over the rim of the Pale Sea. She'd been in the outer chamber every morning at sunrise to watch the drama unfold before her: the gauzy veil splitting open, the dark river water coursing by, and the ghostly figures crossing to the other side, followed by a second group of figures struggling across, and one by one, failing to reach the far shore.

One morning she'd seen an entire boatful of childish figures sailing across the water, and she wondered whether there'd been a school accident. Another morning more boats than usual crossed the water, each filled with clusters of men, women, and children. She thought perhaps a village had been raided somewhere.

Linden wasn't alone in her fascination with the portal. Everyone had been drawn to the outer chamber, waiting for the sun to light up the room and for the veil to open. Each morning she'd taken up a different position in the cave, looking into the portal from various vantage points. Moving around the chamber didn't seem to have any impact on how much she was able to see, and the angle always appeared the same regardless of where she stood. Every scene unfolded in the same orderly fashion, until the end when the people who weren't supposed to cross to the other side wound up pushing, fighting, and falling into the water.

This final morning she stood on a boulder that jutted into the river, her back to the rising sun. Corbahn stood beside her. Jayna, Remy, and Mara were clustered a little closer to the nearest wall, chatting quietly as they waited. Vas, Nahn, and Tam stood on the opposite side of the river, lounging against the smooth rock face of the chamber. Katrine arrived in the nick of time, wearing her golden rope looped around her left shoulder, and stood closest to the passageway that ran between the chambers.

Katrine had brought her rope with her each morning to watch the portal open and then close again. When Linden asked her why, Katrine had shrugged. "You never know when you'll need a bit of ensorcelled rope to wrestle something back to where it belongs."

Linden had frowned at the explanation. "But the spirits don't seem to be aware of the portal. None of them even look our way."

Katrine gave her a half-smile. "Best to be prepared when it comes to the realms of the dead."

The sun rose behind Linden, splashing the chamber with golden light and triggering the portal. As the silvery veil slid open, a loud clap rent the air, like the crack of a whip, followed by screeching and yowling that sent shivers down Linden's spine. She'd heard those sounds before, and they hadn't come from anything living.

Mordahn materialized in the chamber, emerging from fay traveling mists directly behind Katrine. He looked worse for the wear, his long-hooded robe hanging in tatters from his rail-thin frame, the hood pulled up over his skeletal head. His face was more bone than flesh, and what flesh remained was pockmarked with decay. Two orange sparks stared from his eye sockets.

Mordahn hadn't arrived alone—his four undead, screeching protectors accompanied him—and Wreyn, who stared straight ahead, eyes glazed over as if in a trance. Before Katrine could do more than half-turn toward Mordahn, he raised his boot and kicked her hard in the back. She yelped and flailed her arms as she fell headlong into the dark waters churning on the other side of the veil. Katrine struggled to swim, her head bobbing up for air several times before she was swept away by the current.

Wreyn didn't react but stood rooted on the spot. Whatever protective wards Katrine had set when they arrived at the Howling Cliffs offered neither protection nor warning against betrayal by another fay—that is, if Wreyn was even acting of her own accord. Linden heard the hobnailed boots of Glenbarran troopers pounding the ground as they filed into the chamber, surrounding Mordahn and his protectors.

Everyone drew their blades at the same time, troopers and resistance fighters. Linden glanced across the river to her brother, standing next to Nahn and Vas. Their eyes locked as he gave her the slightest of nods. Linden flexed her legs, every muscle tensed and ready to fight. She opened her mouth to yell, "Evakunouz," but no words came out. Confused, she tried to shout the war cry again as she charged Mordahn, but nothing happened. Her legs, like her voice, remained frozen. Her sword, normally glowing with green hieroglyphs around this much dark magic, remained a dull gray.

Linden realized with something like panic that Mordahn had cast a spell to freeze everything, magic, voices, and limbs. His magic was precise as a laser—he'd frozen only the resistance fighters in place. Their five ensorcelled weapons should be blazing green, gold, purple, blue, and red, but not a single colorful spark pulsed along their blades. *So much for the Legend of the Five Swords*, she thought grimly.

The troopers were still on the move, jogging over to Tam, Vas, and Nahn. Other troopers ran toward her and her friends. Linden had never encountered any magic this powerful. It left her feeling as vulnerable as a first-year apprentice.

The Glenbarrans surrounded them, their swords pointed at them with deadly intent. When the troopers were several feet away, a pair of junior officers approached Corbahn and Linden, dragging them farther apart. The officers unwound what looked like a length of black rope that hung from a loop on their belts. As one of the officers tossed the rope over Linden's head, it snaked around her torso several times, until her arms were clamped to her sides and her sword dangled uselessly from her fingers. She realized the rope was woven with twisted steel filaments, making it impossible for her to cast even the simplest of incantations, once Mordahn's freezing spell wore off.

A Glenbarran grabbed her sword and added it to the growing pile of resistance weapons stacked on the ground in front of Mordahn. Mordahn toed the swords with his boot, and then barked a command. Two troopers bent down, grabbed the stack of swords, and tossed them through the portal, where they landed with a splash, sinking immediately into the dark water. Linden couldn't move her head to catch Corbahn's eye, because he'd been shoved several feet behind her, but she sensed his quiet fury.

The officer who'd tossed the rope over her head now pointed his sword at her chest. Two troopers came alongside her and dragged her forward. Linden considered resisting, but without the use of her limbs or her magic, what could she accomplish? As they dragged her across the chamber, she scanned the activity inside the portal, wondering how much longer it would remain open. Most of the boats had crossed over the water, delivering their ghostly occupants to the far shore. Linden prayed the portal would close before Mordahn found a way to tap into the elemental magic inside the gauzy veil. Something about the way he stared into the portal made her think perhaps he'd already found a way, and her heart sank.

The Glenbarrans rounded up the rest of their resistance team, pushing and pulling them until they stood in a cluster on the same wide limestone ledge where Mordahn had kicked Katrine into the portal. Someone shoved Corbahn and he bumped into Linden, his hand grazing hers. She felt a surge of desperation, her hopes and dreams fracturing, as useless as her frozen magic.

Linden expected Mordahn to say something when she approached him, perhaps even strike her down on the spot. After all, she'd been ultimately responsible for dispatching him to the realms of the dead. Plus, she'd destroyed the places of power he'd used for his crossbreeding program. Instead, Mordahn grunted to his troopers, "Spread out the prisoners so they're facing the portal. Make sure they can't step out of line. It's almost time."

Linden felt the tip of a blade pressed against the small of her back and debated whether Mordahn planned to toss them into the actual river flowing out toward the sea, or the dark waters within the realms of the dead. The end result would be the same either way; without the use of their arms or their magic, they'd surely drown.

One of the troopers spun her around roughly and dragged her until she was lined up facing the portal. She stood directly behind Mordahn, who watched the action unfold inside the portal, no longer concerned with a small band of disarmed resistance fighters. Her legs felt rubbery, with the barest hint of feeling coming back into them. Soldiers dragged Corbahn, Jayna, and the others into place on either side of Linden.

Mordahn ignored the shuffling behind him. He stood in front of the water with Wreyn, staring into the portal. His creepy protectors surrounded him, two on his left and two on his right. Glenbarran troopers flanked everyone—Mordahn, his protectors, and Linden and her friends—keeping an eye on the portal while ensuring the resistance fighters remained in place. Given the freezing spell Mordahn had cast, that wasn't difficult.

The last of the boats landed on the shore, and the new arrivals were welcomed with song and ghostly embraces. As the music and figures faded from view, another set of spirits arrived on the opposite shore, and as before, the arguments and fighting started. A few boats managed to launch in the choppy water, their occupants struggling to row across the rapid current.

The gauzy veil started to close; it was nearly halfway across the portal when Mordahn hissed an incantation.

"Offer songs of praise, raise your voice in welcome:
Spirits at the river, spirits on the shore,
Cease your mindless worries, gather now as one—
Follow your new leader, travel to new shores."

Nothing happened. The chamber grew quiet, a pregnant pause that lengthened into a full thirty beats. Linden wondered whether the incantation, or the magic itself, had failed. Then Wreyn began to hum the same melody the figures on the far shore had been singing. She added words to the strange lilting tune, chanting in what sounded like the same ancient language. Her perfect pitch and tone seemed to be having an effect because the veil stopped closing. The portal was stuck halfway open.

Mordahn shoved Wreyn ahead of him until they stood mere steps from the portal opening. Linden spotted a thin silver collar encircling Wreyn's throat, as if Wreyn were bound to someone, indentured to serve a Fallow master. Linden shuddered at the thought of her proud, spirited fay friend being under Mordahn's control. A loud squawk rent the air, and Kal hurled himself at Mordahn's face, pecking at his eyes with his beak. Mordahn screamed, raising his hands to his face. One of his protectors threw a dagger at Kal, hitting the griffin in the side. Kal screeched and dropped like a stone into the portal.

Linden screamed Kal's name, but no sound came from her lips. She scanned the portal, searching the water for Kal, but he'd disappeared out of sight. Tears streamed down her cheeks as she screamed again. This time the hint of a whisper escaped her lips, more of a whimper than the wailing noise she was making inside her head. She realized the freezing spell was starting to wear off. Linden shuffled her feet, testing whether she could move her legs. They felt leaden but moved ever so slightly.

When Mordahn had raised his arms to cover his face and eyes from Kal's pecking, Wreyn stopped chanting, and the portal's gauzy veil started closing again. The protectors began screeching as one voice, the sound so loud and discordant it hurt Linden's ears. Mordahn looked around as if dazed, and then he raised his hands in the air, palms upward, the sleeves of his raggedy robe fluttering around his bony arms. His focus seemed to snap back into place. He gripped Wreyn's shoulder with one grayish, skeletal hand. The fay started right up again with her perfect chants, and the portal stopped closing once more.

Linden moved the toe of one boot slightly, confirming the freezing spell was indeed unwinding itself. She concentrated on swiveling her head to her right, her eyes locking on Corbahn's. She saw the love behind his glance, and the compassion. He knew how much Kal meant to her. Linden could see he was struggling to move, but the spell still had him firmly in its grip.

She turned back toward Mordahn, who inched closer to the portal with Wreyn. Linden began to suspect his plan—cross to other side, find the source of the magic, figure out how to mine it for himself—and she wouldn't let him do that. She flexed her knees and then gingerly put one foot in front of the other. With a burst of adrenaline and speed that surprised even her, she ran at Mordahn, head-butting him in the back.

He yelped and tumbled into the portal, dragging Wreyn along with him. Linden leapt through the gauzy veil, determined to stop Mordahn and search for Kal and Katrine. As she fell, she passed through layers of smoke, vapor, and watery mists. She heard voices call to her, but she couldn't make out the actual words or even identify who was calling.

Linden landed on a sandy bank next to a body of water. She rolled over and pushed herself up to a seated position, stunned to find the twisted steel rope lying on the beach next to her—apparently the steel was no match for whatever elemental magic ruled in this realm—but at the same time, she felt as if *her* magic had drained away. In fact, she felt nothing at all, no psychic intuitions, no tingling sensations, no sense of magical energy coiled up inside her, ready to be called upon at a moment's notice. It wasn't as if she felt like an apprentice again when her magic had been unruly and scattered. No, her magic was simply gone, vanished somehow during her fall.

Then Linden remembered she hadn't exactly fallen, but she'd jumped into the portal after Mordahn. She quickly glanced around, worried Mordahn could attack her at any moment, but he and Wreyn were nowhere in sight. Linden rose slowly, feeling disoriented and a bit unsteady on her feet. She scanned the shoreline for Kal, searching for any spot of chestnut brown on the pale beige sand, but she didn't see so much as a speck of color.

In front of her, instead of dark, roiling waves, she stared at a vast grayish river flowing lazily past. There were no boats, no ghostly figures, nothing to mar its surface. Linden turned around and frowned at the sand dunes behind her, surprised at how far back the beach extended. She'd landed on a completely deserted stretch of sand. Even her griffin was nowhere in sight.

Linden blinked away fresh tears, her heart aching for Kal, wondering where he could have landed. She brushed the sand from her hands and clothes and used her sleeve to wipe her tear-stained face. She knew she'd landed on the other side of the portal but had no idea where—would she have to travel to the other side of the river, or had she already arrived—or worse, would she have to fight with others for a spot in a boat?

Linden shook her head and pinched herself. "Ouch!" she hissed. She examined the veins on the back of her hand; she certainly seemed to be made of flesh and blood.

Linden tipped her head back to stare up at the dunes and made her decision: she'd climb up the tallest dune. If nothing else, it would provide her a better vantage from which to survey the area. Maybe she could spot Kal, or Katrine, or Mordahn from the top of the dune. Linden started the climb, her boots sinking into the soft sand with each step. About halfway up, as she paused to catch her breath, she started having second thoughts about tackling the tallest dune. Linden pushed on, her legs aching by the time she reached the top of the dune, which was nothing more than a mound of sand and rocks, punctuated with a few clumps of spindly grass.

Standing at the highest point, Linden surveyed the area below and gasped. She was standing on a tiny, deserted island in the middle of the river, which seemed much wider here than it had appeared through the portal, and not as dark or wild. This river was silvery-gray and moved at a turgid pace. *Did I land in a completely different part of the river when I jumped through the portal? Maybe I didn't actually travel through the portal, but wound up somewhere else entirely?*

Linden glanced up; the sky itself was the same silvery gray as the river and the gauzy veil that hid the portal from view. There were no clouds, no sun, nothing but silvery gray. She was definitely on the other side of the portal, which meant Kal and Mordahn and Katrine were somewhere in here with her. And Wreyn—she'd have to find some way to break Mordahn's hold over Wreyn—that is, if she could find her. *How am I supposed to do anything, stuck in the middle of a river without a boat and without my magic?*

Linden squinted at a speck of dark gray on the beach below her, certain it hadn't been there before. She started hiking down the opposite side of the dune, determined to check out the only thing that looked out of place on the monochrome beige sand. Linden kept the speck of dark gray in sight as she descended, and about two-thirds of the way down, her eyebrows peaked in surprise. *A boathouse? A weathered gray boathouse, large enough to store maybe two small boats, suddenly pops up on a deserted island in the middle of a mythical river, inside an otherworldly magical realm?*

Shrugging, Linden jogged the rest of the way down the dune and hurried over to the boathouse. As she approached it, she noticed the side of the boathouse facing her had a large, open window. An old man, his gray beard reaching halfway to his waist, leaned on the broad window ledge and stared at her impatiently.

"Took you long enough," he grumbled. His long gray hair, streaked through with blue, was pulled back neatly from his face.

Linden took a step back, confused. "Brother Hume? What are *you* doing here?" Brother Hume had been her fencing master on Sanrellyss Island. The crafty old monk had tested not only her swordfighting skills, but her wits and her magic as well. She had to face Brother Hume, and defeat him, every morning before breakfast. Some days, she had missed breakfast entirely and had to settle for lunch.

"I could ask you the same question, lass. But since you asked first, I'll answer." The monk reached down for something beneath the counter, his long silver-and-blue braid swishing over his shoulder. He brought back up two mugs, which he placed on the ledge. Pushing one of the mugs toward her, he said, "Coffee?"

Linden nodded and picked up the steaming mug. She inhaled the aroma of fresh coffee, took a sip, and glanced up at her wily old mentor. *Wait a minute, if Brother Hume is here, does that mean he's—*

"I ain't dead yet, if that's what you're wondering," grunted the monk. "I was climbing up a ladder to fetch Brother Carmine's cat off the rectory roof, when my foot missed a rung and I fell. Last I recall, I was lying in the infirmary. I even heard Brother Carmine say I was too ornery to be passing on just yet." Brother Hume chuckled. "Since I don't believe much in coincidences, I'd say I'm here because of you."

"Because of *me*?"

"Aye. Seeing as how I'm currently unconscious, I guess I'm here—temporarily anyway—to set you to rights." Brother Hume drew his bushy silver eyebrows together and waved his hand at her empty scabbard. "Where's your blade, lass? Don't tell me you lost your weapon again. Didn't I teach you anything whilst you were at Sanrellyss?"

Linden frowned. Healers told stories of patients who'd been unconscious for days or even months, and when they'd finally woken, the patients claimed their spirits had traveled to the realms of the dead. Linden supposed Brother Hume's presence was no different. She had to admit she was glad to see him, even though he'd folded his arms and glared at her, his eyes steely, waiting for a reply. She sighed. According to Brother

Hume, losing one's weapon was akin to losing one's life. A master mage never lost her sword. Ever.

"Mordahn surprised me and my friends. He appeared without warning and cast a spell I'd never seen before." Linden described what happened, using the back of her sleeve to wipe her eyes when she got to the part about Kal.

The old monk's bushy eyebrows rose halfway to his hairline. "And so you head butted a powerful, undead Fallow sorcerer and followed him through the portal?" When Linden nodded, Brother Hume burst out laughing. He sobered quickly and added, "Katrinareus and young Wreyn are also in here somewhere, along with Kal?"

"Aye," said Linden. "So I have to get off this island and find a way to rescue them. I need a boat and some idea where to start looking. Can you help me?"

The old monk raised his hand. "Whoa. Let's take this one at a time." Brother Hume put one beefy finger in the air. "First, Katrinareus is a fay reaper. She can take care of herself in the realms of the dead—in all of the realms—better than you, better than anyone living."

"Fine," she mumbled, turning over what he said. She'd never bothered to ask Katrine how many "realms" existed beyond the portal. The idea of multiple realms actually made sense, given she'd landed somewhere that looked nothing like what she'd glimpsed earlier through the portal. "How many realms are there?"

Brother Hume shrugged. "No idea. But you've landed in the first, or highest, realm. This is where most people wander when they're injured and unconscious, like me, though some will travel lower. Enough about the realms."

It didn't matter to Linden how many realms existed; she needed to know where to find the others. "What about Kal? Did he fall to a different realm? And then there's Wreyn and Mordahn, though I guess I'd need to find my sword first before

I take on Mordahn. Unless—" Linden stood on her tiptoes to peek behind Brother Hume's bulk, wondering what the boathouse actually contained, but he shifted, blocking her view.

"Second—" Brother Hume held up two fingers "—your griffin. Tell me again exactly how Kal was wounded."

Linden recounted everything until the moment Kal fell into the portal. The old monk scratched his beard as he listened, interrupting her periodically to ask a question. Linden blew out a puff of air, frustrated she couldn't answer his detailed questions about Kal's injury. "Because of the angle, I didn't see exactly where the dagger pierced Kal—only that he squawked and dropped like a stone into the portal."

"From what you've described, my guess is the dagger struck your griffin's wing. That would explain his sudden fall."

Linden had been staring glumly into her mug, but her head snapped up. She gazed at the monk, feeling hopeful for the first time since she jumped through the gauzy veil. "So you don't think Kal is dead?"

Brother Hume shook his head. "I can't say for sure. But griffins are magical creatures—not to say immortal, mind you —although only a direct hit to their hearts is enough to kill them. From what you described, I don't think that happened to Kal."

Linden whooped out loud. "Well then, I need to find him right away. Kal needs my help."

The crotchety old monk grunted. "Kal definitely doesn't need your help to heal. What part of 'griffins are magical creatures' don't you understand?"

Linden scowled. "But I thought—"

"Kal's magic, like this place, is elemental. Griffins, unicorns, and yes, even fays, all are part of the elemental magical system. Your healing skills are unnecessary. Kal will heal himself, unless he was mortally wounded, in which case there is nothing you can do for him." Linden's face fell, and Brother Hume hastily added, "But I think your griffin will be fine. And when he's fully recovered, *he* will find *you*."

Linden sighed, desperately wishing she could find Kal and look out for him while he healed, that is, if he could be healed. She shook her head, deciding she wouldn't allow herself to spiral into negative thinking. She thought about what Hume said; something nagged at her. Actually, many things were vying for her attention, but she needed to focus on the most important. "Wait a minute, what did you mean when you said fays have elemental magic inside them?"

The old brother clarified, "I said fays are part of the elemental magical system."

Linden considered all she'd learned about fays, from her grandmother and Pryl, from Efram and Wreyn, and more recently from Katrine. While the fays she knew tried to do the right thing—they studied, practiced, and protected Serving magic—other fays had turned to Fallow sorcery in the past. A fay sorcerer had killed Katrine's mother. Linden nodded slowly. "I think I have a lot to learn about elemental magic."

"Aye, and—" Brother Hume hesitated, as if he'd lost his train of thought. His eyes became less focused, and his head wobbled on his neck. Suddenly he leaned forward on the window ledge, his eyes sharp as usual and boring into Linden's. "We haven't much time. I'm being called back to my body as we speak, by a combination of strong-smelling salts, heady incense, and a dozen of my brother monks crowded around my bed, caterwauling."

"Caterwauling?"

Brother Hume waved his hand impatiently. "Singing hymns. They know I'm the least musical of all the monks on the island. They figure if anything will bring me back from the realms of the dead, it's their infernal chanting."

His body shuddered, and he slapped the ledge with his

palm. "Now listen here, lass. You have everything you need to defeat Mordahn. Remember who you are, and what you are. You'll know what to do when you need to do it. Follow the sand, wind, and river to the lower realms."

The old monk became less corporeal, more translucent. With one ghostly finger he pointed at the river. "The tide is going out now." Brother Hume flickered in and out a few times before disappearing in a bright flash of light, taking with him the two mugs of coffee, the window ledge, and the weathered boathouse.

"But wait, please," called out Linden. She threw her hands into the air and yelled at the gray sky. "I have everything I need? I'll know what to do when I need to do it? Why can't someone just tell me what to do?" She stomped around where the boathouse had stood, kicking the sand in disgust. A breeze swirled around her feet, lifting the sand she'd kicked and depositing it closer to the water's edge. She stopped kicking the sand and the wind died down.

Linden started kicking the sand again, marching in the direction of the riverbank. Small eddies of wind picked up the sand as she dislodged it, carried it to shoreline, and dumped it into a growing pile. She walked over to the pile of sand and realized with a start it wasn't a random mound at all. The wind was forming the sand into a staircase—well, several stairs to be exact—and as each step formed, the river receded at bit farther.

Linden tried recalling Brother Hume's exact words. *Follow the sand, wind, and river to the lower realms. The tide is going out now.* She realized the old monk was telling her to conjure a passage down to the lower levels, using the elements of earth, air, and water. Somehow, she was able to use—to command— the elemental magic in this place. *But how can this be? How can I possibly command the elements and they obey me? I'm not a magical creature like Kal, nor a fay like Katrine.*

The air grew still, as if waiting for Linden to start kicking and yelling again. Shrugging, she balled her fists at her sides and put all of her energy into kicking sand and hollering into the air. "What are we waiting for? Earth, air, and water, construct safe passage for me to the lower realms, now!" Linden could almost hear her mother admonishing her to be polite in all circumstances, and so she added, "Please."

As Linden kicked and shouted, the wind and sand continued building the staircase, and with each step that formed, the river receded. Linden continued kicking and shouting until the sand stopped swirling, and the water level remained steady. She'd been so busy commanding the elements she hadn't realized how many steps she'd conjured—or how far the river had receded. She looked across the tidal flats, where a few pools of water collected in the damp sand. The tide was as low as it was going to go, and it was time for her to use the stairway she'd just constructed.

Linden hadn't been paying attention to exactly how deep the stairwell extended. She edged closer to the hole in the sand and peered down, then quickly stepped back, her heart pounding in her chest. The stairs seemed to go on forever, a narrow, spiraling staircase descending all the way to the lowest, final realm of the dead. *Where are you, Kal?* she whispered.

Linden didn't really want to go into that deep, dark hole by herself. But she didn't know how long the tide would be out, or how long the stairwell would hold up. Besides, she had nowhere else to go, except down. Linden swallowed hard.

She started to jog down the steeply twisting stairwell, intent on reaching the bottom as quickly as possible. As she rounded the turn on the next level, she found herself staring at a scene unfolding some distance away, as if she were watching a live drama from a box seat in an auditorium.

Something about the scene seemed vaguely familiar, and Linden found herself drawn into the action. Thugs dressed as palace guards pushed and shoved a small group of prisoners toward the dungeon. There was no doubt in Linden's mind the prisoners were falsely accused, and she held her breath, waiting for someone to object. Then it happened: one brave boy about her age reached for a sword. The nearest thug swung his sword in a powerful arc and brought it down toward the boy.

"Oh no," shouted Linden, completely engrossed in the action. "Look out!" Suddenly, one of the other prisoners, an older woman, her hair pulled back into a neat bun, stepped in front of the boy. The sword struck the woman instead of the boy, killing her instantly. Linden stumbled to her knees as recognition dawned. She'd lived through this gut-wrenching scene, recalled the exact moment when she saw her grandmother struck by an enemy blade. "No, Nari, no!" Linden cried, swiping at her face with her sleeve as the scene receded from view.

She took a shuddering breath, her stomach in knots, unwilling to stand there any longer, but afraid to see what came next. She stood up and forced herself to put one foot in front of the other, her legs wooden as she continued her descent. Linden rounded the next turn in the stairwell and found herself staring at the great hall in the Valerran Museum. Glenbarran troopers and grihms poured into the hall, overwhelming the exhausted mages in the final battle for Bellaryss. She wept as she watched Uncle Alban, Ian Lewyn, Mayor Noomis, and so many other brave, decent Serving mages fall to Glenbarran swords.

At each twist and turn of the staircase, she witnessed another gut-wrenching scene from her own past. She stood on the Aurorialyss after Mordahn had attacked the Faymon ship, the bodies of friends and enemies sprawled side-by-side on the deck.

Her sword in her hand, she was running in the Arrowood forest, the air thick with smoke from the burning trees. She heard a shout as a volley of arrows whizzed by, and Haydahn, Corbahn's father, threw himself in front of her. Haydahn died saving her life.

Then came the scene that haunted her nightmares, one she relived so often she knew every beat. She was hiding in an alcove in the basement of Zabor Prison, along with her friends. They'd just successfully cleansed the place of power beneath the prison and were fresh from that triumph, although still in danger. Toz accidentally knocked over an empty cage and stepped out of the alcove to retrieve it, unaware of the danger. A Glenbarran guard, startled by the noise, ran Toz through with his sword. Linden screamed, her heart splintering again, as the blood bloomed from Toz's chest.

One more turn of the staircase, and she saw herself running alongside Vas and Nahn, climbing over the bodies of prisoners and Glenbarrans, troopers and grihms, inside the base camp prison.

Linden paused on the stairs to wipe her streaming eyes and try to figure out what was happening, why she was a silent witness to the worst scenes of her life. She wondered whether a heavy heart, pierced through with painful scenes from her past, was required of every living person who traveled into the realms of the dead. Perhaps. But this descent through the realms felt so *personal*. It was about her and Mordahn, and the atrocities he'd committed.

A woman screamed somewhere below her. The hair on the back of Linden's neck stood up. She squinted down the stairs into the darkness, confused by the screams, which sounded as if they came from a living person. There was another scream, accompanied by the sound of someone gagging.

Whether it was Katrine, Wreyn, or a complete stranger, this woman needed help, and fast. Linden jogged down the steps toward the screamer. Her hand went to her empty scabbard, and she silently cursed Mordahn as she ran.

CHAPTER 29

Linden reached the bottom of the long, winding stairway. She'd arrived at the lowest, the final realm of the dead. She was warm from running and at the same time chilled to the bone. This last realm was dark, or perhaps her eyes hadn't adjusted yet. At least she wasn't witnessing scenes from her painful past.

She stepped down, the ground beneath her feet feeling spongy, waterlogged, and she wondered whether it had something to do with the tides. Was it no longer low tide? How much time could she spend here and still return through the portal?

A gloved hand clamped her mouth closed, and an arm wrapped around her upper torso, gripping her tightly. As Linden started to struggle, she heard a hiss in her ear, "It's Katrine. Not a word." She took Linden's hand and led her away from the stairway. They walked along a damp path. As Linden's eyes slowly adjusted to the gloom, she saw the river in the distance, boats lined up along the edge, waiting for new arrivals. This was a different angle, but the same view she'd seen through the portal above.

Katrine pushed her off the path, behind some scraggly trees, their black, leafless branches twisting skyward, toward the grayish gloom overhead. Katrine tugged Linden down to the ground, a finger to her lips. They lay flat on their stomachs, watching the same scene unfold as they'd seen previously, when the gauzy veil had opened for them. Willowy spirits stood on the far shore, singing their haunting melody. Translucent figures glided down the path toward the boats. Once the boats were full, they sailed effortlessly across the water to the other side, where there was a joyful reunion of kindred spirits.

After the singing and the spirits faded from view, another group of ghosts surged down the path, pushing and shoving to reach the few remaining boats. Linden expected to watch as they struggled in vain to make it to the far shore. Instead, a slender, hooded figure appeared on the riverbank, singing the same melody as the spirits on the far shore, only this person sounded an awful lot like Wreyn. She pointed to a spot farther along the shore as she sang. The ghosts stopped fighting long enough to listen, drawn by the music. The singer-enchanter began to move farther downriver, toward the location where she'd been pointing, and the ghosts followed her until they all passed out of sight.

Linden glanced at Katrine and whispered, "Who was that? And what was that?" Linden was sure of one thing; whatever just happened wasn't good news for their side.

Katrine sat up and leaned against the tree trunk with a sigh. Linden rolled over and sat opposite Katrine, drawing her knees to her chest, waiting for the fay to explain. She didn't have long to wait.

Katrine rubbed her face, her weariness showing in the dark circles beneath her eyes. "I'll start by answering your first question. That hooded figure was Wreyn." Katrine paused and took a deep breath. "She's gone, I'm sorry to say. Mordahn killed her."

Linden gasped, then brought her hands to her mouth to keep herself from crying out loud. She closed her eyes, trying to get a grip on her raw emotions. She took a ragged breath and asked the question she dreaded knowing: "When? And what is Wreyn doing with those unsavory ghosts?"

"As best as I can make out, Mordahn captured and killed Wreyn before they arrived at the Howling Cliffs. He must have raised her immediately and compelled her with his magic. Mordahn was able to use Wreyn's fay traveling mists to arrive inside the cavern, undetected by my protection wards. The wards weren't set up to warn against fay magic."

"But Wreyn must have been alive at that point, although under Mordahn's influence. They couldn't have traveled on her mists otherwise."

Katrine shook her head. "Nay. Did you notice that silver collar around Wreyn's neck?"

When Linden nodded, Katrine continued. "The only way to compel a fay is to infuse an object with Fallow sorcery, and then force the fay to wear the magical object. Mordahn infused that silver collar around Wreyn's neck with his dark sorcery. Once Mordahn killed her, he would have placed that collar around Wreyn's neck and then raised her. At that point, he would have had complete control over Wreyn and her magic. He could travel on her fay mists as easily as Wreyn herself. 'Tis one of the darkest aspects of necromancy, and why it's so dangerous. The undead version of Wreyn is entirely bound to Mordahn by his dark magic."

Linden bit her bottom lip and shuddered, the implications of what Katrine said sinking in. The woman she'd heard screaming must have been Wreyn, killed by Mordahn sometime before they arrived together at the Howling Cliffs. The realms of the dead had shown Linden shadows from the past, up to and including Wreyn's dying moments.

Linden frowned, thinking out loud. "So Mordahn is now

using Wreyn's voice to draw the unworthy ghosts away from the river, where normally they would be swept away to whatever their final destination entails. But what is Mordahn doing with them?"

"With Wreyn and her perfect fay voice under his control, Mordahn can keep the portal open indefinitely as he recruits an unlimited supply of undead soldiers."

Linden shook her head. "And he's recruiting the worst of the bunch, ghosts who were unsavory at best while they lived."

"This undead army will be far more potent and wicked than the undead riders and troopers Mordahn has been using. He's been raising anyone who'd once served in the cavalry or infantry, most of whom were decent men and women, at the mercy of his necromantic skills. This time around—"

"This time around, he's upped the stakes again." Linden paused and grimaced. "He'll be reuniting those nasty spirits with their bodies."

Katrine stood up. "Aye. And we've got to stop him now, before he recruits so many we'll never defeat him."

Linden rose to her feet. She noticed the boats were lined up on the shore again. "How often are there new arrivals?"

"Too often," grumbled Katrine.

Linden compressed her lips, glancing around. "Have you seen Kal?"

Katrine frowned. "No, should I have seen him down here?" Linden explained about his injury, and about her visit from Brother Hume.

"I haven't seen Kal, but that doesn't mean he won't find us when he's healed and ready," said Katrine. She pointed at the stairs behind them. "So you managed to build a stairwell using elemental magic, all by yourself?" When Linden nodded, Katrine looked skyward. "And the old monk says you'll know what to do, when you need to do it?"

"That's what he said, but other than doing something with

earth, air, and water, like build a staircase, I'm fresh out of ideas."

"We need the rest of our group, and I don't think that staircase is going to function for anyone other than you."

"And our swords," said Linden. "We need something more than your rope. Where should we start looking?" Something thudded in the darkness, followed by more thuds and grunts.

"May as well start over there," hissed Katrine.

They jogged toward whatever was making the racket, which sounded more like hand-to-hand scuffling. Linden slowed down as she and Katrine approached the grunts, groans, and scuffles, unsure what she'd find. When she heard the clanging of metal, followed by yelps of pain, she picked up speed again. *What or who had followed us through that portal?*

Then Linden heard a familiar voice say, "Thanks, I don't think they'll be giving us anymore trouble." She put on a burst of speed and bumped smack into Corbahn's chest. He stepped back, his fists up in fighting stance, until he realized who had run into him. Corbahn breathed her name, "Linden," and wrapped his arms around her. She took a deep breath as she cradled against Corbahn's chest, savoring his solidness and strength. Reluctantly, she pulled her head back so she could look into his eyes. Linden ran her fingers along a gash on his forehead, frowning. "That needs to be treated."

Corbahn took her hand in his and squeezed. "Later. We need to track Mordahn."

Linden glanced behind Corbahn's shoulder and noticed Jayna and Mara for the first time. They stood over two fallen guards, holding Glenbarran swords. Mara spotted Linden first and ran over to her. "Queen's Crown," she hissed. "We couldn't figure out where to start looking for you."

Jayna carefully scanned Linden head to toe, looking for any obvious injuries, before giving her a quick hug. "Any sign of Kal?" Linden shook her head, her eyes growing moist.

Katrine pointed at the guards on the ground. "Did any more follow you through?"

Mara waved behind her. "One more. Vas and Remy went after him."

"How did you evade the guards long enough to make it through the portal?" asked Linden.

Corbahn bowed his head at Katrine. "Our resistance leader had a secret backup plan. Farleigh and his grihms showed up—and I don't mean just a few of them—I think at least two dozen armed, angry grihms arrived at the Howling Cliffs. The grihms made quick work of the guards, except for the few that managed to escape through the portal."

"We went right after them," explained Jayna, "to make sure they didn't harm you and Katrine or find Mordahn to tell him what was happening."

Linden realized everyone was accounted for, except her brother and Nahn. A fistful of dread slammed into her stomach. She knew Tam would have followed her into the portal if he was able. "What about Tam and Nahn? Where are they?"

Mara stared down at her boots, while Jayna looked at Linden steadily, her eyes clouded with worry. Corbahn spoke first, his voice gentle. "Tam was injured by one of the guards when the fighting started. Nahn stayed behind to watch over him and maintain a defensive shield around the cliffs. Everything happened so fast, Linden. I'm sorry."

Linden squeezed her eyes shut, not wanting to hear more or see more in her mind's eye. She'd seen enough on her descent through the realms. Corbahn put his arm around her and drew her into his side. Tam had to live; they'd not come this far, been reunited again after nearly a year, for him to die now.

Remy's voice broke through Linden's thoughts. "Look at what we found!" He dumped an armful of weapons onto the ground. Vas came up behind him, dropping the remaining blades onto the pile.

Vas nodded at Linden. "Good to see you, lass." He turned to Katrine. "And you as well, my fay friend."

"Did you catch the guard?" asked Mara.

Remy carefully sifted through the blades on the ground, withdrawing his ensorcelled sword. "Vas took care of him."

Vas looked directly at Linden when he replied. "Aye. He'll not be harming any more of my friends." Linden nodded, a silent acknowledgement of the meaning behind his words.

"We haven't much time," said Katrine, who gave a quick rundown of what she'd discovered. Then she explained about Linden's staircase, which she'd constructed from elemental magic, and her passage through the upper realms of the dead.

Jayna's eyes widened. "We only fell about ten feet, onto soft sand that cushioned our fall. It's so strange you landed on a completely different level." Linden knew they'd have some late-night discussions about what she'd seen, if and when they got out of the realms of the dead.

Remy scratched his head. "And the timing is all off. How can you have done all that, when you've only been here for like, twenty minutes?"

Katrine shrugged. "One of the many mysteries of life and death. Time is elastic. But enough about all that. We need to stop Mordahn, here and now."

"And free Wreyn's spirit," said Linden softly, "so she can cross to the other side." She bent down to pick up her sword and dagger from the pile and slipped them into their scabbards on her belt. She felt them thrum with their fay-born power, their elemental magic still intact inside the realms.

"Aye," said Katrine grimly. "It's the least we can do for Wreyn. Dragging Mordahn into the deepest part of the river will do it. The currents will take care of the rest. Once his Fallow sorcery unwinds itself, any undead that he's raised will be set free. Except, of course, for the necromancers who protect him. We'll have to get rid of them the same way as Mordahn—they'll need to go into the deep waters of the river."

"So just dragging them to the water's edge and getting them wet isn't enough?" asked Mara.

Katrine shook her head and then glanced around the group. "Let's quickly go over our escape plan and the rules of this realm."

"We have an escape plan?" asked Remy.

"Aye," said Vas. "We have an escape plan, but it's going to be tricky."

"Why am I not surprised?" sighed Remy.

Vas ignored him and continued. "I've been timing the portal for the past couple of mornings, and it stays open for twenty minutes. That's how long it takes for the full cycle: for the singing spirits to arrive, for the boats to fill and depart, and for the fighting to start and die down. The portal should be closed by now, but Wreyn's voice is keeping it open."

Linden was beginning to see where this was going, and she didn't want to think about it. Corbahn cleared his throat. "So how much time do you figure we'll have, once Wreyn stops singing?"

Vas sighed. "I figure the portal will start to close right away. If we're at the start of a cycle, where the singing spirits have just begun arriving on the far shore, then we'll likely have twenty minutes. But if we're nearing the end of a cycle, then…"

"Then we'll have very little time," Corbahn finished Vas's sentence. "Perhaps five minutes, ten if we're lucky."

"So what is the plan then?" asked Remy.

Vas said, "Farleigh has posted grihm guards at the portal. They are watching for any sign of change. When the portal begins to close, Farleigh is going to do three things: he's going to shout into the realms of the dead, hoping we will all hear him; he's going to shine a torch into the gloom, for as long as the portal stays open; and he'll toss a rope ladder down to us. He and his grihm friends will haul us out of the portal by way of the ladder."

Mara tucked a chunk of wheat-colored hair behind her ear. "So once we hear Farleigh hollering, or we see that Wreyn's spirit has been freed, we should make haste for the portal."

"And we'll have anywhere from five to twenty minutes to make it back through the portal before it closes for good, or at least, for the next fifty years," said Jayna. "That's not much of a window.

"Aye, but we haven't any choice. Alright, I want to cover the rules of this realm, and then we need to move out." Katrine pointed to the far shore. "The singing spirits are beginning to assemble, and that means Wreyn will be showing up soon, and we can track her back to Mordahn."

Everyone nodded, and Katrine waved her hand at the river. "The dark waters of the river pose no harm to us. We can stand in the river and even swim in the water safely, but we won't be able to cross to the far shore. There's an invisible barrier preventing the living, and those deemed unworthy, from reaching the other side."

"That explains why none of the 'unworthy' ever make it across the river," said Linden.

Katrine nodded. "Now this is important, so listen up. The river bends sharply farther downstream, and the current moves much faster after the bend. If you're on the river anywhere near that turn, make sure you get to the shore. You'll hear it before you see it." Katrine paused, seeming to lose her train of thought.

"Hear what?" prompted Jayna.

"The waterfall. If any of us goes over that fall, we'll not be coming back."

"Is it a long drop?" asked Corbahn.

Katrine shrugged. "No one knows for sure, because none of

the reapers have ever returned once they've gone over the edge. However, I think it's not so much the fall itself as what we'd be falling into that would seal our fate." Katrine ran a hand through her short curls, staring at the river. "Reapers who've neared the bend of the river but managed to crawl to shore before hitting that waterfall, all tell the same story. They hear weeping and wailing from the other side of the fall, but they say the smell is even worse, of burning tar and acrid smoke. Reapers believe there's a lake of fire beyond the waterfall, which is the final destination for the unworthy."

"No wonder everyone tries so hard to reach the far shore," said Linden. She didn't feel sympathy for Mordahn and the others who'd committed horrible deeds while living, but she could understand why they wanted to avoid the lake of fire at the bottom of the waterfall. She shuddered.

Corbahn squeezed her shoulder, as if sensing her inner thoughts. "I can't think of a more worthy destination for Mordahn and his protectors. Just desserts for all the heartache and misery they've fostered."

"Well said," agreed Katrine, as the haunting melody of the spirits on the far shore surged around them. "It looks like the singing spirits have all arrived. That's our cue to get moving." She removed one of the thick coils of gold rope from around her shoulder and handed it to Vas. "Remember, Vas and I will start by picking off the protectors. We'll need the rest of you— with your Swords of Five—to keep everyone else, including Mordahn, at bay."

Katrine took point, Vas closely behind her, followed by Linden, Corbahn, and the rest. They jogged, single file, toward the boats lining the shore. Crouching behind tree trunks, they watched as the first group of spirits glided down the path toward the river, entered the boats, sailed across the river, and were joyfully greeted on the other side. The second group of ghosts arrived, pushing and shoving each other for a chance at one of the boats.

"Here comes poor Wreyn," whispered Linden, heartsick all over again at the sight of her fay friend huddled inside her cape, walking along the shoreline, singing the haunting melody. As before, the remaining ghosts stopped their fighting and followed Wreyn.

Katrine unwound the coil of rope from around her shoulder and held the large loop in her right hand. Vas mimicked her move, both of them ready with their lassos. Linden withdrew her sword and held it crosswise across her chest, as Brother Hume had instructed her on Sanrellyss Island all those months ago. Her fingers grazed her left pocket, where she felt a small lump. The Sollareus crystal. Linden had forgotten she'd tucked it into the pocket of her jacket.

"Let's go!" hissed Katrine, who crept swiftly along the shoreline, using the scraggly black trees for cover.

Mordahn was easy to spot, the tallest of the hooded, undead necromancers, standing near the water's edge, his protectors flanking him on either side. Mordahn watched as Wreyn led her charges past him, to long tables made of weathered driftwood. Although the tables were empty, the ghosts eagerly sat down, grabbing at imaginary plates and mugs.

Katrine and Vas pointed to the protector standing the farthest from Mordahn, agreeing he was the target. The fay turned to give Linden and the others a quick head nod, and then she broke from the trees, swirling her lasso. Vas followed closely behind with his rope.

Linden's heart thundered in her chest as she charged toward Mordahn, with Corbahn running alongside her. Jayna, Mara, and Remy focused on the remaining protectors, who immediately withdrew their swords. The five fay-spelled blades lit up, pulsing with green, gold, purple, blue, and red hieroglyphs. Linden took that as a good sign in the lowest of the realms of the dead. She could do this, she could defeat Mordahn once and for all.

Mordahn scowled at Linden and Corbahn, his orange eyes glowering from beneath his hood. "The spawn of Nari Arlyss and my dear nephew, teamed up once again. How sweet." He brought his sword up with both hands and swung at Corbahn with more force than Linden thought possible, given Mordahn's age and undead condition. Linden knew his power was limited to what he'd managed to bind to himself before coming through the portal. The undead were still bound to Mordahn, but he couldn't conjure fresh Fallow spells inside the realms of the dead, just as she couldn't rely on Serving magic. In that sense, they were more evenly matched than anywhere else.

Corbahn met Mordahn's first lunge, deftly deflecting the old sorcerer's sword and pushing him toward the river. Mordahn's left boot landed in the water, and he hissed. He reached into his robe, withdrawing something in his gloved hand. With a loud yell, he whipped a metal disc at Corbahn, catching him in the side of his neck. Corbahn dropped to his knees, dazed, his hand going to his neck and coming away bloody.

"No, no! Corbahn, hold on, don't you dare leave me!" screamed Linden. Their eyes met, Corbahn's pupils dilating. He toppled sideways onto the sand.

Linden wanted to run to Corbahn, check his wound, scream for help, but instead she rounded on Mordahn, who cackled. "One down, one to go." Linden watched Mordahn carefully, her senses alert to his slightest hand movement.

He brought up his sword, whipping the tip toward Linden's face. She knocked his blade away and returned the thrust. They parried for several long minutes, lunging and blocking in a strange, deadly dance at the water's edge, their boots kicking up sand and water as they fought. He managed to nick her forehead, the cut deep enough to be a nuisance. She had to keep wiping the blood out of her eyes. Linden backed up a few times, attempting to draw Mordahn a little deeper into the surf, but he shook his head at her and remained on the shore.

She heard the sound of multiple blades colliding around them, the yells of her friends and the screeches of the protectors. Out of the corner of her eye she noticed Wreyn, standing on the shore, still singing, insensible to the sights and sounds around her. The ghosts remained at their driftwood tables, equally oblivious.

At some point, Katrine and Vas managed to lasso two of Mordahn's four protectors, who yowled at the top of their undead lungs. Tossing them into a boat, Vas and Katrine rowed toward the center of the river. They dumped their charges into the dark water, which surged around the two necromancers, dragging them down into the depths and drowning out their shrieks.

Linden heard Mara cry out, and Remy yelling something. As much as she wanted to turn around and help her friends, she remained focused on Mordahn. His left hand dipped inside his cloak and she braced herself, expecting him to throw another metal disc. Instead, he charged her, his long blade aimed straight at her heart. As she pivoted out of the range of his sword arm, she felt something slice her thigh. Mordahn had tricked her; he'd transferred his sword to his left hand when she pivoted, cutting her leg deeply. Linden groaned from the searing pain, stumbling to one knee. She used her sword to push herself up, turning around in time to block Mordahn's blade as he swung it at her neck. She ducked beneath his arm and punched her sword into the air, catching Mordahn in his side. He shrieked and stepped back, his eyes fiery in their sockets.

Clutching his side, Mordahn charged her again, swinging

his sword wildly. Linden blocked each fresh lunge of his sword, trying to work out how she would get him into the deep part of the river. Suddenly the entire realm was silent, except for the splashing of the water at their feet, and someone quietly weeping on the shore. Was it Jayna or Mara? Linden couldn't tell. But the silence disturbed Mordahn. He dragged himself onto the beach, waving his arms wildly. Only one protector was left, and Katrine lassoed him while Mara held a sword to his throat. They dragged him to the boat.

Linden quickly surveyed the beach. Wreyn was lying on the ground, silent. Jayna stood over her, a dagger in her hand, weeping. Lying on the sand next to Wreyn was the silver collar, broken apart. Jayna must have figured out the collar connected Wreyn to Mordahn's dark magic. Jayna had knocked Wreyn out, and then severed the silver collar around the fay's neck. Wreyn's pitch perfect voice was no longer under Mordahn's control. *When Wreyn regains consciousness, she'll find herself undead, her spirit unable to cross to the far shore, unless I can lure Mordahn into the river's currents.*

Somewhere in the distance, Linden heard Farleigh hollering. She saw the flicker of a torch, and a rope being lowered, as Vas and Remy carried an unconscious Corbahn toward the portal, his arms dangling on the ground as they ran. Linden vaguely wondered how much longer the portal would be open. She brought her sword across her chest in a defensive posture, realizing she couldn't chase Mordahn down; she could barely stand on her leg. She narrowed her eyes at the grisly old sorcerer, her nemesis for so long, and waited, wiping the blood from her forehead. Pryl told her she'd have to face Mordahn alone, and here she was. Katrine and Mara, having dispatched the last protector, dragged Jayna back to the portal between them. Jayna was shouting at Linden, screaming at her to run.

Linden nodded calmly at Jayna, and a look passed between them. Jayna understood. This was goodbye; Linden would not be leaving the realms of the dead. Jayna sobbed as Katrine and Mara pushed her onto the rope ladder and Farleigh hauled her up through the portal.

Mordahn turned back toward Linden. His protectors were gone, the portal nearly closed. The unsavory ghosts on the beach were fighting with each other over the last boat. Mordahn yowled in anger and flapped his wrist, shooting a dagger out of the sleeve of his cape. Linden tried moving out of the way, but she felt sluggish from blood loss, and worn raw from the inside out. His dagger struck her shoulder and she cried out, "What are you waiting for? Come and get me!" She turned and dived into the river, letting the swirling current take her downstream, hoping to lure Mordahn into the middle of the river.

Mordahn laughed and moved surprisingly fast. He grabbed Linden by the hair and yanked her backward, closer to the shore. "Not so fast. Since we're stuck here together, I'm going to make sure you suffer for a very long time. I'm already dead, so there's not much you can do to me."

Mordahn plunged Linden's face into the water, holding her head down as she struggled, her arms flailing, her lungs bursting for air. He yanked her head up and she spit up water, gasping for air. "You're not really so powerful now, are you little Liege?" He cackled and pushed her head into the river again. She fought him, punched him, but she felt herself drifting away. What was the point? How much longer could she do this? She thought about giving up, inhaling the dark water and floating down the river.

But Mordahn released his grip on her hair and flopped backward into the shallow water with a loud curse. Linden came up for air, sputtering. A creature soared overhead, with the body of a lion and the head of an eagle. He clicked his beak furiously at Linden. "Kal! You're alive!" Kal squawked and dived again toward Mordahn, landing on top of this head. Mordahn flapped his hands, screeching, "Get off me, you mangy half-breed. I swear, I'll rip your soul from your body if I catch you!"

Kal taunted Mordahn, flying just out of his reach, and then swooping in from behind him to peck at his head. The more Mordahn tried swiping away at Kal, the less he noticed the river picking up speed. Linden saw the bend in the river before Mordahn and tried to scramble up the riverbank. Mordahn grabbed at her, and they both stumbled back into the river, the current sweeping them away from the beach.

Mordahn lost his footing and fell. He yelped and splashed, trying to keep himself from getting caught in the undertow. Linden tried paddling toward the beach, but with her leg and shoulder injured, she made no progress against the surging river. As Linden and Mordahn swept past the bend in the river, the sound of the waterfall roared ahead of them. Linden heard wailing and sobbing and smelled the sulfurous odor Katrine had described. Numb with the certainty she'd not make it out of the portal alive, Linden's sole goal now was to avoid the lake of fire. She didn't want to be stuck anywhere with Mordahn and his cronies for all eternity.

Kal started swooping in front of Linden, clicking his beak frantically. "I know, she shouted, "I'm thinking." She thought of the staircase she'd constructed with elemental magic and looked around for something she could use. She spotted a crooked tree perched on the beach and focused on the ground beneath the tree, and the light breeze around it. "Air and earth, topple that tree near to me." The tree creaked as its roots tore from the ground; it fell over into the water, directly in front of Linden. She gratefully grabbed onto its branches and began hauling herself toward the beach, using her good arm to pull herself forward.

"Brilliant, little Liege!" cackled Mordahn, who reached a sodden arm across her head and grabbed onto the tree. "But this tree won't support two of us." He kicked her hard in the stomach, and Linden doubled over, nearly losing her grip. Kal flew at Mordahn's head, flapping his wings, and pecking at Mordahn's arms.

Mordahn lifted his hand to wave Kal away and lost his grip on the tree branch. He screamed, swept under by the current. As he struggled in the water, he lunged at Linden, wrapping his arms around her legs and pulling her under with him. He gripped her tightly as the river churned and sped toward the waterfall. Linden's heart raced, her brain panicked, her lungs nearly out of air.

Everyone kept telling her she would know what to do when she needed to do it. What could they possibly have meant? She had nothing left to fight with, her sword and dagger gone, her strength nearly spent. Mordahn still gripped her firmly around the legs, determined to take her with him over the waterfall. Linden heard the crashing surf in her ears, felt herself tumbling into the river's maelstrom, and Mordahn still held on. She fingered her pocket, her hand grazing the Sollareus crystal. Recalling Sollara's story and how she'd overcome the giant, Linden grasped the crystal firmly in her hand and plunged it into Mordahn's mouth.

A bright white light exploded from Linden's fist, shooting sparks through what was left of Mordahn's less-than-mortal frame. He collapsed into bone and ash and sank with a final whimper into the churning foam. The river flipped Linden around, spinning her away from the white foam of the waterfall. A powerful jet of water lifted Linden into the air, pushing her up toward the silvery grey sky.

Linden glanced at her fist, still pulsing with a white light so brilliant it hurt her eyes. Kal circled around her, keeping pace with the surge of water. Linden felt her energy draining as she fell back into the water. She couldn't break her fall; she had no strength left. She splashed down in shallow water, landing on her back. Linden's eyelids fluttered a few times, so heavy she gave up the struggle and let them stay closed. Kal landed nearby, flapping his wings and pecking at her uninjured leg.

As Linden slipped away, she thought she heard Corbahn calling to her from a great distance. She moved her lips to answer, but no sound came out.

CHAPTER 30

Linden dreamt for days, weeks on end. And for the first time since the raid at Quorne twenty months earlier, not one of her dreams contained Mordahn. She didn't relive any of her nightmares either. She dreamt of her grandmother, but they were happy dreams, the two of them laughing together over a cup of tea. She dreamt of Toz, a gleam in his eye as he told her the latest school gossip. Her Uncle Alban visited her dreams, and his hair was gleaming black again, streaked through with blue and sprinkles of gray, and his posture was straight, unbowed by all that came later, with the Glenbarrans and the fall of Valerra. Wreyn visited her too, an impish grin on her face, as she whispered something about Corbahn in Linden's ear.

Tam was the only visitor who seemed unsettled, still suffering in some way. His lips were pinched, his skin drawn tightly across the damaged side of his face. Linden saw that his physical injuries from their last battle with Mordahn had healed, but something was preventing him from coming fully alive. She realized, then, the gift she'd been given as she passed through the realms of the dead, reliving the horror of each loss, and releasing the pain as she descended the stairs to the final realm. Her brother was still snared deep inside each of his battles, his pain as evident and tenacious as the scars on his face.

First, last, and throughout the weeks she lay in a coma, Linden's broad-chested warrior, the chief of Arrowood and of her heart, visited her dreams. Each time, he brought a single rose, a different color with each visit. Somewhere in her subconscious she knew Corbahn had been injured, but not in her visions of him. No, he stood tall and strong, a scar on his neck where Mordahn's disc struck him, but otherwise healthy and vital. His eyes, the color of the Pale Sea in summer, gave the only hint that something still troubled him. She wanted to reach out and take his hand, tell him all would be well, but she didn't have the strength to lift a finger. As each of his visits came to a close, the Corbahn of her dreams leaned over and brushed his lips against hers, and her heart thudded in response.

As another of his visits drew to a close, Corbahn took her hand and clutched it to his chest. "Linden, if you can hear me, wake up, please." She heard a sharp intake of breath. A single sob escaped from Corbahn, and when his lips brushed hers, she felt moisture on her cheeks. Linden focused on the hand he was gripping and moved her fingers. Corbahn paused, and then squeezed her hand again. She wiggled her fingers and opened her eyes.

Corbahn scooped her up in his arms. "You've come back to me," he breathed into her hair.

"How long?" she whispered.

"Twenty days."

All she could think about was water. Not the dark river waters in the realms of the dead, but crystal-clear water. "Water, please." Corbahn reached over to a pitcher on the stand by her bed, poured her a glass, and helped her to a few sips. She noticed a vase next to the water pitcher, filled with roses, each rose a different color. She leaned back against her pillow and pointed at them. "I dreamt you visited me each day and brought a rose."

"This has been the longest battle of my life, right here, beside your bed, hoping each day you would open your eyes. Jayna feared your spirit had been left behind in the realms of the dead. I couldn't even fathom it." Corbahn kissed her cheek. "Let me get Jayna."

Linden gripped his hand. "Where am I?" She glanced down at her narrow bed. The roof above her head was made of canvas. Thick cotton curtains formed the walls on either side of her. She heard someone coughing on the other side of the cloth room dividers.

"Katrine transported you to a field infirmary north of Bellaryss, away from the fighting. Tam is here too, and Jayna."

"And everyone else?"

"Mara and Remy stayed behind with Vas and Nahn, and the rest of the resistance. They're rounding up the last of the occupiers inside the city. The fays now control Wellan Pass. We're winning, Linden. You did it."

"We did it," she smiled and reached up to trace the fresh scar on the side of his neck. "All of us. At long last, your crazy Uncle Mordahn is well and truly dead."

Corbahn kissed her again, and then left to find Jayna. Kal hopped onto the bed, clicking his beak and nestling against her side. "It's good to see you too." The griffin sighed happily as Linden scratched his mane. "I'm glad to be back among the living." She glanced around her small infirmary room and noticed her sword and dagger, back inside their scabbards and lying beside a wooden chair. She shook her head, amazed at the magic of the Sollareus crystal, which reduced Mordahn to bone and ash, and then freed her, her weapons, and her griffin from the realms of the dead.

Jayna drew aside the curtain separating Linden's area from the other patients. Her normally smooth brow was creased as she hurried over to the bed. Jayna stared into Linden's eyes, her full lips downturned.

"What is it? Why do you look so grim?" asked Linden crossly.

Jayna didn't answer, but changed the dressings on her shoulder and leg, and checked to see whether Linden had a fever. She gave Linden more water before plopping herself in the chair next to the bed. Jayna pointed at her best friend, her dark curly hair wild around her face. "You've had me worried to a frazzle. And poor Corbahn, he's been beside himself. And Tam, and Pryl, who's popped over here every so often just to see if you'd woken up yet."

"I'm sorry?" Linden sputtered.

"Well you should be," huffed Jayna, who wiped a tear from her cheek. "I honestly didn't know what else to do. Your wounds were healing, you didn't appear to be in any pain, and yet you slept on, and on, and on. We were all beginning to think you might never be fully yourself again. Do you have any idea what was happening?"

Linden shrugged. "Not really, but I dreamed a lot." She told Jayna about her dreams, pausing when she got to her brother. "How is Tam doing?"

Jayna looked away. "Physically, he is healing fine. But he's not himself. He's jittery and jumps at every sound. He talks about going home all the time."

"Home?"

"To Delavan. But didn't your grandmother shield it with a spell?"

"Aye, Nari shielded the estate for five years. But I wonder..." Linden thought about one of Nari's last spells, which she'd cast to preserve Delavan Manor for her and Matteo. But Nari had repeatedly told Linden in those final months leading up to the war that she would need to find her "second home." Linden had no idea what Nari meant at the time, but she later learned her grandmother was referring to Faynwood. The same would not be true for Tam, however. While he'd be welcome there, as the Liege's brother, he'd have no actual role in Faymon society. He'd be almost as unhappy there as Stryker. Linden realized that Nari had always intended to preserve Delavan Manor for her grandson. She wanted Matteo to have a place to call home after the war with Glenbarra was over.

Jayna flapped her hand at Linden. "Go on, what were you saying?"

"I'm wondering if maybe there's a way for Matteo to go home."

⁓

Over the next three weeks, Linden received a steady stream of visitors at the infirmary. Servants scurried at times to squeeze a few extra chairs into her small hospital room. Corbahn was by her side each day, with a fresh rose and news from the clans. Inside Faynwood, Linden was being hailed as the most powerful Liege since Hanalorah, the first Lady Liege. "Mm-hmm," Linden would say, and Corbahn would move on to other subjects, realizing his Lady Liege had no interest in that sort of praise.

Mara and Remy visited, bursting with news of the Glenbarrans' retreat from Bellaryss. The occupation was in disarray, and Vas was pulling together a provisional government from the ashes the Glenbarrans left behind. Remy whispered something to Mara before pulling aside the curtain. "I'm going to visit Tam for a bit," he said. "I'll stop back to say goodbye."

Linden quirked her eyebrows at Mara. "What was that about?"

Mara waved her hand. "Nothing. It's just that Remy and I

have decided to stay here in Bellaryss and help Vas with the reconstruction." Linden had learned from Jayna that Vas would be leading the provisional government for the time being, at least until order could be restored in the capital. "There's so much work to be done in Valerra. And for us, this is home. Faynwood is lovely, but it's not the same. You understand, don't you?"

"Of course I understand." Linden leaned against her pillow. "I'll miss you, but I get it." Linden narrowed her eyes at her friend. "But I think there's more."

Mara's face clouded. "One more thing," she glanced at the floor, and then met Linden's eyes. "I felt so guilty, leaving you behind in the realms of the dead. All of us felt terrible about it —we had to literally drag Jayna out of there. But Katrine told us you had to face Mordahn alone, and we couldn't intervene. I'm sorry."

"Don't be, it all worked out. And Katrine was right, even Pryl told me I had to face Mordahn alone in the end."

Katrine and Pryl popped in for visits, although never at the same time. While they clearly got along better than they had in the past, the half-siblings were also set in their ways and equally stubborn.

Katrine sat next to Linden's bed one afternoon, shortly after Linden had awoken, and gave her a curt nod. "Well done, lass. I didn't know if you could beat Mordahn, but I knew if you didn't confront him on your own, you'd never be at peace with yourself."

Linden frowned. "I thought you told Mara all the prophecies said I had to battle him alone, if our side ever hoped to win."

Katrine shook her head. "There was only one prophecy that predicted something like it, and even that was open to interpretation, as all prophecies are. Nay, I misled Mara and the others because I knew this was your battle, against your nemesis, and once we'd cleared away the protectors, it was your fight to win or lose."

Linden nodded slowly. She did feel more at peace than at any time she could remember, or least since she'd been a young girl. "You are a wise one, Auntie Katrinareus."

Katrine pointed at her. "Don't you start getting sassy with me, girlie. My name is Katrine." They both chuckled and Katrine gave Linden a quick, businesslike hug when she left.

Pryl split his time between Tam's hospital bed and hers whenever he visited. During one visit, after they'd been discussing Tam's condition, Pryl drew his eyebrows together and cocked his head to one side. "You're going to try to break Nari's spell, aren't you? You want to help Tam re-enter Delavan."

Linden nodded. "He's so homesick and battle weary; I have to try. I don't think there's any way to actually break the spell—besides, I don't want to undo it entirely. I want to uncover enough of the key so I can open the protective wards and let Tam slip inside. Any thoughts on where to start?"

Pryl rubbed his beard, considering her question. "Nari always loved the woods at the southern end of the estate. There's one tree in particular, with an oddly shaped trunk, at the very edge of the property. Nari used to center her wards and spells at the tree."

"I'll start there." She glanced at her grandfather. He seemed more rested than she'd seen him in many months. In fact, like her, he seemed more at peace. "You look...more relaxed than I think I've ever seen you."

Pryl nodded. "'Tis true, I'm sleeping better these days now that Fallow sorcery is on the decline. And I'm vastly relieved the council has decided the Fay Nation will remain tethered inside Faynwood. You can't imagine the amount of work and magic involved in relocating Havynweal. It's been more than a millennia since anyone's even tried." Pryl rubbed his beard, lost in thought. Then he snapped back to himself and waved his hand in the air, as if to emphasize his next statement. "I feel like I've earned a holiday, and I aim to take it."

"A holiday?" Linden couldn't imagine Pryl slowing down long enough to do any sightseeing. Besides, where would a fay chief go on vacation that he couldn't simply translocate himself to whenever he wanted? "Where will you go?"

Pryl gave her a wistful smile. "To find Ric and Kamden. It's time I tell my son who I am, and why I left him when he was a wee boy. I've been so busy taking care of everything else, I've neglected my family, and my sons most of all. It's time I finally take care of family business."

Linden had so many questions for her grandfather, she didn't know where to begin. She wanted to travel with Pryl, when he made the trip to The Colonies, but she also believed Pryl and her father deserved time alone, to get to know one another as father and son. Besides, she and Corbahn were just getting reacquainted, and she was the Liege of Faynwood, with plenty to do once she recovered and returned to Faynwood. This wasn't the time for her to be going anywhere. "When will you leave? And who will be handling your duties while you're gone?"

"I've spoken to Captain Raffindor. He and his ship will make its first voyage to The Colonies in spring, after the last of the snows. I'll sail with him, onboard the Aurorialyss. As to my duties, Katrinareus is going to cover for me while I'm away. I'd always hoped she'd show more of an interest in fay affairs, and I think the trip she made back home with you helped. At least, she's willing to give me a hand while I take my vacation."

"You spoke to Raff?" asked Linden softly. "How is he doing?" She often wondered how her ex-fiancé had adjusted to life at sea. After Stryker had been convicted of misusing his magic and banned from Faynwood, he'd been sent to work aboard Raffindor's ship, without any real choice in the matter.

Linden believed the punishment had been just, given his crime. Stryker had come dangerously close to harming Corbahn, his sister, and a lot of innocent bystanders. Still, Linden hoped he had been able to adjust to his new life.

"Raffindor tells me Stryker is doing well. He's a regular member of the ship's crew and seems happy."

"Good, I'm glad. I hoped he could find a way to be happy again." Linden looked at her fay grandfather and smiled. "You seem happier too."

Pryl leaned over to kiss her cheek and rose to leave. "My granddaughter defeated the worst Fallow sorcerer in generations. Of course I'm happier. I want you to be happier too."

"But I am," protested Linden.

Pryl seemed unconvinced, but he smiled. "Very well, if you're happy, then I'm happy for you."

Linden didn't answer her grandfather, but she thought about his words afterward. Being with Corbahn made her happy, she knew that. On the other hand, she'd been avoiding any more conversations about their future together, but why? She loved Corbahn. Was she still hung up on the old prophecies about the Arrowood Chief and the Faymon Liege?

On a cold, gray winter morning, less than a week before Winter Solstice, Corbahn, Tam, and Linden finally left the infirmary. They traveled on horseback to the southern boundary of Delavan, to the woods that Linden and Nari loved so well.

Ashir pawed the frozen ground, his breath a frosty stream, and Linden leaned forward to pat his neck "You're right, this is a beautiful spot," she whispered. "Another time, we'll come stay for a while." Ashir whinnied, and Linden laughed, grateful to be riding her horse in this special place without fear.

Glenbarra's beleaguered army had officially surrendered the week before. The only thing marring the Valerrans' celebration was that King Roi himself had escaped. Corbahn was certain the war criminal would eventually be caught and brought to trial for the atrocities he'd committed. Linden wasn't so sure; she sensed the Glenbarran king would create trouble again for Valerra and Faynwood.

Corbahn dismounted and helped Linden down. Her leg and shoulder were nearly healed, but she still needed help getting on and off Ashir. Linden didn't object to wrapping her arms around Corbahn's neck as he lifted her from the saddle and set her on the ground. His scent of wood smoke and leather felt like home to her.

Corbahn held their horses' reins and waited. Tam and Linden stepped up to the invisible boundary set in place by Nari more than a year earlier. All they could see was the woods, Delavan Manor itself hidden beyond the trees, shielded from the inquiring eyes of friend and foe. Linden reached out her hand and touched a large tree, its trunk bent in an *L* shape. The tree thrummed with powerful protection charms, and something else —the ghost of a key, a way inside that invisible boundary. Nari's spell came to her then, and she knew what to do.

Linden turned to Tam. "I can lift the shield for you, but you have to be sure this is what you want. Once I let you in, you won't be able to leave until the spell runs its course, which is another four years."

Tam nodded. "I'm fine with that." He raised bloodshot eyes to Linden. "Thank you, for doing this, and well, for everything. Mother and Dad would be so proud of you."

Linden smiled, her heart squeezing at the thought of their parents, somewhere in The Colonies. "I think we'll get to see them again one day."

Tam nodded. "One day."

She said, "Ready?" Tam nodded again, and Linden asked him to place his hand on the other side of the tree trunk.

She pressed her palm against the curve of the trunk and incanted, "Open what's closed, for one minute thirty, permit entrance to Delavan, to Matteo Arlyss only. Resume all protections once he's inside, all as before, until this magic unwinds."

A twig snapped, and a girl of about twelve stood in the woods on the other side of the boundary. An older man stood alongside her. The girl was slender, with large hazel eyes and shiny chestnut hair that fell to her waist. "Jorri? Is that you?" asked Linden.

Jorri waved. "Aye, well met, Linden Arlyss of Valerra and Faynwood." She looked beyond Linden to Corbahn. "You are with the right man, now, I see."

Jorri, like the old woman in the Arrowood enclave, was a psychic. Apparently, this twelve-year-old psychic preferred Corbahn as well. Linden cleared her throat. "The last time I saw you, you said we'd be meeting again, but not for a while. I wondered what you meant at the time."

"'Twas this vision that I saw."

The man next to Jorri removed his cap. "My daughter told me we had to come to these woods and wait in this spot, because the young master of Delavan would be coming home today." He bowed toward Tam, who stood rooted in place, gazing at Jorri in confusion.

The girl reached her small hand out toward Tam, who took it. Jorri guided Tam past the *L*-shaped tree and through the boundary shield. The older man took the reins of Tam's horse and led the animal toward Delavan, tipping his hat to Linden and Corbahn.

Jorri said to Linden, "Don't worry, we'll take good care of your brother. Healer Gracyn has already prepared his rooms for him, and Cook has his favorite meal waiting—roasted venison with root vegetables and mince pie for dessert." She glanced up

TONI CABELL

at Tam and said, "Did I get that right? I based it on Linden's memories when I last touched her hand."

Tam nodded, awe etched on his face. Linden saw something else there too, a deep sense of gratitude that he could go home again. Perhaps, with time, he would find peace at Delavan. Linden had no doubt her brother would have many stories to tell her one day, about Delavan, and the families who lived on the estate, and about a certain young psychic.

Tam and Jorri waved goodbye. Linden blew them both a kiss and called out, "Remember, I'm the first person you're going to visit when the four years are up, Matteo Arlyss!"

The tree branches closed behind them, Tam and Jorri hidden by Nari's spell.

Corbahn placed a hand on Linden's shoulder. "Are you alright?"

Linden looked up at him, her eyes shining. "I'm fine, happy really, that I could help him get back home."

"And now it's time we think about getting home ourselves. Jayna and Reynier have already left."

"Home? Where did you have in mind?"

Corbahn smiled, his sea-green eyes dancing. "Tanglewood, of course, the ancestral home of the Liege of Faynwood.

"And would the Arrowood Chief be happy, living so far from the forests and bluffs of his own clan?"

Corbahn peered into her eyes. Linden felt her insides melting at the heat behind his gaze. She had no doubts about her feelings for Corbahn. She was more than ready to spend an eternity of bickering, wrangling, and loving this gruff, gorgeous clan chief. "We could split our time, half the year in Tanglewood, and the other half in Arrowood. What do you think?"

Linden gave him a soft smile. "You've thought of everything, Chief Corbahn Erewin of Arrowood."

"Aye," Corbahn sighed, "except my lady still hasn't entered

into the rites of binding with me. I grow weary with the waiting."

"What season did you have in mind for our rites? Spring perhaps? Or maybe summer would be best?" Linden teased, biting her bottom lip to keep from smiling. Corbahn's eyebrows rose at the idea of waiting until spring or summer to hold their binding rites.

"Not exactly." Corbahn cleared his throat. "I propose, ah, I'd like for our rites of binding to occur much earlier, five days hence to be exact."

"On Winter Solstice? You want to be bound together on the shortest day of the year?" Linden tilted her head up at him. Now that she'd made up her mind, she was as ready as Corbahn to be married, but she couldn't understand why he would choose the Winter Solstice.

"Aye my lady, it is the shortest day." Drawing her into his arms, Corbahn gave her a sly wink. "But, my love, it's also the longest night."

THE END

Thanks so much for reading *Lady Liege*! I hope you enjoyed it. Please consider taking a moment to share your thoughts by leaving a review. Reader reviews help other readers discover new books.

If you are new to the world of Serving Magic, these are the other books in the complete series:

- Lady Tanglewood, Prequel
- Lady Apprentice, Book 1
- Lady Mage, Book 2
- Lady Liege, Book 3
- Lady Spy, Book 4
- Lady Reaper, Book 5

For more action-packed fantasy, please check out my Water Witch Series, about a young woman with the rare gift for water divining:

- The Lightness of Water
- The Way of Water (coming soon)

I love to stay in touch with my readers. Please sign up for my newsletter to learn about giveaways and new releases at https://tonicabell.com or visit me at https://www.facebook.com/ToniCabellAuthor.

-Toni Cabell

Made in the USA
Columbia, SC
06 April 2025